continued . . .

Ace Books by Erin Lindsey

THE BLOODBOUND
THE BLOODFORGED

THE
BLOODFORGED

Erin Lindsey

ACE BOOKS, NEW YORK

ACE

An imprint of Penguin Random House LLC
375 Hudson Street, New York, New York 10014

THE BLOODFORGED

An Ace Book / published by arrangement with the author

ISBN: 978-0-425-27629-7

PUBLISHING HISTORY
Ace mass-market edition / October 2015

PRINTED IN THE UNITED STATES OF AMERICA

10 9 8 7 6 5 4 3 2 1

Cover art by Lindsey Look.
Cover design by Lesley Worrell.
Interior text design by Kelly Lipovich.
Map by Cortney Skinner.

Penguin
Random
House

For my mother,
Billie,
the fiercest cheerleader any daughter could hope for.
With all my love and appreciation.

ACKNOWLEDGEMENTS

I knew going in that *The Bloodforged* was going to be the most challenging book I'd ever written, it being much more ambitious than anything I've tackled before, so I was prepared to hit a few potholes along the road. Or at least, I thought I was. But it ended up being even tougher than I'd expected. There were roadblocks and detours. Moments when I ran out of gas, or was tempted to take a shortcut. I might still be stalled on the side of the road if it hadn't been for the patient but firm encouragement of Lisa Rodgers and Joshua Bilmes. I'm enormously grateful for that, and I hope they're as proud as I am of the result.

Readers desiring a little extra information on people, places, and culture can refer to the glossary at the back of this book.

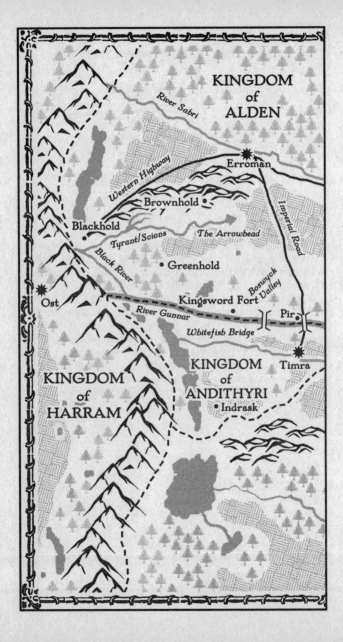

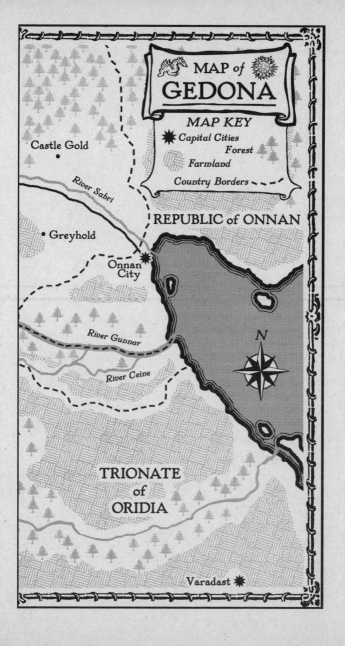

ONE

† Boot heels rang out under the high ceiling. Stiff. Precise. A military gait. The oratorium stood dark, its hearths unlit. Sunlight slanted down through arched windows on either side of the vast hall, but the stained glass filtered it into near irrelevance. Only when the gleaming surface of spaulders passed directly through a shaft of jewelled light was it possible to make out the figure moving along the wall.

She reached out, letting her hand trail along the stone until a flaw in the smooth surface caught her fingertips. Its contours were familiar to her now. It scarred the stone at thigh level, slanting upward from left to right. A left-handed swordsman, she judged, looking to open his enemy's flank. She'd often tried to picture who might have dealt the blow, but the battle had been too frenzied, her part in it too brief. Her duty had been to get the king to safety. Whoever left this mark, whether guardsman or Greysword, might be alive or dead. His blow might have landed or not. Only the walls knew. These walls knew so much. They'd presided over weddings and funerals, coronations and banquets. They'd presided over treachery too. But that would never happen again. Not on her watch.

She paused under the stained-glass image of Ardin's flame. Crimson light spilled over her, bloodying her armour and setting her copper hair afire. She gazed up at the magnificent window, frowning. A crack had appeared in the yellow band of flame. *When in the hells did that happen?* No more than a week ago, or she'd have noticed. She knew every inch of this room. Every knot in the gallery rail, every whorl in the polished stone floor. She'd studied it for days on end, in light and in shadow, with eyes and ears and hands, until she could be absolutely certain that she would notice anything, *anything*, out of place. Eldora herself, with her all-seeing eye, couldn't know this room any better than Alix Black.

"Godwin." Her voice echoed coldly off the stone.

A rustle of armour sounded behind her. Godwin hurried over from the door where he'd been hovering in anticipation of her orders. Alix always did the first sweep alone, the better to avoid distractions.

"Captain."

She pointed. "Do you see that?"

Her second squinted, cocked his head. "Afraid not, Captain. What am I looking for?"

"There's a crack in Ardin's flame. Look there."

He grunted. "How do you reckon that happened?"

"That's what I want to find out. Fetch Arnot. I want someone up a ladder on either side of that window."

"Shall I ask for the braziers to be lit on my way out?"

"Please."

Godwin held a fist to his chest in salute and hurried out, leaving Alix to scowl up at the offending glass. It was almost certainly nothing to worry about. Glass did crack occasionally, especially centuries-old glass. The cold, most likely. But Alix wasn't taking any chances. By this time tomorrow, the most important lords and ladies in the realm would occupy this august hall. A tempting target in peacetime, let alone in the middle of the fiercest war the Kingdom of Alden had ever known.

Alix was about to resume her sweep when she sensed a presence behind her. Tensing instinctively, she turned. The shadow of a hulking beast darkened the doorway; yellow eyes met hers from across the room. It took a halting step forward, muscular frame pausing midstride. It waited.

Alix smiled. "Hello, Rudi."

The wolfhound padded over, nub of a tail wagging enthusiastically. Alix dropped to her haunches.

"I wouldn't do that," said a voice from the doorway. "He's liable to tear your throat out."

Alix laughed, tugging the hound's ears. "Yours, maybe."

Footfalls tracked across the hall. "What's your secret, anyway?"

Alix glanced up to find her husband looking legitimately put out, arms crossed over the white wolf emblazoned on his breast-plate. Liam was in dress armour already, improbably shiny, the hated white cape fixed to his left shoulder with a sunburst clasp. That explained the mood.

"There's no secret to it," Alix said, straightening. "Unless you count not being terrified of him. Dogs can smell fear, you know."

"I'm not *terrified* of him. I just don't trust him." Liam gestured irritably at the wolfhound, a movement too sudden for Rudi's liking; he growled. Liam spread his hands, vindicated.

"He's still a puppy. He'll settle down."

"He's the canine equivalent of a brooding adolescent, and he weighs ten stone. Such a delightful combination."

"Maybe he resents you naming him *Rudi*."

"Rudolf is a strong, wolfy name."

"Which you shortened to *Rudi*." Alix resumed her sweep, Liam tagging alongside. Rudi trotted ahead, slipping under the gallery rail to sniff at the benches. "If you didn't want him," she said, "you shouldn't have got him."

"Like I had a choice. Highmount was on me day and night about it. I was given to understand it was practically a matter of duty."

"You could have said no. You are a prince, after all."

He made a face. "Don't remind me."

Alix left that alone. She focused on the task at hand, running her gaze from floor to ceiling and back again, as systematic as a servant with a feather duster.

"Why do you do this in the dark, anyway?" Liam asked. "Isn't it hard to see?"

"I only do the first pass this way. It's not completely dark, and you notice different things than when the room is well lit. See there?" She pointed. "That nail in the bench, the way it catches the light? You'd never notice that if the braziers were lit."

Liam looked at her sceptically. "It's just a nail."

"The king's life is my responsibility, Liam. There's no such thing as *just a nail*."

As she spoke, a soft glow climbed the walls, spilled out under their boots. The servants had arrived with torches to light the braziers. And they did not come alone. A thin voice piped across the room. "Oh, *dear*!"

Rudi raised his head from between the benches and growled.

Arnot stood in the doorway, wringing his soft white hands. "Cracked, Lady Alix? Are you certain?"

"I'm afraid so," Alix said, motioning the steward inside. Like all the servants, he knew better than to enter the oratorium without express leave from the king's bodyguard.

"This won't do at all." Arnot rubbed his balding pate in distress, a nervous gesture that probably accounted for much of the baldness. "The banner lords will be here tomorrow!"

Alix couldn't help sighing. "Not all the banner lords. Rig won't be here."

Arnot fluttered a pale hand dismissively. "Yes, but your brother doesn't . . ." He caught himself, if not quite in time, at least before it got any worse. "That is, Lord Black has never shown much care for matters of courtly prestige." He cleared his throat primly.

"You mean he thinks it's bollocks," Liam said.

Arnot managed to look horrified and apologetic at the same time. "Your Highness. I'm so very sorry, I did not see you there. Er . . . by your leave . . ." He gestured at a servant hurrying by and made his escape.

"Very princely," Alix said in an undertone.

Liam shrugged. "Bastard."

"Being a bastard gives you licence to behave boorishly?"

"It's got to have some perks, doesn't it?"

Alix rolled her eyes and kept walking. "You'd better be on your best behaviour tomorrow, love. Erik's court is still getting used to you as it is. You don't want to give people an excuse to dismiss you altogether. And you don't want to embarrass your brother."

Liam's grey eyes clouded over, the petulant look returning. "I don't know why I have to be there."

"This is the most important council meeting Erik has ever convened. We're at war, Liam. Facing imminent conquest. Of *course* you have to be there."

"But it's a political discussion, not a military one. I don't see what use I'll be."

"You give yourself too little credit. Besides, you're not there in your capacity as commander of the White Wolves. You're there because you're prince of the realm." *Whether you like it or not.* Sometimes, she wondered whether Liam regretted letting his brother acknowledge him. Not that it made any difference; there was no going back on it now. Especially since, for the moment at least, Erik had no other heir. If anything were to happen to him . . .

Now there's a thought. Alix took up her task with renewed focus.

"I might be prince of the realm," Liam said, "but I'm still a bastard. They'll never see me as one of them."

"You're worrying about it too much. It never bothered me. It doesn't bother Rig."

"You two are different."

Alix snorted. Few of the other Banner Houses would disagree with that assessment. "Raibert Green and Rona Brown have both ridden into battle with you. That's three banners in your camp. And Sirin Grey . . ." She paused awkwardly. "Well, you helped her once."

"Oh, right, you mean the time I stopped her collapsing after my brother executed her true love? I'm sure she remembers that incident fondly."

"The point is, most of the banner lords know and accept you. The lesser nobility will follow their lead eventually—unless you give them an excuse not to. It's only been six months." Saying it aloud, Alix had to pause. Had so little time really passed? It seemed an age since the Oridians surrounded the city walls. The Siege of Erroman had already acquired the lacquer of legend, as though it were the climactic end of a great and glorious war, instead of merely a punctuation point in an ongoing, bloody struggle. So much had happened since then. Rig's appointment as commander general of the king's armies. Alix and Liam's wedding. The dismantling of the Greyswords and the division of half that family's estates. Most of all, the war, dragging on and on, as much a feature of Aldenian life as the harvest or the Moon Festival. As though it had always been, would always be.

But of course that wasn't true. The war couldn't go on forever. If Rig's reports from the front were anything to go by, it wouldn't even last the summer. The Warlord had them by the throat; all he had to do was squeeze, and the Kingdom of Alden would be lost. Alix felt a familiar buck of panic at the thought.

She was grateful for the interruption of Liam's voice. "It's just . . . I belong at the front, Allie. I'm a soldier. What good are the White Wolves if they stay cooped up in their barracks? If they don't see some action soon, I'm going to have a mutiny on my hands."

"Don't even joke about that." Alix gripped his arm, glancing around furtively to see if anyone might have overheard. The loyalty of the White Wolves was still a touchy subject, given their role in the treachery at Boswyck. The Raven had been their commander then; after his execution, most of the officers serving under him had been dismissed. Still, the Wolves would carry that stain for a long time.

Liam growled under his breath. "There, you see? How am I supposed to manage a war council when I can't even get through a conversation with my own wife without saying something stupid?"

"Do what I do and keep your mouth shut." The voice was nearly as familiar as Alix's own, but she could just as easily have recognised him by the authoritative toll of his boots as he made his way across the hall. Rig didn't walk. He *strode*. Alix turned around, grinning. "Since when do you keep your mouth shut?"

"Don't I? I always mean to." Rig gathered her up in a bear hug. He smelled of leather and steel and the dust of the road. As always, Alix felt small and safe in his arms. His deep voice rumbled in her ear. "How's things, little sister?"

"Suddenly better." Alix had learned to cope with Rig being at the front, but it was never far from her mind. His visits, too short and too few, lifted a weight she was barely conscious of carrying, like shucking her armour at the end of a long day.

"They told us you weren't coming," Liam said, clasping arms with his brother-in-law.

"Well, *they* obviously didn't see the summons I received from Albern Highmount. Apparently, missing a council of this magnitude simply isn't done. Unbecoming of a banner lord, so on and so forth."

"You'll have to add that to your list of behaviours unbecoming of a banner lord," Alix said.

"I don't need to keep a list. Highmount is doing it for me." Rig shook his head, dark eyebrows drawn into a scowl. "Can either of you explain to me how a *meeting* can possibly be more important than commanding Alden's armies at the front?"

Alix sighed. "Not you too. Look, both of you, this isn't just any meeting. We're in serious trouble."

Rig laughed humourlessly. "There's an understatement. My men are exhausted, and the spring thaw is just around the corner. The war is about to come out of hibernation. We'll be lucky to hold the enemy at the border until the Onnani fleet arrives on his doorstep."

"That's just it," Alix said. "They may not be arriving anytime soon. Word is that they're well behind schedule. The Onnani ambassador hasn't been able to give us a clear indication of when they'll be ready to launch, but it sounds like it'll be months yet."

Rig swore and rubbed his jaw, beard bristling beneath his fingers. "*Bloody* fishmen. I can't hold them off that long, Allie. What in the Domains am I supposed to do until then?"

"That's what you're here to discuss, you and the rest of the council. There aren't many options."

"You don't say." He shook his head. "What about Harram? What's the latest on that?"

"Bit of flirting," Liam said, "but no action."

"So much for the fierce fighters of Harram," Rig said bitterly. "We'll be halfway through the afterlife before those cowards join the war."

Alix didn't bother arguing. Aside from a westerner's natural suspicion of foreigners, Rig harboured a particular dislike for the Harrami, whose failure to control their mountain tribes left the Blacklands vulnerable to raids. He'd faced Harrami tribesmen in battle, and it had marked him. It had also taught him hit-and-run tactics and the rare art of true horse archery, both of which the Blackswords had put to good use in the first six months of the war. But Alix doubted he would see the positive side.

"What's with the shine?" Rig said, gesturing at Liam's dress armour.

Liam grimaced. "In honour of your esteemed selves. Most of the banner lords are arriving tonight."

"Is there a banquet?" Rig asked, brightening.

"There is," Liam replied with considerably less enthusiasm.

"Thank the Nine Virtues. I'm lucky if I get a bite of venison these days. The Imperial Road is a mess this time of year."

"Looks like it," Alix said, inclining her head at her brother's muddy boots. He'd left a trail of it across the polished stone floor. Arnot would not be pleased. "You'd better get cleaned up. You might even consider cutting your hair."

Rig ran a careless hand through his coal-black locks. They were almost to his shoulders again, hanging in the same lazy waves as Alix's. "Do you think it'll annoy Highmount if I don't?"

"Definitely."

"In that case, I think I'll leave it."

Liam grinned. "A man after my own heart."

Rudi padded over, having concluded his own sweep of the oratorium. He snuffled at Rig's boots, but otherwise gave him a pass. "Holy Scourge of Rahl!" Rig held out a callused hand for the wolfhound to sniff. "Is that *Rudi*? He's a monster!"

"Yes," Liam said, "he is."

"I can't believe how much he's grown! We could use a few like that at the front. Put some fear into those gods-cursed Oridian warhounds." Rig gave the animal's flank a solid thump, setting Rudi's nub wagging.

"You want him? He's yours." Liam started to reach for the wolfhound, but Rudi bared his teeth.

"All right," Alix said, "out of here, all of you. I need to finish this and get back to Erik."

"Come on, Rudi," Rig said, "let's find something to eat." The wolfhound trotted alongside him as happily as if Rig had reared him from a pup. Liam looked after them in disgust.

"Bye, Allie." He dropped a kiss on Alix's cheek. "See you at the banquet."

Alix shook her head ruefully. A banquet. In the middle of war. She understood the politics of it, but even so, it felt wrong somehow. Like a death feast. A final indulgence before the execution.

She raised her eyes to the stained-glass window, watching detachedly as the servants tried to repair the crack. She no longer saw the symbol of Ardin's passion. Instead, she saw the flames of war.

Erik White stood at the window of his study, gazing out over the rose garden. A light glitter of snow dusted the burlap sacks covering the rosebushes, giving them a sombre cast. *Like a row* *of tombstones*, he thought. An endless row, twisting back on itself and back again, an army of tombstones in tight, ordered ranks. Was that what the graves at the front looked like?

Don't be ridiculous. They have no time to erect monuments to their dead.

Erik sighed, his breath fogging the glass. It was no good, giving himself over to grim thoughts like this. He knew it, but he could not seem to help himself. The longer the war dragged on, the less Erik could think about anything else. He was climbing the walls here in the palace, futile and frivolous, throwing banquets and convening council meetings while hundreds, thousands of his men died at the front. It was almost enough to make him long for the days when he commanded his own forces in the field. His kingdom had been torn in half then, its lands overrun by enemy forces, but at least Erik had not felt as though he were burrowed down, snug and safe, like a hedgehog waiting out the winter. At least then, he could face his enemy head on. If his kingdom was destined to be conquered, Erik would rather die on the point of a sword than be captured in the palace, forced to his knees in front of the Warlord. Thrown in the Red Tower, or worse, given his freedom in exchange for surrender.

Stop it. We are not conquered. Not yet.

"Your Majesty."

Her voice was a welcome interruption. Erik turned.

"The oratorium is clear. There's a crack in one of the windows, but the servants assure me it's just ordinary wear and tear. It'll be repaired by tomorrow."

"Thank you, Alix. And what of the banner lords? Have they begun arriving?"

She smiled. Erik knew what that meant, and he smiled too. "So he did come, then?" He had been told not to expect Riggard Black.

Closing the door to make sure they were alone, Alix strolled into the room and threw herself casually into a chair. "Apparently, he got a letter from Highmount."

"Ah." Erik pulled out his own chair. "I suppose I shouldn't be surprised. My first counsel is convinced this is the most critical decision we've had to make since the siege."

Alix toyed with the pearl-handled seal knife on his desk. "Is it?" she asked quietly.

"I think perhaps it is," he said, just as quietly. "But the truth is, I'm not sure it's really a choice at all. If our allies don't enter the war, and soon, it's over for us. We must do whatever it takes to see that they do."

"And you and Highmount have an idea how to do that?" The barest hint of frost touched her voice. Few would have noticed it; Alix had grown better at concealing her thoughts these past months. Time at court did that to a person. But Erik spent at least twelve hours a day with this woman, and he could read her as easily as a favourite book. She was annoyed, and he thought he knew why.

"We've discussed it in detail, yes. And no, you were not present. That was deliberate, Alix." Hardly likely to appease her, but he wanted her to understand. "I needed to discuss the options freely, without worrying about those whom it might affect."

She gave him a wary look. "Meaning?"

"I see only one possible solution, and you're not going to like it."

"That sounds ominous."

"Ominous." He sighed again, rubbed his temples. "That is how we live our lives, is it not? Ominously?"

Her expression softened; she reached across the desk and took his hand. Instinctively, Erik's fingers tightened around hers.

"It won't last forever, Erik. It can't."

For half a heartbeat, he let himself take comfort in her voice, in the warmth of her hand. Then he released her and sat back. "No, it can't. It must end. My duty is to make sure it ends well, no matter what. I hope I can count on your support tomorrow, even if you don't like what I have to say."

The wary look returned. "In that case, maybe you'd better tell me now."

"We will discuss it at length tomorrow, I promise. And I'm not asking you to agree with me blindly—just hear me out, without jumping to conclusions. If you still have concerns, you are free to air them, as always. I daresay you won't be alone."

She shifted uncomfortably. "This proposal of yours—it's really that bad?"

"Bad? I sincerely hope not. Call it desperate, rather."

She swallowed. "Are things really that . . . Are we desperate?"

His gaze moved back to the window, to the glitter of snow and the marching ranks of tombstones. "Yes, Alix, we are."

TWO

† "My lady?" Arnot poked his head in, a little warily. He'd grown accustomed to Alix's mood on days like this, and learned to tread lightly.

She nodded distractedly, her gaze raking the oratorium one last time. Though she had no reason to expect trouble, she knew better than to take anything for granted. She'd taken plenty of precautions last summer, on that fateful day when Erik and his brother had met in parley to decide the future of the crown, and it hadn't helped. Roswald Grey had still managed to smuggle his men inside. Erik had nearly been killed. Alix would never make a mistake like that again, not ever.

Having secured her leave, Arnot led a small army of servants into the room. Under his capable command, hearths and braziers were lit, flowers arranged, refreshments placed close at hand. The wood had been waxed, the floors polished. A new rib of lead had been added to the window bearing Ardin's flame. Silk cushions of green and black, brown and gold and grey were carefully positioned so that each banner lord might know where to sit, in a position commensurate with his prestige. Everything was ready.

Albern Highmount was the first to arrive, as always, to do his customary inspection of the preparations. "Your Highness," he said, acknowledging her with a grave nod. The first counsel was the only person at court who referred to her that way—possibly because he knew how much it annoyed her. She had been born *Lady Alix*, appointed *captain of the royal guardsmen*. These titles were her own, one a birthright, the other something earned. *Your Highness*, on the other hand, was something she'd acquired through association. The honorific belonged to Liam, not her. It didn't speak to who she was. Not really.

"I am pleased your brother was able to join us," Highmount said. *I am pleased your brother saw fit to do his duty*, was what he meant.

"It's fortunate he found a window to do so, what with the *war* and all."

"Wars are not fought with swords alone, Your Highness. Indeed, in many cases, they are not decided by swords at all."

Alix treated herself to a brief, diverting vision of Highmount slipping on the freshly polished floor.

The first counsel concluded his inspection and departed, heading for his post at the main doors of the palace. Protocol demanded that he greet the banner lords personally. Alix was not sorry to see him go.

Godwin appeared at her side. "All clear, Captain?"

She nodded. "Let's do this."

A moment later, the herald announced the first arrival. "Lord Raibert Green."

A familiar figure appeared in the doorway. As bearer of the kingdom's oldest and most venerable banner, Green was first among his peers, and thus preceded them into any official gathering. One might expect such an august person to carry himself haughtily—but only if one had never met Raibert Green. He looked solemn as always, his thin face wise and world-weary, but when he spied Alix, a smile burst over him and set his gentle eyes sparkling. "My lady. It's good to see you."

She embraced him as if he were a favourite uncle. "You're looking well."

"As are you," he said. "Married life agrees with you, I see."

Alix started to reply, but the herald's voice cut her off. "Lady Rona Brown."

The newest of the banner holders entered tentatively, glancing around as though not quite sure what to do with herself. This was only her second council since inheriting the banner. At nineteen years old, a knight for barely a year, she had yet to fully grow into her office. Alix had no doubt that she would, though, judging by her attire. Rona had elected to wear ceremonial armour, a daring choice that would no doubt set Albern Highmount's teeth on edge. A rampant white wolf, smaller but otherwise identical to Liam's, adorned her breastplate, marking her an officer of that elite unit. Her only concession to her birthright was a brown satin cape over her left shoulder. To flout tradition barely six months after inheriting the Brown banner spoke volumes about her sense of independence.

It spoke of something else too, Alix judged. Wearing her White Wolf armour was a mark of Rona's loyalty to her commander. Loyalty, and perhaps something a little more. It wasn't the first time Alix had noticed this . . . devotion. Well, that was all right. After all, who could blame her? Liam was handsome, witty, and as talented a sword as any in the realm. Also, he was a prince. Banner lady or no, Rona Brown had every right to be smitten. So long as she kept her hands to herself.

"Lord Riggard Black."

Rig wore armour too, but in his case, not even Highmount would have expected anything else. Like his predecessor, Arran Green, Rig was every inch a soldier. That meant he had a soldier's sense of solidarity, so when he spied Rona Brown hovering awkwardly near the door, he went over and clapped her shoulder. Rona smiled, relaxing a little.

Norvin Gold was next to arrive, looking even more ancient than the last time Alix had seen him. Thin hair drifted in wisps over his spotted scalp; angular cheekbones threw shadows down over gaunt cheeks. Even his doublet looked worn. *They have fallen on hard times*, Alix thought. They all had, and none more so than the final arrival.

"Lady Sirin Grey," said the herald.

Alix and Raibert Green exchanged a look. Sirin was not the holder of the Grey banner; that honour belonged to her mother, Alithia. To send a lower-ranking member of the family to a council of this importance could be taken as a slight. The Greys were already disgraced, thanks to the treachery of Sirin's brother. It surprised Alix that Lady Grey would risk offending the crown barely six months after her son had plotted to wrest control of it.

"Perhaps Lady Grey is ill?" Alix ventured in an undertone.

Raibert Green shook his head. "I saw her only yesterday. She looked hale enough to me."

Alix regarded him in surprise. It was none of her business, but as usual, she found it difficult to hold her tongue. "You had business with the Greys?"

The barest hint of a sigh passed Green's lips. "Lady Grey was so gracious as to offer me the hand of her daughter."

Alix looked down at her boots for the handful of moments it took to master herself. "That's . . . unexpected."

Green shrugged. "Lady Sirin is the daughter of a Banner House. All things being equal, she should have been married long ago."

All things being equal, she should have married Erik. Alix couldn't bring herself to be sorry that hadn't happened, though she did pity Sirin her circumstances. Being in love with her fiancé's brother was bad enough; seeing her lover beheaded for treason was a misfortune she surely did not deserve. Still, to suppose that she could still be worthy of a Green, the most illustrious of the Banner Houses . . . It was wildly ambitious. Politically, it would have made far more sense to offer her to Rig. Not that Alix would have welcomed that; having Sirin Grey as a sister-in-law would have been more than a little awkward.

"Lady Sirin is still young, and very beautiful," Green said. "And I do not think it fair to hold her responsible for her brother's sins, or the Raven's. The fortunes of her house are not her doing, and their standing will recover in time."

"But . . ."

He shrugged again. "But she doesn't love me. We barely know each other. We both need heirs, it's true, but I am not so desperate as to enter a marriage with someone in mourning. It's been barely six months since Prince Tomald was executed. I know what it's like to lose the one you love. Six months is not nearly enough time, Alix."

Sirin Grey acknowledged the others with a nod and moved to find her seat. She carried herself with grave dignity, gaze straight ahead, acutely aware that every pair of eyes followed her across the hall. Silent steps moved her pale silk dress in dreamlike wisps, as if she were a ghost. In a way, Alix supposed, she was; a ghost of the influential figure she'd once been.

"That's everyone," Alix said as a few minor lords and

ladies made their way in. Now that all the Banner Houses were represented, the rest of the council members were permitted to enter. That left only His Majesty the king and His Highness the prince.

She found them in the king's study. Liam perched on the edge of Erik's desk, looking casually beautiful in his dress armour. Erik sat with his head bowed, absently stroking Rudi's fur, his gaze a million miles away. The wolfhound, for his part, had his eyes closed in bliss. Erik was his favourite—to Liam's vast annoyance.

The sound of Alix's footfalls drew the king's head up. "Are we ready?" He looked nearly as tense as he had the day of the parley with the Raven, the day the stone walls of the oratorium had acquired an upward-slanting scar.

"Ready," she said. "The last of the lords and ladies are just filing in now."

Erik rose, revealing a white doublet with sky blue embroidery that brought out the bright, clear topaz of his eyes. "To work, then," he said, and headed for the door.

Liam strode at his side, Alix trailing just behind. Even after all these months, it felt strange to follow in Liam's footsteps. For so long, he'd been the one to follow her, tracking her footfalls through the brush as she led them on a scouting mission. Figuratively, too, he'd always taken Alix's lead—*like a puppy*, Arran Green had once said. But that was when he'd been merely Liam, a no-name commoner, a scout like any other. Things were different now. *So different*, Alix thought.

The high lords and ladies of the realm stood arrayed behind their designated seats, waiting. Erik acknowledged them all with a crisp nod, gestured for them to sit. Alix alone remained on her feet, hovering just over Erik's right shoulder, close enough to rest a hand on it if she'd wanted to. No doubt many in the room would consider that overkill. Insulting, even, implying as it did that the king's bodyguard didn't really trust them. Alix didn't give a flaming flea what they thought. This was war.

Erik's solemn gaze took them in one by one. "My lords. Thank you for gathering on such short notice. Some of you have travelled great distances to be here, and the roads are difficult. The crown salutes your loyalty and service. Be assured that I do not presume upon them lightly. The matters we discuss today are of vital strategic importance to the realm." He turned to Rig, who sat second from his left, with only Lord Green between them. Barely a year ago, such a position of honour would have been unthinkable, but the Blacks had come a long way since then. "Lord Black, perhaps we might begin with an update from the front."

"As you wish, Your Majesty." Rig raised his voice a little above his customary rumble. "The winter has been difficult, as predicted. Things have been relatively quiet on the battlefield, but our supply lines have grown stretched. Aside from the usual difficulties of the season, our stores are at an all-time low following last year's lost harvests. On top of which, banditry is rife on the Imperial Road, and worsening every day. We've been obliged to double the escort on our supply wagons, diverting men who are sorely needed at the front."

"With your permission, General," said Rona Brown. When Rig nodded, she continued. "The problem is even worse in the Brownlands. Highwaymen roam the farmsteads and villages, looting and preying on the people. It's been especially hard on the womenfolk. They sometimes . . . That is, there have been several cases . . ." She swallowed, dropping her gaze.

"Yes," Rig said, his eyes hard with fury. "That too."

"Every sword we can muster goes straight to the front," Rona said. "I have none to spare on law and order."

"In the Greenlands too," Raibert Green added. "Nearly a dozen untimely deaths reported this winter, and half as many disappearances. And those are just the incidents that have reached my ears. The real numbers are almost certainly higher."

Rig's hands balled into fists on the table, forearms twitching into cords of stiff muscle. He would consider all this a personal failure, Alix knew. She wanted to say something, to tell him it wasn't his fault, but now was not the time.

"Please continue, Lord Black," Erik said.

With a visible effort, Rig relaxed his hands. "The winter has been hard on the enemy too. Their supply lines are secure, thanks to their foothold in Andithyri, but disease has torn through their ranks. Some sort of cough, I'm told. Probably the same one our men had last winter. Meanwhile, their reinforcements have slowed."

"Perhaps I might interject here," said Albern Highmount. Unlike Rona Brown, he didn't wait for Rig's leave. "My spies report that the Oridian populace grows weary of war. They have been at it for much longer, of course, and with the Priest slain, their religious fervour has dimmed. They begin to question the purpose of unending expansion."

"Even if the people are weary," Rig said, "their soldiers are not. And neither is the Warlord. He'll not stand down, not unless Varad forces him to."

"That he is unlikely to do," Raibert Green said. "Varad may be King, but with the Priest gone, his position is weakened. And it would not do for the two remaining Trions to appear divided. The King will support the Warlord for the time being, if I am any judge."

"Agreed," Erik said, "but even so, the news is welcome. The people are the backbone of any war effort. It may take time, but if the Oridian public opposes the war, it will sap their strength."

"In the meantime," Rig said, "we have thirty thousand soldiers on our doorstep, and only half that number to defend it. We've been plodding through the winter, but spring will set things galloping again."

"How long do you estimate you can hold the enemy at the border?" Highmount asked.

"The raiding will begin straightaway, I expect. As for a full-scale invasion, it's impossible to say, but I'd measure it in weeks rather than months. For the moment, the river is doing most of the work; otherwise, the Warlord would be halfway to Erroman by now. We've managed to destroy most of the bridges, but there are still a couple of fords the enemy could cross. Needless to say, my men are piled up at those points."

"The spring thaw will help you out there," Alix said. She remembered how dangerous the Black River became in spring, swollen with snowmelt.

"For a while," Rig said. "The water levels have already risen enough to close off a few crossing points, but it won't last. By midyear, two fords will become five, and I don't have the men to plug that many holes." Though his voice remained level, Alix knew her brother well enough to detect the hint of desperation creeping in. "I don't know any other way to say this, Your Majesty: If we don't find a way to strengthen our ranks, we won't last the summer. We need solutions."

"Yes," Erik sighed, "we do. And that is why we are here." He turned to his first counsel. "Lord Highmount, if you will."

Highmount inclined his head ponderously. "Certainly, Your Majesty. First, a bit of good news. My spies have assured me that the enemy continues recruiting the old-fashioned way. That is to say, the Trionate has not resumed making thralls."

Rig sat forward a little in his seat. "You're absolutely sure? How do we know they aren't busily bewitching peasants behind enemy lines?"

"My spies have assured me," Highmount repeated coolly.

"We've problems enough without an army of mindless drones throwing themselves against our walls. We'd never survive another attack like that."

"True," said Highmount, "but fortunately, it would appear that the Priest kept his secrets close. The Trionate's bloodbinders continue to forge bloodweapons at an alarming rate, but there is no sign they have learned how to warp their art into controlling men. Madan seems to have taken that knowledge to his grave. However, though the Priest's secrets are not yet known, Nevyn tells me that a number of his fellow bloodbinders in Harram and Onnan are busily trying to discover it. It is only a matter of time before someone succeeds. It might be days or it might be years, but it will happen eventually."

"And what about Nevyn himself?" asked Norvin Gold. "I presume he is also trying to work it out?"

Erik shifted in his chair. Alix knew he was deeply uncomfortable with the idea of Alden wielding such a dark power, no matter how desperate the cause. *Controlling another man's mind is an abomination*, he'd told her once. *I want no part of it, ever.* Erik had lost much of his principled idealism over the course of the war, but there were still some lines he was not prepared to cross, and enslaving men's wills through dark magic was foremost on the list.

Not everyone shared his scruples, however. "If he managed it," Lady Stonegate mused, "it could turn the tide of the war, especially if we were alone in mastering the technique."

Raibert Green frowned. "You would win this war by bewitching thousands of innocents?"

"If that is what it takes to bring an end to it . . ."

Green started to object, but Highmount raised a hand. "Let us not descend into debate, my lords. The point is moot; Nevyn does not know the secret." Alix noticed that he hadn't answered Lord Gold's question. Not for the first time, she wondered if Highmount might be pursuing the matter without Erik's knowledge.

"Good to hear we won't be facing thralls anytime soon," Rig said, "but that doesn't change the fact that we're outnumbered two to one. We need our allies to move."

"Indeed," Highmount said. "On that front, I fear the news is less positive. Ambassador Corse has informed us that in spite of previous promises, the Onnani fleet will not be ready for launch by spring. Instead, they are predicting midsummer at the earliest."

A ripple of despair went round the table.

"How can that be?" cried Osmond Swiftcurrent. His outrage was understandable; his family had done more to finance the expansion of the Onnani fleet than any house save the Whites themselves. "It's been nearly six months! How long does it take to build a bloody ship?"

Highmount gave him a reproving look. "There is no cause for coarse language, Lord Swiftcurrent."

"I disagree," Rig growled. "There's plenty of cause. If that fleet doesn't start pressing the enemy soon, we're finished. I can't hold them at the border unless a new front opens up, and they've conquered everything to the south. With Harram still dithering away, that fleet is everything."

"Onnani bloodbinders are working day and night to help supply bloodweapons," Highmount said, "and they have promised to send a battalion to join you at the front."

"A whole battalion? Lucky me."

Highmount opened his mouth to reply, but Lady Stonegate beat him to it. "Have the Onnani given any explanation for the delay?"

"They have offered an explanation," Erik said, "but I think it's fair to say that Lord Highmount and I did not find it especially satisfying."

That was an understatement. Alix had been present for that meeting, and the Onnani ambassador had been slippery as a fish. Something was up in Onnan City—that was clear. Something the ambassador wasn't keen to admit.

"Ambassador Corse suggested that their early efforts were not satisfactory," Highmount said, "and they were obliged to start from scratch."

Liam gave an incredulous little laugh. "What, like they've never built a ship before? They don't call them *fishmen* for nothing."

"They do not call themselves *fishmen* at all, Your Highness," Highmount said, "a fact you must remember at all costs." An odd remark, Alix thought; she and Liam exchanged a bemused glance.

"From scratch indeed," Swiftcurrent said disgustedly. "Well, what does Woodvale have to say about it?"

"Rather too much, unfortunately," Highmount said. "Lord Woodvale has quit Onnan City following a somewhat . . . *effervescent* appearance before the Republicana."

"They've expelled our ambassador?" Norvin Gold's moustaches quivered in outrage. "How dare they?"

Erik sighed. "Not quite expelled, but they made it clear that he would no longer be an effective envoy. I was obliged to recall him. He should be back in Erroman within the week."

"But who will replace him?" Green asked. "We cannot leave his position vacant at a time like this. We need someone looking into the situation with the fleet."

"Quite so, my lord," said Highmount. "That is among the issues we must resolve today."

"In due course," Erik said. "But first, the rest of the news, thankfully of a more positive nature. The Harrami have indicated that they are willing to discuss entering the war."

"Willing to discuss it?" Rig smiled thinly. "They really shouldn't overcommit themselves."

"It's been a frustrating dialogue, I admit, but Lord Highmount and I agree that King Omaïd is showing more openness to the possibility than ever before. After months of exchanging letters, he has agreed to receive a diplomatic mission to confer over the matter."

"That is a good sign," said Green. "A more committed isolationist has never been. I cannot recall a single diplomatic mission to Ost since Omaïd assumed the throne. He would never invite a delegation if he were not prepared to seriously consider what it had to say."

"Agreed," said Highmount. "It is the opening we have been waiting for, and we absolutely must capitalise on it."

"Easier said than done," Green said. "How will we get there, with things as they are? The usual route is in enemy hands."

"It will not be easy," Erik admitted, "but we cannot afford to let this chance pass us by. If the Harrami do declare war, it could change everything."

Norvin Gold hummed a sceptical note. "No one can doubt that the Harrami are skilled fighters, Your Majesty. I have seen their horse archers with my own eyes, and their fearsome reputation is well deserved. But they have known only a single war in their entire history. Their failure to subdue their own mountain tribes stands testament to their ineffectiveness as a coherent fighting force. What makes you think their role would be so decisive?"

Rig answered for him. "They don't have to be particularly effective. It's enough for them to open another front, put just enough pressure on it that the Oridians have no choice but to deploy. It will stretch their forces even more thinly."

"If we can get the Harrami to declare," Erik said, "it could dramatically change the complexion of the war."

"So how do we do that?" Liam asked.

Erik cleared his throat.

Here it comes, Alix thought.

You're not going to like it, Erik had said. And from the way he was looking at his brother, it was obvious Liam wasn't going to like it, either.

"I want us all to be absolutely clear about what is at stake here," Erik said. "It may be nothing less than our survival as a nation. Which means that this mission to Ost, however difficult, may be the most important diplomatic undertaking in our history."

A moment more was all it took for Alix to realise where he was going with this. Her eyes rounded in horror, and she seized the back of Erik's chair in a white-knuckled grip. *Oh, please, Erik, no. Stay your tongue. Let me talk to you first . . .*

But she knew him better than that. He'd made up his mind to table this, and so he would. What followed would be in the hands of the gods, but Alix knew one thing for certain: Her job was about to get much, much harder.

THREE

† Erik glanced briefly over his shoulder, but otherwise ignored his bodyguard's silent outburst. "I propose to lead the delegation to Ost myself," he said. "As soon as possible."

They all stared.

"You can't be serious," Liam said.

"I am perfectly serious. Despite the obvious risks—"

"Obvious risks?" Rig echoed incredulously. "It's *suicide*, Erik!"

Highmount *tsk*ed. "Let us not be dramatic, Lord Black."

The look that came over Rig did credit to the family name. Not for the first time, Alix feared her brother might leap across the table and throttle the first counsel.

"I'm afraid I quite agree with the commander general," said Norvin Gold. "Unless my geography fails me, I don't see how you mean to reach Harram without crossing enemy lines, of one sort or another. The southern road takes you straight into the arms of the Warlord, and the west into the mountain tribes. Quite frankly, I'm not sure which is worse."

"I am," Rig said. "I've fought off more than a few tribal raiders in my time. They're hard enough to defeat when you catch them out in the open, and you want to try your luck on their home territory?" He shook his head. "Suicide."

"Crossing the mountains in spring is dangerous at the best

of times," Lord Swiftcurrent added. "It's avalanche season, not to mention those unpredictable springtime blizzards . . ."

Erik listened to it all patiently, hands folded on the table in front of him, gaze shifting levelly between speakers. He'd been prepared for these objections, Alix knew. He'd been through them all with Highmount, probably more than once; he was just waiting for the council to reach the same inescapable conclusions he had.

"Is there any chance we could cross the mountains without the tribes knowing?" Rona Brown asked.

"You might get that lucky once," Rig said. "Not twice. Even if you somehow managed to make it to Ost, you'd never make it back."

"What if Omaïd were to send an escort?" Swiftcurrent asked, demonstrating a poor grasp of regional politics.

"That would draw the mountain men like moths to a flame," Green said. "The tribes take any opportunity to strike at Harrami soldiers. The only hope is to pass unnoticed."

"Which is exactly what I propose to do," Erik said. "It will require a small force composed mainly of scouts, relying on stealth. Fortunately, the stealthiest scout in the land happens to be my personal bodyguard." He didn't turn around, but Alix felt her skin warming all the same. "What's more," Erik said, "she also happens to hail from the Blacklands, and knows the terrain."

"The foothills aren't the mountains, Your Majesty," Alix said, "and I've never dared set foot across the border, for obvious reasons."

"Isn't this what ambassadors are for?" Lady Stonegate asked, adding wryly, "Or have the Harrami ejected our envoy as well?"

"Lord Sommersdale has devoted an entire year's worth of diplomacy to this sole matter," Highmount said. "Visibly, he is not succeeding."

"Perhaps he should be replaced."

"A brand-new ambassador, a stranger to Omaïd's court, to negotiate the most important agreement in the history of our two nations?" Highmount raised his eyebrows.

Her Ladyship sighed. "I suppose you're right."

"Aside from which," Erik said, "the invitation has been

made, and it comes from Omaïd himself. Were we to refuse it now . . ."

"So we have no choice," Rig said. "Wonderful."

"There is always a choice," Erik said. "But inaction has consequences, and these must be weighed against the risks."

"This is not a quandary, my lords," Highmount said, "it is an opportunity. As you said only moments ago, Lord Black, we are in dire need of military support. This is our chance to get it."

"But why does it have to be His Majesty?" Alix felt her grip tighten on the back of Erik's chair. "Surely someone else . . . Lord Green, perhaps . . ."

Highmount was shaking his head before she even finished. "The Harrami are very proud, Your Highness. Anything less than royalty at the head of the delegation would be a slight."

"Then let me do it," Liam said. "I'm a member of the royal family, and I'm a lot more expendable than the king. The Wolves are hungry for action anyway."

"Before you volunteer yourself, brother," Erik said, "hear me out. We have another task in mind for you."

Liam's eyes narrowed. "Why do I think I'm not going to like this?"

"I would indeed have you as my envoy, but not to Ost. I would see you travel to Onnan City to oversee the construction of the fleet."

Liam's mouth dropped open. "But that makes no sense! I don't know the first thing about ships. I've never even seen the sea!"

"I need eyes and ears in Ost," Erik said, "and fortunately, we have an opening. After the ugly incident with Woodvale, the Republicana felt obliged to extend an invitation to me personally, to show there was no ill will."

"Perfect. You go to Onnan, I'll go to Harram."

"I'm afraid that is impossible, Your Highness," said Highmount. "As I mentioned, the Harrami are"—he cleared his throat—"very proud."

"Oh, I see." Colour crept up the back of Liam's neck. "A half-breed isn't good enough for them, is that it? But it's good enough for the Onnani?"

Silence dropped over the hall. Alix squeezed her husband's shoulder. All around them, lords and ladies acquired an abrupt interest in the grain of the oak table.

"Well, that's just great," Liam growled.

"*Someone* had better find out what's going on over there," Rig said. "I can't emphasise it enough: *I need that fleet.*"

"You have made that clear," Erik said. "As to whom, in spite of certain ill-considered intimations to the contrary"— he fired an icy look at his first counsel—"the Onnani are also very proud. As they see it, we are their former imperial masters. We must tread carefully, especially following the incident with Woodvale."

"His Majesty is right," Green said. "The Onnani have been staunch allies. If we send a royal delegation to Ost, but not to Onnan City, the Republicana will certainly take offence."

"So you see," Erik said, "both of our allies demand royal blood, and I cannot be in two places at once."

Rig snorted. "Tell me again we aren't in a quandary, Highmount."

Erik ignored that. He spread his hands, offering the floor. "You have heard my proposals, my lords. If there are others, now is the time to air them."

Alix's mind whirred, searching for something, *anything*, that might pass for an alternative. She came up empty-handed. Worse, she could tell from the grim expressions around the table that she wasn't alone. "It's too dangerous, Your Majesty," she said feebly.

"I will not deny the risks," Erik said. "That is why I convened this council. If the stakes were any less, I would have taken the decision myself. Believe me, I would like nothing better than to find another way."

Raibert Green sighed. "For my part, I cannot offer one, sire, though it pains me to admit."

"Nor I," said Norvin Gold, "though if you ask me, our allies are behaving like spoiled children."

"Spoiled children with a toy we badly need," Rig said. "*Bloody* fishmen . . ."

Highmount *tsk*ed again. "If Lord Black is quite through indulging himself, are there any other suggestions from the council?" He raised his eyebrows, met only silence. "So we are decided, then?"

"So it would seem," Gold said, "may the gods help us."

"Excellent. Then let us discuss the details. First, Onnan."

"I'm not a diplomat," Liam said sullenly.

"That is well understood, Your Highness," said Highmount, "which is why I recommend that you take Lady Brown with you."

One could say so much with silence. In the ensuing pause, Highmount transmitted three things: One, Liam was going to Onnan whether he liked it or not; two, Highmount didn't trust him not to cock it up without help; and three, Rona Brown had been bred at court and would hopefully keep the bastard prince from stepping into what Liam typically referred to as *a steaming pile of politics*.

Gods, Alix wanted to wring his neck.

"What is more," the first counsel continued, "it will be necessary for you to appoint someone of Onnani stock as your second."

Rig snorted, offering a soldier's opinion of political appointments in the military.

"I *have* a second," Liam said through gritted teeth. "Ide earned her place. What am I supposed to do, demote her?"

"The symbolism is important." Erik, at least, had the grace to look uncomfortable. "It will ease your way, I promise you."

"And just where am I supposed to find an Onnani knight?"

"I have one," Rig said. "A damned good one too. Former Brownsword. I'm loath to part with him, but he's yours if you want him. But for the record, this is *bollocks*."

"The record so notes," Erik said dryly.

"Excuse me, Your Majesty," said a smooth voice. Sirin Grey hadn't spoken until now; Alix had almost forgotten she was there. Erik's former intended sat perfectly poised, pale face composed, keen eyes unreadable. "Since we have decided that both you and His Highness will go abroad, might I enquire who will govern the kingdom in your absence?"

A question so fundamental that Alix couldn't believe it hadn't occurred to the rest of them until now.

"His Majesty intends to appoint me chancellor," Highmount said, "to rule in his absence."

Rig burst out laughing, bleak and humourless, fingers pinching the bridge of his nose as though to ward off a terrible headache. The other lords and ladies exchanged glances.

"That is not *quite* how I put it," Erik said with a wry look at his first counsel. "I ask that this council serve as advisors to

Chancellor Highmount throughout my absence. Decisions of importance will be taken by two thirds majority, not by fiat. The chancellor will not be ruling so much as presiding, much in the way First Speaker Kar presides over the Onnani Republicana."

"Democracy?" said Lord Gold, looking very much like a man who has just discovered a rat in his soup.

Erik smiled faintly. "I wouldn't go that far. I have always relied on the wisdom of this council. Chancellor Highmount will do the same."

Alix pursed her lips to forestall an outburst she would regret. It was so very like Erik to portray all this as a minor affair, a trivial, cosmetic thing. *Oh, I'm just abdicating for a while. Don't fuss about it.*

"I will have the details drawn up," Erik continued, "and delivered to your chambers. Take the evening to read them, carefully. We will reconvene tomorrow, at which point you may address any questions or concerns to Highmount and myself. And now, my lords, all that remains is for me to thank you for your voices in this matter. I trust we are all comfortable with the decisions we have reached here today."

Comfortable was surely a stretch; the council members looked more dazed than anything, as if they couldn't quite believe what they'd just agreed to.

Erik rose, indicating the session was over. Chairs scraped across a taut silence. The council members bowed and took their leave. All except Rig and Liam, both of whom hovered over their seats, glaring at their king.

"Godwin," Alix called, "please seal the doors."

The four of them stood staring at each other as the guards shuffled out, the rustle of armour echoing off the walls. They waited until the doors sounded with a muted *boom*. Then they all started talking at once.

"Erik, you can't—"

"It would have been nice if you'd—"

"Have you lost your—"

"Stop." Erik raised his hands. When he was certain he commanded silence, he said, "I know you're angry, but you all know me too well to imagine that I tabled this lightly."

"You should have warned us," Rig said. "The Broken Mountains, Erik? You can call it a *diplomatic mission* all you like, but you're not fooling anyone. This is nothing less than a stealth incursion into hostile territory."

"Yes," Erik said, "it is."

"Oh good, well I'm glad we cleared that up." Rig took two ringing strides toward the door before whirling back around. "What are you going to do when you run into some glory-hungry tribesmen looking for easy prey? Not to mention the half a hundred other dangers of a mountain pass in springtime?"

Erik scowled. "Is this Riggard Black lecturing someone on taking calculated risks? You of all people?"

Rig blew out an oath, ran a hand roughly over his beard. "No. The fact is, I don't see any way around it, either. I just wish it didn't have to be you. Or my sister."

"But it does, and we both know it."

Alix steadied herself against the heavy oak table and drew a deep, calming breath. Erik and her brother were right; there was no alternative, at least none any of them could see. Still . . . "It could hardly be a worse time for you to leave the capital," she pointed out. "The White Ravens might be broken, but that doesn't mean we're out of danger. The nobility is divided." That was putting it politely. The families that had thrown their lot in with Tom and Roswald Grey had been punished, some of them harshly. Scions in prison, lands confiscated, fines levied . . . Some of them, surely, would be only too happy for a chance at revenge. "What if your enemies use the opportunity of your absence to try to wrest control?"

"Why do you think I've delegated so much power to the council? Now each of those lords and ladies has a personal stake in maintaining the current order. If one begins to gain supremacy, he does so at the expense of the rest. They will keep each other in check."

Or they will ally against you. Alix didn't bother to say it aloud. Erik knew the risks better than anyone. But here again, he had no choice.

"Let me come with you," Liam said. "The Pack can protect you."

Erik shook his head. "We've discussed this. I need you in Onnan. That fleet is everything. You must find out what the delay is."

"How am I supposed to do that? 'Hey, look, chaps—I see

your problem.'" Liam pointed at an imaginary spot in the air. "'The thing hanging from the other thing is loose, see? There you go—problem solved.'"

"I haven't told you everything," Erik said. "There are certain details I did not wish to make public before the council." He threw a look at Alix.

"Ambassador Corse wasn't telling us the truth," she said, keeping her voice low. They were alone, supposedly, but one could never be too careful. The ears at court were notoriously keen. "Not all of it, anyway. His whole manner was off. Whatever's holding up the fleet, it's not a technical problem. I'd bet my eyeteeth on it."

"It's almost certainly a political issue of some kind," Erik said.

Liam scowled. "Well, that's a relief. Here I thought I was being sent to fumble my way through something I know *nothing* about."

"You are a prince, Liam. Politics is in your blood. You'll have to get used to it."

The anger drained from Liam's eyes, replaced by a resigned look. "I know. I just wish it didn't have to be today."

Erik flashed an anaemic smile. "We all wish a lot of things, brother. And now, if you'll excuse me, I have a letter to write to His High Lordship King Omaïd." Alix started to follow, but Erik waved her off. "You can join me in my study later. The two of you should take some time together."

There will be little enough to come. The words hung, unspoken, in the air.

Rig swore quietly. "That's it, then. My king off to try to sneak through enemy territory, my prince exiled to a political viper's nest, and Albern sodding Highmount left in charge. Did I miss anything?"

"Just those thirty thousand enemy soldiers at our doorstep," Liam said.

"Blessed Farika." Rig headed for the door, shaking his head. "We'll be lucky to last a month."

It isn't right, Allie," Liam murmured, touching his forehead to hers. His hands went to her waist, drawing her in until they tangled together. "If I can't go with you and Erik, then I should at least be at the front. I'm a soldier. I'm not—"

"Yes, you are. And you'll be fine." She spoke the words with such conviction that she almost believed them. Almost.

It should be me.

The rebellious thought raced through her mind for only a moment before she wrestled it down. *Your duties lie elsewhere,* she told herself firmly. *You are the king's bodyguard. Whatever else you might have been, those doors are closed now.* The choice had been made. It was as unchangeable as Erik's decision to go to Harram, as Liam's adoption of the White name. They had all made their choices, and this was where it had led them.

"You have to believe in yourself," she said. "If you don't, they'll see it, and they'll take advantage of it. Just remember, you're a White."

"Half."

"It doesn't matter," Alix said, struggling to keep the exasperation from her voice. "If anything, they'll like you better for being a bastard. If there's one thing the Onnani hate, it's a haughty Aldenian. Their pride is still recovering from the time they spent as slaves, no matter that it was centuries ago. Your humility will go over well with them. You'll see." She smiled. "So long as you don't call them *fishmen.*"

Liam groaned softly. "I wish you could come with me. You're so much better at these things than I am."

Alix knew she should argue, but she couldn't.

His lips dropped to her ear. "I don't know how I'll even sleep without you." She felt a gentle tug at her side as Liam pulled at the laces of her undershirt.

"Now?"

"Now. Later. As often as we can. Who knows how long it'll be until we . . ." The tugging stopped. He stood motionless, his breath uneven in her ears. Alix swallowed against a growing ache in her throat.

"We'll be fine," she whispered. A promise or a prayer? If only she knew.

A warm hand slid into the gap in her shirt, along her skin, fingers trailing up the back of her rib cage. His thumb moved over the swell of her breast and found its mark. Alix sucked in a breath.

"Swear you'll come back to me, Allie." His fingertips brushed the scar on her back, the one left by the assassin's dagger. When he spoke again, his voice was ragged. "Swear."

"I promise." His thumb moved, and she gasped again. "I *swear*."

He let out a long, resigned breath. Then he reached down and swept her legs out from under her, cradling her as easily as if she were a child. "Right, that's your part done." He started toward the bed.

She gazed up at him. Mischief pooled in the slate grey of his eyes, a flammable substance about to take light. She shivered with anticipation. "What's your part?"

"Incentive."

FOUR

"**D**isturbing news indeed," the rasping voice said. A plume of breath vented from the hood, the only evidence of the face obscured in its depths.

"Don't give me that," Alix said. "You already knew this, or you aren't worth nearly what I pay you."

She sensed the smile within the hood. "Then why bother to tell me?"

"In case there were any missing pieces in the account you received." She glanced at him. "From someone whose identity you will give me one day."

A dense cloud accompanied the laughter. "I doubt that, Lady Black."

Alix didn't bother to correct him. For some reason, it amused the spy to refer to her as *Lady Black*, as though it were she, and not her brother, who held the banner. It seemed to be a sign of respect, albeit of a mocking sort. "We'll leave as soon as possible," she said. Huddling deeper into her cloak, she added, "Hopefully it will warm up soon."

"Don't be too eager to greet the warm weather. With spring comes war."

"I know." Rig had ridden out that morning. It was never easy, but this time had been especially difficult. Alix had barely been able to keep her tears in check when he'd planted a rough kiss on her forehead. *Be good, Allie,* he'd told her, just as he'd done when she was a child. *Let Eldora be your sign,* she'd replied. And he'd said what he always did: *She doesn't fancy me.* So Alix had called on Olan instead—as though her brother had ever lacked for courage.

"As difficult as you will find the mountains," Saxon said, "Prince Liam may have the more challenging task before him."

"How do you figure that?"

"The politics of the Republicana are . . . complex. Even seasoned diplomats find themselves lost in the maze."

"How complicated can it be? Court is court, surely, whatever you call it. If anything, things should be simpler there. The speakers have only five years to build alliances and make enemies, and then their terms in office are done. Here, the same families have been plotting and scheming for centuries."

"As they have in Onnan. Do not be fooled by lofty talk of democracy, Lady Black. The Onnani have their dynasties, whatever their pretensions to the contrary. The same handful of families has been churning out speakers for generations. Nor is family the only claim upon their loyalties."

"The leagues."

The hood rippled in assent. "That is another, though by no means the most influential. True power lies with the secret societies, and those cut across league lines. A speaker who represents the Worker's Alliance might be a Son of the Revolution, while another Alliance member is a Shield. If forced to choose, they will side with their society brothers rather than their league members."

"Seems simple enough. All you have to do is find out what a secret society's agenda is, and you know where its members stand."

The grating laughter sounded again. "Discovering a secret

society's agenda is a quest akin to finding the Lost Kingdom. They are called *secret* for a reason, my lady. Even their membership is kept in the strictest confidence. Those in my trade do a brisk business in Onnan, as you can imagine. And then there is the religious angle. Most high-ranking members of the Republicana are also priests."

Alix swore under her breath. Liam had enough trouble fitting in at his own brother's court. How in Eldora's name was he ever going to navigate his way through *that*?

"I could accompany His Highness," Saxon said, as though reading her thoughts. "I have a strong network in Onnan City, even stronger than in the Trionate. I could be of tremendous value to him."

"I have no doubt, but unfortunately, I need you here."

Saxon gave a thoughtful grunt. "You fear instability in His Majesty's absence."

"Wouldn't you?"

"Things are not as uncertain as they once were. War has a way of bringing a nation together."

"The king's position may be more stable than it was, but that isn't saying a whole lot. He nearly lost his crown. However much the war may have glossed over the cracks, they're still there."

"Indeed."

"I need you to keep an eye on Highmount and the council." She paused, threw him an arch look. "Good thing you have your tick to help you."

"My tick may change his mind about feeding me information once he realises how much power he holds under the new dispensation. His ambition is what allowed me to recruit him in the first place. It could turn him from an asset to a liability very quickly."

"In which case, you'll know what to do."

The hood twisted to face her. Dark eyes stared out from the shadows, glinting like moonlight on coal. "Be careful, Lady Black. Some stains never wash away. Some paths, once set upon, cannot be turned from."

"You're giving me advice now?"

"I've been giving you advice from the beginning, and you would do well to heed it." He turned, vanishing within the hood once again. "I will do whatever you ask of me. It is the privilege for which you pay. But consider carefully before you choose the way of blood, because it only ends in one thing."

"And what's that?"

"Blood."

Alix looked away. Her gaze wandered over the glittering burlap that lined the rosebushes to fall upon the fractured glass surface of the frozen duck pond. She flexed her shoulders, as though banishing a chill. "It's tempting, though, isn't it, to think that all our troubles could be ended at a stroke, if the right person were to die? Sadik, for instance, or Varad."

"Killing the Priest did not prove so very decisive. Why should it be any different with the Warlord or the King? Wars are rarely ended by assassination."

"Too bad." There was a stretch of silence. Alix shivered again. "Speaking of the Trionate, what news from your contacts there?"

A shrug. "Little of consequence. The squabbling among the priests for the right to succeed Madan continues. Meanwhile, the people mourn their Trion. They grow weary of war."

Highmount had mentioned that too. Erik had thought it useful information, but Alix wasn't so sure. "Not much to go on," she said. "Maybe your network isn't as strong as you think."

"Does that mean you no longer wish to hear from them?" The rasping voice was heavy with sarcasm.

"I wish to hear from *you*, and as often as possible. You can reach me through any of the post stations along the western highway, all the way to Blackhold. After that, we'll be out of touch until we reach Ost. I'll see to it that you have access to the royal pigeons. You can write to me care of the palace in Ost, if you need to."

"A sensible measure, one that works both ways. If you require anything of me, do not hesitate to send word."

"In the meantime, what do you know of Harrami politics?"

"Less than you, I imagine. The Harrami hold themselves aloof of Gedonan affairs, which means they are rarely a worthwhile subject of research for those in my trade. You would do better to ask a scholar."

"Maybe I will."

"In that case," Saxon said, rising, "I wish you good day,

Lady Black. We both have research to do. You on Harram, and me on my tick."

"You haven't researched him already?"

"Of course. But something tells me I will need more on him in the days to come." He smiled. "Or her."

Alix squinted up at him against the glare of a winter sky. "Tell me something, Saxon. Are politics any less cutthroat in peacetime?"

The spy expelled a puff of vapour, something between a laugh and a snort. "Good gods, no, my lady. They are much, much worse."

"Notes," Liam said, eyeing the scroll doubtfully. "From your spy."

"Think of it as a sort of encyclopaedia of Onnani politics. It'll be helpful, I promise."

He unfurled it and scanned the page, brow creasing as he read. "Holy Hew, Allie, this is a mess!" He groaned and sat back heavily in his chair. "I can't do this."

"Yes," Alix said firmly, "you can. Look, it's not that complicated." A bald-faced lie, based on what Saxon had told her, but one Liam needed to hear. "The Onnani elect their leaders every five years, right?"

"Right," Liam said sullenly.

"There are three main leagues that vie for power." She ticked them off on her fingers. "The Worker's Alliance, the Union for the Republic, and the People's Congress. The Worker's Alliance has been in power for two consecutive terms, under First Speaker Kar."

"Who's a priest."

Alix heard the anxiety in his voice, and she couldn't blame him. The idea of priests meddling in politics had never sat well with Aldenians, and their experience with the Priest of Oridia had only cemented that distrust. "Erik says you could never be elected in Onnan without being a member of the clergy. All the major players are ordained."

"But it says here they're also members of secret societies." Liam shook his head as he read. *"The Sons of the Revolution. The Shield.* Gods, I thought the Trionate was complicated!"

Alix had never considered the Trionate's politics especially complex, but then, she'd had a proper education. Liam had been tutored, but only in the basics; foreign political systems were utterly beyond his ken. "Our system is simpler than most, that's all," she said.

"Our system makes sense." He held up a finger. "One king. One decider. He consults, sure, but at the end of the day, the decisions are his. Having three leaders is a recipe for disaster. What happens when the Trions disagree? And then there's these Onnani blokes!" He rapped the scroll with the back of his hand. "*Dozens* of them, Allie. How do they decide anything?"

"Well, they vote."

He went on as though he hadn't heard. "And this business about secret societies—what does that even mean?"

"I'm not sure," she admitted. "I guess what's important is that you can't assume you know where an Onnani politician stands just because of his league affiliation."

"Then how am I supposed to know? How am I supposed to figure out *any* of this?" The helplessness in his grey eyes pierced Alix's heart.

She took his hand, gave it a reassuring squeeze. "You will, love. I know you will."

"That makes one of us."

Alix dropped into his lap and curled her arms around his neck. "You really have to stop talking like that. You're wilier than you give yourself credit for." She nuzzled his shoulder. "You don't really think I'd have married a fool, do you?"

It was her secret weapon. Liam simply couldn't resist. The playfulness returned to his eyes, and he gave her an arch look. "You might have, if you wanted him to be a slave to your will."

She laughed. "Now why would I want that?"

"I can think of several reasons."

"Hmm." She gazed at him teasingly, brushing her thumb along his lip. "I'm starting to think of a few myself."

He needed no further encouragement, reaching up and twining his fingers in her hair. He sighed as his lips met hers, and she felt his shoulders relax. He kissed her slowly, lingeringly, letting the tension drain from his body, and soon he was lowering her back against the cushions, thoughts of Onnani politics long forgotten. Alix let herself sink into the moment, wrapping her limbs around him, wishing she need never let go. But even as her body awoke to his, something else was settling inside her, grey and quietly mournful, like a thin blanket of ash. Tonight would be their last together. After that . . .

After that, there was no telling.

Alix tightened the cinch on her saddle, yanking the leather with more force than was strictly necessary. The gelding grunted and shifted a little in protest. She slipped the strap end through the buckle and patted his neck in apology. *Not his fault you're in a mood*, said a voice in her head that sounded suspiciously like Gwylim's.

Gwylim. How she wished he were here now. Aside from the fact that they could have used his scouting skills—not to mention his healing skills, or the myriad of other useful tricks he knew— Alix had always found his presence comforting. Gwylim never let himself get rattled by anything. He'd seemed to absorb the emotions of those around him the way a cloth mops up a spill. He was the man everyone went to for advice, all of it delivered with kindness and empathy. *The world lost something special when it lost Gwylim.* Something that could not be replaced.

Certainly not by Kerta Middlemarch.

"Oh, Alix, this must be so awful for you," Kerta said, fussing with her own horse. "Taking the king into danger. Being separated from Liam." She shook her pretty blond head mournfully.

"Yes, it is," Alix said, doing her best not to growl. Kerta was a friend, and she meant well, but at times like these, Alix resented her syrupy brand of sympathy. It was hard enough dealing with this situation without someone narrating her misery.

Kerta reached over and gripped her arm. "We'll protect him, Alix. And Liam will be fine. You'll see."

Alix let out a long breath. Nodded. Taking the horse's bridle, she led him away from the scouts and across the yard to the main doors, where she handed him off to Godwin. She mounted the steps the way a condemned man climbs the stairs to the gallows. Inside, Liam and Erik awaited her. When she gave the word, they would leave. They would ride out together as far as the south gate. And then they would part, for the gods only knew how long. Liam would head east, Alix and Erik west. Not for the first time, Alix's heart and her duty would tear her in two.

She hesitated outside the door to the study, but there was no point in putting it off further. Nodding to the royal guardsman on the door, she stepped through.

"It's time, Your Majesty."

Erik looked splendid in his armour and white leather, the garnet-studded pommel of his bloodblade jutting out from his hip, and Alix realised how long it had been since she'd seen him dressed for battle. The sight was at once inspiring and disconcerting.

"Don't look so downcast, Alix," he said. "You're going home."

She managed a smile. "I do look forward to seeing Blackhold again. Though . . ." The smile faded. "I wonder what I will find."

Liam looked away, his mouth pressed into a thin line. She could guess his thoughts. He wanted to be there for her when she stepped through the doors of her childhood home. A place she hadn't seen for nearly two years, that had fallen to the enemy, with gods knew what consequences for those beloved halls.

I wonder if I will even recognise it.

She pushed the thought away. "After you, Your Majesty."

It was chaos in the courtyard. Grooms and squires bustled between horses stamping and snorting with impatience. The White Wolves gathered near the armoury, the scouts near the cistern. The supply wagons were islands of stillness in a sea of moving horseflesh. Near the gate, the honour guard was already mounted up, the White banner dangling from gilded spears propped in their saddles.

The king's arrival brought a hush over it all. Heads turned. Some faces were apprehensive, others merely expectant. If Erik noticed, he gave no sign; he mounted up as if they were merely heading out for a leisurely hunt.

The Street of Stars had been cleared for the procession, but the common folk were permitted to gather along the fringes. And gather they did, in gutters and side streets, on rooftops and balconies. It seemed to Alix that every man, woman, and child in Erroman lined the route, watching in an eerie near-silence as the king and his retinue rode past. She was reminded forcibly of last summer, when Erik and the banner lords had returned from the front. The streets had been quiet then too, the people unsure how to react to the unexpected sight of their king, a man whose crown had nearly been wrested from him by his own brother. That ride had ended in triumph, with joyful crowds all but carrying them to the palace gate.

Alix felt as though she were reliving that day in reverse.

The crowds bore sombre witness all the way through the south gate and onto the old temple road. Alix hadn't been this way since *that day*, and she couldn't suppress a shudder. The gate had been repaired, the bodies long since buried, but it seemed to Alix that an aura of death remained, like a foul odour that never quite goes away.

The others felt it too, she could tell. Erik's gaze roamed over the ruins, grim and thoughtful. Liam, meanwhile, wouldn't even look at the pile of rubble that had once been the Elders' Gate. He stared straight ahead, unblinking, as though he could pass the place where Arran Green had died without it tugging relentlessly at him, like a fishhook catching at the weeds.

The column drew to a halt at the crossroads. Erik, Liam, and Alix dismounted.

"I guess this is it," Liam said.

"Guess so." Alix longed to bury herself in his arms, but felt as if every pair of eyes in the procession were trained on them.

Including Erik's. Looking from Alix to Liam and back, he sighed. "I'm sorry for this. I wish there were another way."

Alix nodded. They'd had this conversation too many times to count. There was no point in having it again now, in front of White Wolves and royal guardsmen and half a hundred others.

She tried for a smile. "At least you'll have Rudi," she said as the wolfhound trotted over.

"Yeah, great." Liam gave his dog a wary look. "If you get word I've been killed, you'll know what happened."

"Death jokes. Perfect." She had half a mind to slap him; lucky for him there were all those pairs of eyes.

"You are an ass, brother," Erik said with a rueful smile, clasping Liam's arm.

He grinned. "It's a gift."

"Just promise me you won't bestow it upon the Onnani."

"I'll do my best."

Erik's smile faded. "I'm counting on you, Liam. We all are." He slung himself back in the saddle. "Let Eldora be your sign," he said before guiding his horse away.

Liam looked at his boots. He shoved a hand through his unruly dark hair. He had nothing to say.

"Good luck." It was the best Alix could manage.

"Take care of him, Allie. And . . . take care of yourself." He looked up, the beginnings of a smile hitching one side of his mouth. "I don't want to hear about frostbite on your toes or panthers in your bedroll."

"Panthers. In my bedroll."

"Cats love to snuggle up with warm things."

"I'll try to remember that."

"Speaking of warm things . . ." He reached into a saddle-bag and drew out a scroll. "Here. Don't open it now. Save it for a really cold night."

She ran a thumb over the wax seal, marked with the royal sunburst. "What is it?"

"It's a letter, you dunce."

"I can see that, but—"

"A really cold night, Allie. When you need to warm up."

She shook her head, baffled.

"Gods, woman, you have no imagination at all." Gathering her into his arms, he whispered something in her ear.

Alix felt her skin warm. "Oh."

His laugh against her ear made her want to cry. The gods only knew when she would hear it again. *If* she would hear it again.

He pulled back and took her chin in his hand. "No, no. Don't do that. If you cry, you might take me with you, and then how will I ever command this fine pack of manly men?"

She laughed. "And women?"

"The women are especially manly."

"Don't let Rona Brown hear you say that."

He glanced over his shoulder. "We'd better get on. We're holding up the war." He planted a soft, chaste kiss on her mouth.

Alix brought a hand to his cheek. Drew in a deep draught of his scent, as though she could bottle it, keep it with her. She was about to pull away when she felt his tongue slip into her mouth. She broke off a moment later, gaze skipping over the assembled crowd. She could feel the fierce blush colouring her cheeks.

"They'll get over it," Liam said. He swept onto his horse with a grace belying the weight of his armour, then reached down to offer Alix a hand onto her own horse.

"What, in front of all these manly men?" She mounted up on her own.

"All right, Wolves," Liam called. "We're for the Imperial Road."

Ide said something Alix couldn't hear, and the Pack turned as one, pointing their mounts south. They'd follow the Imperial Road as far as the river, then swing east onto the Onnani Highway.

"I think I'd rather face a horde of thralls," Liam said in parting.

"There's no such thing as thralls anymore," Alix said. *But I'll be facing the next best thing in the mountain tribes.* If she'd been Liam, she would have made a joke of it. But Alix didn't feel like joking. She was leaving behind the man she loved, and all that lay ahead of her was bitter winds and bitter memories.

And the deadly mountain tribes of Harram.

FIVE

There were certain constants in the world. Absolutes. Things you could count on, whatever twists and turns fate might take. Dogs obeyed their masters. Knights fought in battle, with swords and arrows and other pointy objects. And commanders got to choose their own seconds—especially if they were *prince* of the sodding *realm*.

So how, Liam wondered, did he end up here?

"Bollocks," he growled.

Ide didn't respond. Admittedly, Liam might have mentioned this before.

"Completely unfair," he added.

That provoked a response, though not quite the one he'd been looking for. "All due respect, Commander, you sound like a five-year-old."

"There's gratitude for you."

Ide hitched a shoulder, her sturdy frame swaying back and forth with the rhythm of the horse. "No use wallowing in it. What's done is done. I don't mind so much anyway. Never expected to be made a knight, did I?"

"You deserved it," Liam said. "You're a better fighter than half the men under my command, and they're the cream of the realm." What was left of them, anyhow.

Ide shrugged again. "I still come out ahead, way I see it."

See, *that* was why he'd picked her in the first place. He'd never met someone so levelheaded. Ide was cool as mint in a fight. Afterward, she could put away enough wine to sink a small ship and still beat you at cards. She could shoot a swallow out of the sky, and that was before she'd got her bloodbow. Now he had to put her aside for some random Brownsword he'd never even met? Good job his new second had been recommended by Rig, or Liam might have pitched a proper fit.

Ide was right, though—there was no point dwelling on it. In less than half an hour, she would be relieved as his second, whether he liked it or not.

The landscape rolled past, a dozen shades of brown under an ash-coloured sky. The horses' hooves drummed rhythmically against dirt packed hard with frost. It was almost enough to put him to sleep. Last night had been spent on the hard earth, and as for the night before that . . . between making love to his wife and staring miserably at the ceiling (fortunately not at the same time, or he might have found himself short one appendage), he hadn't had much sleep. He wondered how the beds at the inn would be. *Nicer than what you've known most of your life, most likely.* Things certainly had changed since he became Liam White.

For the better, mostly. But when it came to things like this . . . diplomatic missions and political appointments . . .

Bollocks.

"There it is, Commander," said Rona Brown, pointing. She'd braided her hair like Alix's, starting behind her forehead and sweeping down one side. Just fashionable enough to mark her as a noblewoman, but subtly. *Smart*, he thought. The Onnani would go for that, if what Alix had told him was true. He was glad Rona had come along, he decided. He hadn't been sure at first. He would have preferred to leave her in command of the Pack, the bulk of which had stayed behind in Erroman. It wouldn't have occurred to him to consult her on courtly matters. It was, he had to admit, a good idea.

"You been to Onnan before, Commander?" Ide asked.

Liam shook his head, taking in the shambling outline of the village as it rose up out of the horizon. "Actually, I don't think I've been this far east before."

"Not much reason to," Ide said, "unless you fancy pig farming."

As soon as she said it, Liam could smell it: the unmistakably delightful odour of pig shit. *This just keeps getting better.*

The village was typical of those along the highways, little more than a glorified hitching post erected for travellers on their way somewhere more important. Its amenities lined the road like a row of soldiers hoping to be picked for some special duty. Liam spotted a smithy, a baker, a cobbler, and a cluster of market stalls selling vegetables and meat. "Do you suppose they have pork?" he asked dryly.

The Boar's Tusk was the only stone structure in the village. A handsome whitewashed building of two storeys capped with thatch, it presided over its collection of modest neighbours with the ponderous dignity of a priest ministering to a rabble of peasants. Cheerful bay windows swelled out from the walls on either side of the door. It was posh, all right. Liam suddenly felt awkward. As much as he looked forward to a nice bed, sleeping apart from the rest of the men didn't seem right. It was easier to ignore at the palace. The Pack barracks were well appointed, as barracks go, and Liam had family to look forward to at the end of the day. Out here on the road, it felt like putting on airs.

Get used to it, he told himself. *You're not one of the lads anymore.*

He dismounted and handed the reins to Stig. "Tell the

stable boy no oats," he reminded the squire. "And take Rudi with you, all right?"

"Yes, Commander." Stig summoned the wolfhound with a shrill whistle and headed off to the stables.

The door of the inn opened to eject a plump, swarthy man in a straining doublet. From his dark complexion, Liam would have taken him for Onnani, but he was obviously of mixed blood, because a moustache the size of a small ferret perched across his upper lip. The innkeep, Liam reckoned.

"Your Highness," the man said, bowing low. "It is a great honour to welcome you to the Boar's Tusk. My name is Cull, your most humble host. Please, come inside. Your supper is on the stove even now."

Liam, Ide, and Rona Brown followed the innkeep into a warm, low-lit common room full of empty tables. For a fleeting moment, Liam worried what that said about the food. Then he realised: *They've cleared the whole place out for us. For you.* He almost sighed aloud, offering a silent apology to the poor sods who'd been relocated to gods-knew-where. His gaze took in the rest of the room. A long, curved bar hugged the far wall, and a fire snapped in the hearth. Something sizzled heartily behind a closed door. Bacon, naturally.

The room's only occupant rose from behind a table near the hearth. He wore Kingsword armour, and had the dark hair, smooth cheeks, and dusky complexion of an easterner. He bowed.

"Commander Dain Cooper, I presume." Liam hoped it sounded warmer than he felt.

"Your Highness." The knight bowed again.

"Wasn't sure you'd make it in time." *Almost wish you hadn't.* "You ride fast."

Dain Cooper made no reply.

"Shall I have the girl draw you a bath, Your Highness?" the innkeep asked.

Liam glanced at his companions. "I think we'd rather eat first," he said, to a vigorous nod from Ide.

The innkeep blinked, surprised by this display of rough manners. Liam was feeling just peevish enough to enjoy that.

The three Wolves joined their newest member at the table. Liam clasped arms in greeting, which seemed to surprise the other man. He introduced Ide and Rona and pulled up a chair.

Then they sat there and stared at each other for a while.

"So," Liam said eventually. "You're my new second."

Brilliant opening. While you're at it, maybe you could try lighting a fire with soggy straw.

"It's my great honour, Your Highness," the knight said.

"Commander, please."

"I . . . beg your pardon?"

Rona Brown came to his rescue. "The commander prefers for us to refer to him by his military rank, not his courtly one. He only goes by *Your Highness* at the palace. Just as I only go by *Lady Brown* at court or at Brownhold."

"I see," Dain said, in a tone that suggested he really didn't. "I apologise, Commander. I didn't realise."

"How could you?" Liam said. *Since I've never clapped eyes on you before they made you second-in-command of my Pack.*

The knight shifted in his seat. He wore a look that Liam knew intimately; he'd been seeing it in the mirror for months. A man out of place. Sent where he'd been told, not where he'd chosen to go. Surrounded by people he feared were judging him.

You, Liam White, are a proper prat.

"So," he said again, and this time he forced himself to smile. "Cooper. First generation?" It was none of his business, and he didn't really care anyway, but he couldn't think of a sodding *thing* to say to this man.

"That's right," Dain Cooper said, a little warily. Dark eyes searched Liam's. He didn't know anything about his new commander's politics, presumably. Like whether Liam was the sort to be offended by the obvious statement of taking a second name, when most commoners had only one.

Of course, he could have figured it out, if he'd thought it through. Liam decided to help him. "Never missed having a second name, myself. I'm still getting used to it." The man's shoulders relaxed. Liam felt oddly proud of himself. "Why Cooper?" he asked.

The knight shrugged. "Thought it sounded better than *Barrel-maker*."

A serving girl appeared at Liam's elbow with a big platter of rashers, and his stomach rumbled appreciatively. There were worse things, he decided, than overnighting in a pig town.

He reached for a bread roll, broke it in half. It shattered like masonry met with black powder. "From barrel-maker to Brownsword to Kingsword. There's an interesting journey."

Dain picked up the basket of stale rolls and passed it to Rona Brown. "After my king's service, I realised I liked handling a sword better than I liked banding oak."

"I never knew my father had an Onnani knight in his service," Rona said.

"He didn't." Dain was using bacon fat to loosen up his bread. Or at least, he was trying to. The things were impervious to all forms of moisture. They could double as ammunition for a trebuchet. "I've only been a knight for a few months. I was appointed by the commander general." There was more than a hint of pride in his voice, but Liam didn't hold it against him. He'd felt the same when Arran Green finally made him a knight.

"Rig . . ." Liam cleared his throat. "That is, General Black . . . speaks highly of you."

"He's a great man." Liam would have taken that for polish had Dain not been so visibly earnest. Somewhat less earnestly, he added, "Also, he owes me half the gold in the Black River."

Liam's bacon froze halfway to his mouth. "How's that?"

"He can rout a battalion with a band of fifty and bludgeon any man in the ring one-on-one, but by Hew, the man *cannot* play cards."

It was right about then Liam decided he liked Commander Dain Cooper.

"Well," Ide said, lowering the longlens, "how do you like that?"

Liam peered down the long metal cylinder, trying to get a sense of their numbers. About fifty, he reckoned, though it was hard to be sure. "Definitely soldiers." He'd known that before he put the longlens to his eye; it was the glint of their armour on the horizon that had drawn his attention in the first place. "I see the Onnani banner."

"An honour escort?"

"Let's hope so, or things are about to get awkward." Liam twisted in his saddle. "All right, Wolves! Look sharp! I want the lines kept nice and clean. First impressions, and all that."

"You heard the commander," said Dain Cooper, turning his

horse and heading down the line. "Let's tighten it up back here. We're representing His Majesty the King of Alden, so let's bloody well look like it!"

Moments later, Liam's pack of fifty riders had been guided into ranks as straight and even as the tines of a comb. His new second was doing well, Liam had to admit. In less than three days, Dain Cooper had taken to his new role like a fish takes to—

No. Not like a fish. Definitely not *like that.* Grumbling, Liam spurred his horse.

"The border post is just over that rise," Dain said.

"Funny they're meeting us on this side of it," said Ide.

"Actually, the Onnani consider that we crossed the border about half an hour ago."

Liam blinked in surprise. "Come again?"

"This section of the border is still technically in dispute. Has been ever since the empire fell."

"But the border post . . ."

Dain shrugged. "The Onnani are willing to play nice and share the fort, but that doesn't mean they accept the Aldenian border demarcation. As far as they're concerned, they're hosting an Aldenian contingent on their territory."

"Huh." Liam hadn't realised the border between the two allies was in any way controversial. *Nothing about that in Saxon's notes.* Alix had assured him the spy knew all there was to know about Onnani politics, that his notes would be an invaluable guide. This little oversight did not bode well. *How many more of those have I got to look forward to?* The thought didn't fill him with confidence.

"You been here before, Dain?" Ide asked.

"We came often when I was a kid. Distant relatives. My father thought it was important that we see the old country."

"Did you like it?" Rona asked.

Dain smiled. "Have you ever seen the sea?" When Rona shook her head, he added, "Well, just wait. Every man should see the sea at least once before he dies."

They were nearing the riders now, and Liam realised there were more than he'd thought. A lot more. Eighty at least. *What in the Nine Domains do they need with eighty men?*

Their leader raised a hand as the Wolves approached. He spoke a word, and the riders all crossed one arm over their breasts and did a seated half bow. Liam had no idea how he was supposed to respond. He waved.

The riders at the front of the column flourished their banners, and slowly, somewhat awkwardly, their horses lowered themselves to one knee. It was, Liam had to admit, a nice trick.

The leader spoke. "Your Royal Highness. In the name of First Speaker Kar and the Republicana, I welcome you to the Republic of Onnan. It will be our great honour to escort you to the capitol." The speaker, one of three riders at the centre of the column who had not forced his horse to kneel, did the waist bow thing again. This time, Liam did his best to mimic it in return.

"Thank you," he said. "I hope one day we can return the courtesy."

"My name is Rellard Mason. I am captain of your honour guard."

"Pleased to meet you. This is my second"—he was about to turn to Ide, but caught himself in time—"Commander Dain Cooper."

Rellard Mason inclined his head politely. If he was surprised to find an Onnani second in command of the fabled White Wolves, he didn't show it. "This way, please, Your Highness. If we keep good pace, we should reach Onnan City by sunset."

Liam was pleasantly surprised. He'd thought they had at least another two days' ride ahead. He knew the map, of course, but it was always hard to get a sense of scale. Apparently, the finger of land separating Alden from the sea was even smaller than it appeared. On a map, it looked as though some giant beast had taken a big bite out of Onnan's western flank. And in a way, Liam supposed, that was what had happened. The Erromanian Empire had fought fiercely to prevent the Onnani secession—not just because of the slaves, but because an independent Onnan would mean the loss of the empire's best seaport. Liam hadn't realised how close the Erromanians had come to retaking Onnan City. *No wonder the border is still contested.*

Liam had never been abroad before, and he'd half expected the frontier to be a physical, visible thing. A line of trees, or a moat. A swath of cleared brush, like a firebreak. Upon crossing it, he'd find himself transported to some wild, alien land full of half-clothed savages and exotically striped cattle. Instead, his surroundings were dull and familiar. If he'd woken up after too many pints to find himself lying on the side of this very road, he'd have assumed he was in the Greylands. Even the people looked like Aldenians, albeit of Onnani descent. He couldn't find a single thing that distinguished them from the folk he'd been riding past for days. They were just . . . ordinary.

The feeling didn't seem to be mutual, though. The Wolves and their escort attracted plenty of interest. In every village, at every roadside inn, people stopped to stare at the riders passing through. It wasn't just their fair skin, Liam supposed, but the trappings of royalty: the barding on his horse, the White banner, the gilded spears. *This must be what Erik feels like wherever he goes.* For some reason, the thought made him uneasy.

They rode in silence. Not the easy camaraderie sort of silence, either; the awkward, wish-you-could-crawl-off-somewhere-and-hide sort. Liam wondered if it was his fault. Maybe they were waiting on him, as prince, to strike up a conversation. But he couldn't think of anything to say, at least nothing safe. Every possible subject seemed full of hidden traps, tripwires and pitfalls just waiting for him to blunder into. In situations like this, he usually resorted to humour, but that was far too risky under the circumstances. So he held his peace, and so did everybody else. Hour after hour, mile after mile, until Liam wanted to scream, just for the sake of it.

He might have done it too, had the city not appeared, finally, mercifully, in the distance. It rose up in a jumble of grey and black, anonymous blocks scattered across the horizon as though cast there by a god playing at dice. A pall of smoke obscured the rooftops, smudging them into a darkening sky. An unfamiliar smell bit at his nostrils, something that might have been the sea.

Liam straightened in his saddle. He took a deep breath and tried to look confident.

This is it, he thought. *Onnan City.*

Gods help him.

SIX

† The closer they got to Blackhold, the less Alix
spoke.

A thoughtful silence, at first. A distracted break in the
conversation, a faraway look in her eyes that told Erik she
had spotted something, smelled something, that drew her back
in time. A secret smile every now and then, which Erik would
find himself echoing even though he had no way of knowing
what had prompted it. This homecoming was nearly as bittersweet for him as it was for her. Witnessing her heart laid bare
like this, its deepest chambers open and vulnerable, was both
painful and irresistible.

Progressively, however, her silence took on a brooding air.
Instead of secret smiles, there were thinly pressed lips, and it
was no mystery what prompted them. Blackened fields. Burnt-
out husks of villages. Pigs rooting at the roadside, far from any
sign of civilisation, already half feral from months of freedom. The central Blacklands had suffered greatly at the hands
of the enemy, and though Arran Green had broken the Oridian
forces eventually, by then the damage had been done. Erik and
his entourage rode for two full days without crossing a single
living soul. By the end of the fourth day, Alix was as silent as
the ghosts she was seeing.

Erik had thought the sight of Blackhold, at least, would be
enough to bring a smile to her lips, but he had been wrong. As
it appeared on the horizon, Alix coiled even tighter, and the
colour drained from her cheeks. She looked as though she
might be physically sick.

"Alix." He reached for her hand, and she took it, gripping
it hard enough to hurt fingers stiffened with cold. Erik was

acutely aware of the eyes on them, but just this once, he would ignore them. Alix needed him. And he could not deny that it felt good.

"I don't know if I can do this," she whispered.

He squeezed her hand. "You can. Besides, it won't be as bad as you fear. It's been months. The servants have all returned, and they've been hard at work. It might not be exactly as you remember it, but it will still be home."

She shook her head. "You don't know that. You can't."

"Yes, I can. You don't really think Highmount would suffer me to stay anywhere that hadn't been fully prepared for a royal visit? We wouldn't want to tarnish the dignity of the crown, after all."

That was a lie. Or at least, a half truth. Highmount hadn't needed to worry about the state of Blackhold, because Erik had already seen to it. He would never put Alix through the pain of seeing her family home in disarray. He had sent servants ahead, with gold and goose down and bolts of fabric, to help the steward of Blackhold prepare for his lady's arrival. Every inch of the castle would have been scrubbed and polished and aired out. Erik had even made sure to supply a generous length of rough black silk, in case the Oridians had defiled the family banner.

Blackhold still showed signs of her ordeal, of course, even at a distance. Her gates fairly glowed, the pale hue of fresh wood standing in stark contrast to her dark stone walls. Blackened, twisted pines tortured by fire edged the forest at the base of her sloping lawns. But she still stood, and proudly, her ancient stone edifice clawing at the majestic backdrop of the Broken Mountains.

Alix closed her eyes, drew a deep breath. Erik thought she was steeling herself, but then, mercifully, she smiled. "Smell that."

He did. Clear mountain air, and a sharp, fresh scent. "Pine."

Her smile widened. "Home."

The gates swung open on freshly oiled hinges. The portcullis had not yet been replaced, Erik noticed, and the bailey was rather barren. A few windows had been boarded up. On the whole, however, Blackhold looked healthy enough.

The servants stood in a row in the middle of the yard, their faces bright with anticipation. A groom rushed up to take Alix's bridle, until an ancient-looking man growled out an order and diverted him in the direction of Erik's horse instead.

There followed a bit of confusion as the servants struggled with the protocol of welcoming their lady and their king at the same time. Alix was oblivious, dismounting on her own and rushing at the ancient-looking man with her arms wide. For a moment, Erik feared she would crush the old boot, but at the last moment she remembered her armour and settled for a tentative half hug instead.

"Henning," she said, "it's so good to see you."

The old man looked equal parts pleased and horrified by this unbridled display of affection. He patted Alix's back awkwardly.

The steward. Erik recognised him now. It had been years, but Henning hadn't aged a day. Mostly because he had already been impossibly old.

"My lady," Henning said, "we are so very pleased to have you back with us."

"Only for a short time, alas. Just long enough for the scouts to reconnoitre the pass, and then we're off again. I'd hoped for warmer weather by now, but we'll have to make do."

"We have taken the liberty of procuring some heavy cloaks for your party," Henning said. "There is nothing like Blacklands furs to keep you warm when the snow flies."

Alix smiled. "I remember. When I was small, I used to pretend I'd been swallowed by a bear."

Henning returned the smile under duress. He shifted from foot to foot. Erik waited, hiding his amusement behind the most solemn mask he could muster.

Belatedly, Alix registered the servant's discomfort. "Oh! I beg your pardon, Henning, please go ahead."

With a look of profound relief, the steward sketched a hasty bow and swept over to Erik. "Your Majesty. It is our very great honour to welcome you back to Blackhold."

That very great honour would normally fall to Rig, but he was not here, and Alix was ill-placed to assume his duties just now. As a stand-in, Henning did his household credit. He was tall and well set, even in the sunset of his years, and his slate-grey hair and beard gave him an air of gravitas. Lines of wisdom, referred to in polite company as *Eldora's graces*, rounded out the effect.

"A pleasure to see you again, Henning," Erik said.

The steward inclined his head, the very picture of propriety. "If you will follow me, sire, the servants will see to your party."

Erik trailed the steward into a vast entrance hall. *It's bigger than I remember*, he thought. Then he heard Alix draw in a sharp breath, and he realised why.

It was virtually empty.

Silk panels dangled along the bare cliff faces of the walls, a hasty attempt to make up for the lack of tapestries. A single ceramic pot stood forlornly in the corner, swallowed by the space around it. Whatever furnishings had once lined these walls, they were long gone. A damningly light patch of stone in the shape of a shield marked the archway above them. Alix paused beneath it, her face pale and unreadable.

"This way, please, Your Majesty." Henning gestured with a rigid arm. The poor man was taut as a bowstring. He wanted Alix out of there, and quickly. Erik did the only thing he could: He hastened his step, obliging his bodyguard to follow.

The view improved when they reached the solar. Whether the furnishings were new, Erik could not tell, but they filled out the room admirably. A fire crackled in the hearth, and above its mantel, the Black banner shone darkly. The original, Erik was relieved to see; he could tell by the patina on the bronze bar holding it in place.

Alix hovered in the doorway, her eyes moving slowly over the room.

"They looted everything of value," Henning said, gaze downcast, "and burned much of the rest. But we were able to bring down most of the contents of the lake house."

Alix nodded mutely. She looked numb. Erik wanted to put his arms around her, but of course he could not—not even if they had been alone. Perhaps especially not then.

"Could you give me a moment, please, Henning?" Her voice sounded small and distant.

"Of course, my lady." He bowed and withdrew. Erik started to follow, but Alix called his name.

"Please stay."

"Are you sure?"

Nodding, she dragged a corner of the bench out from under the table and dropped onto it. She laid a hand against the empty space beside her, but Erik pretended not to see; he sat across from her, his back to the hearth. The firelight licked the contours of Alix's armour, threw blazing copper highlights into the thick rope of her braid.

She said nothing at first, her gaze as far away as her voice had been. Erik watched her trace little circles on the wood grain of the table. "It was so beautiful," she said eventually.

"It will be again. And until then, it's home, isn't it?"

She didn't answer. Erik wondered if she was thinking about Liam, wishing he were here instead.

Perhaps I made a mistake, he thought. *Perhaps bringing her here was cruel.*

"Rig will be pleased to hear that the banner survived," Alix said. "The shield . . . that's . . ." She did not finish the thought. The words, Erik suspected, would not come.

"I'm surprised you didn't already know. Did you not write to Henning for news?"

"Rig did, but I think he stuck to the basics. Whether the castle would be inhabitable and so on. I don't think he had the heart to ask after specific things. When you're far away, you can almost pretend it never happened." She let out a long, deliberate breath. "It's not as bad as I feared, though. That's something, at least. And you're right—it will be restored in time. It might not be exactly as it was, but I'm used to that by now. War never leaves things as they were."

That was surely Destan's own truth.

Hazel eyes met Erik's. As always, it sent a shiver through him, like a haunting strain of music. "I'm so glad you're here," she said. "It means a lot to me."

The words lodged in his breast. Made camp there, built a small fire. He hated himself for that. "I'd better go," he said, rising. "You should"—his mind raced through half a hundred excuses—"spend some time with old friends."

A hint of confusion flickered through her eyes, but she only nodded. "Thank you."

Erik headed off in search of Henning. A hot bath, something to eat, and then to his letters. He had not quite settled on his strategy with the Harrami; he needed to bandy a few more ideas with Highmount. Not so long ago, he would have consulted Alix, instead of sending some half-exhausted pigeon to the capital. But those intimate discourses were in the past. It was better that way.

It was the only way.

Alix drifted through the knot garden, her fingers trailing along the perfectly flat top of the boxwood. Freshly trimmed, she noticed, yet another of the dozens of small measures taken to purge all evidence of the fall of Blackhold. The Oridians had been pressed for time when they'd taken the castle, just passing through on their way to their next conquest. That and a generous covering of snow over most of the grounds had spared Blackhold the worst of the enemy's wrath. They'd lost the armoury and the stables. They'd lost Alvan, their master-at-arms, and a dozen other stalwarts too stubborn to flee when Rig gave them the chance. But on the whole, Blackhold had endured. Scarred, its insides filled with dark, empty spaces, but much the same could be said of Alix. Of everyone who had suffered in this war.

The garden was as lovely as she remembered, even in winter. The boxwoods formed an intricate knot over sparkling white quartz, a marvel to behold from the wall walk or the upper windows of the castle. Down here, the meticulously pruned shrubs shone a waxy deep green, offsetting the bright red berries of the rowan trees. The smell of cedar and snowdrops and the rhythmic crunching of gravel beneath her boots lulled Alix into a pleasant sort of trance, like walking through a memory.

She'd wanted to show Erik these gardens, but he was shut up in his chambers. As he'd been yesterday, and the day before. Whatever weighed on his mind, he dealt with it alone. That bothered Alix more than she cared to admit. She hadn't looked for many bright spots on this journey, but at least she'd hoped it would bring her back into Erik's confidence. Not that she'd *lost* it, exactly, but he didn't rely on her the way he used to. There had been a time, not so long ago, when it had seemed like the two of them against the world. Alix's opinion had meant more to Erik than anyone's. Now, she was lucky if he consulted her at all. He kept his distance, figuratively at least. It wasn't that things were awkward between them—that would have been unbearable—but they weren't the same, either.

Nothing will ever be the same.

How many times was she going to have to tell herself that before it truly sank in?

"Alix?"

She started. For a moment, she couldn't place the voice, but by the time she'd turned around, she was grinning like a fool. "Edolie!"

A flutter of silk and rose perfume plunged into Alix's arms. "It's so good to see you!" Edolie squeezed Alix's neck so hard it hurt.

"I can't believe you're here! I thought your family would have sought refuge in Erroman long ago, or I would have come calling."

"And I'd have been here sooner, had I known you were passing through. Henning didn't tell me, the wicked man."

Alix gave her childhood friend a once-over. Edolie's delicate frame was shrouded in folds of silk and velvet, petal upon petal layering her skirts in the cheerful hues of spring. She looked like an inverted rose. Alix wondered if the effect was intentional, to go with the perfume. "Good gods, Edolie, you must be freezing! Where's your cloak?"

Edolie flicked a dismissive wave. "Furs are simply not possible this year, Alix. Surely you noticed it in Erroman? It's velvet or nothing, darling."

Alix laughed ruefully. "No, I'm afraid I didn't notice. I can't tell you the last time I was allowed to think about fashion."

"But, Your Highness! It's your *duty* to be gorgeous!" She didn't quite make it through before she burst out laughing.

Alix hugged her again. She'd forgotten how much she missed Edolie's sharp wit. Too well bred to ignore her station, but too clever not to have a laugh about it. *Liam could learn a thing or two from her*, Alix thought.

"I couldn't believe it when I heard," Edolie said. "Her Royal Highness, Alix White." She bowed.

"It came as a bit of a surprise to me too," Alix said dryly.

"To think, all this time, another White brother . . ." Edolie flashed a coquettish smile. "And you snared him!"

"I snared him before I knew he was a White." It felt important to say, somehow.

"A secret identity! How romantic!" Edolie tucked her arm through Alix's. "You must tell me all about it."

Alix permitted herself to be guided toward the gazebo. "Are we gossiping now?"

"Good gods, yes. You must be *starving* for it."

Alix laughed. It was even true, after a fashion. She'd spent so much time dwelling on war and death and betrayal; it would be nice to talk about something trivial for a change. They settled in the gazebo, Alix in her furs, Edolie shivering away like a flower in a stiff wind. "Are you sure you won't put on something warmer?"

Edolie shook her head. "In these times of war, Alix, we must be brave. Though . . ." She glanced at the castle. "Perhaps tea?"

Alix smiled. "You stay here. I'll fetch a servant. In the meantime"—she shrugged out of her cloak—"please protect this for me."

"Oh, yes, I shall. With my life." Edolie draped the fur over her shoulders with a wink.

Tea arrived, hot and pleasantly bitter. They ate cakes and traded meaningless trifles, as was proper. Matters of any importance simply were not discussed over sweets. Alix chewed slowly, knowing that Edolie would pounce on her the moment they were through. But she couldn't draw it out forever, and when she brushed the last crumbs from her fingers, Edolie said, "Now."

Alix checked a sigh. "What would you like to know?"

"All of it. From the beginning."

All of it. Alix couldn't possibly cope with that. But she gave her best summary, from the moment she left Blackhold to the moment she found herself back here again. She skipped only the most painful parts.

Or at least, she tried to. But apparently court gossip reached as far as the western foothills, because Edolie said, "Aren't you forgetting something?"

"Am I?"

"Don't pretend you don't know what I'm talking about. You and the king." All traces of humour were gone from her now;

she regarded Alix with steady brown eyes. "Did you really save his life?"

"Yes. That's how I came to be his bodyguard."

"And then?"

Alix shifted on the bench. Dropped her gaze.

"It's true, then," Edolie breathed. "You *were* lovers."

"Not exactly."

Edolie's eyebrows flew up. "Not exactly? You sound like a priest wrangling over technicalities."

"Edolie . . ."

Hearing the misery in Alix's voice, Edolie tried for light-hearted. "Prince Liam must be something to look at, because I've met the king, and it doesn't get much better than that. Did you know I danced with him once? Those blue eyes . . ." She swooned melodramatically over the back of her chair. "Icicle daggers straight to the heart!"

"Edolie, please. He's just on the other side of that wall, for gods' sake."

"Is he? Do you think I should say hello?" When Alix didn't take the bait, she sobered. "Honestly, I didn't think it could be true."

Alix's shoulder twitched in an irritable shrug. "I don't know what you've heard, so I can't tell you if it's true. There was talk of marriage, if that's what you mean. But it was mostly political." *Mostly.* The word glinted like a coin half buried in the dirt.

"I have to ask . . . why didn't you do it?" Edolie reached over and took Alix's hands, as though to blunt the edge of her question.

"Marry him?"

"I don't know anything about Prince Liam, but if there was even a chance that you and King Erik . . . Why wouldn't you take it? There could be no better match."

"I wasn't thinking about matches. I was thinking about my heart."

Edolie looked almost pitying. "Alix, darling, you're a Black. Marriage isn't about your heart. Besides . . ." The pitying look deepened. "Your heart wouldn't have objected too loudly. I can see that even now."

Alix jerked away. She started to pour more tea. Stopped.

She folded her hands in her lap. "I love Liam." It was the truth. So why did it wedge in her throat like something sharp?

Because you hurt Erik.

That was why he kept her at arm's length, of course. It wasn't that he no longer valued her advice; it was that he couldn't allow himself to be vulnerable in front of her. She'd seen it before. With Liam, when he thought she would choose Erik.

I just can't be around you. Liam's words, that day by the river.

Erik hadn't gone that far. He was more restrained than his brother, more accustomed to hiding behind a mask. He'd been doing it all his life. But Alix had seen behind that mask. He'd taken it off for her, and she'd rewarded him with a slap in the face. Small wonder he'd donned it again.

"I'm sorry, Alix," Edolie said gently. "I don't mean to question your decisions. It's just . . . this war . . ." She shook her head. "I suppose it has me thinking about duty more than I used to."

"You think it was my duty to marry Erik?" The question came out sharper than she'd intended.

"I didn't say that. But you have to admit, things would be easier if he had a queen. An heir on the way." She looked up. There was no accusation in her eyes, only concern. "That's all I'm saying, Alix. I'm sure Prince Liam is a wonderful man, and I'm sure you made the right choice for your heart. I'm happy for you, truly. I hope you can believe that."

"I do. And I hope you can believe that my choice wasn't just right for me. It was the best thing for all of us in the long run." Even as she spoke the words, Alix wondered which of them she was trying to convince.

Edolie nodded. Then she slipped her shoulders out from under Alix's cloak and handed it back. "I'd better go. The roads aren't safe after sundown."

"Thank you for coming," Alix said, embracing her. "It was wonderful to see you."

"And you. Travel well. And . . . be careful, Alix."

Alix tried for a smile. "Panthers and frostbite. Liam already warned me."

Edolie glanced up at the ice-fringed windows of the guest quarters. She looked as though she might say more, but instead she gave Alix's arm a final squeeze and headed up the path.

SEVEN

† He wends his way through the moving tapestry of colours, tucking his shoulders in so that his armour doesn't accidentally brush up against anyone's finery. The dancers don't notice him. They keep moving, twirling and swaying in time to the music. The oratorium thrums with their energy. It's almost hypnotic, the patterns expanding and collapsing, forming and re-forming, mixing and matching in a kaleidoscope of silk and satin.

He can't find Alix. He knows she's here, but she's melted into the crowd. She's one of them, indistinguishable from the rest. He tries to catch someone's attention, to ask after her, but it's as if the dancers can't see him. As if he's not even there.

He spots Erik. The king is standing near the musicians, laughing at some joke or another, a crystal wineglass half raised in salute. He shines out like a candle in a dark room, the faces surrounding him seeming anonymous, inconsequential. His posture is straight and regal, and though he's not the tallest of the men gathered around him, he seems to tower over them. Yet for all that, Erik is somehow the most relaxed and unaffected person in the room. It's effortless. Beautiful, even.

He starts to make his way over, but a royal guardsman steps into his path. "Where do you think you're going?"

"To talk to my brother."

"Your brother?" The knight shakes his head. "You must be mistaken."

The dancers have started to notice him now. One by one, they turn to stare, eyes hard with disapproval. They back away from him, as if afraid they might become soiled by his nearness.

Erik is still laughing. The men and women around him are laughing too, pressing in close, as if hoping to absorb just a little of his grace.

"You shouldn't be here." The knight blocking his way is Alix, he realises. She follows his gaze. "You can't really think he's your brother," she says, pityingly.

Liam looks at this golden being, this . . . king. "No," he says, "I suppose not."

It wasn't the kind of dream you woke up screaming from, but it wasn't exactly fluffy clouds and songbirds, either.

Liam threw the covers aside and got up. He went to the window, passing the foot of the bed where Rudi lay curled on the floor in a heap of wiry fur. The wolfhound raised his head and growled. Liam shot back a two-syllable retort. They resumed ignoring each other.

Liam pushed the curtain aside. The valley spread out below him, a glowing bed of coals under a blushing dawn. Fisherfolk rose early, he knew; the lamps had probably been lit for hours already. To the east, the orange lights stopped abruptly in a curving line, beyond which there was only darkness, a pool of spilled ink stretching all the way to the horizon. *The sea.* In a few moments, he'd be able to see it. It had been dark by the time they reached the city, so he had yet to form much of an impression of his surroundings. For now, all he knew of Onnan City was that its wealthy and powerful preferred the fresher air of the hills, and that was where they'd decided Liam and his retinue should stay. The Ambassador District featured dozens of estates as impressive as any temple, and one of these, a sprawling, whitewashed complex called Bayview, was to be home for the next few weeks.

Liam opened his balcony door and stepped out. A cool breeze rushed in to meet him, bringing an unfamiliar tang to his nose. He closed his eyes and listened for the sound of the waves, but he couldn't hear anything. Maybe they were too far away.

He watched the sun come up over a limitless expanse of grey. He'd always dreamed of seeing the ocean, maybe even taking a swim in the waves. But this was not the sea of his imagination. In paintings and tapestries, it was a playful, frothing thing, blue and white and capricious. The water below him was utterly flat, dark and brooding, as if lying in wait. And vast—gods, it was *beyond* vast. From his vantage in the hills, the city looked small, insignificant, a swath of rubbish left by a receding wave. The sea, meanwhile, seemed to stretch to the very edge of the world. How far had the Onnani sailors ventured, he wondered, before turning back in fear? What was it like to deliberately set sail for infinity?

I certainly wouldn't know. It occurred to him that the sea was an apt metaphor for his task here: vital, unfathomable, utterly alien.

He set about finding something to wear. He'd taken a bath last night, soaking away most of the dirt and aches of the road, so he should be presentable enough—provided he didn't insult his hosts by wearing something too casual, or provoke them by wearing something too grand. Ordinarily, he would have been sent with a valet and half a hundred other attendants to worry about this sort of thing, but Erik and Highmount had agreed that it would be a mistake to drape Liam too heavily in the trappings of royalty. The fiercely republican Onnani would find it pretentious at best, imperious at worst. Better to keep things simple. That meant Liam was on his own. He went through his trunk gingerly, careful not to disturb the neatly ordered piles Alix had prepared. Each one represented an *ensemble*, for a specific *affair*, the conduct of which would follow a strict *protocol*. If he was unsure, he should ask Rona Brown. Under no circumstances was he to reconfigure the ensemble. Improvisation, he'd been given to understand, was not a good idea.

Today was especially important, as his first formal presentation to the Republicana. For this occasion, his wife had decreed that he should wear a heavy brocade doublet. When he'd enquired whether perhaps it wasn't a bit . . . *puffy*, he'd received a look that could curdle milk.

He put on the puffy vest.

He'd just finished donning the rest of the ensemble when a quiet knock sounded. Rudi shot to the door like a quarrel from a crossbow. Grimacing, hoping he wasn't about to lose a hand, Liam grabbed the wolfhound's collar.

"Your Highness?"

"Yes. Er . . . just give me a . . ." He dragged a scrabbling

Rudi over to his trunk, found the lead, and tied the infernal beast to the bedpost. "Stay."

The young man on the other side of the door was visibly relieved to find Rudi tied up on the far side of the room. "Good morning, Your Highness," he said with a bow. "May I show you to breakfast?"

Liam followed the servant through a maze of echoing corridors lined with gratuitous furnishings. He was lost within moments. It just went on and on, like one of those endlessly repeating dreamscapes where every corner you rounded led you back to the place you'd just left. He'd have sworn they'd turned left five times in a row, and he'd definitely seen that sideboard at least twice. *Good job you're going to have an escort everywhere you go.*

When at last they reached the dining hall, Liam was surprised to find himself alone with the servants. "Where are the others?" he asked, surveying the table dubiously. There were no rashers that he could see, no eggs of any sort. Bread, cheese, and some sort of shrivelled fish appeared to be what passed for the morning meal in Onnan.

The servant gave him a surprised look. "Does Your Highness normally dine with your guards?"

"My *officers*, yes."

The servant coloured a little. "I'm very sorry, Your Highness. We won't make that error again."

And now he felt guilty. Wonderful.

After breakfast, Liam was shown to the courtyard, where he found Dain Cooper and Rona Brown waiting for him. The rest of the men would remain barracked in one of the outbuildings, under Ide's command.

Rona Brown smiled at him from atop her horse—a little nervously, he thought, whether for her commander or herself, he couldn't tell. She'd braided her hair again, and her armour was freshly polished. Dain's too. They would be his bodyguards as well as his counsellors on this mission, not that Liam expected any trouble.

Rellard Mason and his honour guard were here too—considerably diminished in number, Liam was relieved to note. He took the reins from his squire and mounted up. "Ready," he said, and wondered if it was true.

They descended from the hills along a cobbled road that wound its way through a gallery of blooming pear trees. The cherries were in flower too, clouds of pink dotting the gardens and strewing their delicate petals onto the shivering surfaces of duck ponds. The slope of the hills allowed a clear view into the gardens of the lower estates, and Liam was amazed at the wealth he saw on display there.

"I never knew Onnan City was so lovely," Rona said, echoing his thoughts.

"The Ambassador District, at any rate," Dain replied. "Wait until we get into the city proper."

Even from here, Liam could see what he meant. The image that had occurred to him earlier of rubbish left on the beach was not far off; farther down the valley, the city had the look of something discarded, half used and left to rot. A warren of twisting alleys cut through low stone buildings crusted with lichen—the remnants of the imperial city, Liam supposed. Here and there, temples imposed themselves on the clutter, but they looked to be modest in size and architecture, nothing to rival the grand monuments of Erroman. Nearer the water, humble timber dwellings vied for space with warehouses and piers. *No pear trees down there*, Liam thought. Not a bit of green in sight, unless you counted the moss flecking the roof tiles.

"There's the Republicana," Dain said, pointing.

Of course. The most impressive building in the valley, it appeared from their vantage as a gleaming white triangle with a gilt dome. The gold leaf flared under the rising sun, as if trying to rival Rahl's splendour. Liam knew enough history to recall that this building had been constructed—proudly, smugly—with materials looted from the palaces of deposed Erromanian nobility. It had seemed fitting to the new republic's rulers that their seat of power should be built from the remnants of a shattered empire.

An empire whose heirs Liam was here to represent. He wondered how that would shape what was to come.

He was about to find out.

Liam shifted from foot to foot, his gaze fixed on the ornate wooden doors before him. He could hear a voice droning on the other side, obviously making a speech of some kind, but the words were too muted to make out. They'd be speaking Onnani anyway, he supposed. He glanced at his officers, Dain on his left and Rona on his right. He hoped he didn't look half as anxious as they did, but he suspected otherwise. He'd been fine, more or less, until his escort showed them into the anteroom. Now he felt his breakfast churning in his belly. (Good job he hadn't touched the fish.) Speakers Hall lay on the other side of that door, the benches packed with every voting member of the Republicana.

This is it, Liam thought. He schooled his features, squared his shoulders, and tried to look regal.

The voice on the other side of the door fell silent. Footfalls sounded, like a countdown to doom, and then the carved panels swung away to reveal the inside of a temple. That was what it looked like, anyway, all marbled pillars and high ceilings and flashes of gold. Tiered benches lined either side of the hall. At least two hundred men sat shoulder to shoulder— every single one of them staring at Liam.

With a final, helpless glance at his officers, Liam stepped into Speakers Hall.

You could have heard a feather drop in that room were it not for the sound of their footfalls echoing under the gilded dome, so conspicuously loud that Liam almost flinched. The man who'd opened the door led them toward a raised dais at the far end. The wall behind it was inlaid with gold, thin bands and broad radiating out from the dais like the rays of the sun, as though it were the holy seat of Rahl himself. There were figures on the platform, Liam saw. Priests, masked, robed in the colours of the Holy Virtues they served.

"His Royal Highness Prince Liam White." The announcement—booming, primly oratorical—came from a small, silver-clad herald at the foot of the dais.

Liam bowed to the priests. Then, on a whim, he bowed to the benches as well.

"Welcome, Your Highness." At first, Liam wasn't sure which of them had spoken; their faces were invisible behind the masks. Then the one in the centre, a priest of Ardin, inclined his head. The delicate points of his spun-glass mask glinted in the wavering light of the braziers, seeming to twist and dance like an actual flame. "In the name of the Republicana, I welcome you. I am First Speaker Kar."

Liam had assumed as much—Saxon's notes had told him to expect it—but he still felt uneasy at the confirmation. In Alden, the priesthood stayed away from politics. They were above it, at least in theory. Here, politics and religion were inseparable, just one more strain in the complex symphony of the Republicana.

And me without my dancing boots.

Belatedly, Liam realised they were waiting for him to speak. He cleared a dry throat. "I thank you, First Speaker, and I bring the regards of His Majesty King Erik. He regrets that he is compelled to be elsewhere, but these are troubling times, as you well know." That bit had been prepared by Highmount. It sounded simple enough to Liam, but apparently it had been carefully crafted. An apology, but a cool one, containing just a whiff of rebuke. Hearing Highmount talk about it was like listening to a cook describing an elaborate dish.

"We know it indeed," said another of the priests. He wore the mask of Olan, a silver disc with narrow slits for eyes and mouth. *Irtok, Chairman of the Republicana. A Shield, fittingly.* Liam had practically memorised Saxon's notes, and knew this man to be almost as powerful as First Speaker Kar, and a rival. "The Republicana deplores the cowardly acts of the Trionate of Oridia, and stands in full solidarity with our Aldenian allies. The people of Onnan offer their sincere condolences for your losses. You are in our prayers."

"Your support is deeply appreciated," Liam said, launching into his second prepared line, "and we know you are doing everything you can to accelerate preparations to join us in this fight."

A new voice spoke then—smooth and dark, languid, like molasses. It oozed out from behind a crude mask of black wood adorned with a single, all-seeing eye. Liam sensed something different about the words, something less than cordial, but he couldn't be sure, because the man was speaking Onnani. *Is he talking to me? How in the Nine Domains am I supposed to—*

The little herald at the foot of the steps spoke up. "It is good to hear you say so," the booming voice said, translating. "In view of your presence here, one might have thought His Majesty had doubts on that score."

And just like that, the atmosphere in the room grew thin and quivering, a drawn bowstring, the arrow pointed right at Liam's chest.

"He doesn't," Liam said—too quickly. He tried for a disarming smile. "If he did, he would hardly send me, a man who knows nothing at all of ships."

Your humility will go a long way with them, Alix had said.

But Alix had never met this priest of Eldora, whoever he was. He cocked his head, the all-seeing eye tilting slightly, and the honeyed voice spoke again. He hadn't waited for a translation. He didn't seem to need one. *I'll bet he speaks Erromanian just fine*, Liam thought sourly.

"Indeed?" The little herald's voice thundered under the dome. "Which of his advisors would he have sent, one wonders? Which captain of the seas would he have selected to advise us?" The translation contained no trace of sarcasm—which made the barb all the sharper.

Sweet Farika. Liam glanced helplessly at Rona Brown, his guide in all courtly things. She stared back at him, her features carefully blank. She could do nothing for him, not without making him look like a fool in front of everyone. Liam was on his own.

Dogs could smell fear, Alix had said. Apparently, so could politicians. Liam had faced battles with more confidence than this. He'd faced death with more cold-blooded determination.

The thought gave him an idea.

"We don't have many captains of the sea, it's true." Liam addressed his words to the priest of Eldora, fixing the all-seeing eye with the same look he gave foes on the battlefield, the one that dared them to come on. "But we do have captains of war. Seasoned and tested, especially in these *troubling times*. And I flatter myself to think that I'm one such." He bowed then, low and deliberate. "I'm not here to advise you, my lord speaker. I'm here to learn, as much as I can, as quickly as I can, so that my king and his commander general have all the information they need to plan our strategy for this new season of war."

To Liam's vast relief, it was First Speaker Kar who spoke next. "And in that task we shall assist you to the best of our ability. For as Speaker Irtok has rightly said, the people of Onnan stand beside our Aldenian brothers. You shall be accorded every courtesy and assistance." The spun-glass flame ducked again, a grave nod to seal the words.

There was a stretch of silence. Something stirred at Liam's elbow. The man who'd escorted them from the anteroom was standing there, waiting. They'd been dismissed.

The pocket-sized herald struck up again, but the words were Onnani, clearly not intended for Liam's ears. He quit the hall with as much princely dignity as he could muster, not daring to breathe until the thick wooden doors came to behind him.

"Holy Virtues," Dain Cooper muttered. "I need a drink."

"I need a cloak," said Rona. "It was *freezing* in there." She didn't mean the temperature, Liam knew.

A few moments. A handful of words. That was all the time he'd merited, apparently. Would they have dismissed Erik so quickly? Liam didn't think so. "The priest of Eldora. Who is he?"

His officers shook their heads. "Do you think we'll see him again?" Dain asked.

"Yeah," Liam said grimly, "I do. And I think it's going to be a problem."

EIGHT

Liam paced the sunroom like one of those bears they keep in cages at the fair. (Probably. He'd never actually been to a fair, but he'd heard.) He was wearing down the shine on the floor, black-and-white marble glossy enough to shave in and with the approximate traction of a frozen lake. It was a miracle he hadn't yet fallen and broken his neck, but that didn't stop him from tearing back and forth, back and forth, the way he'd seen Erik do a hundred times when he was agitated and needed to think.

Not that it was helping. They'd been back at Bayview for over an hour, and Liam was no closer to figuring out what in the Nine Domains he was supposed to do next. His officers watched him in silence, their expressions ranging from bored (Ide) to worried (Rona) to mildly embarrassed (Dain).

"Maybe we should get drunk," Ide suggested.

Rona blinked at her in astonishment. "I hardly think that would help matters."

"It'd pass the time. You ever seen the commander tippy? He giggles. Worth seeing. More entertaining than this, anyway."

"He needs to think," Rona said. "This is a very serious situation."

"Not to mention confusing," Dain put in. "I don't see how he's going to make top nor bottom of all this—"

"You all realise I'm *right here*, don't you? I may be thick, but I'm not deaf."

"You're not thick, Commander," Rona said, rising. "You're doing fine. Anyone would be overwhelmed by this."

Erik wouldn't. Liam kept the thought to himself.

"The important thing is not to *seem* overwhelmed," Rona continued. "Diplomacy is all about crafting an image. Carry yourself as if you belong here, and soon enough, you will."

She sounded a lot like Alix just then, and it comforted him. He nodded, forcing himself to stop pacing.

"Excuse me, Your Highness." The servant who'd escorted him earlier—Shef, he'd said his name was—appeared in the doorway. "You have visitors. First Speaker Kar and Defence Consul Welin are in the entrance hall."

Liam stiffened in surprise. "Here? Now?"

"Yes, Your Highness. Shall I . . . ?"

"Of course. Show them in."

Rona Brown swept over to the window seat, arranging herself in a posture that was dignified, but relaxed. She gave Liam a meaningful look.

Diplomacy is all about crafting an image. He needed to look confident, as if he belonged here. He cast a glance around the room, settled on a pitcher of wine, and stationed himself near the table.

First Speaker Kar and his consul of defence entered the sunroom to find the prince and his officers pouring wine, reclining, and leafing casually through old books, to all appearances passing a pleasant afternoon. The speakers had brought a third man with them, Liam saw, the only one of the three not robed as a priest.

It was Rona Brown who set the tone. She rose and bowed—cool, unhurried, not a servant genuflecting, but an equal paying respect. She was pitch-perfect—as good as Alix, maybe better. *Thank Farika she's here*, Liam thought, not for the first time.

"Speakers," he said. "Welcome."

"Your Highness." The first speaker had shed his formal mask, thankfully; Liam could see his face now. That sat easier with him. Liam didn't trust anyone he couldn't look in the eyes.

"May I introduce my secretary, Ash Bookman." The third man, the one Liam didn't know, inclined his head. "Ash will be at your service throughout your stay with us. He will organise your schedule and arrange any meetings you desire."

"Thank you."

"I must apologise, Your Highness, if my learned colleague was less than civil this morning. Speaker Syril is a staunch republican, and no ally of the war effort. It was, I fear, a case of shooting the messenger." He smiled then, an expression so artfully crafted that Liam had the impression of a pantomime. *He's still wearing a mask after all*, Liam thought. One of flesh instead of spun glass.

"I'm not familiar with Speaker Syril," Liam said.

"Entirely understandable." It was Welin who replied, disdainfully. He was a round, wrinkled man of medium complexion; the overall effect was that of a large walnut. Right down to the bitter insides, judging from his sneering expression.

"What Speaker Welin means," Kar said, "is that Speaker Syril came to his position only recently. The People's Congress had something of an internal power struggle last summer, and when the dust settled, Syril was their new leader. He is"—the painted smile again—"sly."

"I see," said Liam, though he really didn't. "Please, take a seat."

Kar settled onto the window seat Rona had abandoned, arranging his priestly robes around him. The walnut rolled in beside him.

"Wine, my lords?" Rona said.

"Yes, thank you, Lady Brown." Kar's gaze followed Rona across the room, his brow slightly stitched. *She confuses him,* Liam thought. Bad enough that she was a female knight, something the conservative Onnani just didn't understand; she was also a banner lady. The Republicana had been informed she'd be part of the delegation, but they probably hadn't realised she was a Wolf. They'd have expected her to come in a fancy frock, with jewels on her fingers. Instead, she'd come in White Wolf armour, with a sword at her hip.

Good. Let them be confused about our politics for a change. Maybe it would even out the battlefield a little. "So," Liam said, "what happens now?"

Kar took the glass Rona offered him. He sipped from it, then set it down, turning the glass a little as though to admire the cut crystal. He folded his hands over his knees and gazed at Liam.

Hardly any drama there.

"Can I be frank, Your Highness?"

I seriously doubt it. Aloud, Liam said, "Please."

"My colleagues and I have reason to believe that the setbacks we are experiencing with the fleet are not entirely accidental."

Liam regarded him warily. "Meaning . . . ?"

"Meaning," said Welin, "that someone is deliberately employing delaying tactics."

"Why would someone do that?"

"To embarrass the government," Kar said. "To make us look like incompetent fools. Next year is an election year, Your Highness. The games are well under way."

Liam stared. His country was at war, thousands dead and dying, bandits marauding over half the territory, raping and stealing . . . and these fishmen were using the fleet as a game piece in their sodding *elections*?

Dain Cooper cleared his throat. "Commander . . ."

"Go ahead." Liam was only too happy to let Dain talk; it would give him a chance to calm down. Thumping the leader of a foreign country would probably qualify as a diplomatic incident.

"Do you have actual evidence of that?" Dain asked. "Or is it just a theory?"

"It is the only plausible explanation," said Kar. "But perhaps you would like to judge for yourselves. Would you care to pay a visit to the shipyard, Your Highness? I know it was planned for tomorrow, to give you a chance to rest from your journey, but—"

Liam was already on his feet. "Let's go."

"And this," said First Speaker Kar, "is Mallik, our Chief Shipwright." He nodded at a thickset man with compact features and leathery skin. "Chief, if you please."

"Happy to, First Speaker." The chief shipwright gestured behind him at a towering structure braced with scaffolding. "After you, Your Highness."

Liam craned his neck until it hurt. The thing was *huge*, its wooden rib cage looming over them like the carcass of some massive sea creature.

Dain Cooper whistled appreciatively. "That's quite a vessel. How many oars?"

"A hundred each side," the chief said with a grin. He glanced back over his shoulder at the first speaker and his deputy. "Biggest galley ever built," he added, apparently for their benefit. "Half again the size of anything the Oridians have."

The air rang with hammer blows and the shouts of workmen. Gulls wheeled and cried overhead, and the smells of pitch and wet sawdust filled Liam's nose, vying for dominance with the salt tang of the sea. A soft, rhythmic pulse of white noise washed over him every few moments. *The waves.* He longed to see them, but he had work to do.

As he approached the galley, he saw that it was only the first in a long line stacked up on wooden platforms. Some looked almost complete; others were little more than a few bowed sticks gathered together, like a barrel before it's banded.

None of them was finished. Not a gods-damned *one*.

"A new design of my own devising," the chief was saying proudly. "See these front turrets? Perfect for archers. And there's plenty of open space on the deck for transporting siege engines."

"How many men can they carry?" Rona asked.

It was the first speaker's secretary, Ash, who answered.

"Four hundred apiece, not counting the crew. Those were the specifications given by the Republicana."

"And cursedly difficult to meet, I don't mind telling you," the chief said. "But we managed."

Liam was about to ask the chief for his definition of *managed* when he felt someone's gaze on him. He turned to find a dock-hand looking at him—staring, really—with a gaze that couldn't be called warm. He wasn't the only one, either. Glancing around, Liam realised that every man on the docks was watching their little party of dignitaries, and none of them seemed especially friendly. Were those frosty looks intended for him, he wondered, or the members of the Republicana?

"Speaker," he said in a low voice, "do we have a problem?"

Kar raised his eyebrows and looked around. "What, the dockies?" He made a dismissive gesture. "Never mind them. They always look like that."

"A more self-entitled group of malcontents never existed," Welin added. "They are almost enough to put me off unions entirely."

Liam glanced at his officers, saw his own confusion reflected in their faces. "What's a union?"

"Do not concern yourself, Your Highness," Kar said. "Ash will explain that and more, at your leisure."

They continued wandering alongside the half-finished hull of the galley, the chief shipwright nattering on about this innovation and that, telling them how many wagonloads of timber had gone into it, how many men, how well balanced it was and how light on the draught—on and on, as if this ship were the single greatest invention in the history of warfare. Which maybe it was—Liam didn't know. He didn't *care*. There was only one thing he wanted to know. "How long does it take to build?"

The chief fell silent. His gaze cut briefly to Defence Consul Welin. "If everything goes as it should, about six months."

"Six months. Meaning a first round of them should have been finished by now, assuming you only started *after* declaring war."

The chief's eyes met his. "If everything goes as it should," he said again, deliberately.

"And how far along are these?"

"About three months, Your Highness."

Liam frowned. "How does that work? My maths may not be top drawer, but—"

"Your Highness." First Speaker Kar smiled and spread his hands. "We can discuss this further back at Bayview. Have you seen everything you wish to see?" His smile was as wooden as the timber planks behind him. Little splinters gathered at the corners of his eyes.

"Sure," Liam said. "I think I've seen enough." *Enough to know I'm not getting anywhere with you around.*

He thanked the chief for his time. Then he followed First Speaker Kar back up the hill to where the horses waited.

"Thank you again, Your Highness," Kar said, bowing. "Ash will return first thing in the morning. He will take excellent care of you, and if there is anything more you need from me personally, do not hesitate to let me know."

Because you've been such a big help so far. Aloud, Liam said, "Bye."

Ide came to join them as they watched Kar and the others ride down the drive. "How'd it go?" she asked.

"Oh, splendid. Perfect. Unless of course the idea was to *learn* anything, in which case, not so well."

"Not very forthcoming?"

Liam snorted. "That bloke is slippery as a"—*Not fish! You can't say fish!*—"marble floor," he finished lamely, avoiding Dain's eye.

"The shipwright clearly had more to say," Rona added. "The question is, why was Kar so keen to hurry us out of there? What didn't he want us to hear?"

"There's so much that doesn't make sense," Liam said. "It looks like they're building everything from scratch down there, but why? What happened to their existing fleet?"

"That's a good question, Commander," Dain said. "I've seen the fleet a few times. It's never been big—the Onnani put more effort into fishing boats and merchant vessels than warships— but it was there. You used to see big galleys anchored out in the bay. A beautiful thing at sunrise."

"So where are they now?"

It was a rhetorical question, of course; none of them had an answer.

They found Shef waiting for them inside. "You have another visitor, Your Highness," the servant said. "Chairman Irtok is waiting for you in the sunroom."

Liam sighed. And here he thought he'd met his quota of politicians for the day.

The chairman rose when Liam and his officers came into the room, his silver robes falling into neat, shining folds. "Your Highness."

If Liam hadn't been told who awaited him, he never would have recognised the man. With his mask on, Irtok had been a grave, imposing figure. Without it, he looked old and querulous, with narrow-set eyes and a disapproving mouth. He was balding, but tried to disguise the fact by casting an improbable wave of grey hair over the crown of his head.

"Please forgive my unexpected arrival," the chairman said. "I would have sent word, but I thought it best that this visit go unmarked."

"Unmarked?" Liam frowned. "You mean you're here in secret?"

Irtok gave a short laugh, setting his jowls quivering. "Nothing so dramatic. I am simply trying to avoid awkward questions."

"Such as?"

"Such as why I felt the need to speak with you in private." He waited. Cleared his throat. When it became clear Liam had no intention of dismissing his officers, Irtok added, "Or, if not in private, at least outside the presence of my learned colleagues."

"And why would you feel the need to do that?" Liam gestured for the chairman to sit.

"I presume the first speaker and his consul of defence offered a theory as to why the construction of the fleet is delayed. I presume they intimated that the opposition is actively sabotaging the efforts of the government." Irtok leaned forward, his voice dropping to a low growl. "I tell you now, Your Highness, that is rank nonsense. The People's Congress may oppose the war, but they would never go so far. Syril would never go so far."

Liam considered him with narrowed eyes. "You're a member of the Worker's Alliance, aren't you?"

"Of course. I could hardly be chairman otherwise."

"I'm just surprised you would speak so openly against your own league." That wasn't completely true. He knew from Saxon's notes that Irtok was a rival for leadership of the Alliance, and with elections on the horizon, it was all but inevitable that his differences with Kar would widen. Liam didn't know much about politics, but it didn't take a career diplomat to work that out.

"I want what is best for this country, Your Highness," Irtok said. "We are at war, and we need competent men at the helm. Alas, that does not include our current consul of defence. I'm afraid that First Speaker Kar is simply doing his best to cover up the failings of his own cabinet. Which makes him just as culpable, I regret to say."

He didn't sound that regretful.

"So you think it's a question of incompetence?" Liam asked. "No one is deliberately dragging his feet?"

"A terrible accusation," Irtok said. "It wounds me to the core that my learned colleagues would deliberately lead you to believe so. They are only looking to deflect blame from themselves, Your Highness."

"So what's to be done?"

Irtok's gaze fell to his lap. He picked at something invisible on his robes. "I regret to say that so long as things remain as they are, there is no solution at hand. If we are to find a way out of this most desperate situation . . ." He shook his head sadly. "I fear significant changes may be called for."

"Ah." Liam saw where this was going. He should have seen it from the start.

"Nothing so dramatic as an early election, of course. We could not afford that kind of instability. But perhaps, if His Majesty, your brother, were to suggest to some of my learned colleagues . . ."

"Got it," Liam said. And he did. He got it all too well.

His point made, Chairman Irtok drained his wine and left. Liam didn't even bother to rise, let alone see him off. He was too bloody *stunned*.

"Well," he said when Irtok had gone, "that was definitely my favourite part of the day."

"What he just suggested to you . . ." Rona was wide-eyed. "If anyone had overheard that . . ."

"What, you mean the part where he asked me to help toss out his own government?"

"Treason," Ide whispered, darting a glance at the door.

"No," Dain said. "This isn't a monarchy. The Worker's Alliance can vote to replace its leadership anytime it likes. Irtok's proposal isn't treasonous, it's just slimy."

So it begins. Liam had been warned about the agendas here, how dangerously complex they could be, but he hadn't expected to be sucked into the mire quite so quickly. He raked his fingers through his hair and swore under his breath. Gods, he hated this. He belonged at the front, with Rig—all the Wolves did. Instead, they were squirming around in this viper's nest.

"Your Highness." Shef again, bearing a scroll. "A messenger left this for you earlier. I did not wish to interrupt . . ."

A blade of fear sliced through Liam. How long had the servant been standing there? What had he overheard? Treason or no, the Onnani were not likely to look fondly on the Prince of Alden conspiring against their government.

If Shef had heard anything, he gave no sign; he just handed over the scroll. Liam took it, hoping his hands looked steadier than they felt. There was no seal on the wax, just an anonymous grey blob. Frowning, he opened it.

As he read, he felt heat rising on the back of his neck, and his pulse started to race. It must have shown on his face, because Rona got up from her chair. "Commander?"

"I spoke too soon," he growled. "This is *definitely* my favourite part of the day."

"What's it say?" Ide asked.

"The handwriting is a bit crude, but I'm pretty sure it says, *Monarchist bastard. You are not welcome in Onnan. You leave now, and your White Dogs with you. You are warned. If you stay, you die.*" He crumpled the parchment in his hand. "Do you think they meant *bastard* literally, or just in the nasty way?"

"How can you joke about this?" Rona had gone pale. "That's a death threat!"

"I got that impression too."

She snatched the letter from Liam's hands, and the three of them clustered around to read.

Liam went for the wine. Then he changed his mind and

threw open the doors to the balcony. He stood outside, breathing deeply of the salt air, letting it ruffle his hair.

If you stay, you die. Pretty unambiguous, that. Clearest thing anyone had said to him since he got here.

He missed Alix. She'd know what to do. She knew how to solve puzzles, how to fight foes you couldn't see. So did Erik. They were alike that way. *In a lot of ways*, a voice inside him whispered. Liam closed his eyes and tried not to think.

He stayed out there until the sun set, ignoring the exhortations to come back inside, to get something to eat. It wasn't until the moon rose and the mist crept up the hill that he finally retreated, damp and shivering, to his room.

Rudi growled from a shadowed corner. Liam was too exhausted to care. He dropped down in front of the fire, and the wolfhound came over, sniffing at his salt-crusted clothes. Liam ignored him. A moment later, a warm mass slumped into his leg. Rudi dropped his head onto his paws with a sigh.

Liam fell asleep with the wolfhound's wiry fur coiled in his fingers.

NINE

There were four of them. They weren't wearing crimson, but he could tell even at this distance that they weren't his, which meant they were the enemy. Scouts, obviously, and a good half day's march from the border—a lot closer to the fort than they had any right to be.

"Bugger," said Riggard Black.

"Have to agree with you there, General." Commander Morris offered him the longlens.

Rig waved it off; he'd seen all he needed to. "I thought we'd have another two weeks or so before the fun started. I'm still freezing my balls off every morning, and we've got at least one snowfall ahead of us. It's too soon."

"Agreed on that too," said Morris. "Reckon we should be grateful they waited until you got back from the capital."

"I'll be sure to thank the Virtues in my prayers tonight."

"Never took you for a praying man, General."

"Oh, constantly. I'm one trial away from being ordained as a priest."

They wriggled back down the hill, their armour carving a glistening trail of black mud out of the undergrowth. They'd be covered in it from knees to shoulders, but that was all to the good; it would make them harder to see when they stole up on the enemy.

Men and horses, eight of them, waited at the bottom of the rise. "Arrows," Rig told them. "Quick and quiet."

Wordlessly, the men readied their bows. Rig grabbed his own bloodbow and quiver from his saddle and motioned for them to fan out. They'd close a little distance, then take the enemy scouts from the flanks. It would be the first bloodshed of the season. Scattered droplets before the downpour.

Rig and Morris split up, each of them leading four men. They picked their way carefully through the undergrowth. The wind was in their favour, rustling the trees and carrying sound away from the enemy. Rig's pulse pounded satisfyingly in his ears. It wasn't that he craved battle—the gods knew he had enough of *those* types under his command—but sitting around all winter waiting for the enemy to pounce was enough to drive a man mad. So when enemy scouts were sighted near the fort, he'd insisted on coming himself. Not a commander general's task, he knew, but his hinges were rusty, and they needed working.

He led his unit in a wide arc, confident that Morris was mirroring the move on the enemy's other flank. He kept them out of sight until he judged they were just short, then swung in to intercept. There was no signal, no elaborate whistle or flash of mirror. Rig would shoot first, then the others would loose their own. Simple. No room for ambiguity. There was nothing ambiguous about death.

The enemy scouts moved slowly, hoping for stealth. That made them easy targets. Rig drew, thumb brushing his beard. The bloodbow creaked. He paused, eyes narrowed, letting his breath settle—as though there were any chance he could miss, any chance that a shaft loosed from an enchanted bow could do other than fly unerringly to its target. Rig could have pierced his enemy's ear from here. But he was too practiced a soldier to take anything for granted, so he sighted, and he breathed, and he waited. And then he let fly.

The lead scout pitched backward with an arrow in his eye.

The enemy scattered like startled deer. For two of them, it was too late; they went down studded with arrows. But communication had broken down in Morris's unit, and the archers all aimed for the same man. The survivor, unmarked, dove through the trees and out of sight.

Rig swore and gave chase. It was only one man, but they'd managed to keep the location of the fort secret until now, and Rig would be damned if a lucky scout lived to betray it. He plunged through the trees, bloodbow pumping in his right hand, sword swinging wildly at his hip. He was a big man, and athletic, but he wore a breastplate and mail, heavy boots, designed for fighting on horseback. The enemy scout, in his lightweight leathers, would outrun him easily. Fortunately, Rig had two scouts of his own, already streaking ahead. He wasn't worried.

Until he saw the rest of them.

Seven in all, only three men short of Rig's unit. Scouts, judging from their leather and light weapons, but they were ready, having been alerted by the noise of ten men crashing through the trees toward them. An arrow whizzed by Rig's shoulder. It caught one of his scouts in the chest; she went down with a cry. Moments later, another shout sounded from the east—one of Morris's. Near even strength now. Rig swore viciously and yanked an arrow from his quiver.

His was the only bloodbow on the field; he could tell by the wild shots flying in both directions. He dropped three men before anyone else drew blood. It wouldn't be much of a fight, but that didn't mean all was well. Rig couldn't see the first scout, the one who'd fled. He must have kept running. And that meant he was still a danger.

Rig loosed another arrow, but his target got lucky, diving to avoid someone else's shot and taking himself out of Rig's line of fire. Bloodbows were deadly accurate, but they couldn't turn corners. "Morris!"

"Here, General!"

"Finish this! I'm going after him!"

A heated oath floated through the trees. Morris didn't like his commander putting himself at risk. But he was a soldier, and soldiers followed orders, so his next words were, "Aye, General!"

Rig hadn't waited for the reply; he'd already broken off from the battle, moving in the direction he'd last seen the scout. He despaired of catching up, but he had to try.

Within moments, the sounds of battle were swallowed by the forest. That was well, because now Rig could hear his quarry up ahead, rustling and snapping. He veered toward the sound, and soon enough he could see the trail. A man blundering through last season's undergrowth was not hard to follow; Rig even allowed himself to slow down some, putting stealth above speed. He couldn't hope to overtake his quarry, but if the scout thought himself out of danger, he would slow, perhaps even stop.

Rig's breath was harsh in his ears. He couldn't remember the last time he'd run like this with armour on. *You'll be feeling that tomorrow*, he thought. Presuming he lived that long.

The trail grew harder to follow. The enemy scout had dropped pace, as hoped, but that meant he left less destruction in his wake. Rig slowed to a walk, using his ears to guide him once more. The noise came from the south, toward the river. The scout had a long way to go, but if he made it across the border, he'd be treated to a hero's welcome. The Oridians had been trying to locate the fort since last autumn. It had been built in haste and was no great fortress, but it gave Rig a foothold west of the citadel at Pir, allowing him to be much more nimble along the border and plugging the gap that had allowed the enemy to invade in earnest last spring. If the Oridians found it, they would smash it easily, and then there would be nothing standing between them and the Greenlands.

Belatedly, Rig realised that the forest had gone silent. He froze. A breath of wind rustled the budding branches around him, but nothing else moved. He closed his eyes, listening. Still nothing.

A squirrel erupted into chatter above him. Swearing under his breath, Rig looked up, thinking to silence it with an arrow; instead he saw a dark shape plummeting down from the branches. It struck him full force, knocking him to the ground and driving the wind from him.

A moment of confusion, the world reeling overhead, a mass of leather and steel piled on top of him. Metal flashed. Rig's hand shot up and seized the wrist above him, gave it a sharp twist. The man grunted, but the dagger didn't fall; instead it continued to inch nearer. They struggled; somehow, the scout managed to get a knee up against Rig's throat, a crushing weight against his windpipe. Panic arced through him, stronger even than the pain. The knee ground into him. A few more moments of this, and he'd never draw air again. He writhed violently, trying to throw his attacker off even as he kept the dagger at bay, his left hand clawing ineffectually at the man's leathers. The scout shifted again, looking to pin Rig's left arm with his other knee.

That was a mistake.

With his legs freed, Rig was able to get the leverage he needed; he threw his left fist into the man's temple, landing a solid blow that stunned his enemy. Another punch pitched the scout sideways, and Rig rolled, putting himself on top. He used all his considerable bulk to pin the man, and then he went to work, driving his fist down again and again with the brutal force of rage and relief.

It wasn't pretty, but it didn't last long. By the time he was through, the face below him was scarcely human.

Rig lurched to his feet over the bloodied form, coughing and fingering his throbbing throat. He couldn't see any pockets, pouches, anywhere the scout might have stashed information of value. The Warlord was too smart for that. Like Rig, he sent his scouts into the field with little more than their leathers and their wits. Which was why so many of them ended up gutted, felled by an arrow, or beaten to death by large, angry men.

Pausing to catch his breath, Rig took in his surroundings. The first thing he noticed was the bright scar on the tree bark beside him, from where the scout had scrabbled up to ambush him. *How did you miss that, you oaf?* He was lucky to be alive.

The second thing he noticed was that he had absolutely no idea where he was.

Brilliant. He was ploughing with a full team today.

He had two choices: head back the way he'd come until he picked up the trail, or make for the road, which had to be broadly northwest of here. He chose the latter. A longer route, but a surer one, and less likely to run him into prowling enemy soldiers.

A good hour went by before Rig found the road. And naturally, it started to rain. A cold drizzle at first, followed by a deluge. Water streamed down his face, soaking his beard and plastering his hair to his forehead. It trailed icy fingers down the back of his neck and under his mail. He might as well have gone for a bloody *swim*. The storm let up after a while, but by then, the damage was done; Rig was shivering down to his bones. If he didn't find dry clothes and a fire soon, he'd fall ill for certain. *Wouldn't that beat all*, he thought. *Survive the siege and bloodbound thralls, only to die of fever.*

It was about then that he realised he was being watched.

He turned, already swinging his bloodbow down from his shoulder. A figure on horseback stood in the middle of the road. The rider's features were obscured within a hooded cloak, but the long black hair cascading over the left shoulder marked her a woman. A brazen one at that, leaving her hair unbound. A noble lady might get away with that, but it surprised Rig that a woman from these provincial parts would be so unabashed.

"Ho there." He slung his bow back over his shoulder to show that he wasn't a threat.

The woman brought her horse closer, turning it aside so she might get a clear look at the stranger in the road. Rig resisted the urge to wipe at the mud on his breastplate. It wouldn't do any good anyway.

"Is that how you greet a woman, soldier? *Ho there?*"

She spoke with a light Onnani accent. An easterner, Rig wondered, or the real thing? Either way, it seemed he'd offended her. He offered his most charming smile and swept into a bow. "My deepest apologies, my lady. I meant no offence. Army life erodes a man's manners."

"Are you lost?"

"Not lost, at least not anymore. I'm not far from home, actually, but the going has been slow." He gestured at the muddy road.

"Are you wounded?"

"Thankfully no, though I did encounter a spot of trouble."

"I can see that. There are spots of trouble all over your breastplate."

Rig looked down and winced. Soaked to the smalls, but some-how he still managed to be spattered with blood. The gods were not on his side today.

"Yours," she asked, "or someone else's?"

"An Oridian scout."

"May he find peace in his Domain," she said gravely.

A number of possible responses occurred to Rig, but he thought better of them.

"You are on your way back to your comrades, presumably. My horse can carry two, if you like."

A woman leaving her hair unbound in public was brazen. A woman offering to ride double with a total stranger—a soldier spattered with blood, no less—was something else entirely. Fortunately, Rig was quite comfortable with brazen women, having more or less raised one himself. "A very generous offer," he said, "one I'm inclined to accept, given that my fingers are turning blue."

Her horse danced up alongside him. Rig could see her face now, gazing down from within the hood, dark-skinned and dark-eyed, quite lovely. His admiration must have shown on his face, because her mouth quirked. "You're staring, soldier."

"I suppose I am." He smiled. "Last chance to back out."

"You don't frighten me. The Virtues protect their chosen." She threw back one side of her cloak, revealing the robes of a priestess. She laughed then, obviously enjoying the look of astonishment on Rig's face. She leaned down, so close that it was all Rig could do not to recoil. "Last chance to back out," she purred.

A priestess. Rig certainly hadn't been expecting *that*. Female clergy were rare in Alden, even rarer in Onnan, and figured prominently in a number of unflattering legends. Under the Erromanians, they'd been branded witches, hanged and burned, and not necessarily in that order. Rig wasn't a religious man, but he'd seen firsthand the terrible magicks a priest could wield. To be sure, Madan, the Madman of Oridia, hadn't been just any priest. But he'd proven that some legends, even the darkest ones, had their basis in truth.

"Why, soldier, you've gone a little pale. Perhaps we'd better get you to a fire." She laid a hand against the saddle. "Front or back?"

"I'm taller," Rig said, his voice suddenly a little gruff. *Get a hold of yourself, Black. She's just a woman. She's not likely to harvest your blood.* "I'll go behind, if you don't mind."

"Sensible. That way, you can keep an eye on me. You never know what foul mischief a priestess might get up to."

Rig wasn't quite sure what to make of that.

The woman laughed again. It was as if she enjoyed his discomfort. He couldn't imagine why, but he had more important things to do, so without further preamble, he swung himself up and nestled in behind her. Putting his arms around her didn't seem like a good idea, so he grabbed the back of the saddle instead.

They rode in silence for a while. Rig's mind started to wander, thinking through his next move now that he knew the Oridians were poised to strike. He'd thought to have more time. He'd have prayed for it, were he the praying sort. Two weeks early meant two extra weeks of trying to hold the enemy off while the bloody Onnani tried to patch together a fleet, something they seemed curiously incapable of managing. *I can't do it*, he thought darkly. *It isn't possible.* He'd told Erik as much, not that it made any difference.

After a time, the woman broke in on his musings. "The enemy will strike soon, I suppose."

He stiffened.

She must have felt it, because she clucked her tongue impatiently. "Relax, soldier. It is common sense, not magic, that showed me your mind. Your armour is decorated with the blood of an enemy scout. You are plainly an officer. What else would occupy your thoughts just now?" Her voice turned wry. "Unless it is your unsettling proximity to a priestess."

"How do you know I'm an officer?"

"I speak Erromanian well enough to know a highborn accent when I hear one."

Plausible enough, he supposed, but that didn't mean he was going to answer her question, not until he knew who she was. "I don't think I caught your name, by the way."

"You did not ask it."

He waited, but she didn't elaborate. Casting a glance skyward, he said, "What's your name, Daughter?"

"I am called Vel." There was something almost musical

about her voice, something intimate, like humming a private tune.

He waited for her to ask his name, but she didn't, so he took his cue from her and didn't offer it. "What brings you to these parts, my lady? It's not safe this close to the front."

"I am no lady. We have no such affectations in Onnan."

The real thing, then. He'd thought so, from the accent. "Onnan, is it? Now I'm even more curious. I feel compelled to warn you that it's not an idle curiosity. We're at war. Foreigners wandering around this close to the front is not a matter we take lightly."

She drew herself up in the saddle. "We are allies, soldier. We are here at the invitation of your king."

"*We*, is it? Are you with the Onnani battalion?"

"I am. I minister to their ranks."

"They arrived two days ago. What are you doing out here alone?"

"I fell behind in the Greylands when I remained in a village to help deliver a baby."

"A courageous decision," Rig said. *A foolhardy one*, he was thinking. "It's not safe to travel the Imperial Road alone, especially for a woman."

"Even for a priestess of Eldora? Would Aldenian bandits not fear my dark powers?" The sarcasm again. It seemed to be a favourite tune.

"They might," Rig said, "if you were lucky."

"And if I was unlucky?" She turned her head so that he could see the sardonic twist of her mouth. "Would they rape me, do you think? Set me aflame?"

"Most likely," Rig said flatly. "They've been doing it to their own women, so a foreigner wouldn't trouble them overmuch."

She fell silent for a moment. When she spoke again, the sarcasm was gone. "Is that true? Are your women being attacked on their own soil?"

"And our men, though they generally have the good fortune to die before anything worse befalls them."

"Can your lords not protect them? Is that not the duty by which they justify their privilege?"

"Every man and woman who can hold a sword, and a few who can't, are already deployed. We're training more, but they're needed at the front, or elsewhere. We're stretched to the brink, and if we make it through the summer, it will be by the grace of the gods alone." He risked nothing in telling her this; it wasn't anything the Warlord didn't already know.

Another silence. "I did not realise things were so grave," she said at length.

"I'm not sure your Republicana realises it either, or we'd have a fleet coming to our rescue by now." Without waiting for a reply, he grabbed the reins and drew the horse to a halt. He jumped down just as a pair of archers stepped out from the trees on either side of the road.

The priestess sucked in a breath, her hand reaching inside her cloak. For a dagger, presumably, as though that would do her any good.

"Afternoon, chaps," Rig said.

The archers lowered their bows and saluted, fists to their chests.

"Blindfold the lady until we can confirm her identity."

Vel went rigid in the saddle. "I beg your pardon? How dare you—"

"Where are your horses?" Rig asked the men, ignoring her. One of the archers pointed. "Half an hour's walk."

"I'll send someone back with it once I reach the fort." Rig gestured behind him at the outraged priestess of Eldora. "Gently, now. She's a friend, I think."

"Is this how you treat your friends?" Vel asked coldly.

"Until I'm sure they are who they claim to be, yes." To the archers, he said, "See to it that she has whatever she needs. As soon as her people confirm her identity, she's free to go." He bowed. "I thank you for the assistance, Daughter Vel, and I hope to see you again. Until then . . ."

Until then, he had a battle to plan, and if he was any judge at all, less than two days to do it.

The season had begun.

TEN

✝ "Here," Rig said, pointing at the map. "Or maybe here."

Morris grunted. "Not sure, General. If what we've heard about the Resistance is true, maybe the Warlord will want to steer clear of their strongholds. It would leave his rear vulnerable. He might decide to try his luck farther west."

"The Resistance won't take on an army on the battlefield. It would be suicide. They'll do like we used to, go for his supply lines, or some other soft spot deeper in their own territory. Sadik will have his pick of the crossings, and if it were me, I'd ford the Gunnar here. Then, once I had enough men across, I'd take Whitefish Bridge." It was the only bridge the Kingswords hadn't destroyed, simply because they couldn't. It had been built by the Erromanians, vexingly wide and stubbornly solid, enough to last through centuries of steady use. It would take a barrel or two of the priests' black powder to bring it down. Even if Rig was willing to use the last of his stock, they'd never get near the bridge with it. Anyone brave enough to attempt it would be blown to dust by a flaming arrow long before he got the barrels into position. The Oridians had been caught unawares by black powder once before; they wouldn't be caught again.

"Still," Rig said, "the bridge is a choke point. They can't get more than—what, fifteen abreast?"

"Fifteen is a lot, especially with their catapults having a go at us from the far bank."

He was right, of course. "Sadik wouldn't even need to cross," Rig said, thinking aloud. "Even a feint would cost us dearly. He could grind us down by attrition and then step over our corpses on his way to Erroman."

They exchanged a grim look and stared at the map some more.

"General." A guard appeared in the doorway. "Battalion Commander Wright is here."

Wonderful. The last thing Rig needed was to play nursemaid to a novice Onnani commander. *I should have just refused*, he thought sourly. A foolish notion, and fleeting; he needed the men, even if they came with such a thick string attached. "Show him in."

Commander Amis Wright strode into the war room, armour glinting in all its unused glory. And he was not alone. A priestess stood at his side, looking cold and proud—and extremely surprised.

"You." She blinked at Rig, eyes round, lips parted.

"Hello, Daughter." He was more than a little surprised to see her too. In his *war room*.

Commander Wright looked from one to the other. "You know each other?"

"Daughter Vel was kind enough to offer me a ride back to the fort yesterday," Rig said. Inclining his head, he added, "Thank you again."

He expected a barbed reply, but it seemed the priestess was too muddled to give one. Rig enjoyed that more than he ought to have.

"Ah!" said Wright. "You were the soldier she rescued on the road?"

Rig frowned. "Well, I'm not sure I would use the term—"

"General." The guard appeared at the door again. "The scouts have returned."

"Thank you. I'll send for them presently."

"General." It was Vel who spoke, warily, as though testing the word. She let out a short laugh and shook her head.

Morris didn't like that. "With all due respect, Commander Wright, this is a war room, and no place for a . . . priestess."

The hesitation was slight, but it was enough to give Morris away. Not that Rig blamed him. A priestess would unnerve any Aldenian, but soldiers were superstitious, especially when it came to planning a battle. Having a priestess in the room was like calling a curse down on them.

"I must disagree with you there, Commander," Wright said. "Daughter Vel does more than minister to my men. She is my advisor in all things, that I might be certain my decisions follow the teachings of the Holy Virtues."

Rig checked a sigh. *Bloody fishmen and their bloody piety.* But he could do nothing about it, not unless he wanted to get off to a bad start with his new ally. He forced a smile. "I might have balked at a priestess of Ardin, but a daughter of Eldora will no doubt give good counsel."

The priestess's mouth quirked, as though she saw right through him. Which she probably did. Well, that was too bad. He might be obliged to let her stay, but he didn't have to like it.

He turned back to the map. "We were just discussing where the enemy is likely to strike. I make it the day after tomorrow, though of course that's just a guess."

"An informed one, judging from the Warlord's pattern," Wright said, leaning over the table. At Rig's enquiring glance, he added, "We've studied everything there is on Sadik's movements to date. Onnan may have only lately entered the war, but we have been following it closely, and there are enough refugees in our lands to piece together much of the story so far. Sadik prefers to rely on speed and surprise rather than giving his enemies time to plan."

"Ardin is clearly his sign," the priestess added. "He is bold and impulsive, and if we plan accordingly, it will be his undoing."

Rig gave a thin smile. "Unfortunately, Ardin is also my sign."

"So I had observed," she returned dryly.

"Do we know whether Sadik has learned the location of the fort?" Wright asked.

Rig shook his head. "He'll have it narrowed down, but nothing firm enough to take action on, or we wouldn't be standing here. I've tried to organise our deployments so as to keep him guessing."

"And what about Sadik's location?"

"We have a rough idea," Morris said. "But with thirty thousand at our border, and another ten holding down Andithyri, there's not much room for our scouts to manoeuvre."

"Are you in contact with the Andithyrian Resistance?" Vel asked.

The question surprised Rig. The Resistance was a relatively new phenomenon, and not openly discussed. If an Onnani priestess had heard of them, it was a safe bet that the Warlord's spies knew a lot more. Not good news. "We've tried," he said, "but we can't find them. They're understandably shy."

"A pity." The priestess's tone was distracted; Rig could see the waterwheel turning in her head.

"What about a preemptive strike?" Wright suggested.

Morris scoffed. "With half the enemy's strength?"

"Actually," Rig said, "it's not a bad idea."

The priestess raised her eyebrows. "Ardin truly is your sign."

Rig shrugged. "It wouldn't be the first time we went at the enemy with a fraction of his numbers."

"Indeed not," Wright said, "which is why I suggested it. You spent the better part of a season harrying an Oridian host with a force of barely six hundred men, to great success. Of course, you did have your famous horse archers, and I'm told each one of them is worth twice an ordinary cavalryman." Seeing Rig's expression, he laughed. "Don't look so surprised, General Black. I told you we've studied the war. We did not confine ourselves to the Oridians."

Rig was beginning to wonder if perhaps he hadn't misjudged the Onnani commander. What Wright lacked in experience, he seemed to make up for in study. Which made him more or less the opposite of Rig, a balance that might come in handy. "If we hit them when they don't expect it," Rig said, "we could make a mess of their plans. It might buy us some time."

"Hardly a sustainable solution," said the priestess.

"Sustainability is a luxury I can't afford with what I have on hand. A well-managed strike will earn us a few more days to plan. It'll also give us a look at their deployment, something a little more up close than what the scouts have managed."

Morris scanned the map, his brow stitched. "What're you thinking, General?"

"Whitefish Bridge." Rig tapped the map. "We're going to blow it."

"But I thought . . ." It took Morris only a moment more to

figure it out. His expression turned rueful. "Can we afford to waste the black powder?"

"We won't be wasting it. This is it, Morris. No point in holding anything back now. Either we'll survive the summer, or we won't. And if we don't, I don't want anything left behind for those animals, not a single rotten leaf of cabbage. Certainly not a barrelful of black powder."

Morris swore quietly. "We need that fleet, General." As though Rig didn't know. As though he could think about anything else.

"It will be here soon." Wright looked embarrassed—as well he might.

"It had better be," Rig said. "Or come harvest, we'll all be speaking Oridian."

Rig passed his sword over the whetstone, steady and methodical, listening to the familiar rasp of a blade finding its edge. The rhythm was a kind of meditation for him, like the breathing of a priest going into trance. It helped him to think.

Unless, of course, he was interrupted.

"Do you not have people to do that for you?"

Somehow, he was not surprised to find the Onnani priestess darkening his door.

"I suppose I do," Rig said, "but a man who lets anyone else polish his bloodblade is not worthy of the weapon."

"Ah, yes, the famous bloodblade. I have never actually seen one. I have never known anyone wealthy enough to own one." She entered his chamber—uninvited—and came over for a closer look. "My, that is a large weapon. One might almost think you were compensating for your . . . shortcomings."

Rig snorted softly. "You have a quick tongue for a priestess."

"You have no idea."

He resisted the urge to look up. She was baiting him, just as she'd done yesterday, trying to get a rise out of him. He thought he knew why. Vel had pegged him as a nobleman from the moment they'd met. Most Onnani had little time for the Aldenian aristocracy, and she'd proven no different; when he'd called her *my lady*, she'd dismissed it as an affectation. Now she was going out of her way to offend his delicate highborn sensibilities. That amused him. It would have amused anyone who knew him.

"What can I do for you, Daughter?" he asked, exchanging the whetstone for another with a finer grain. He ran a thumb over it to make sure there was enough oil before setting to work.

"I could see you felt cornered earlier," she said. "Obligated to let me stay. You needn't be. If you wish me gone, say so. I will find a reason to excuse myself from the planning. I can minister to the men and Commander Wright in their encampment. You and your men need never see me."

Rig ran the blade back and forth, his touch feather light. Not the easiest manoeuvre with a greatsword, but he'd had years of practice. "Why should I want you gone?"

She laughed bitterly. "I am well used to it, General. In my own country, and especially in yours. I am a *priestess*." She fairly spat the word, and there was enough acid in it that Rig half expected his floor to start smoking. "A witch, or a harlot, or both. Fear and derision have followed me all the way from Onnan City."

"I'm surprised it bothers you. From what I've seen, you court it."

Her gaze settled on his, dark and unreadable. "I would not expect you to understand, *Lord Black*."

"Oh, good. I do so hate not living up to people's expectations."

She frowned. "A glib reply."

"I'm known for them." Rig grabbed a cloth and wiped his blade down. He set it across his knees. "Look, Daughter, I'll not deny I was surprised to find you in my war room this morning. I've never been much of a religious man, and it's not common practice in Alden to have a priest, much less a priestess, involved in military planning. But I'm not a superstitious man, either. I'm a pragmatist, and if it makes Commander Wright feel better to have you there, absent any practical concerns of my own, it makes no sense to banish you."

"What about Commander Morris?"

"Oh, he dislikes you enormously," Rig grinned. "He generally feels that way about things that terrify him."

"And?"

Rig shrugged. "And he's a good officer. He focuses on the

task at hand. Don't worry about Morris." He rose, propping his sword against his chair. "Wine? It's mulled."

"Yes, thank you. I'm freezing."

"Spring's late this year. I thought that might buy us more time, but . . ." When Rig turned, he found her trailing a finger lingeringly along the garnet embedded in the pommel of his sword. "Pretty rock, isn't it?"

She straightened suddenly, as if he'd caught her with a hand in her money purse. "It's huge," she said coolly. "It could feed a village for a year."

"Maybe it could, if there was any grain to buy." He handed her a cup.

"Another glib answer."

He shrugged. "Like I said—"

"You are known for them, yes. I'm beginning to see." She sipped her wine. Hummed in satisfaction. "Andithyrian."

"Do I detect a familiarity with fine wine? Not to mention a fascination with large gemstones. Better not let that get out, Daughter. Someone might think you weren't a proper republican."

That earned him a withering look. "Just because I admire fine things does not mean I approve of a system that hoards them in the hands of a privileged few."

"Relax, Daughter, I was only teasing."

She wouldn't be placated so easily. He'd piqued her pride; now she had to put him in his place. She pointed at his greatsword, then at the shortsword propped in a corner of the room. "Two bloodblades. I do not even care to speculate what they cost. Meanwhile, most of your men lack even one. Does that strike you as fair?"

He regarded her in amusement. "The military isn't known for being egalitarian."

"So it has nothing to do with you being highborn?"

"It has everything to do with it. Are you telling me there's no concept of rank in Onnan? I doubt that very much, Daughter."

"Of course we have rank," she said, tossing her head proudly. "But it is earned, not born into."

"Well, here it's both. Would it surprise you to learn that my second is common-born and has a very nice bloodblade? He earned his rank by virtue of his competence, and his weapon by virtue of his rank. I'd love to put one in the hands of every man and woman in my army, but we have one bloodbinder, and it just isn't possible." He gestured with his cup at the bloodbow sitting beside his shortsword. "I've had that bow since I was twelve years old. The greatsword since I was eighteen. The shortsword—that's new. A commander general spends most of his time on horseback, which makes my preferred weapon a bit impractical. So I had that made." He arched an eyebrow. "Does that explanation meet with your approval, Daughter?"

She hitched a shoulder. "You don't need my approval, obviously." Her tone was sullen, but there was a stubborn cast to her mouth that Rig found more than a little appealing.

"I might not need it," he said with a grin, "but it's nice to have. Not unlike fine wine."

"You're making fun of me again."

He didn't deny it, but he did make a peace offering. "Earlier," he said. "You had an idea, I could tell. I'd be interested in hearing it."

She narrowed her eyes over the rim of her cup, wary of more teasing.

"Something to do with the Andithyrian Resistance," he prodded. "Tell me."

She hesitated, took another sip of her wine. "If you truly wish to know, I was wondering if I might do better."

"Meaning?"

"Contacting the Resistance. I thought perhaps I might have more luck."

He blinked; he certainly hadn't expected *that*. "And how would you propose to make that happen?"

She gave him a flat look. "A dark spell, naturally. Or perhaps a well-targeted seduction. I am undecided."

"I thought we were having a serious conversation."

"By going there, obviously. How else?" She gazed boldly into his eyes, daring him to mock her.

"By going where? Andithyri is a small country, but it's not that small."

"Where have you been sending your spies?"

"Spies? I don't know what you're talking about. More wine?"

She sniffed, but handed over her cup. "It's not so outlandish. The Andithyrians are strong in their faith. They might trust me, even if I am a woman."

"They might, assuming they ever laid eyes on you." Rig headed to the mantel and poured more wine. "The Oridians would pounce the moment they saw you. You have bronze skin and black hair. Not an asset if you're in the business of espionage in the land of the white-hairs."

"I'm sure we could come up with an appropriately convincing story."

He paused, a cup in each hand, the sweet-smelling steam tickling his nose. "You're serious about this, aren't you?"

"Why shouldn't I be?"

He handed her the wine. "Take no offence, Daughter, but it's a bit early in our relationship to be planning espionage."

Something flitted through her eyes, something Rig couldn't place. It was gone almost instantly, replaced by a coy little curve of her mouth. "Do you expect our relationship to advance, General?"

Rig knew a shield when he saw one. Whatever she'd been about to say, she'd lost her nerve, and now she was hiding behind the sultry priestess act. That didn't mean he had to play along, though. "I'll consider it," he said. And he would—at his own pace. He'd just met this woman, and her commander. He wasn't about to entrust so important a task to just anyone, especially someone he had as much trouble reading as this mercurial priestess of Eldora. "We'll talk about it again another time. Assuming we survive tomorrow, that is."

She turned her gaze on the fire. Sipped her wine. "Do you think it will work? This preemptive strike of yours?"

"Defensive provocation. You seem to be well familiar with the tactic."

"You know nothing about me."

"I know enough for today." He smiled to soften the words, took her empty cup. "If you'll excuse me, I need sleep. Tomorrow's sort of an important day for me."

"For us all," she said solemnly. "If I do not see you on the morn, may Eldora be your sign, General."

Rig started to make his customary reply about Eldora not fancying him, but thought better of it. Somehow, he doubted

Vel had much of a sense of humour where the Holy Virtues were concerned.

When she'd gone, he picked up the greatsword, slid it into its scabbard, and set it in the corner with his shortsword. He dropped onto his bed fully clothed. The firelight cast strange shadows on the ceiling; they seemed to take the shapes of borders and coast-lines, mountains and rivers, a giant map that shifted every time he got a fix on it. By the time he fell asleep, thoughts of espionage and prickly priestesses were far behind him.

He dreamed of war.

ELEVEN

The ram raised its head, nostrils twitching, scenting the air. A glorious specimen, with great coiling horns as thick as a man's arm. Its glassy black eyes stared in Erik's direction, but he was downwind and well hidden, invisible to the animal. Only the creak of his bloodbow had given any sign of danger. The ram stood on a rocky outcropping, framed against jagged peaks and a clear blue sky, barrel-chested and posing like the symbol of Destan himself. Erik's arms started to ache, his eyes tearing against the glare of the melting snow. Still he hesitated. Such a magnificent creature . . .

But his men were hungry and half frozen, and this was the first decent game they had spotted in days. Sighing inwardly, Erik let fly. The enchantment guided his arrow straight between the animal's eyes; it pitched to its knees with a grunt before slumping to the ground.

He approached the carcass warily, bow nocked in case he should stumble upon another ram ready to charge. Cresting the rock, he found the rest of the herd grazing contentedly along a grassy slope down into the valley, clustered around their lambs and blissfully unaware of anything amiss. Erik debated dropping another, but the ram weighed at least twenty stone, difficult enough to carry back to camp.

"Need a hand with that?"

He glanced over his shoulder. Alix already had her knife out, blade glinting in the ever-present sunshine of the Broken Mountains. "Thanks," he said. "It will go faster."

Alix considered the fallen ram. "A nice one. We used to keep a couple of these mounted on the walls at Blackhold."

"The horns are impressive."

"And useful. The tribes make all kinds of things from them. Jewellery. Cups. Even blades."

"And warhorns," Erik said—and immediately regretted it. Alix was tense enough without the reminder of the lurking danger of the mountain tribes. She tried not to show it, but she was too exhausted to fool anyone, least of all Erik.

She knelt and took the ram's hind leg, splaying it out and slicing open the abdomen. It was a gory scene against the snow, crimson and purple and steaming, but they worked efficiently. They needed to finish and get back to camp as quickly as possible; they were too exposed out here.

"You've done this before," Erik remarked.

"Once or twice. Mostly, I watched Rig do it. I used to come along on hunting trips as often as he'd let me. I enjoyed the stalking part." She straightened, examining her bloodstained hands. "This part, less enjoyable."

"Agreed."

They cut off the head, washed the cavity out with snow, and trussed up what was left of the carcass. Alix tried to dig a hole with her knife, but the ground was still too frozen, so they kicked snow over the mess. With luck, by the time it was discovered, they would be well gone from this place. A flock of carrion birds or a pack of scavenging wolves would be certain to draw the attention of any passing tribesman—just the sort of thing to get them all killed.

"This isn't going to be easy," Erik said, staring ruefully at the carcass. "Next time, we should bring the horses."

"Too easy to spot at a distance. We'll take turns. I'm strong enough. I carried you over my shoulder once, remember."

As though he could forget. "I daresay this ram still weighs

more than I do, even without his guts." That, and Alix was not as strong as she had once been. Aside from ordinary exhaustion, she was still recovering from the fever. Two days on, and she could barely keep her food down. She tried to hide that too, but of course Erik noticed.

As it turned out, however, they did not have far to go. After less than half an hour of walking, a figure stepped out from behind a rock and into their path and, at the sight of what they were carrying, clapped her hands in a manner rather at odds with her function as a concealed sentry. "Oh, Your Majesty, how wonderful!" exclaimed the little blond scout called Kerta.

Erik let the carcass slide off his shoulder and rolled his neck, wincing. He would be feeling that for days. "If you don't mind, I'll let someone relieve me from here. How much farther to camp?"

"Another half hour or so," Kerta said. "Alix, help me drag this behind the rock while I fetch Frida. She's just over that rise . . ."

Alix wasn't listening. Instead, she stared grimly at the footprints they had left in the snow. "I suppose it would be too much to ask for a light snowfall. That trail's going to be there for days. Weeks, if it gets cold again."

"It can't be helped," Erik said. "Let's worry about the things we can control, Alix."

"It's my duty to worry about everything, sire."

Erik was too tired to argue.

They made their way down into the valley and the protective cover of the pines. The Condor's Nest was not the easiest pass through the Broken Mountains, but it was thought to be less frequented by the tribes. So far, that intelligence had proved reliable; the only evidence they had seen of human activity was the shaft of an arrow embedded in a fir tree. At least two seasons old, if Erik was any judge, and perhaps a good deal older.

Even so, he worried. Of course he worried, and not just about the tribes. Five days out from Blackhold, and already they had lost a man after a patch of melting snow gave way beneath his feet. Then there was the fever, striking a handful of them, including Alix, virtually the moment they quit civilisation. Morale was low. That obliged Erik to be even more cheerful, even more sanguine about their success, though he risked looking the fool.

Already they were falling behind schedule. Erik could feel the time slipping through his fingers like fresh-fallen snow, and with it, their chances of salvation. If they did not reach Ost in time . . .

He shook his head. It did not bear thinking about.

They arrived at camp to find the tents already pitched, the horses rubbed down and fed. The men clustered around a single fire built deep in a pit. It was warmer down here in the pines, but still barely above freezing, even by day. "Mutton tonight, lads," Erik called, and was rewarded with brightened expressions. "Enough to go around and then some."

One of the men came over with a basin of warm water for washing. "Saw some panther tracks down by the creek, sire," he said. "Fresh ones."

Erik smiled, as if the news delighted him. "If you see it, I'd happily take the pelt off your hands. It would make for a handsome cloak, don't you think?"

The guardsman grinned and promised to deliver it if he had the chance.

"Not good news," Alix said in an undertone when the guardsman had gone.

"No. Would it dare attack the camp, do you think?"

"I doubt it, but with the scent of food around, you never know. A scout on her own, or a man relieving himself in the dark . . ."

Erik sighed. Just one more thing to worry about.

But not tonight. Tonight was for roast meat and warmed wine, and maybe, if they were lucky, just a little bit of cheer. The gods knew they needed it.

Alix filled her lungs with pine. The smell of home. Something familiar, comforting. This forest could be in the foothills of the Blacklands, just a little above the birch and the poplars and the heart-shaped aspens, those well-loved woods where Alix had learned to move silently through the brush, soggy leaves squelching beneath her boots and wild roses snatching at her clothing.

It could be, but it wasn't. Instead it was hostile territory, untamed and ungovernable, full of prowling barbarians and natural booby traps. It had claimed one of them already. It would claim more, Alix felt sure.

She sighed. *When did I become such a pessimist?* About the moment she'd agreed to be the king's bodyguard, presumably. She'd aged a decade overnight.

So had Erik. She looked over at him, riding silently beside her, gaze abstracted as he mulled over the task ahead of him. War had aged him too. Not physically—if anything he was stronger, fitter—but in spirit. Erik carried the weight of the kingdom on those broad shoulders of his. All those smiles and blithe predictions of success—he didn't fool Alix for a moment. He was every bit as anxious as she was. How not, with the survival of his kingdom at stake, and their party falling further behind schedule with each passing day?

"Last night was nice," she said, to break him out of his thoughts.

"Hmm?"

"Supper. It was nice."

"It was, wasn't it? Though I feel badly for the advance party. It hardly seems fair they should miss out after working so hard to scout the way for us."

"Don't worry about them. They're being relieved tomorrow, and I've saved them all a taste. It'll keep in this temperature."

Erik smiled. "You're a good leader, Alix."

"I learned from the best."

He looked away, staring off into the trees. Silence fell again, broken only by the horses' hooves punching through a hard crust of melting snow, the trickle of water at the edges of the ice. The snow lasted a little longer here in the shade of the pines, but even that would be gone soon, leaving only the peaks above them wreathed in white.

"How much longer until we're out of the mountains, do you suppose?" Alix thought she knew the answer, but she'd be damned if she let that silence, whatever it was, sit between them.

"About a week, I should think. It takes about ten days from Blackhold in summer, so I suppose it takes half that again in conditions like these."

She'd thought as much, but she couldn't help the sour turn of her mouth. A week . . . it might as well have been forever.

And then another three days after that to get to Ost, though at least they'd have an escort at the foot of the mountains.

"A long time," Erik said, reading her expression, "but we'll be heading down soon, and things will warm up. That should make things easier. Warmer nights, more plentiful game."

"Fewer tracks in the snow."

He sighed. "Alix . . ."

"Though I suppose if they know these mountains as well as Rig says, they don't need footprints to track us. They'll see it in the lichen on the rocks, or the scatter of pine needles, or some such."

"Honestly, Alix, I hardly think it helps to—"

A crack of thunder sounded in the distance, trailing a low rumble. Alix swore and looked up. The last thing they needed was a storm descending on them. The rain would freeze on top of the snow, making it even more treacherous, and . . .

She frowned. "Did you hear that?"

"The thunder?"

"But look—not a cloud in the sky."

He glanced up. "On the other side of the peaks, perhaps."

An airy hush settled over the pass, soft and unblemished, like a blanket of fresh powder. Then a cackle of ravens drew Alix's eye up the slope. A clutch of them had burst from the pines, rising like a cloud of smoke. Black wings swept the sky, a dozen or more, grating voices scolding the silence.

Alix looked from the blazing blue of the sky into the blazing blue of Erik's eyes.

Seeing her fear, he paled. "Alix, what—"

The thunder returned, a low, steady growl on the slopes above them. But this time, it didn't go away; instead it grew louder, deeper, and now the horses were whinnying, dancing, and there was shouting from the men behind them.

Alix's blood froze in her veins.

"Ride, Erik! Go, go, go!"

But it was too late. A roar unlike anything Alix had ever heard broke over them in a wave, drowning out the shouts of men and the screaming of horses and the panicked calls of the ravens. The pines shuddered and bowed, sending a sheet of snow down upon them, and a heartbeat later, the ground gave way.

Alix went down, swept into darkness, tumbling in a torrent

of ice and branches. Her hip cracked against a stone. Snow rushed into her mouth and up her nose. She tried to grab hold of something, to brace herself, but a frigid, smothering weight pressed down on her from all sides, pinning her arms and legs against her. She was in a coffin of ice, banded in iron, layer upon layer piling on top of her in an ever-deepening grave. Panic flared through her, a mindless, numbing terror that stole every thought until all that was left was a silent scream.

She slammed up against something hard, light exploding between her temples. The thundering roar filled her head, her chest, crushing, freezing, dragging the world over top of her.

And then, gradually, the rumbling died away, the shifting slowed, until all that was left was a soft *hiss* and the crowding dark of oblivion.

Stillness.

A crack of light over her shoulder.

Alix twitched. The crack widened, snow spilling away. Drunk with panic, she took a moment to react. Then she was bucking, twisting, clawing her way free of a prison of pine branches. The tree she'd been swept against lay half buried; Alix couldn't get a foothold in the loose snow. She scrabbled and swam, fighting not to be drawn back into the dark.

"Erik!" She looked around wildly, but all she could see was a smooth white slope peppered with broken branches. The windy hush had settled again. It was as if the mountainside had been scoured clean, as if none of them had ever been there.

"Erik!"

Somewhere down the slope, a horse screamed. Alix twisted, still waist-deep, but she couldn't locate the source. There was no sign of her own horse. She'd managed to pull her feet from the stirrups just as the snow hit; the animal had been torn out from under her. She waded away from the tree, gaze raking the scene for any sign of clothing, flesh, anything that might stand as a marker of the place where her friends lay buried. She called Erik's name again and again, her voice splitting the terrible silence.

Movement caught her eye. Alix dragged herself toward it and saw a hand wriggling free. Too small to be Erik's. Too small to be anyone's but . . . "Kerta!" Alix scrabbled at the snow. "Kerta, I'm here!"

Another hand appeared. Alix grabbed them both and pulled. She fell back; Kerta tumbled into her arms, gasping.

"I can't find Erik." Alix's throat closed on the words.

Kerta lurched unsteadily to her feet, shaking her head to clear it. "We will."

"He was right in front of me." Alix started back toward her tree, weaving like a drunkard. "Right there . . ."

Farther down the slope, the screaming horse had managed to struggle free. It lay on its side, thrashing, broken. Alix recognised it as Godwin's. Of the man himself, there was no sign.

"There!" Kerta pointed. The ground moved just below Alix's tree—another horse kicking its way out from under the snow. Alix recognised the glorious silver coat, and her heart leapt.

"Erik!"

They threw themselves down the hill, half swimming, half leaping, until they came to Erik's horse. The stallion had almost freed himself now. He watched them, white-eyed, ears pinned, grunting and heaving. His right flank was exposed, the stirrup empty.

They started digging just above the flailing stallion. They tore bodily at the snow, nearly burying themselves in the process, pausing only to kick loose powder out of the way so they could keep moving. Their progress was achingly slow, and Alix despaired a little more with each hard-won step. How long had it been since Erik went under, since he'd been without air? Even if they found him . . . Cold tears blurred her vision; she ploughed on, carving a trench in the snow.

They came to a stand of trees, three young pines clustered together, and there, amid a wreckage of boughs, Alix found a scrap of fur—black, like the lining of Erik's cloak. She dove at it, and after what seemed like forever, she found herself clawing snow away from leather. A few more inches, and a patch of red-gold hair appeared. Erik shook his head free, revealing a pocket of air between the boughs of a tree. The left side of his face was badly scored; a trickle of blood ran from his temple to his jaw.

They dragged him out by the shoulders. Alix threw her arms around him, sobbing. His skin was cold as ice and he trembled like a newborn calf, but he had strength enough to clutch her to him. "Thank the gods you're safe," he whispered.

"Look, up there!" Kerta started up the slope. Alix glanced after her, then back at Erik uncertainly.

"Go," he said. "I'll be fine, just give me a moment." Still she hesitated. "*Go*, Alix. There are others to think of."

Reluctantly, she did as her king commanded.

They dug six more bodies out of the snow that day, none of them alive. The rest, including Godwin, were lost to the mountain. Of the fifteen men who'd left Blackhold, six remained, including the three who'd been scouting ahead when the avalanche hit. They had one horse, few supplies, and a long, treacherous journey ahead.

They had, in other words, no chance.

TWELVE

"Well?" Liam said, holding out his arms and presenting himself for inspection.

Rona smiled warmly. "You clean up very nicely, Commander."

Liam wasn't convinced; turning back to the mirror, he eyed his reflection unenthusiastically. "You're sure the leather one is a *no*."

"The hunting jerkin? Yes, I'm quite sure."

"Don't know what you're complaining about," Ide put in from her perch on the window seat. "Fine wine, good food . . ."

"And a room full of politicians," Liam said. "Yes, it promises to be a delightful evening."

"Do you suppose they'll have those little snails?" Ide asked wistfully.

Liam made a face. "I certainly hope not."

"Whatever they serve," Rona said, "you'll have to eat it. You wouldn't want to give offence."

"This reception is supposedly in my honour. Shouldn't I get to decide what I want to eat?"

"It doesn't work that way, I'm afraid."

Liam knew that, of course, but the thought of sucking steamed snails out of their shells wasn't doing wonders for his already unsettled stomach. He hated these kinds of events, especially when they revolved around him. There hadn't been many formal occasions since he'd come to Erik's court, but it hadn't taken him long to realise that they weren't his idea of a good time. In fact, he'd reached that conclusion after the very first banquet, the one Erik had thrown to welcome him to court. Liam would rather streak through the oratorium in his smallclothes than be forced to endure another evening like *that*, watching Alix and Erik tripping over each other to cover his gaffes. On the plus side, he'd built up an impressive repertoire of excuses for why he couldn't *possibly* dance just now, thanks anyway, but perhaps another time. He reckoned those were going to come in handy tonight.

"Stay away from the lillet, if you can," Dain said. "I've never met a westerner who could stomach it."

"I don't even know what that is," Liam said with growing alarm.

Dain held his thumb and forefinger a couple of inches apart. "Black fish, about this long. Dark and oily and strong enough to start hair growing out your ears."

"Sounds delicious."

"Does to me," Ide said. "See if you can bring us back some nibbles to try."

Liam gave her a flat look in the mirror. "I'll just stuff my pockets with steamed snails and oily black fish, shall I?"

"We should go," Rona said, all business now. She smoothed the folds of her gown, skimmed her fingers over the slender braids of her upswept hair. Unnecessary gestures both; she looked immaculate. Beautiful, even, as poised and self-assured as Alix. Once again, Liam found himself thanking the gods she'd come along. Her rank made it impossible to exclude her from such an event, and that meant Liam wouldn't have to face this ordeal alone. "After you, Commander," she said, gesturing at the door.

Dain and Ide accompanied them to the courtyard, where a carriage waited. Liam froze a moment on the steps as he took in the contraption. The body of the carriage was bad enough, draped with velvet and tassels and crusted in gold leaf. But the horses . . . "Dear gods," Liam said under his breath, feeling a stab of pity for the animals. The poor sods were positively *festooned* in lace. They stood with their heads bowed in shame, flanks shuddering in disgust. They almost seemed to hide behind their blinders, as though avoiding embarrassing eye contact. "That should be illegal," Liam said.

Rona stifled a laugh. "Well, we put war paint on our horses."

"Yeah, but that's different. It's just a bit of paint, for tradition's sake. *That* . . ." He shook his head emphatically. "No."

"You should be flattered, Commander. It's probably the finest carriage in Onnan."

"I've half a mind to cut the poor chaps loose and ride them all the way to Erroman." He grinned at Rona. "What do you say? Just you and me?"

Her smile turned shy. "If only."

"All right, let's get this over with."

The first speaker's residence wasn't far. Everyone who was anyone in Onnan City, it seemed, lived in the Ambassador District. The carriage juddered along the cobbled streets for less than a quarter of an hour before coming to a halt, the thick velvet curtains drawn aside to reveal a handsome gravel drive edged with cedars. A gloved hand reached inside; Liam watched in amusement as Rona took it, lifting the hem of her dress and letting herself be led gingerly from the carriage as if she were some fragile debutante. It would have been hard to reconcile this version of Rona with the knight he'd seen slashing her way through enemy ranks if he hadn't seen his wife undergo a similar transformation on more than one occasion.

They were ushered into an elegant courtyard of arched alcoves and carved wood doors, a theme that was echoed on the second and third levels by ribbed butterfly windows that gave onto vine-draped terraces. Roses climbed the pillars, and a trio of pear trees thrust up between the flagstones, white petals shivering in the breeze. In the centre of it all, moonlight sparkled off the watery plumes of a fountain in the shape of a leaping fish. People were scattered about the courtyard in close-knit clusters, laughing softly and sipping at something that glittered like the fountain. Thus far, no one had noticed the newcomers.

"Beautiful," Rona murmured. When Liam didn't reply, she glanced over. "Commander? Something wrong?"

"What? Oh, no thanks, I'm fine. It's just that this reminds me a little of a dream I had recently." More than a little, actually, but he had no desire to recount his nightmares to Rona Brown. "So"—he glanced around—"what do we do now?"

"We mingle." Rona paused, gazing up at him expectantly.

"Oh, right." Liam offered an arm. "Sorry. A bit flustered, is all."

"Don't be. Or at least, don't look it."

"Right," Liam said again, feeling foolish. He took a deep breath and escorted Rona into the courtyard.

Heads started turning straightaway. This, too, was like the dream, and Liam couldn't help squirming a little. *You're being stupid*, he told himself. For one thing, this wasn't Erik's court. Nobody here cared that he was a bastard; if anything, it was a point in his favour, at least according to Alix. On top of which, the looks he was getting weren't hostile. On the contrary, the beautiful people in the courtyard were smiling at him diffidently, as though hoping he might bestow a little attention on them.

"Your Highness. Lady Brown." Liam turned to find First Speaker Kar standing with a striking woman of middle age. "It is an honour to welcome you both to my home. May I present my wife, Lyn." The woman inclined her head, showing off a thick rope of braid coiled at the crown of her head. She was tall for an Onnani, standing at nearly Rona's height, and when she spoke, her voice was low and smoky.

"A great pleasure to meet you both."

"And you, my lady," Rona said. "You have such a lovely home."

"Thank you." Lyn wore a gown of silver silk with pearl buttons, its unusually high collar serving to emphasise her height. Or maybe not so unusual, Liam realised; a quick scan of the courtyard revealed that all the frocks had modest necklines. Most had sleeves, too. Liam wasn't exactly an expert on fashion, but he couldn't recall Alix ever having worn a gown with sleeves. But wait, wasn't Rona wearing . . . ? He cut a discreet glance at Rona's gown, and sure enough, it had a high collar and cap sleeves. She'd taken care to choose something that wouldn't offend the conservative Onnani. Of course she had. He beamed at her in silent thanks; she smiled back, a little bemusedly.

"You look absolutely radiant, Lady Brown," Kar said, gesturing at her as though she were something miraculous.

"You're too kind."

"I must admit, it is difficult to imagine you wielding a sword. If I had not seen you in full armour with my own two eyes, I might not have believed it."

"Our traditions are a little different," Rona said.

"I daresay that is an understatement," Lyn remarked dryly.

"I should be very interested to hear of your exploits," Kar went on with an oily smile. "Perhaps you will indulge me later."

Rona inclined her head demurely. "If you like, First Speaker."

Motioning for a servant, Kar said, "Let me get you something to drink." A young man hurried over with a selection of drinks on a gleaming silver platter. Kar chose a pair of cut crystal glasses filled with a golden, sweet-smelling liquid that Liam assumed was wine. "One of our local varietals," he explained as he handed it over. "I think you will find it pleasantly fruity."

"Is this your first visit to Onnan, Your Highness?" Lyn asked.

Liam resisted the urge to sniff at the wine. "First time abroad, actually."

"Really?" Sculpted eyebrows climbed Lyn's forehead. "I would have thought a prince had many opportunities for travel."

Was that a gibe? Surely she knew of his background, that he'd been a prince for all of six months? Liam had no idea how to respond without making his hostess look ignorant, or rude, or both.

"All things being equal, perhaps," Rona cut in smoothly, "but His Highness is also Commander of the White Wolves, and in these times of war, he is sorely needed at home."

"Indeed," Kar said. "I know it was not easy for you to come here, Your Highness. We are so grateful that you managed it."

I'll bet. Liam smiled and sipped his wine. It was fruity, all right, and sweet. Like swallowing liquid jam. It was all he could do not to grimace.

"And how are you finding our city so far?" Lyn asked, smiling politely.

A potentially tricky question, but one he'd been prepared for. "I haven't had a chance to see much of it yet, but I did get down to the seaside with your good husband a couple of days ago, and that's something I'll never forget. I'm sure it seems like stale bread to you, but if you come from a landlocked country . . . well, there's nothing like it back home, that's for sure."

"We must get you out on a ship, Your Highness," Kar said.

"I'd like that." *Especially if it was a war galley bound for Oridia.*

Kar glanced over his shoulder. "Please excuse me for a moment, Your Highness. I must welcome some more of my guests, but I'll be back in a moment to make introductions." He held out an arm to his wife. "Come, my dear."

Liam took another sip of his wine, just to calm his nerves.

"You're doing well," Rona said in an undertone, as though reading his thoughts.

"You think? The question about travel caught me off guard."

She hummed a low note of agreement. "I'm not sure what she was getting at. It's hard to imagine that she isn't aware of your background, but I can't think of any reason why she'd want to insult you." Sighing, Rona shook her head. "There are so many agendas here, it's difficult to keep track."

"Glad to hear you say so. Makes me feel less of an idiot."

"You're not an idiot, Commander. It's as I said before: Anyone would feel overwhelmed by this. I mean, look around." She made a discreet gesture encompassing the courtyard. "See how people are standing? How tight the clusters, how little they mix?"

It was true, Liam realised; though everyone seemed relaxed and jovial, there was remarkably little intermingling of the groups. "What's that about?"

"Politics. Each of those groups must represent a bloc of some kind. League lines, maybe, or secret societies. I've seen a similar phenomenon at court from time to time, especially when there's a major decision looming, but never quite this rigid. I thought the Aldenian aristocracy was divided, but this . . ."

Liam looked more closely. He didn't know many people here, but there were a few he recognised. Defence Consul Welin stood in the largest group, and he appeared to be the ranking member, judging from the way others had positioned themselves around him. He was doing most of the talking, his discourse punctuated by the occasional bark of sycophantic laughter. The second largest group, meanwhile, was presided over by Chairman Irtok. The Sons and the Shield, Liam wondered, or some other configuration of power as yet undocumented by Saxon and his spy friends? The whole thing gave him a headache.

He heard Rona murmuring behind him, and he turned to find her consulting a servant about something. "I thought so," she said as the servant walked away.

"Thought what?"

"Don't look too suddenly, but there's a man over by the fountain who's been staring at us since we got here. Speaker Syril, apparently."

"The priest of Eldora?" As casually as he could, Liam turned.

He needn't have bothered with the subterfuge; Syril was looking right at him. Without the mask, he revealed himself to be a distinguished figure with silver-flecked hair and serious, intelligent eyes. Those eyes fixed on Liam from halfway across the courtyard; by the time he looked away, Liam felt as if he'd been leafed through like a book.

"I can tell we're going to be the best of friends," he said, tossing another mouthful of jammy wine down his throat.

A few moments later, Kar returned to collect them, and they began making the rounds. Liam kept his smile tacked on the whole time, repeating the same banalities about lovely homes and how enchanting he found the sea. He fantasised about slashing his wrists with the cut crystal glass.

Eventually, they came to Speaker Syril. Walking up to him was like getting a bucket of cold water in the face; Liam drew himself up, tense and alert.

"And this is Speaker Syril, whom you've already met." Kar's smile was bland and unreadable.

"Speaker," Liam said with a stiff nod.

"Your Highness. I trust you are enjoying the evening." As Liam had suspected, he spoke Erromanian perfectly well. The translation at the Republicana had been pure posturing.

"Lovely," Liam said. "I'm so grateful for the chance to meet you all." And if he couldn't keep just a *hint* of sarcasm out of his voice, really, who could blame him?

Syril's expression didn't budge, but a glint of amusement touched his eyes. "The pleasure is ours, Your Highness. It is not often we have a chance to rub shoulders with royalty."

"Better not rub too hard. Some of it might come off."

Kar laughed. Rona flashed a tight smile. Speaker Syril tilted his head, as though examining a curious specimen. "So fragile, is it?"

"New coat of paint," Liam said, holding Syril's gaze defiantly, like a too-firm clasping of arms.

The speaker's mouth quirked. "Indeed. One wonders what is underneath."

"Will you listen to that!" Lyn appeared at Liam's side, resting her hand on his elbow. "This is positively my favourite piece of music this season." She gave his arm a meaningful squeeze.

Oh, dear gods. There was no way he could escape it this time, not unless he wanted to continue this delightful chat with Speaker Syril. What was that Onnani saying—*any port in a storm*? Swallowing a sigh, Liam said, "Would you care to dance, my lady?"

"I would be delighted, Your Highness."

"Well then, Lady Brown," said Kar, "shall we join them?"

Liam turned from Syril to the dancers. From the anvil to the forge.

It wasn't that he was a *bad* dancer, exactly. Physically, it wasn't so different from battle. Someone took the initiative, then it was move and countermove. Keep light on your feet. In battle, though, no one was *staring* at you. No one was *judging.* Dancing felt like a test, one he was bound to fail. Admittedly, a lot of things felt like that lately.

"I apologise if my intervention seemed abrupt," Lyn said as Liam led her through the steps. "I sensed a certain . . . tension."

"Speaker Syril and I seem to have got off on the wrong foot, and I'm not sure how to fix it."

"Perhaps you cannot. Syril is a difficult man." She smiled up at him, pivoting in time with the music. Seen this close, her cosmetics seemed thick and harsh, like someone trying much too hard. "But let us not talk politics. Both of us have had more than enough of that, I think." They parted, came together, parted again, filtering through the other couples. When they rejoined each other, Lyn said, "Lady Brown seems lovely."

"She's great."

"A knight. How extraordinary. Is she a skilled fighter?"

"She holds her own," Liam said, grateful for a topic he was

comfortable with. "Not as strong as some others, obviously, but she's canny. Knows where to hit you and when."

"Yet she seems like such a sweet girl. Delicate and refined. Not classically beautiful, perhaps, but compelling, in her way."

Liam glanced down at his dancing partner, puzzled by this turn of conversation. Then he saw how wooden Lyn's smile had become, how her gaze continued to follow Rona and her husband.

Ah.

He'd sensed Kar laying it on a little thick with Rona earlier, and apparently so had Lyn. Then again, *she'd* been the one to suggest dancing, so there was no point in getting jealous about it. "I think she's very beautiful," he said, a little irritably. "She's a lot of great things, actually, and a huge help to me." He really ought to tell her so sometime, in fact.

"How wonderful," Lyn said.

Thankfully, the music stopped soon after, and Liam was free to regroup with Rona. "How was that?" she asked, raising her wine to her lips.

"Oh, fine. Except I think Lyn wants your braid for a trophy."

Rona froze midsip. "Pardon?"

"Didn't like seeing you in her husband's arms, I think."

She *tsk*ed quietly. "Ridiculous."

"To be fair, he *is* a priest of Ardin."

Rona's eyes widened, a frisson of disgust rippling through her.

"Excuse me, Your Highness." A servant appeared bearing a small scroll. "This just came for you."

"Came?" Liam frowned. "From whom?"

"I'm sorry, Your Highness, I don't know." Bowing hurriedly, the servant withdrew.

Liam and Rona exchanged a glance. He broke the seal and unfurled the note.

"It's not another death threat, is it?" she asked in a low voice.

If you want to know the whole story, come to the Ship and Anchor. Come at noon, alone. Wait at a table in the back. I will find you.

"Not a threat," Liam said. "It's an invitation."

"An invitation to what?"

"A meeting of some kind, from the looks of it."

She shook her head. "I don't understand. A meeting with whom? What for?"

"I don't know. I don't have any answers." Judging from the note, though, he was about to get some at last.

THIRTEEN

"I don't think this is a good idea, Commander," Rona said.

Liam didn't think it was a particularly good idea either, but it wasn't as if he had much of a choice. He needed answers, badly, and the note had promised he'd get some. So here he was, strolling down the boardwalk with his officers, searching for a sign with a ship on it and trying to avoid eye contact with the locals.

"Thought you would've had your fill of anonymous notes, Commander," Ide said.

"They do seem to be fond of them here, don't they? But I've got a feeling I know who this one came from."

"I hope you're right," Rona said.

Liam hoped so too.

"There it is." Dain Cooper pointed.

Liam could see it now, a faded sign swinging on its hinges in the light breeze of the quay. "Here goes nothing. Now remember, stay out of sight unless I need you."

"And how are we supposed to know that?" Rona asked irritably. She really wasn't happy about this.

"Not sure," he admitted, "though my getting thrown through the front window is probably a sign."

"You jest, Commander," Dain said, "but from what I've

heard, that's a real possibility. The Ship is notorious for being the rankest, rowdiest tavern in the city."

Which reputation was entirely deserved, Liam decided an hour later, after he'd had a chance to take the place in. He was no stranger to taverns; like most soldiers, he'd spent an evening or two in some of the rougher places in Erroman. That was where he'd first become acquainted with sailors—crusty, foul-mouthed men who left their vessels anchored at the mouth of the Sabri to pilot small craft upriver to Erroman. Those men liked nothing better than drinking, fighting, and whoring, and they preferred to do it in the sorts of places that had men crawling under the tables and vermin crawling under the men. Those places were bad. But this place had them all beat as far as Liam was concerned, claiming the title by virtue of its smell (vomit and fish guts), the taste of its ale (same), and the completely unidentifiable gruel they served, which looked suspiciously like . . . well, suffice it to say the place had a *theme*.

Thankfully, an hour was all he had to wait before his mysterious correspondent appeared at the door. They recognised each other immediately. They had, after all, met before.

"Hello, Chief," Liam said, feeling a bit smug. He'd guessed right. It was nice to be one step ahead for a change. "Lovely spot you've picked here."

Mallik, Chief Shipwright of the Onnani Republican Navy, dropped his broad frame onto the bench across from Liam. "Sorry, Your Highness, but I wanted to make sure no one would see us. You came alone?"

"No. My officers are loitering somewhere nearby."

The chief's face darkened. "But we agreed—"

"We didn't *agree* anything. You sent me an anonymous letter. Not my preferred means of communication, incidentally."

The barmaid appeared, but Mallik declined her offer of ale. (He'd obviously been here before.) "I didn't know who to trust. I could be dismissed just for speaking to you."

"Why? What doesn't Kar want me to know?"

The chief regarded him with shrewd, dark eyes. "It's not just the first speaker. No one wants me to talk to you. They would all rather give you their own theories, recruit you to their cause. You are a powerful man, Your Highness."

So powerful that people are threatening my life. Liam kept the thought to himself. Like the chief, he didn't know whom to trust; so far, there weren't a lot of promising candidates. "What about you?" he asked. "You must have more than a theory. You're the one responsible for building for the fleet. What in the Nine Domains is going *on*?"

"I wish I knew. I'm the one responsible, as you say, so I'm the one who looks like an incompetent fool."

"Your note said you had the whole story."

"One whole story, anyway. But that is not the same as having all the answers."

Liam suppressed a growl. *Even the shipwrights in this country talk like priests.* Aloud, he said, "Go on, then."

The chief propped his elbows on the table, as though settling in for a long tale. "You have to understand, Your Highness, it started so gradually that none of us noticed at first. Myself, I've had my suspicions since last summer, but it must have started before then, maybe even before the Siege of Erroman. Back then, the Republicana was still debating whether to join the war. The mood on the docks was bad. People were divided. Some of us thought it was our duty to go to war. Others . . . well." He shrugged. "I suppose it was the same in Alden after the invasion of Andithyri."

Liam stared. Was the man trying to be clever, or did he genuinely not know that Prince Tomald had betrayed his own brother—had been sodding *executed*—over this very issue? *Maybe Erik doesn't want that part of the story getting around.* Belatedly, it occurred to him that he might need to be careful what he said, how much he divulged, about affairs in his brother's kingdom. As if he didn't have enough to worry about.

"Anyway," the chief went on, "what I noticed first was the *Seaspear*." He raised his eyebrows significantly.

"The . . . er . . . ?"

"The *Seaspear*!" The chief was visibly aghast at Liam's ignorance. "The flagship of the naval fleet! A more glorious ship never was! Until the new models, at least . . ."

"All right, so where is it now, this ship?"

The chief stabbed a finger at him. "Exactly."

"Wait, you mean it's missing?"

"I mean it's gone. They're *all* gone. A dozen galleys, more than a thousand oars in all, just—" He spread his hands.

"But what . . . *How?*"

"Only two ways." The chief counted them off on thick fingers. "One, they're taken out to sea. Not very likely, that; it would take too many men. Two, they're sunk. Dropped beneath the waves." He looked mournful as he said it, like the idea pained him. "Could be a combination of the two. Take her off somewhere close by, somewhere you don't need a full crew to reach, then punch a few holes in her belly to take her down. Not easy, but it could be done."

Liam knew his mouth was hanging open, but he couldn't help it. "Wouldn't someone have seen? Heard?"

The chief shrugged. "Docks are pretty quiet at night."

"You're telling me that the entire Onnani navy—"

"Keep your voice down."

Liam darted a look around, dropped his voice. "That the entire Onnani navy was either *sunk* or *stolen?*"

"That's what I'm telling you. It happened over the course of a few days. People saw the number of ships dwindling, of course, but nobody thought anything of it. Figured it was manoeuvres, you know? Getting ready for war, supposing the vote would go that way. By the time we realised something was wrong, it was too late."

"What about the commander general in charge?"

"Admiral. He was brought before the Republicana. Lectured and dismissed. He swore up and down he had nothing to do with it, and neither did his captains." The chief shrugged again. "I believe him, but who knows? At the least, he let it happen right under his nose."

Liam slumped back against the wall, stunned. "That's . . ." As it turned out, he didn't have a word for it. "No wonder First Speaker Kar didn't want me to hear this."

"There's more." The chief reached for Liam's jug of ale, took a swig, grimaced. He muttered a curse in Onnani and continued. "After I got the word to start building, in those final days just before the vote, things started happening straightaway. Strange things."

"Such as?"

"Streak of bad luck as makes a man think it's no luck at all. It started with the timber. Burned up right in the shipyard. Lightning, they say. You tell me, Your Highness, what are the odds of lightning striking a pile of timber when it could have struck a mast not a hundred paces away?"

"Not good," Liam said, since that seemed to be the expected answer.

"Then the dockies go on strike, leaving our supplies stranded. Took us weeks to gather enough men to replace them. And then, when we finally get the first of the new galleys done and take her out into the bay, she sinks. *Sinks.*" He pounded a fist on the table, sending Liam's jug two inches in the air. He lowered his voice to a growl. "No ship of mine *sinks*, Your Highness, not unless she's been sunk."

"Meaning sabotage."

The chief leaned back and folded his arms, looking well satisfied with this conclusion. "Meaning sabotage."

"But who?"

"That, Your Highness, is the golden question. Add to that *when will he strike next* and *how do we stop him*, and you and I are riding the same wind."

"The Oridians," Liam said. "It has to be."

"Possible, but they would have to be damned clever. Takes a dozen hands to move a warship even a few miles. That many pale-skinned folk running around the docks would get noticed. Me, my gold is on someone homegrown. Working with the Oridians, maybe, but a local, and with friends."

Liam cursed under his breath. This was so much worse than he'd thought. "And you have no idea who it could be?"

"None." The chief smiled, his leathery face crinkling. "I'm counting on you to find out, Your Highness."

I'm counting on you, Liam. Erik's words at the crossroads. It felt like a lifetime ago. Liam had promised to do his best, but he'd feared, even then, that his best wasn't going to be enough.

At least he'd been right about *something*.

Liam sat on his balcony, letting the breeze ruffle his hair in what had become a nightly routine. In the distance, the sea sighed rhythmically, like a lover sleeping peacefully at his side. It relaxed him. It washed over his mind, drowning out the voices that said he wasn't smart enough, wasn't subtle or experienced enough. The voices that reminded him that two people who were all of those things, his brother and his wife, were far away, over plains and mountains. Together.

Facing what, he wondered?

No. Don't do that. He didn't want to think about Alix and Erik in danger. He didn't want to think about them *not* in danger, either. He didn't want to think about them at all. Just her. Alix. The love of his life. A woman so impulsive, so deeply passionate, that she didn't always make good choices. She was a Black, a true child of Ardin. He loved that about her, but he also feared it. It wasn't that he didn't trust her. He did. He trusted Erik too, maybe even more so. Somehow, though, it didn't help. Not after what had happened between them last winter, how close they'd come to . . .

He growled, grinding the heels of his hands into his eyes. This wasn't working. He needed a different distraction, something more active. He went inside and sat down at the writing desk. Grabbing a quill and unstopping the inkpot, he wrote,

Dear Allie . . .

When he was through, Liam folded the letter into a tiny envelope and sealed it. He'd give it to Shef in the morning, ask for it to be sent to Ost.

Feeling better, he stepped back out onto the balcony . . .

. . . and nearly died of heart failure.

A figure stood shadowed against the moonlight. Instinctively, Liam's hand went for his sword, but of course it wasn't there. He glanced over his shoulder, gauging the distance to the balcony door.

"Do not be alarmed, Your Highness."

Liam didn't recognise the voice. On the other side of the door, Rudi barked. *Too late for that, you useless mutt.* Liam took a step back toward the door. "Who are you?"

"A friend."

"A friend of whose?"

Laughter in the dark. "A fair question."

"Pleased you think so." He took another step back.

"I am a friend of Saxon's, Your Highness, here at his request."

Liam relaxed a little. Just a little, mind. Spies were not high on his list of favourite creatures.

"I have been keeping an eye on you from a distance," said the voice, lightly accented. "From what I saw today, however, I thought it time to be a little more . . . direct." The figure stepped forward, just enough that Liam could make out a sketch of his features in the soft glow of the bedchamber window. He was of middling height and build, with nothing much to distinguish him. Liam wondered if this was what Alix meant when she said it was impossible to describe Saxon.

"What did you see today?" Liam asked warily.

"You, at the docks. With the chief shipwright." The man paused, presumably to let that sink in. "A productive meeting, was it?"

"I suppose so." Liam wasn't about to start serving it up just yet, whoever this man claimed to be.

"You understand the situation, then?"

"I wouldn't go that far."

The man hummed a low note. "I suppose not. Still, presumably you are convinced by now that whatever else might be happening, the delays with the fleet are not accidental. I have known that for a long time, but I have struggled to learn anything new. Your arrival has stirred the pot. I have heard more theories over the course of this week than in the past six months put together."

"Glad I could help."

"First Speaker Kar came to see you." It was not a question. "And Chairman Irtok. The first will have told you that the opposition is to blame. The second will have denied it, naming it simple incompetence." The man smiled. "How am I doing?"

Liam made himself shrug. "All pretty obvious so far."

"Chief Mallik, meanwhile, will not have dared an opinion on who is to blame, except to suggest that it was unlikely to be the enemy. No great feat of deduction, that. From what I hear, the Warlord could not be less concerned with Onnan. A tiny, yapping dog, easily kicked to a corner."

Liam scowled. "No offence, but if Saxon sent you to help me, you're letting him down. I don't really need a narration of my week. I need new information. Do you have any?"

"Not as such. What I have is intuition and experience, and both tell me that everything you have heard so far is misdirection, men pointing the finger at one another in service to their own narrow interests. They are opportunists, using this crisis as an excuse to destroy their enemies. No one has yet had the spine, or the incentive, to tell you the truth: that whatever is going on here, it has nothing to do with league politics or international espionage. This is not about Alliance versus Congress, or Oridia versus Onnan. There is some other game at play here."

"The secret societies?"

"A reasonable supposition. The true power struggles in this country always come back to the Shield, or the Sons of the Revolution, or both."

"But how am I supposed to find out what I need to know? If men like Kar won't even admit to belonging to these societies, how am I supposed to find out what they're after?" Liam had been feeling helpless before, but this—this was a whole new level of futility. He almost didn't want to hear it. It was all he could do not to stick his fingers in his ears and hum a tune.

"That is where I come in, Your Highness." The man sketched a brief bow. "I have connections in both societies. Men of influence. I can try to get you a meeting."

"Great," Liam said. It came out more sarcastic than he'd meant it to.

"No promises, but give me a few days."

"How much will it cost me?"

The man smiled. "No charge, Your Highness. Having Saxon owe me a favour is more than enough compensation."

Liam decided he didn't want to think about that too much. "How do I get in touch with you?" he asked. *How do I know I can trust you?* he wanted to add.

"You don't. I will get in touch with you. Just be ready. You may not be given much notice. And whatever you do, do *not* carry arms into the den of a secret society. It will be the end of you." So saying, the man bowed again and, without further ado, swept over the balcony.

Liam could only watch him go, wondering if things had just looked up, or gotten much, much worse.

Candlelight flickered over the map, a wavering orange glow that spread hungrily over the towns and forests of Alden, as though a great inferno devoured the land. The image pleased Sadik. Almost as much as it pleased him to move the final cluster of crimson blocks into place, representing the battalion of cavalry he'd called up that morning. Together with the infantry, they formed a crescent around the forlorn little white blocks at the border, a bloody curved blade poised to strike off the head of an enemy on its knees.

He grabbed a tankard of ale, took a long, frothy pull. He lived for moments like these, savoured them as nothing else in this world. Victory was sweet, but the anticipation of victory . . . that was ecstasy. Nothing else came close to it, not even the touch of a woman. Not every man would agree with him in that, he knew, but he was not like other men. He was a Trion, high warlord of an empire that stretched from sea to sea. He'd earned his place through moments like these. Small wonder he gloried in them as no other man.

Reaching into the pitifully small cluster of white blocks, he plucked out a single black one. *General Riggard Black*. A name he had known only a few months, one that meant little to him. Who had this man been before being named commander general? What had he done to distinguish himself on the battlefield? No Arran Green, that one.

Sadik's mouth took a sour turn, as it always did, when he thought of *that* worthy name. He had been robbed of that victory, and the anticipation of it. If he could have, he'd have killed the man who took Green's head. It had not been his to take. That skull belonged above Sadik's mantel, where the shattered skulls of all his best enemies were kept. It could not be replaced, not by King Erik White, and certainly not by this Riggard Black.

A matter of small consequence, he supposed, in the larger picture. It would all be over by summer. The Trionate of Oridia would spread his glorious mantle over poor little Alden, offer his protection, and then have his way with her. Varad would have another crown to add to his pile. A meaningless trinket. It was Sadik who would truly profit from the conquest of Alden. He would have her timber, her gold, her single paltry bloodbinder. She would make him stronger. She would have made Madan stronger too, offering up more souls to his altar, but he had pushed himself too far, and paid the price. No matter. The Priest had passed on his secrets before he died. Sadik had seen to that. And he would put those secrets to better use than his fellow Trion ever had.

Not that he needed such dark devices. With seven blood-binders in his army and a fresh spy in his enemy's pocket, he had more than enough strength to crush the armies of Alden. Still, a wise general makes use of all the resources at his disposal, and Sadik was more than a wise general. He was the greatest warlord the Trionate had ever known.

Gently, Sadik placed the little black block on the north side of the river, at Whitefish Bridge. *I wish you luck, General, with your surprise attack. Though I fear the surprise will be yours.*

With a blissful sigh, Sadik drank his ale.

FOURTEEN

† "Well," Rig said, "this should be fun."

Commander Wright flashed a tight smile. "You have unusual ideas about fun, General."

"I have unusual ideas about a lot of things." Unusual enough, he hoped, to catch the Warlord by surprise. He was about to find out.

Wheeling his horse around, Rig addressed the ranks. "I won't lie to you men. A lot of blood will be spilled today. It won't take the enemy long to realise what we're up to, and when he does, he's going to come at us hard." He paused, surveying the faces before him. Fearful eyes stared out from under half helms; white knuckles curled around the hafts of pikes and poleaxes. A trill of birdsong filled the silence, incongruously bright in the grim chill of dawn. "That's what's going to happen," Rig continued. "That's what's *supposed* to happen. Remember that when you see your enemy bearing down on you. Remember it, and draw strength from it. When he comes at you, when you see the whites of his eyes, you brace your feet, grip your weapon, and you thank the gods that Oridian swine is doing just what we want him to do." Rig tore his sword from its scabbard. *"And then you take his gods-damned head!"*

The men roared and brandished their weapons. Rig gave them a moment to vent their tension before turning his horse back around to rejoin Wright. "Ready?"

"As I will ever be," Wright said, remarkably poised for a man on the cusp of his first real battle.

"Right. Let's get going." Slamming down his visor and putting the spurs to his horse, Rig led the vanguard through the trees toward Whitefish Bridge.

The ancient structure lay in no-man's-land between the armies, well covered by archers on both banks. Each side knew that the other was watching, ready to strike down anyone attempting to cross the wide open expanse of the Gunnar. Ready, but not really expecting it, because it would be foolish to try. If Sadik were to attempt it, he'd find himself pinned at a choke point, able to throw only a narrow column of attackers against a wall of defenders—a waste of good men. For Rig, it would be worse than a waste; it would be suicide. He'd be trading the relative safety of his own side of the border for a head-on meeting in enemy territory with a force twice the size of his own, leaving that same choke point between him and retreat.

So naturally, that was exactly what he meant to do.

A stutter of hooves ricocheted off the trees as they approached the bridge. They would meet resistance here, but how much? How many of Sadik's men watched the bridge, and how many prepared to ford the Gunnar upstream? Everything hinged on that question. It had been pure guesswork. If Rig had guessed right, many of his men would die today. If he'd guessed wrong, they all would. And so would he.

The arrows were the first to meet them.

Silent as wind, near-invisible in the shadows of the trees, they slanted down from the sky on crimson feathers, ringing off armour and embedding themselves in horseflesh. Rig hunkered low behind his horse's neck, raising his shield as high as he dared without leaving his flank completely open. Behind him, he heard unluckier men cry out as the missiles found flesh. Kingsword archers answered from the near bank, their bows pointed skyward to send a volley of shafts arcing up over the trees.

He could see the bridge now, tantalisingly close. Getting over it would be a trick, but Rig had fitted his cavalry with as much armour as he dared without sacrificing too much manoeuvrability. For his horse, that meant so much barding that the animal was a weapon all its own, a four-legged battering ram capable of crashing through infantry like a boar through brush. For Rig, it meant a full helm—something he normally disdained for its restrictive field of vision—and a thick gorget that made him feel like a slave in an iron collar.

That gorget earned its place, though; an arrow that would otherwise have found his throat bounced harmlessly away, and he rode on undaunted, the first to clatter across the smooth, cold stones of Whitefish Bridge. From his vantage at the halfspan, the far bank looked thinly defended. Crimson-clad archers, of course, loosing a steady hail of arrows, but no sign of cavalry, no pikes or halberds to skewer him or drag him off his horse. Rig's pulse started to race.

Clatter turned to thud as his horse's hooves met the riverbank. Hauling on the reins, he veered through the trees in search of prey. Archers continue to harass him, but it looked as though Sadik hadn't posted a single unit of infantry, much less cavalry, to defend the bridge. The Kingswords continued to flow across, fanning out, cluttering the southern bank of the Gunnar. The enemy archers were all but defenceless, falling to the gleaming blades of Kingsword cavalry.

Rig's heart hammered in his ears. *Nobody here. Every last man of them upriver at the ford.* He'd guessed—

"General!"

Wright's voice, bright with fear. Rig risked a glance over his shoulder and saw the Onnani commander pointing downstream. Ducking out of the way of an arrow, Rig looked.

A wall of horses surged between the trees. A battalion, maybe more, a thundering horde of cavalry headed straight for them. Rig's mouth went dry.

That was when the infantry appeared.

Up out of the brush like the fae folk of legend, materialising from the shadows brandishing polearms and axes and swords. Upstream, downstream, surrounding them in a deadly arc of crimson. Every enemy soldier that should have been fording the river to the west had been here all along, lying in wait to spring a trap on the Kingsword commander general who'd been foolish enough to test his luck at the bridge. Reining in his horse, Rig uttered every curse he knew, plus a few he invented on the spot. Then he cast his eyes skyward and gave a silent prayer of thanks.

He'd guessed right.

"Close ranks!" he cried, knowing it would be too late for many. Already, the enemy was moving to cut them off at the bridge, blocking their escape. Their only hope was to tighten up, protect each other's flanks, and pray.

Enemy infantry closed in on Rig's side. The first to come at him wielded a polearm of a sort he'd never seen before: bladed on one side, hooked on the other, studded with barbs designed to snag his sword. A clever innovation—unless the rider you were facing had a bloodblade. Rig focused his gaze on one of the narrow spaces between the barbs, then swept down, letting the bloodbond guide his hand. The stroke fell perfectly, dashing the weapon in half. Throwing the now-useless bits of wood aside, the infantryman tried to flee. Rig rode him down under the destrier's hooves.

His next opponent lasted a little longer, keeping light on his feet and darting under blows like a prizefighter facing a much larger opponent. But he was armed only with a shortsword, not much of a weapon for a man on foot; Rig relieved him of his head without ever having to deflect a stroke.

He was just turning to engage another foe when something hooked him under the arm, wrenching him from the saddle. He went down hard. The impact blasted the air from his lungs, and he lay there for half a heartbeat, stunned and vulnerable. Then a flash of metal caught his eye: a halberd swinging down at him in a murderous arc. *That* brought him round quickly enough. He threw himself into an awkward roll, cursing his heavy armour even as the blade whistled past his ear. It bit deep into the half-frozen soil, forcing the man wielding it to wrestle it free. That bought Rig just enough time to scramble to his feet. His attacker repositioned and lunged, his movements surprisingly quick; Rig barely managed to avoid being spitted, the spear tip glancing off his breastplate. He stumbled back and cast a frantic look about for his shield, but he couldn't see it anywhere.

The Oridian coiled for another lunge. Rig read it in his stance, so that when the halberd came at him, he was already moving, snapping his body sideways to let the spear tip dart past harmlessly. Now his enemy was overextended, his weapon exposed; Rig dashed off the head of the axe, spun, and hacked into his opponent's shoulder, sending him down into the rotten leaves with a scream of agony.

Rig turned to find his destrier pawing the ground restlessly, as though impatient to continue. Slinging himself back in the saddle, Rig dared a quick scan of the battlefield. They were surrounded from three sides, backed against the bridge but unable to retreat without opening themselves up. It looked very grim indeed.

Now would be a good time, Morris.

It was as if his thoughts carried on the wind. A chorus of shouts went up from the west, and there was Morris, south of the Gunnar where he had no business being, driving his battalion into the enemy's unprotected flank like a shaft loosed from hiding. So cleanly did they cut that Rig actually watched his second ride across his view, crashing through men whose polearms were pointed uselessly in the wrong direction.

Chaos erupted in the Oridian ranks. Officers shouted conflicting orders, sending their men scattering in all directions. Morris split his host and confused them still further, harrying them from two sides while Rig and his vanguard pressed the attack. A tiny, glorious space opened up between the Kingswords' rear lines and the foot of Whitefish Bridge. Rig couldn't resist glancing over his shoulder as he fought, snatching quick looks at an opportunity so irresistible, so unexpected, that he nearly lost a hand lusting after it. He jerked his arm out of the way just in time to avoid a well-placed cut; turning his horse sharply, he dealt a death blow at an awkward angle across the destrier's neck. Coincidentally, the move pointed him straight at Whitefish Bridge. Rig paused, reins in one hand, gore-stained blade in the other.

As bold as a Black. It had got him this far, hadn't it? He spurred his horse.

"Morris!" He couldn't get as close as he would have liked, but close enough for his second to hear over the clash of steel and the screams of dying men. "The bridge! I'm going to do it!"

Morris's favourite curse travelled across horses and men to meet him. "Aye, General!"

"Can you make it back to the ford?"

More cursing, unintelligible through the visor. "Bloody well have to, won't I?"

That hadn't been the plan, of course. Blowing the bridge had been a ruse, a way to lure Sadik's men away from the ford upstream. By pretending to be rash, Rig had tempted the Warlord to abandon his own plans in favour of capitalising on his enemy's supposed foolishness, allowing Morris and his men to cross virtually unchallenged. Rig had brought the black powder, had every intention of using it, but only as a means of covering their escape. That had been the limit of his ambitions.

But now here it was, staring him in the face: a chance to bring down the last remaining bridge, the only way for the enemy to get siege engines across the Gunnar. Rig would be damned if he squandered that chance, even if it cost him hundreds of men. "Hold them off as long as you can!" he ordered Morris before wheeling back to the bridge.

He met little resistance on the way. The Oridians swarmed about like panicked ants, no longer capable of mounting any organised manoeuvres. Rig ignored the enemies in his path, swerving to avoid them as he made his way to the rear of the Kingsword lines. He passed Commander Wright on the way, and shouting, "With me!" rounded up the Onnani knight and started across the bridge. His horse's hooves struck out a furious rhythm against the cobbles. They had only a few moments, a handful of heartbeats before the confusion righted itself and his opportunity expired.

Kingsword archers lined the north bank, bows curved, ready to rain death upon anyone in crimson. Somewhere just behind them stood the decoy wagons.

Decoys no longer.

"Black powder! In position, go!"

A moment's hesitation as the Kingswords exchanged glances, unsure if they'd heard right. Then a whip cracked, and an oxcart lumbered into view, loaded up with two barrels of black powder. By the time Rig hit the bank and turned his horse, they'd lit a torch. The soldier holding it glanced back at him, hesitating, knowing that if he put flame to fuse, he'd cut off his comrades' escape.

"Do it! The rest of you, fall back!" Rig dug in his heels and flattened himself against the destrier's neck, hoping it wouldn't throw him.

A breath passed, and another. When the blast came, it sent a sheet of wind whipping against Rig's back. His horse found a new speed, fleeing the terrible fury of a five-hundred-year-old bridge in its death throes. The rumble followed him through the trees, deep and deafening, drowning out the rattle of armour, the stutter of hooves—everything but the distant, triumphant cry of the Kingswords.

"And another to Commander Morris!" cried Rollin, hoisting his flagon, "for being able to *find* the sodding ford at a flat-out gallop with a thousand howling Oridians on his arse!"

The men cheered and drank.

"And to Herwin, for giving our friends such a warm reception on the north bank!"

More cheering and drinking.

Rig hefted his own flagon from across the room, though he doubted anyone saw. They'd given up on him at last, leaving him to observe at a distance. A stretch of shadow separated him from the rest of the men. Figuratively, as well as literally.

"It's quite impressive, really," said a musical voice in his ear. "I'd have thought they would have run out of toasts hours ago."

Rig laughed quietly, watching as a visibly drunken Rollin tried to hoist an equally sodden Herwin onto his shoulders, only to pitch both of them over into the crowd. "When it comes to celebration, soldiers never run out of ideas."

The priestess settled in beside him, arranging her robes around crossed legs. "If that is so, why do you sit apart from them like this? Why not join in? You deserve this more than any man here, surely."

Rig grunted into his flagon. "I sent a lot of men to their deaths today, Daughter. Spent their lives on a gamble."

"A fruitful one, it would seem. Your ruse was successful. I'm told the destruction of the bridge is quite the boon to our cause."

"That it is. But it could have gone very differently." It *would* have gone differently if he'd been wrong, and Sadik hadn't been expecting them at the bridge. But Sadik *had* been expecting them. He'd known of Rig's plans, or at least part of them, and that could only mean one thing.

Vel looked over at him, a half smile pulling at her lips. "Why, General, is that what you're doing in this dark corner by yourself? Brooding?"

"I wouldn't call it brooding. I'm thinking."

"About what comes next?"

"I know what comes next."

"Nothing good, judging from your tone."

He shrugged. "We won a victory today. It bought us—what, a week? Threw a wheel off Sadik's wagon? It won't be enough. He'll find a way to get those siege engines across the river. I would."

Vel gave him a funny look. "I believe you would, General."

"It all comes down to how many lives we're prepared to spend on that crossing. Him to take it, and me to keep it."

"Does it bother you, all this death? Your part in it?"

He shrugged again. "One day, maybe. Right now, I don't have the luxury. What's that saying—when the winter is done, the birds will flock home? It'll come back on me eventually. Maybe I'll be one of those tortured old men who can't sleep for the nightmares. But not now. I'm too busy worrying about the living to dwell on the dead."

Across the room, Morris was regaling the men with a tale— a meandering, slurring version of the time he and Rig led a few hundred Blackswords against a much larger Oridian host, only to find themselves coming to the rescue of another outnumbered force (*the sodding* King of Alden, *that's who*) and routing the enemy in the bargain. A bit of an exaggeration, and every man in the room had doubtless heard the tale a dozen times by now, but they listened raptly all the same. As for Rig, his mind wandered, hazy with drink and spent battle frenzy.

"Sadik is not as fearsome as you think," the priestess said at length.

"No? He didn't become the Warlord by being passably capable. He's not like the other Trions. He wasn't born into his place, or appointed by his peers. He *earned* it. He had to kill for it."

"What difference does that make? It's not as though you have to face him in single combat."

"He's a clever bastard too," Rig muttered, almost to himself.

"You tricked him."

"This time, but he won't fall for it again. And that trap he laid for us was brilliant. If we hadn't been expecting it . . ." Rig shook his head; it didn't bear thinking about. "His men appeared out of nowhere, dressed in forest colours with mud spread all over their faces. I've seen that before, in the Broken Mountains, but I've never seen a conventional army use tactics like that."

"Except yours."

He turned, his eyes meeting hers. "Not for a long time," he said carefully. *And I've never talked openly about those tactics with anyone.* Even Morris's drunken tales never made mention of details like that. It wasn't exactly a secret, but it wasn't the sort of information that just fell into one's lap, either. "You're very well informed, Daughter."

She looked away. Brought a cup of wine to her lips.

"It was you," Rig said, the truth dawning on him even as he spoke. "You're the one who read up on the battles." He couldn't deny it—he was impressed.

It must have come through in his tone, because she flushed with pleasure. "Commander Wright and I studied together. He admires you greatly, you know. Though," she laughed, "he was not very happy with you today."

Rig grinned. "I do regret that, but it couldn't be helped."

"It was amusing to see him after the battle. So angry, so thrilled, practically shaking with it. He couldn't tell if he wanted to kiss you or hit you. Both, I think."

"I have that effect on people."

"I readily believe that, General." Her mouth curved into a teasing little bow, the sort of look that sent a man's imagination on flights of fancy.

Is she doing that on purpose? Most likely, Rig decided. She was baiting him again, trying to shock him with her forward behaviour. He considered her: those clever dark eyes, that coy look, so intent on knocking him off balance. "Why are you here, Daughter?"

"What, here? In this room?"

"Here in Alden. At the front. Why subject yourself to fear and ridicule just to minister to some soldiers? You could do that back in Onnan City. Then you wouldn't have to hide in a dark corner with me."

That seductive smile again. "Perhaps I like being in dark corners with you."

"If you want to flirt with me, Daughter, you're most welcome, but it won't get you out of answering my questions."

Her expression closed down. "I don't owe you answers, General," she said coolly, looking away.

"Fair enough." He started to rise.

She clucked her tongue impatiently. "But you are a *contrary* man. Do you really wish to know?"

"I do."

"Then I'll tell you, but if it sounds foolishly romantic to you, I'll thank you to keep that to yourself."

The idea of the waspish priestess of Eldora being *foolishly romantic* struck Rig as highly improbable, but he kept that to himself. He leaned back against the wall and gestured for her to proceed.

"Have you ever heard of *Zan and Adra*?" When Rig shook his head, she continued, "It's one of our most famous tales, dating back to the time of the Erromanian Empire. Zan was a slave and a freedom fighter. A foot soldier at first, but over the course of the tale, he rises through the ranks of the rebellion to become one of its leaders. Adra is his wife. She stays behind in his village, raises his children, finds ways of getting supplies and messages to her husband and the rebels." Vel made a dismissive gesture. "It ends tragically, of course. Zan is caught and tortured. Adra must soldier on, as it were, without her husband. The rebellion does what it can for her, but eventually she dies of grief."

"Heartwarming story."

"We have many such tales, as you can imagine. *Bar of the Seas*, have you heard that one?"

"Can't say I have." Rig was starting to feel a little awkward. He knew a few legends from Harram, and from Andithyri of course, but his tutors had not seen fit to teach him anything of the folklore of the former slaves, an omission he hadn't noticed until now. He had an idea what Vel would say about that.

Fortunately, she was too caught up in her tale. "About something other than the empire and slavery, for once. Bar goes on a long sea voyage, leaving his wife and children behind. He's on a quest to find the lost island of Tarsin and its fabled waters of everlasting life. If he succeeds and brings the waters back with him, he can save Onnan from hunger and disease. Yila—that's the wife—does everything she can to keep his household and business healthy while he's gone. Another tragic ending, with Bar and his crew going down in a storm." Vel looked at him, arched an eyebrow. "Do you see the common theme, General?"

"Sure. Man goes off to do great deeds, woman stays at home to mind the fire."

When she spoke again, her voice was low and vehement. "I will not simply mind the fire while my countrymen die for me and mine. I have something to contribute, even if it is not a blade or a bow, and I will do it at the front lines, just like Commander Wright."

"Commendable."

Vel's eyes narrowed sharply. "Are you mocking me again?"

Rig laughed. "Put your stinger away, Daughter. No one's mocking you. I said it was commendable and I meant it."

"Then let me do more," she said, leaning forward intently. "Let me get in touch with the Resistance."

Rig looked at her. Scratched his beard. Gods, he was almost tempted to do it. They needed the Resistance working with them, now more than ever. The fleet would take too long, the Harrami even longer. He needed help now, or they weren't going to make it. *Therein lies the problem.* The Resistance was too important. An underground movement of Andithyrians working behind enemy lines to undermine their conquerors . . . having them as allies would be an incredible boon. Rig would get only one chance to make that happen, and if he failed, the Resistance would go deeper into hiding—or worse, fall into the hands of the enemy. Rig needed to be absolutely certain that whomever he entrusted with this was up to the task. Vel was smart, and she was determined, but could he trust her? *After what happened today . . .*

"I've heard you, Vel," he said, using her name to soften the words, "but I'm not ready just yet."

"Take your time, General," she said coldly, rising. "I'm sure Sadik will wait."

He sighed as he watched her go, hoping he hadn't just made an enemy. The gods knew he had enough of those already, on both sides of the border. For all Rig knew, he had enemies right here in the fort.

One thing was for sure: He had at least one spy.

FIFTEEN

Erik dropped a pine bough at his feet and reached for another. He was dimly aware that his shoulder ached, that the fingers of his gloves were glued together with sap, but his task was not yet done. He paused a moment to catch his breath. Then he put the dulling edge of his dagger to green wood and began to saw. He worked blankly, mechanically. The cool hush of the mountains filled his ears, scouring the landscape of his thoughts and chasing the shadows into corners. Branches piled up at his feet. His breath bloomed in steady pulses of vapour. He knew nothing else.

When he deemed he had enough, Erik put his dagger away and gathered the pine boughs in his arms. He carried them to the pit fire, arranging them as close to its heat as he dared, one atop the other in a loosely woven pattern. He pushed down on them to test their depth; satisfied they would provide enough of a barrier against the chill of the ground, he turned to the bundle of furs beside him.

"Alix." She didn't stir right away. Erik shook her gently. "Alix, let's get you onto the mat." Still nothing. Swallowing, his heart skipping unpleasantly, Erik pulled off his glove and touched her forehead. *Better,* he decided, but perhaps that was wishful thinking. The sweat matting her hair showed that the fever had not yet broken. The cool hush of his mind was fading away, shadows rolling in like fog over a lake.

Alix's eyelids fluttered open. She focused on him, hazel eyes scanning his features. A weak smile pulled at her lips. "Liam."

He wilted a little. "No, Alix, it's—"

She reached up and touched his face, her fingers sliding into his hair.

Erik shivered against a toxic brew of emotions, worry and guilt and an unmistakable twinge of longing. He slipped his arms under her and gathered her against him. "*Shh.* Never mind. Go back to sleep." Easing her onto the pine boughs, he arranged the furs around her. Then he found a reason to be on the other side of the camp.

A short while later, Kerta returned from her hunt. "Any luck?" Erik asked her.

She hefted a limp rabbit by way of answer. "There were two of them, but I couldn't get another arrow off in time. I'm sorry, sire."

"Don't be absurd. A rabbit is a great victory compared to squirrel."

She did her best to smile. "You know, it wasn't as bad as I thought. A bit sinewy, perhaps."

The guardsman Alfred eyed the rabbit hungrily. The poor man had been on watch for hours now and looked even more exhausted than the rest of them. There was no help for it, though; with a scout moving out ahead and another at their rear, he was the only one left to guard the camp.

Kerta cocked her chin at the slumbering form across the fire. "How is she?"

"Better, I think, but still confused. She . . . mistook me for Liam." The words surprised him; he hadn't meant to say them.

Kerta knew it. She saw it all, Erik realised; he could tell by the pitying look that came over her. "I'm sorry," she said.

"It's just not a good sign," he returned briskly. "I'd hoped we were past this." *I'd hoped I was past this.*

"I can't understand how it came back like that," Kerta said, "and so suddenly. She seemed to be over it, and then . . ."

"The stress, I suppose."

Kerta drew her knife, readying to dress the rabbit. "I just wish there were something more we could do."

"She'll be fine."

"I know, but . . ." *But she's slowing us down.* Kerta would never say it out loud, but she didn't have to. They all knew it. And they all knew the consequences of delay. The longer they lingered in this gods-forsaken pass, the more likely they were to be discovered. Meanwhile, Erik had no way of knowing what was happening back home, how close they were to losing the war. For all he knew, it was already over, his friends dead, his kingdom conquered . . .

The familiar panic began to well up inside him, but he tamped it down ruthlessly. "One more day ought to do it," he said. "Then hopefully we can pick up the pace."

"Farika willing."

Erik did not join her in the prayer. He was not feeling terribly close to the gods at the moment.

They made a quiet, modest meal of the rabbit. Erik tried to get Alix to eat some, but of course she would not. Frida came in from the rear guard to join them. Of her fellow scout, Leola, there was no sign.

"I'm sure she's just late," Kerta said with her usual optimism.

But when nearly dark gave way to fully dark, and still no sign, it was clear the missing scout was not merely late. Something was wrong.

"We can't risk going after her," Erik said. "There isn't enough moonlight to see by, and we don't dare light a torch. Whatever has befallen Leola, we can't help her until dawn. Hopefully, she has simply lost her way." He did not believe that for a moment, of course. More likely, the scout had been injured somehow, fallen on loose rock or melting snow. Perhaps she had met a bear, or a panther, or something else that forced her up a tree or out of her way.

There was another possibility, of course, by no means the least likely, but Erik did not care to think on it. Not that it mattered what he cared to think on. His mind was through taking orders from him today; it explored whatever dark corners it liked.

He fell asleep, as he had nearly every night, to the image of a tribal warrior standing over him, face smeared with concealing mud, sword curved like the sickle of a too-dark moon.

Dawn found Erik upright, well armed, and giving orders.

"Alfred, you stay behind and keep watch on Alix. If she wakes, try to get her to eat something. Kerta and Frida, you're with me. If Leola is out there, we'll find her." *Unless someone else found her first.*

Were their situation any less dangerous, he would have left the missing scout behind, however reluctantly. Time was too precious, their task too desperate, to risk falling even further behind. But he could ill afford to lose another man. It was worth looking for her, if only briefly. "She would know better than to go chasing after someone on her own, wouldn't she?" Erik asked as they walked.

"Oh yes, Your Majesty," Kerta assured him with wide-eyed earnestness. "That would be completely against protocol!"

Alix would do it, Erik thought. She *had* done it, nearly getting herself and Liam killed in the process. Thankfully, most of the scouts had cooler heads.

When they reached the place where Leola should have been posted, and still no sign of her, they agreed to split up. Kerta headed up the slope, Frida down. Erik kept on straight, bloodbow in hand, eyes scanning the trees for any sign of . . . anything.

His boots scraped noisily against loose rock, or so it seemed to him. Unlike the scouts, he had not been trained for stealth. He had no skill at tracking, or climbing trees, or half a hundred other things that seemed like terrible oversights now. If his bowstring had not been boiled in his own blood, he doubted he would even be much of a shot. He was as out of place here, he reflected, as his brother was in the halls of the Republicana. *Perhaps Liam was right after all. Perhaps he should be here, and I there.* Liam was a trained scout, and a good one, according to the late Arran Green. He would be better at this. Better at taking care of Alix, too.

The thought brought a fresh twinge of pain. When she'd reached for him, her fingers twining in his hair . . . *Like a bittersweet memory.*

Erik cursed himself quietly. The thought was a betrayal. So many of his thoughts felt like betrayals, especially lately. His mind, usually so disciplined, was a tumult of doubt and guilt. Anxiety scratched at him like a cat at the chamber door.

He paused. A stone in the path lay at an odd angle, a dark band of moisture marking the place where it had once been buried in moss. It did not take a tracker to understand what that meant. Someone had passed through here recently, though whether man or beast, he could not tell. He crouched, listening to the whisper of the pines, scanning the slope above and below.

There. A scar in the moss on the slope below, glistening black, as though a boot heel had scraped it aside. Erik made his way carefully down, arrow to bowstring, every sense alert. He saw more of what might have been tracks, but he could not be sure; the snow had only recently melted, leaving the undergrowth crushed and wet.

A raven cackled to his left. Looking up, Erik's heart sank. Half a dozen of the vile creatures perched in a single budding poplar, and when he took a step toward them, several more took flight from the undergrowth. Certain now what he would find, Erik made his way over.

It was a grisly sight. The scout was half eaten, torn open from navel to neck. Her entrails lay strewn about her, dragged there by the ravens. Her bow, in splinters, was still slung over her shoulder, and her knife was sheathed at her hip. Whatever had taken Leola had caught her completely by surprise. It looked as though the beast had made some effort to bury her, perhaps intending to come back to finish its meal. That, and the scarred bark on a nearby tree trunk, left little doubt as to what was responsible.

There was nothing to be done but chase off the ravens and try to cover the remains as best he could. That done, he started back up the slope.

"Erik."

He swung, bow taut, to find Alix standing in the trees. Cursing, he lowered his weapon. "What in the Nine Domains are you—"

"You shouldn't be out here alone." She looked like death walking, pale and tatty, shoulders drooping. Even so, she had still managed to sneak up on him without a sound.

"*I* shouldn't be out here? You shouldn't even be on your feet!"

"I didn't have much choice, since my king saw fit to wander off without me."

Erik stared at her incredulously. After all this time, the woman still managed to astonish him. She wasn't just impudent; she was bloody *impossible*. "Alfred shouldn't have let you leave," he growled, somewhat irrelevantly.

"I outrank him." She scanned the brush around them. "You're looking for Leo, he said."

"Not anymore."

She started to ask a question, but then her brow smoothed, grim understanding coming into her eyes. "How?"

"Panther. Yesterday afternoon, by the look of things."

She sighed. "Gods, that's awful."

"Yes," Erik agreed, "it was. But there's nothing to be done now. Let's get you back to camp."

"I'm fine."

"Obviously. That's why you keep rubbing your eyes. By the Virtues, Alix, would it kill you to be sensible for once?"

She scowled. "That's rich, coming from you."

"What's that supposed to mean?"

"You're the *king*, Erik. You can't be running off on rescue missions in the middle of enemy territory."

"I'm not *running off* anywhere," he said coolly. "It wasn't as though we had the luxury of sending someone else. In case you haven't noticed, we're a bit thin on the ground here."

"Have I noticed we're in an impossible situation?" She made a furious, sweeping gesture. "Why yes, Erik, I have. We *shouldn't* be, but we are, and it's my duty to make sure we survive it, no matter how ill I might be feeling. So when my king goes off into the woods alone, I'm obliged to follow."

They glared at each other, standing there on a slope in the middle of nowhere. They rarely argued, and never like this. Erik found it strangely liberating. "You blame me for this, then? Is that it?"

Something drained from her eyes. "Of course not. It's just . . . I wish you didn't always have to take everything on your shoulders, yours and yours alone. You have a whole court, Erik. A council. Ambassadors. And yet here we are"— she gestured about them again, wearily this time—"in the Broken Mountains, being picked off one by one."

"You think I want this?" He could hear something perilously close to a tremor in his voice. He could not remember the last time he had been this angry, this . . . *inflamed*. "Do you honestly believe I would have put myself through this if I saw any other choice? Don't you think I'm tired, so *gods-damned tired*, of doing what's necessary, instead of what I want?" He was vaguely aware of taking a different path now, of wandering away from where they had begun, called there by an irresistible song that had been echoing in his ears for what seemed like forever. If he was not careful, he would say something he could never take back, that would hang around their necks for the rest of their lives.

"Then why?" She closed the distance between them, utterly oblivious, gripping his shoulders and gazing searchingly into his eyes. It felt like falling. "Why do you do it?"

How do you always manage to be so good? Her voice again, reaching across the void of time, dashing over him like cold water.

"Because I have to." Turning away, Erik started back up the slope.

For a long moment, Alix could only stand there, trembling, wondering what had just happened. She'd been insolent, lashing out in her fear and discomfort. That was, it pained her to admit, not unusual. But Erik's reaction . . . He was always so measured, so composed. *Almost always*, she amended. She'd seen him this raw once before: on the day of the parley, when he'd confronted her about her relationship with Liam.

Liam. Something tugged at her memory, too hazy to make out. Could that be it? Had she inadvertently reopened old wounds? She couldn't see how. "Erik," she called, "please stop."

He ignored her. In a few moments, he would disappear over the lip of the hill. Alix hurried after him—or at least, she tried to. Her head swam, and her mouth felt like something had laid eggs in it. She should never have come. She was no good to him in this state, no good to anyone until she recovered her strength. Dragging herself up the slope was like slogging through shin-deep mud.

She crested the hill to find him a good twenty paces up the path. Her shoulders sagged in defeat; she would never catch him now. Resignation opened the floodgates: Dizziness crashed over her, sending the world on a mad tilt. Grabbing hold of a tree, she clung there as spots chased one another across her vision. *Don't faint. Don't you dare faint . . .*

And then strong arms were around her, steadying her. "I've got you. Here, sit down."

"We can't . . . We have to keep moving . . ." In spite of her words, Alix slumped gratefully into his arms.

"In a moment. You need to sit." Erik started to ease her down.

"I'm sorry . . ."

He sighed, a gentle breath in her ear. "You don't even know what you're sorry for, Alix."

She started to reply, but a *snap* from the trees nearby drew her head sharply around. Her hand whipped up, demanding silence.

Erik eyed her warily, quietly shrugging his bloodbow off his shoulder. Alix scanned the shadows between the trees. *It's Kerta*, she thought. *Let it be Kerta.*

An arrow whizzed over her left shoulder. Alix was moving before it had even buried itself in the tree trunk behind her; she threw herself at Erik, sending them both tumbling over the crest of the slope. The moment she'd stopped rolling, she gave Erik a hard shove. "Take cover!"

He obeyed, diving behind a tree, an arrow already nocked to his bow. "Tribesmen," he growled, as though she needed to be told. She'd seen the fletching on the arrow, the distinctive stripes of falcon feathers.

Fear lit up every nerve in Alix's body, sending a shock of strength through her limbs. She scrambled behind a tree and drew her bloodblade, though it would do her little good at range. Not for the first time, she cursed herself for not taking Nevyn up on his offer to prepare a bloodforged dagger for her. She could have thrown it with deadly accuracy; instead, she faced the prospect of charging an unknown number of archers.

She held her breath, listening. Erik shifted behind his tree, trying to peer through the branches for a glimpse of their attacker. Wind sighed through the pines, but all else was still. "Go," Alix whispered. "I'll cover you."

He gave her an incredulous look. "With what?"

"I'll think of something."

"I'm not leaving you, Alix." As if to emphasise the point, he drew back on his bowstring, though he still didn't have a target in sight.

Alix cursed under her breath. There was no point in arguing. Erik had many kingly instincts, but self-preservation was not among them. "Stay here, then." Lowering herself onto her belly, she started to worm her way along the slope on elbows and knees. If she could outflank them, come up from behind . . .

Then what? She had no idea how many there might be. Even if she could get the drop on one of them, a second would take her out easily. But what choice did she have? Erik wouldn't retreat, not without her, and she was in no condition to outrun anyone. So she pressed on, crawling as silently as she could through the undergrowth, praying for a miracle.

The air hissed, twice in rapid succession. An exchange of arrows. Alix propped herself on her elbows, hoping for some sign of the enemy archer. A moment later, Erik took another shot, loosing a shaft into a dense cluster of pines about a hundred feet up the slope. Alix pointed herself toward it, creeping forward with agonising slowness, pausing every few feet like a cat stalking its prey.

She'd covered half the distance when a rustle in the undergrowth drew her head up. She could see something, a bit of brown moving between the trees a few feet away. She waited, head swimming, pulse hammering in her ears.

The brown thing shifted. An elbow, drawing back on a bow. Alix gauged the distance. *Ten strides. Maybe less.* Cold sweat trickled down her temple. She could feel the surge of strength ebbing away as the shock wore off. The fever was closing in on her again; any moment now, it would pounce. *Ten strides*, she told herself. *You can do this.* She tensed, breathed a silent prayer, and sprang.

She didn't make a sound—she would have sworn it before the gods themselves. Yet somehow, the archer sensed her coming; he turned, bow drawn, the point of his arrow glinting in the sun. Alix's heart froze in her chest, as though it could hide.

A stinging pain pricked the back of her neck. She ignored it, letting her momentum carry her through the undergrowth. For some reason, the archer hadn't fired; instead he just stood there, watching her barrel through the brush toward him.

She didn't make it. A wave of dizziness crashed over her, and suddenly her legs wouldn't carry her another step. She fell at the archer's feet; her sword tumbled from clumsy fingers. The tribesman loomed over her, dark and alien and terrifying. He sneered at her before turning away as though she were of no consequence.

The back of her neck burned; instinctively, Alix reached up to touch it. Her fingers brushed feathers. *An arrow,* she thought. *They've shot me . . .* But no, this was too small to be an arrow, and anyway, she'd be dead.

She heard movement behind her. She tried to turn, but her body wouldn't obey. She tried to call out to Erik, to tell him to run, but her jaw had seized shut. Darkness crowded her vision. *Poison.* She'd felt this once before, she realised groggily, on a distant battlefield in the midst of a siege . . .

A voice cried out. Erik. He sounded as if he were a half a hundred miles away . . .

Alix pitched forward onto her hands, onto her face, into blackness.

Sixteen

The spy found him alone on the balcony, breathing the salt air.

Rudi sprang at the rose window, scrabbling and barking with such ferocity that Liam actually jumped. Just a little, mind.

"Your dog . . ." The spy drew back a step. "He is secured?" Liam didn't blame him for asking. The wolfhound looked absolutely terrifying through the warped prism of the stained glass, like some kind of mythical monster.

"Let's hope so. I'm not sure which of us he'd go for, frankly."

The spy didn't find that comforting; his hand strayed to the rail. "Why do you keep him, if that's so?"

"Long story." Liam crossed his arms, a move that coincidentally positioned his hand just above the dagger in his belt. After the spy's last visit, Liam had vowed never to be caught unarmed again. "What can I do for you?"

"I'm here to escort you to your meeting, Your Highness."

He arched an eyebrow. "What meeting?"

"You may recall, Your Highness, that you asked me to arrange a meeting with one of the secret societies."

That was days ago; Liam had assumed it wasn't going to happen. "You actually managed it, then?"

"I am humbled by your confidence," the spy said dryly.

"No offence, I just thought it would be more difficult. I mean, they're *secret* and all."

"With respect, Your Highness, you have no idea what it took for me to arrange this meeting."

Liam supposed that was true. Indeed, the fact that it had taken several days did suggest a certain amount of fuss had gone into it. "You didn't have to threaten anyone, I hope?" *Or worse?* Liam wished he'd thought to ask before, when it might have made a difference.

The spy shrugged him off. "All you need know is that the Shield has agreed to hear you this evening, at their lair."

Lair. Why did they have to make it sound like some fetid cave where a scaly beast perched atop a pile of human bones, picking meat from its teeth with an elegantly curved claw? The Onnani, Liam decided, were awfully dramatic. "Let me wake my officers and we'll go."

The spy shook his head. "Just you."

"Worth a try, anyway," Liam muttered.

"The dagger, Your Highness. You must leave it behind."

Liam opened his mouth. Closed it. Scowled. "Fine, but if I get killed on this little outing, I'm going to be quite put out."

The spy was unmoved.

"Just let me put it inside." He squeezed through the door, driving Rudi back with his knee. For once, he was glad of the wolfhound's presence; it gave him an excuse to close the door behind him. As soon as he was out of sight, he tucked the dagger into his boot. He recalled the spy saying something to the effect that carrying arms into the den of a secret society would be the end of him, but he decided that was just more drama. Probably.

"All right," he said, slipping back out. "Let's go."

The spy disappeared over the rail. Liam peered after him, decided the drop wasn't too bad, and climbed up. He felt ridiculous, like a squire sneaking out of the barracks after curfew. (He'd done that precisely once. Arran Green had *not* been amused.) Sitting atop the rail, one leg dangling over into the night, Liam looked down again. Seen from this angle, the slope below didn't look quite so benign, but there was no help for it; he jumped.

He hit the ground with an ungodly racket, scrabbled to his feet with ungainly haste, and brushed himself off. He glanced around him, as though searching for his dignity.

"This way, Your Highness." The voice carried just a hint of dryness.

Liam followed the spy through the woods at the back of the garden. The wall at the foot of the property was rough stone, which Liam scaled easily enough to soothe his pride. After that, there were more gardens, and more walls, all the way down to the city. It wasn't until they reached the old battlements that they set foot on a proper street.

"Here," the spy said, tossing a cloak at Liam. "Put this on, with the hood up."

Liam complied, even though the wool smelled like a wet dog had slept on it following a spot of grave robbing.

"This way."

They headed toward the gate. Liam tensed when he saw the guards, but the spy just nodded at them, and they passed without a word. Which wasn't much comfort, really. *This place really is a viper's nest*, he thought.

The spy led him into an alley and said, "Stop." The light from the street barely reached them here; only the man's mouth and chin were visible within the hood. "Do not be alarmed, Your Highness."

Something stirred behind him. Liam was fixing to be properly alarmed when he felt the swatch of fabric go over his eyes. "Oh, come *on*. A blindfold? Is that really necessary?"

"I'm afraid it is."

There followed an absurd interlude of fumbling blindly through the alley, after which there was a very long wagon ride, followed by still more blind fumbling. Finally, after what seemed like hours, Liam was led up some steps, and he heard a door open. The sound of his boots went from flat to echoing, and a crack of light appeared at the bottom of his blindfold. *Thank Farika.* They were finally here.

He was escorted down a long corridor and through a heavy set of doors. The air seemed cooler here, and the sound of the sea washed over him. *Outside?* But no—his footfalls still echoed, albeit differently.

The hands guiding him pulled him to a halt. Footsteps withdrew. Liam stood there in the dark, not daring to speak or even to remove the blindfold. A gentle, salt-scoured breeze tousled his hair. He could feel eyes upon him, as if from every direction at once, but he could hear nothing. He had never felt so alone, so vulnerable, in all his life.

"You may remove the blindfold, Your Highness."

Haltingly, Liam reached up and pulled it free. For a moment, all he could do was blink in the searing glow of torchlight. He was in some sort of chamber, but when he glanced up, stars pricked the darkness above. Columns stretched up from the four corners of the room as if to support a ceiling, but there was none; instead, they reached into the sky like ancient trees. As his eyes adjusted, Liam found himself at the centre of a ring of figures, all of them robed and masked, but not in the raiment of priests. The masks they wore were similar to Olan's, but instead of a silver disk, they were black, as glossy as mirrors. Onyx, maybe, or jet. The torchlight rippled liquid orange on their shining surfaces. The figures behind were still, silent, utterly inscrutable.

"Hi," said Liam.

"We apologise for the means by which you were brought here," said a voice as smooth and dark as the masks. "We rarely entertain outsiders."

"I appreciate you making an exception." Liam couldn't help glancing around, taking in the robed figures surrounding him. Somewhere among them, he supposed, was Irtok, but he didn't know the chairman well enough to identify him by build alone.

"An exception, yes," said the same voice, "and not lightly made. Why did you wish to see us, Your Highness?"

Right. So much for the pleasantries. Liam cleared his throat. "Well, I assume you know why I'm here. In Onnan City, I mean."

"We know why you're here." A hint of impatience in the voice now.

"Then you know how important the Onnani fleet is to the war effort. I am commander of the White Wolves. A soldier, in command of an elite battalion of soldiers. We should be at the front right now, protecting home and hearth. Instead, I'm here, trying to find out why a fleet that should already be at sea is still at least three months from completion."

"And what makes you think the brothers of the Shield can help you answer this question?" A new voice this time, a thicker accent.

Liam steeled himself. He was fairly certain his next statement wasn't going to go over well, but there was nothing for it—he had to put his cards on the table. "The fact is, I've already learned the answer. It turned out to be fairly simple: It's sabotage."

He'd expected murmuring. Shouting, even. What he got was silence, torchlight flickering off the glassy black surface of shield-shaped masks.

"What I don't know is *why* it's happening, or who's behind it. I'm hoping men of your stature can help me find out."

"How shall we do that?" asked a third voice.

Liam scowled. It was like a bad game of volley. Wasn't *he* supposed to be the one asking the questions? "I was told that the Shield had a finger in every pie around here. If that's not true, tell me now, and I'll stop wasting your time. But if it is true, then you probably have a good idea who's behind this thing."

Orange light glinted off the masks as they looked at one another. Sibilant whispers carried across the room. After a brief discussion, the masks turned back to Liam.

"We are sorry, Your Highness." The first voice again, sounding about as sorry as if he'd accidentally deliberately stepped on Liam's foot. "We would like very much to help you, but we cannot tell you what you wish to know."

Liam felt his jaw twitch in anger. "Can't, or won't?"

"Very well. We *won't*."

"Why in the Nine bloody Domains not?"

He knew the moment he said it he'd made a mistake. The robed figures stiffened, and a palpable chill descended over the room. "I will thank you not to blaspheme in this hallowed chamber, Your Highness."

Of course. Half these men were probably priests. "Sorry," Liam said, cursing inwardly. "I meant no offence."

After a suitably reproachful silence, the voice continued. "Rest assured that the man responsible for this evil deed will be punished. But he is Onnani, and must face Onnani justice."

Liam felt his scowl returning. "Why hasn't he, then? What are you waiting for?"

"We were not certain of his crimes until you arrived. But your presence has spurred various parties into action, some of them rash, thereby shedding light on the matter."

The spy had mentioned something similar, Liam recalled, about his presence stirring the pot. Still, there was something that didn't smell right about this. It was all a bit . . . *fishy*.

There, he'd said it—if only in his head.

Aloud, he said, "Why would anyone do something like this? Doesn't he realise that hundreds of thousands of lives are at stake? Aldenian *and* Onnani?"

"Desperate men do desperate things, Your Highness. The

Trionate of Oridia is the wealthiest nation in Gedona. Their gold would go a long way to restoring the fortune of a man who has lost it all."

"That is enough, I think," said another voice, gently admonishing. One black mask turned to another, as if enjoining silence. "We have no more to say on the matter, Your Highness. We wish you a pleasant evening, and may Olan be your sign."

Liam stood there, powerless, listening to footfalls approach from behind. They'd make him put the blindfold back on, escort him out of here whether he liked it or not. "Do I at least have your word?" he asked, hating how desperate he sounded. "You will stop this man, whoever he is?"

"We will do what is possible within the confines of the law," said a voice that might have been Irtok's.

And then there was a hand on his arm, a dismissal as clear as the one he'd been given at the Republicana. Liam's blood spiked; for a dangerous moment, he almost resisted. But his better sense prevailed, and he allowed himself to be led, blindfolded and helpless, out of that roofless hall and into the night.

They left him at the foot of the road leading up to Bayview. There was no sign of the spy; Liam wondered if he'd ever see the man again. Olan shone like a beacon at the top of the hill, as though beckoning him home. The sight left him cold and embittered.

Onnani justice. If there was any justice to be had, whoever was responsible for sabotaging the fleet would be drawn and quartered, or pinned to one of those horrid devices the Erromanians had devised.

That was his first thought, anyway. Then he found himself squirming at the uncomfortable, all-too-familiar image of an Onnani meeting his gruesome end on the points of some imperial torture device. That was extreme, he decided. But still— the miserable cur should be made to *suffer*. The idea that Alden could be conquered because of one man's lust for gold was more than he could bear. It didn't just make him angry; it made him *sick*.

Desperate men my arse. From the way the Shield had spoken of him, this man had been rich once. Going from rich to poor didn't make you desperate, not in any way Liam understood the word. It just meant you had to claw your way through life like everyone else.

His step faltered.

Hang on.

A formerly rich man who'd lost it all. Onnan was a small country, with a small elite. How many men could possibly fit that description? And he'd have to be connected too, wouldn't he? Just having a reason to destroy the fleet wouldn't be enough; he'd have to be in a position to make it happen. If he didn't have money, he'd need some other kind of leverage, or access, to do what he'd done. That narrowed the field even further, surely?

"I'm going to find you," Liam murmured into the night. "I'm going to find you, and I'm going to drag you back to Erroman behind my horse."

He found a new spring in his step as he made his way up the road. For the first time since he'd arrived here, he didn't feel completely lost. *Mostly* lost, maybe, but not completely. He had the scent now, at least. That was something, wasn't it?

The first thin rays of dawn crept into the sky. By their light, Liam saw a figure standing in the road. He took a few more steps, then knelt casually, as if to tie his laces. He'd been told the Ambassador District was safe after dark, but he was too much a soldier to take any chances. As he straightened, dagger tucked into his sleeve, he saw another man materialise from the shadows to stand with the first. He seemed to be clutching a cudgel of some kind.

Which was just how you wanted to greet a new day, really.

"Maybe you cannot read the note?" said the shorter, stockier of the two in heavily accented Erromanian. The pair started to walk toward Liam.

"I'm not so great with my letters," Liam said, stalling as he manoeuvred the dagger into position. "Do you want to tell me what it said?"

"It said you to *leave*," the short man hissed. "It said you to take the others and go." That was definitely a cudgel in his hand, the kind city guards sometimes used to break up brawls.

"You were warning," he continued in his broken Erromanian. He pointed the cudgel at Liam. "Now you pay."

Liam snapped the dagger into his hand and said, "Please go away."

They rushed him together, ready to bash his skull in. Liam liked his chances well enough until a third man stepped out of the bushes and joined the fun. That just felt *excessive*.

The one who'd jumped out of the bushes reached him first. Liam cracked his nose open with an elbow, then landed a heavy blow to his temple, dropping him to the dirt. The thin one was next, just two steps ahead of his stockier friend, but Liam ducked easily under the cudgel and twisted away. He planted his feet, dagger raised, ready. His pulse was steady in his ears, his breath even. He knew this dance. Every step, every variation, a geometry as familiar as walking. Politics and intrigue might be beyond his ken, but *this* . . . this he knew.

The first man was on his knees, still sluggish. Liam focused on the other two. They spread out, trying to flank him. Liam waited until they lunged, then spun around behind the stocky one and opened a nice big gash across his shoulders. When the thin one darted in, Liam threw the sort of punch that usually resulted in fewer teeth. The man weaved for a moment before dropping unceremoniously onto his arse.

Liam backed up, dagger raised. "This isn't going anywhere, lads. No offence, but it looks like it'll take a lot more of you to get this done."

He must have convinced them, because they tore off down the road, leaving behind a few spots of blood and a discarded cudgel.

Liam straightened, stretched a kink in his neck. Not the best way to wake up, but it could have been a lot worse. It probably *would* be worse, he reflected, and soon.

But not today.

SEVENTEEN

Erik woke to a blinding headache. For a moment, he
could not recall where he was or how he came to be
there. Then the memories rushed back in, and he sat bolt
upright.

Or at least, he meant to. But when he tried to brace his hands
at his sides, he found that his wrists were bound. His ankles too.

"Be still."

Erik froze. His eyes raked the gloom, eventually settling
on a dark shape crouched nearby. Somewhere behind him,
a fire snapped. "If you move too suddenly, you will vomit." A
woman's voice, cool and matter-of-fact. She was speaking
Harrami, but with a strange accent.

Another voice spoke, a man this time. Erik could not understand what he said.

"Who are you?" Erik barely managed to force the words past
his dry mouth. Speaking Harrami gave him a sore throat at the
best of times, with its rolling *R*s and hard-edged consonants.

He heard a sharply drawn breath. The man spoke again,
sounding surprised.

"Yes," the woman said, "he does. That is why I used it just
now. I heard him speaking it in his sleep."

Erik cursed inwardly. He must have been dreaming about
Ost, though he had no memory of it. *What did I say?* Nothing
too damning, or he would be dead already.

"Where did you learn that, dog?" The darkness shifted, a
looming shadow in the vague shape of a man. Beside him, the
woman remained crouched, watching. Erik could just make
out the edge of her jaw, framed by long, dark hair. "Why do
you speak the tongue of the *mustevi*?"

Erik shook his head, trying to clear it. The darkness swam around him. "Alix. My friend. Where is she?"

"She sleeps," said the woman.

"What did you do to us?"

"You do not ask questions, dog!" A boot blasted into Erik's side, sending a bright arc of pain through his skull. He curled over himself, coughing, fighting a wave of nausea.

The woman shot to her feet with a string of sharp words. Erik tried to understand, but though it sounded like a form of Harrami, he could not make it out. It seemed to be a different dialect from the one he had been taught.

Footsteps scraped heavily against loose rock, someone storming off into the night. There was a stretch of silence. Then: "He should not have done that." The woman's voice.

Erik swallowed against the nausea still threatening to overtake him. "Do you have water?"

"Here. Sit up."

A curtain of black hair brushed against his face as she helped him to sit. He felt a weight in his lap, and his hands curled around a waterskin. He brought it to his lips and gulped it down.

"Not too much. You will be sick."

Reluctantly, he heeded the advice, passing the waterskin back. "The dart you shot me with. It was poisoned?"

"*Hrak*. Spider venom. We use it for hunting."

"Why did you attack us? Why am I prisoner?"

The woman snorted quietly and uncoiled from her crouch. "You know why."

"We have done no wrong. We are just passing through."

"You should not be. These are not your lands. Imperials are not welcome here."

"Imperials?" Erik shook his head. "I do not . . . I am from Alden."

"Erroman." She spat the word, as if it tasted foul on her tongue. "The Imperial City."

"It has not been that for centuries," Erik said, but he knew he was wasting his time. When it came to matters of war and conquest, memory was eternal.

The woman did not bother to reply. She moved behind him, busying herself with something near the fire.

"My friend," Erik said. "She is not well."

No response.

"She needs water. Let me wake her."

A sizzling sound, as of meat being put on the fire. A moment later, he could smell it; his stomach turned over. "Please—"

"She sleeps. You should sleep, if you wish to feel better. The poison lingers many hours."

Erik tested the bonds at his wrists, but they were securely tied. Besides, his sword and dagger had been taken, and there was nothing to hand he might use as a weapon. The rocks were too small to do much good, even if he had not had poison in his veins. *Patience*, he told himself. *The time will come.* He twisted around to look at the woman. She crouched over a fire, roasting something thin and grizzled-looking on a spit. Erik's mouth watered, which made him want to throw up. He looked for Alix, but it was too dark to see more than a few feet beyond the greedy glow of the flames. "What will you do with us?" he asked.

"You will be brought to the *pasha*. They will decide your fate."

Pasha. He didn't know the word, but it sounded like a council of some kind. "Are they far from here?" he asked.

She took the spit of meat from the fire. "Sleep," she said, and she left him.

Erik tried to defy her in that, but found he could not; with the smell of food gone, his stomach settled, leaving empty exhaustion behind. He fell asleep to the snap of the dying fire and the cold, distant whisper of the mountains.

"Erik."

He opened his eyes and immediately regretted it. Sunlight knifed through his eyeballs. That part, at least, had not improved since last night.

"*Erik.*"

Alix's voice, barely more than a hiss. She lay only a few feet away, looking pale as death. "Thank the gods," she breathed.

Erik glanced around. What he could see of the campsite appeared to be deserted. From the angle of the sun, it was still early. "Where are they?"

"I don't know. They were gone when I woke up. Do you suppose they've left us?"

Erik wriggled his wrists: still bound. "No. They'll be back."

"Kerta's here." Alix gestured with her chin. Rolling over, Erik saw blond curls spilling out from under a bundle of furs. He tried calling to her, but she didn't move.

"What about the others?"

"I don't know." Alix started to sit up, but something stirred out in the trees, and she dropped back down and squeezed her eyes shut. Erik did the same.

A voice spoke; it might have been the man from the night before. Erik opened his eyes a fraction and saw two men making their way out of the trees. The one who had spoken—a tall, raven-haired tribesman with a bow slung over his shoulder—gestured at the camp and said something in a tone of disgust.

"Lazy," said the other one, and both men laughed.

The first man spoke again. Erik found he could make out a word here and there, once he got past the accent. His head had been too muddled last night, but he was certain now it was a form of Harrami, though a different dialect, instead of the High Harrami he had been taught. The men were discussing their prisoners; specifically, how much longer they were prepared to wait before they kicked them awake. Erik decided not to test them; he sat up.

"The dog awakens!" said the tall one in High Harrami, sounding amused. Erik recognised the voice from last night. "Lucky for you. I was going to piss on you."

Alix opened her eyes. She lay with her back to the two men, body tensed and ready. She was thinking about trying something, Erik could tell. He could also tell it was not a good idea. "Can you sit up?" he called to her, deliberately giving her away.

She stared at him incredulously for a moment before wriggling upright. She started to reply, but the tall man swatted the back of her head. "No talking!"

Erik strained against his bonds, but of course it was no good. Alix froze, head bowed, copper hair spilling over her face. For a long, tense moment, Erik feared she was going to do something foolish. In the event, however, she settled for an icy glare.

The shorter of the two laughed. "Look, Fahran, she is . . ."

He spoke his own language now; Erik didn't recognise the word that followed.

The tall one, Fahran, agreed. Grinning, he knelt and grabbed Alix's chin. He made a great show of looking her up and down. He repeated the word, and the two men laughed.

Erik's breath quickened. He had to glance away so the tribesmen would not see the death in his eyes. It would only earn him a beating, or worse. *Patience*, he reminded himself.

Alix jerked her face away. "Water," she said in High Harrami.

Fahran sneered. "So, she speaks the language of the *mustevi* too." He spat in the dirt.

"I speak some small," Alix said. "Your kind attack my home." It was halting, her accent poor, but she made herself understood. Erik was relieved. It had not occurred to him to ask her if she spoke Harrami; given her breeding, he had simply assumed she would.

Fahran certainly had no trouble taking her meaning. His expression darkened, and he jabbed a finger at her chest. "Lies. My people never go into the valley."

Alix's lip curled, but she did not otherwise dignify that with a response. "Water."

"Dabir," the tribesman called over his shoulder.

The other man frowned. "Where is yours?"

Fahran made an impatient gesture, and Dabir threw him a waterskin. He unstopped it and held it out, making as if to hold it to Alix's lips. But instead he upended it over her head, letting it dribble down her face and over her chin. Alix blinked, but she didn't open her mouth. She was too damned stubborn.

"Don't be a fool, Alix," Erik said quietly. "There's no telling when you'll get another chance."

She opened her mouth, letting the water run into it. Then she spat it in the tribesman's face.

Erik was already scrambling to his feet when the blow fell, snapping Alix's head brutally to the side, but Dabir had seen it coming too; he had his knife out, pointed at Erik's chest. *"Sit."*

Fahran grabbed a fistful of copper hair and snarled something Erik could not understand. Alix spat again, blood this time, into the dirt. Fahran released her roughly and rose. Levelling a finger at her, he said, "Remember that. Next time, I will mean it."

Alix shook the hair out of her face. Blood reddened her already-swelling lips, and her cheekbone blossomed where she had been struck, rosy against pale skin. The effect was perversely beautiful.

Erik fought down a surge of fury—and not just at the tribesman. *Why must you be so hotheaded, Alix?* If she didn't learn a little self-control, and soon, she was going to get herself killed. They had argued about it more than once. It was, in fact, the first thing they had ever argued about, a quarrel that had ended with her in his arms, fingers twined in his hair . . .

He shook his head fiercely, banishing the memory. *Where did* that *come from?* It was ridiculously inappropriate—disturbing, even, under the circumstances. Apparently, Alix was not the only one who lacked self-control today.

Fahran stood over Kerta now, grinning. "Time to wake up," he said, and threw the rest of the water in her face. She gasped and tried to sit up, but instead she rolled onto her side, retching. The tribesman laughed roughly. Meanwhile, Dabir shoved another bundle of blankets with his boot; it rolled over, groaning.

"Look," Erik said. "It's Alfred."

Alix nodded, spat again in the dirt.

"Are you all right?"

Another nod, and a guilty look. She knew what she had done was foolish. She always knew—too late.

Kerta sat up, looking pale and miserable. "Is everyone all—"

"No talking!" Fahran whipped around, hand on the curved sword at his hip. Kerta quailed and fell silent.

Dabir dragged them to their feet one by one, cutting the bonds at their ankles so they could walk. Erik looked for Frida, but didn't see her. He hoped that meant the scout had escaped. From what he could see, everyone and everything else had been taken. Their horse stood at the edge of the camp, their armour and weapons piled nearby. *Quite a haul*, Erik thought grimly. It would be the second bloodblade he had lost.

"Erik." Alix gestured at the far end of the camp. An animal carcass hung from a tree, skinned. A panther, he judged.

Dabir noticed them looking at it. "Man eater," he said. "It had the rage."

It must be the same one that killed Leola, Erik thought. "You were tracking it?"

Dabir's eyebrows darted up in the Harrami gesture of assent. "It killed Uthal. Then it led us to you."

Erik cursed their luck. Encountering tribesmen had always been a risk, but they had taken every possible precaution to avoid it, and had very nearly succeeded. If that panther had not had rage . . . if it had not attacked a tribesman, setting his kin on the hunt, leading them here . . . *We were so close. We might have made it.* The accident. The fever. The avalanche. And now this . . . Calculated risks, each and every one; threats known and planned for. Yet to face so many of them, to have them stack up one after another . . . *This mission has been blighted from the start.* Erik wondered what he could have done to offend the gods so.

He looked over what remained of his party. Alix, Kerta, and Alfred all looked sick, but steady. As for Erik, a vicious headache still throbbed between his temples, but he let no hint of it touch his features. His people needed him to be strong. He stood straight, brow smooth, shoulders square, looking each of them in the eye with a calm, cool gaze that said, *Patience.*

Fahran had nearly finished packing up the camp. "Where is Sakhr?" he asked irritably.

"Here." A third man stepped out of the trees, a brace of birds slung over his shoulder. Like the others, he was tall, raven-haired and dark-skinned, beardless. He was also strikingly handsome, moving with a grace that reminded Erik of his dead brother. Like Tom, there was a coiled power about him, like a panther ready to pounce.

Solemn golden eyes scanned the prisoners. "They are ready?" Erik did not catch Fahran's reply—he was still having trouble with the dialect—but it sounded scornful. The new-comer, Sakhr, listened impassively. Then he said, "Qhara is still tracking the other one. She will meet us."

The other one. Erik hoped they meant Frida, and that they never found her. Qhara, he decided, must be the woman he had spoken to the night before.

Fahran gestured at Erik and said something about his tongue.

"Does he?" Sakhr's golden gaze fell on Erik. "Is that common in the imperial lands?" he asked in High Harrami.

"Fairly common," Erik lied. It wouldn't do to let on that he was anyone special.

"Is that so?" Sakhr eyed him shrewdly. "All of you know it, then?"

Kerta spoke up immediately. "Of course. Except Alfred here, who is from a humble family and does not read or write."

Erik said a silent prayer of thanks—for Kerta's quick wits, and her nearly flawless accent.

"And you?" The tribesman turned to Alix.

"Enough."

"A pleasant surprise. It makes things easier." Sakhr turned to Fahran and rattled off a set of instructions, pointing at the captured Kingsword horse, which was now serving as a pack animal. Fahran scowled, but did not object.

A clear pecking order here, Erik thought. Fahran over Dabir, Sakhr over them both. He wondered where the woman, Qhara, fit into it. He would find out soon enough, and he would file that information away too.

They struck out onto the path, heading—Erik glanced at the sun—east. The realisation hit him like a body blow. After everything they had been through . . . So many dead, so far behind schedule . . . And now they were retracing their steps, moving *away* from their goal. "How far is it to reach the *pasha*?" he asked, doing his best to keep the urgency from his voice.

Sakhr glanced over his shoulder. "Save your strength. I will not tell you anything that puts my village at risk."

"We pose no risk to your village. We are on our way to Ost."

"To commune with the *mustevi*, yes. That is obvious."

"Mustevi." Erik shook his head. "I do not know this word."

"It means those who impose their will on others. There is no word for it in the language of Ost. This is ironic, no?" Sakhr glanced back again; the eyes that met Erik's were deepset and clever.

"We have no interest in Harrami politics. We are here to—"

"Save your strength," Sakhr said again. "Save your words for the *pasha*."

Erik's hands curled into fists. There must be *something* he could say to this man, something that might convince him they were not a threat. "The *pasha* . . . how will they decide what to do with us?"

Sakhr shrugged. "They will ask you questions. Then they will decide. It will not take long—there are only two choices."

"Death," Erik guessed.

"That is one choice, yes."

"And the other?"

"If they decide you are no threat to us, that you did not come here to aid the *mustevi*, they will send you home."

Erik swallowed down a cry of dismay. "We cannot go home. You do not understand. It is a matter of life and death, not just for us, but—"

Sakhr turned abruptly, looming over him with his imposing height. "You are lucky to be alive. We could have killed you. Some of us *wanted* to kill you." He looked pointedly at Fahran. "You are still breathing because Qhara insisted. She knows the *pasha* will want to see you, to learn whether you are alone or merely the first of many. If you are lucky again, *very* lucky, the *pasha* will spare you. Do not insult your gods by demanding more." So saying, he continued along the path.

Do not insult your gods. Erik had the inescapable feeling that he already had, for whichever way this went, he would never make it to Ost. He would never convince King Omaïd to enter the war. He had failed, and his men had paid the price in blood.

Eighteen

"That," said Commander Morris, wiping the back of his hand over a bloodied mouth, "was dirty."

"There's no etiquette in war, Morris. No whinging, either." Laughter rippled through the handful of onlookers. Rig rapped his wooden sword against the edge of his shield. "Let's go."

Morris spat blood onto the dirt and squared his feet. His lip curled into a half snarl, a look Rig had learned to respect. Like his commander, Morris fought best when he was in a bit of a temper. *Probably shouldn't goad him, then.* The thought came too late to do Rig any good. A family trait, that.

Morris circled him, closing a little distance with each step. He was taller than Rig, and stronger with a one-handed blade, taking full advantage of his reach. Rig would have felt better with his greatsword, but he'd opted for the blade and buckler today, precisely because he was less comfortable with it. He had a feeling he was going to pay for that choice.

Morris lunged. Rig raised his shield, but at the last moment, Morris reversed the blow and came up under, forcing Rig to twist awkwardly away. He tried to take advantage of his momentum to jab at the neck, but Morris anticipated him and danced aside. Rig carried himself through the turn to come full about, his back to the fort. He barely had time to dig in before Morris was on him again, cutting across his body to come at Rig longside. Wooden swords met with a mighty *crack*. They traded blows, feet shuffling, throwing up dust as they circled and dove, thrust and parried. Sweat stung Rig's eyes and salted his lips; his breath rasped harshly in his ears.

The lead weight in his hand grew heavier, and his right thigh started to protest the lunging.

If there was a better way to get the blood flowing in the morning, Rig hadn't found it.

Admittedly, it lost some of its charm when Morris rang one off his rib cage, hard enough to send a jolt through his whole body. "Nice cut," he grated between clenched teeth. Morris didn't even pause. He came at Rig's injured side, hoping to score another in the same place. That got Rig's blood up. He deflected, but it still hurt like hell. He spat out a curse and went hunting for revenge. He found it in a blow that landed in just the right spot to send a spasm of numbness through Morris's arm; it dangled for a moment, useless. A moment was all Rig needed: He drove his shield into Morris's shoulder and hooked his foot out from under him. The tall man went down with a crash of armour and a blistering oath.

Laughter from the onlookers, men thumping the rail in approval.

Rig braced his hands on his thighs, panting. "Are we done?"

"Depends. Do you want me to be able to take a piss without bleeding?"

Rig grinned. "Your piss is your business, but it would be nice to be able to get on a horse later." He offered a hand.

Morris took it. Then he swept Rig's feet out from under him, bringing him down hard.

"Dirty," Morris growled.

Rig grimaced and clutched at his bruised ribs. "Point taken."

They hobbled over to the rain barrel. Morris washed first, dipping his hands in and throwing a sheet of water over his face. Rig started to dip his own hands, then changed his mind and plunged his whole head in. He came up dripping like a shaggy black dog.

"The next man'll thank you," Morris said dryly.

"Commander general's prerogative."

They headed for the stables. In the foreyard, cavalrymen had already begun saddling their horses, readying for the morning's mission. Rig wanted a look at the upstream ford, to make sure his orders had been carried out precisely. It had been four days since the battle at Whitefish Bridge, and though he doubted the Warlord would be ready to strike again so soon, he wasn't taking any chances. *Not that there's anything to be done if he's as ruthless as they say.* Rig could set up whatever defences he liked, but if Sadik was willing to sacrifice enough of his men, he would get across eventually. Rig simply didn't have the manpower to stop him. He needed that fleet. Needed the Harrami too, though it pained him to admit it. He thought of his brother-in-law in Onnan City, of Erik and Alix in the mountains. *Hope you're getting the job done, you lot, or we're finished.*

In a corner of the yard, Vel was holding service. Men gathered around her, heads bowed, listening to the rise and fall of her musical voice. Rig couldn't hear much at this distance, especially with the wooden mask muffling her words, but it sounded like Erromanian. Scanning the cluster of men, he recognised a few faces. "Look at that," he said to Morris. "Almost as many of ours as Wright's." In the beginning, the Kingswords had given the Onnani priestess a wide berth. Lately, though, her following had grown, apparently to the point where she felt obliged to hold her services in Erromanian. Vel's powers of persuasion, or the men's growing fear of what lay ahead? A little of both, perhaps. "If she keeps up at this rate, the priests are going to get jealous." He was only half joking; already, Reverend Son Orton—also a disciple of Eldora—had come to him complaining about Vel. Apparently, he didn't like having to compete with a foreigner for his following.

Morris eyed the crowd darkly. "I don't like it, General. It's not natural, having a priestess around."

Rig laughed. "Afraid she'll turn them all into rats?"

"I don't see what's funny about it. You and I have seen priestly witchcraft with our own eyes."

"Fair to say Madan was exceptional."

Morris grunted. "And then there's the rest of it."

It took Rig a moment to figure out what he meant. "Ah. It's her feminine wiles you fear."

"You know as well as I do what goes on in the clergy."

"Why, Morris, I had no idea you were such a prude."

"It's nothing to me what religious types get up to in the dark of night. They can commune with their gods any damned way they please. When they become a distraction for the men, that's when I have a problem."

"Haven't heard you complaining about the priests."

Morris gave him a flat look. "A sweating fat man and a balding old codger. Not likely to distract the women, let alone the men. And then there's *her*." He gestured at Vel's undeniably lovely form. "Any surprise her following is growing?"

"What do you suggest I do, Morris? Forbid the men from seeking spiritual solace? That would go over well, I'm sure."

"Send her home."

"Commander Wright would be pleased."

"I don't give a damn what he thinks, begging your pardon, General. And neither should you."

Rig stopped, regarding his second with narrowed eyes. "I'm not buying it. You might be an ill-tempered bastard, but you're no bigot. What's this really about?"

Morris glanced around uneasily. Lowering his voice, he said, "There is a spy among us, General."

"I know."

He frowned. "You never said anything."

"I figured it was obvious. You think it's Vel, I take it?"

"Awfully suspicious that word of our surprise attack gets out almost the moment it's planned. She and Wright were the only other people in the room."

"It's occurred to me." Rig shot a look at the other man and said no more. Morris got the message; he dropped it.

The stablemaster met them near the gate. "Which one will it be today, General?"

"Alger, I think. He acquitted himself well at the bridge."

The stablemaster nodded and withdrew to prepare the destrier. A pair of squires hurried over with Rig's weapons, while a third tended to Morris. Commander Konrad arrived to discuss the formation. When the storm of preparation cleared, Rig was surprised to find Vel leading her own horse out of the stables.

"Good morning, Daughter," he said, a little warily. "Going for a ride?"

"I thought to accompany you." She raised her eyebrows. "Unless you object?"

Rig started to do just that—until he saw the sullen look Morris was directing his way. That annoyed him. He wasn't going to be bullied, least of all by his own second. "No objection," he said, staring Morris down. "So long as you remember that this is a military operation. I can't guarantee your safety, and I can't have you in the way if something unpleasant happens."

Vel bowed her head. "Understood, General."

They rode out with an escort of twenty knights, a formation light enough to be almost symbolic. Rig didn't see any point in wasting good men on escort duty; they were put to better use defending strategic locations like the ford. Morris started out riding abreast of Rig, but when Vel fell in beside them, Rig's second decided he would rather be in the vanguard; he spurred his horse and moved away.

He left behind an awkward silence. It endured for a long while, until Vel said, "This is the place."

"Sorry?"

"That day, on the road. This is where I found you."

Rig glanced around. "I suppose it is."

"It was much colder then." As if to illustrate the point, she unfastened her cloak and slid it off, revealing . . . rather a lot, actually. The neckline of her robes swept off her shoulders and plunged down her back, exposing a smooth, dusky expanse of flawless skin.

"You're staring again, General."

There was no point denying it; he *had* been staring. It had been a long time since he'd seen that much of a woman's back, and he'd always found that particular part of the female form incredibly alluring. The sleek ridges of the shoulder blades, the furrow of the spine, a delicate trail of promise curving all the way down to those wonderful dimples at the base . . .

Still staring, Black.

Rig laughed and looked away. "My apologies. It seems that something drew my eye."

"Does my attire shock you?"

You'd like that, wouldn't you? Aloud, Rig said, "I do wonder how you manage to be warm enough."

"The mere proximity to you is enough to warm me."

"Please."

"I could prove it, if you like." She flashed him a seductive smile.

He left that alone. Eventually, she'd learn that her efforts to scandalise him were a waste of time.

"Thank you for allowing me to come along," she said. "I

needed to get out of there. I have never coped particularly well with being cooped up in one place for too long. Though"—she glanced at the surrounding trees—"I'm not sure this is helping. Do you not find it awfully close in this wood? A little . . . what's the word . . . stifling?"

"These woods are keeping us alive, Daughter. If we were out in the open, Sadik would take us all the more easily."

"I know that, of course. I just miss the sea. I miss its breath on my skin, its sigh in my ears. I have never been without it for so long." A tiny crease appeared between her eyebrows, as if she were annoyed with herself for divulging so much. "You would not understand."

"I might. I feel the same about the mountains sometimes."

"I don't see how it could be the same."

He shrugged. "Okay."

"The mountains are practically the opposite of the sea." She paused, as if waiting for a response. When none was forthcoming, she went on, "A mountain range is a barrier. A wall. The sea is our path to eternity." When Rig still didn't respond, she frowned. "You are very sure of yourself, aren't you?"

He laughed. "How have I offended you, Daughter? By not arguing with you?"

"You haven't *offended* me. I am trying to make conversation, and you just . . . sit there."

"My mother taught me never to disagree with a lady. Especially one who plainly doesn't like to be disagreed with."

"Ah." Vel straightened in her saddle. Rig had a sinking feeling he'd just stepped in it. "You will not engage me because I'm a woman."

"That's not what I meant and you know it."

"I know nothing of the kind."

Rig growled under his breath. This woman's insecurities were *not* his problem; he would be damned if he let himself be goaded into a fight. "Just stop it, all right? You've been trying to catch me out since we met. Get me to prove what a spoiled aristocrat I am, how much I disapprove of you. It's not going to work. You're used to being judged—I get it. But it's nothing to do with me. You want to shield yourself with righteous indignation, that's your business, but leave me out of it."

The rest of the journey passed in icy silence. Vel stared

straight ahead, spine rigid, shoulders square, seemingly oblivious to everything around her. When they reached the ford, she remained astride her horse while Rig and Morris surveyed the defences. She feigned disinterest as Commander Herwin explained his preparations, pretending not to notice the nervous looks he kept shooting her way. *Morris was right*, Rig thought. *I shouldn't have let her come.* She made the men uncomfortable. That might not be right, but it was a fact. One she was all too accustomed to, had learned to expect as a foregone conclusion, and so armed herself preemptively against it. Rig understood that, but it didn't make her any easier to deal with.

The ride back was equally pleasant, especially once it started to rain. Between the cold, Vel's silence, and the sadly inadequate timber palisades he'd just surveyed, Rig was in a foul humour by the time they reached the fort. His boots had hardly hit the dirt before he stalked off to his quarters for a change of clothing and some warmed wine. That went some way to improving his mood, so when the knock came, he managed to receive it with something approaching civility. "Who is it?"

"Vel."

He swore under his breath. So much for his mood clearing up. He didn't bother to disguise his annoyance when he opened the door. "What is it, Daughter?"

"I came to tell you that you're wrong." She said it matter-of-factly, as though she were reporting on the weather.

"Yeah, all right, thanks for letting me know." He started to close the door, but Vel jammed a foot in it.

"Wait."

He raised his eyebrows expectantly.

The corner of her mouth twitched, hinting at a smile. "Do you really want to discuss this in the common room, General?" She cast a meaningful glance over her shoulder at the men milling about.

Sighing, Rig stood aside to let her in.

"Thank you." She hovered for a moment, as if waiting for something. When Rig didn't react, she shrugged and went for the wine.

"Help yourself," he said dryly.

Her back was to him as she poured, the V of her neckline

framing a smooth canvas of caramel skin. "You are wrong, you know."

"So you said."

"I'm not trying to catch you out." She turned, sipped her wine, dark eyes gazing at him over the rim of her cup. When she lowered it, she moistened her lips with her tongue. "It is true that perhaps I have made certain . . . assumptions . . . about you. About what you would think of me. If I have been wrong about them, I'm sorry."

Rig rubbed his eyes. It was early afternoon, but he was exhausted, and this conversation wasn't helping. "Okay. Is that all?"

"Headache, General?" She sidled up to him, lashes lowered, mouth curved like a barbarian's blade. "I can help with that, if you like."

"I'm not in the mood for this, Vel. What do you *want*?"

The coy look vanished. "What I want is for you to let me help you. You need me, whether you realise it or not. We both saw the state of those defences today. Little more than a thicket of sharpened logs. You will be lucky to hold the Warlord for an hour with that."

"And how to you propose to help me?" He reached past her for the wine jug, and when he leaned in, the scent of perfume hit his nose. She hadn't been wearing it before, he was sure of it. It was a stirring fragrance; he would have noticed.

She lifted the jug from his hands, her fingers brushing his as she took it. She stood just close enough to offer a glimpse of the perfect valley between her breasts. "If the Andithyrian Resistance were to keep Sadik busy, it might give you time to build something more permanent at the ford." She gazed up at him through those long lashes.

Rig laughed. "I give you full marks for persistence, Daughter, but subtlety is not your strong suit."

Her sultry look collapsed into a scowl. "You think you have it all figured out, don't you?"

"Maybe not all of it, but enough."

"I'm trying to seduce you in order to get my way, is that it?"

"You tell me."

"I suppose you think I'm the spy too."

Rig's smile vanished. He set his cup down on the table, carefully. "Who said anything about a spy?"

She made a dismissive gesture. "Of course there is a spy. How else would Sadik have known of your plans to blow the bridge? Except that wasn't *really* the plan, a fact you kept secret from the foreigners, perhaps because you already knew you had a spy in your ranks." She closed in on him again, her chin turned up defiantly. "What do you think, General? Which of us is it? The commander, or his pet witch of a priestess? *Oh!*" Her eyes rounded, and she brought her fingers to her lips. "Maybe it's *both!*"

"Are you through?"

She sniffed and turned away. Snatching up her wine cup, she filled it again and threw back a mouthful.

"Are you sure you're in the right robes, Daughter? Maybe Ardin would suit you better."

Her shoulders tensed, and for a moment, Rig fully expected to get a cup of wine in the face. Instead, she blew out a resigned laugh. "If you think these robes are scandalous, you should see what the priestesses of Ardin wear."

"Scandalous? Those? Hardly."

"Not in Alden, perhaps, but my people are more conservative. Back home, these are barely decent."

"Which is why you wear them, of course."

She smiled wearily. "Defensive provocation, I think you called it."

Rig took her cup and filled it one last time. "I'll let you in on a secret, Daughter. You might not be able to tell, what with my refined manners and my soft, manicured hands"—he held up a calloused palm for her to inspect—"but I'm actually a bit of a brute. So the next time you go out of your way to shock me, just remember it's going to take a lot more than a dip in your dress."

She smiled again, only this time, it reached all the way to her eyes. "That sounds like a challenge."

He sipped his wine, letting what was left of the ice between them thaw while he chose his next words. "As for the rest, I agree with you. I do have a spy on my hands, and bigger problems besides. We can't hold the border with timber palisades and a few makeshift towers."

"Sadik will throw everything he has at you, as many men as it takes to break through your defences."

"And he'll still outnumber us when he's through. I know." Rig paused, giving himself one last chance to back out. But it was no good—he was out of options. Sadik had seen to that. Rig could either sit here and wait for death to come to them, or he could risk it all. Again. Taking a deep breath, he said, "Which is why I've decided to let you go."

Vel stared at him, as if she couldn't quite believe it. Not that Rig blamed her—he could barely believe it himself. "Truly? You will let me seek out the Resistance?"

"I don't have much choice. My spies aren't getting anywhere, and I need a breakthrough, fast."

"You will have it," Vel promised, her eyes bright and eager.

"I can get you across the river, but after that, you're on your own." He fixed her with a long, grim look, a deliberate counterweight to her enthusiasm. "Are you sure about this? If you're caught . . ."

"I won't be."

"No unnecessary risks. We need this, Vel. We need it very badly."

"I won't let you down, General." She stood on her toes and planted a kiss on his lips, like a child who'd been given what she wanted for her birthday. "I will start preparing immediately."

She left him standing by the hearth, sipping warmed wine, wondering if he'd just made a terrible mistake.

NINETEEN

† "**I**n the middle of the night," said Rona Brown. *"Alone."* She shook her head, dark eyes flashing with anger. When she looked at him like that, she reminded him of Allie.

"I asked if I could bring you along." Liam's gaze took in his officers, all three of whom sat across from him, looking annoyed. "The spy refused. What choice did I have? We need to get at the truth here, whatever it takes."

Rona scowled. "Even if it takes you being jumped by assassins?"

"Let's not be dramatic. If they'd really meant to kill me, they would have been armed with more than sticks. They were just some thugs sent to scare me, that's all, get me to back off."

"And what about the spy?" Rona persisted. "When were you going to tell us about him?"

"Er . . ." Liam raked his fingers through his hair.

"Pretty reckless, Commander," Ide put in. "Starting to think maybe Alix is a bad influence."

"Funny. Look, this is the first good lead we've had. I don't plan on making a habit of it."

"That's what you said when we went to see the shipwright," Rona reminded him.

"What if the spy comes back?" Dain asked. "What if he offers to take you to the Sons of the Revolution, or the Freemen?"

"What if," said Rona, "he comes back to *kill* you?"

Liam sighed. "All right, I'm properly chastised. Now is anyone interested in hearing what I found out, or shall I just go chat to Rudi?"

An exchange of sulky glances. "Go on, then," Ide said.

"The Shield didn't come right out and say it, but they know who's behind this. They promised to try to stop him, but I'm not holding my breath. I say we take care of this ourselves."

"So who is it?" Dain asked.

"They didn't give me a name. Wanted him to face Onnani justice, they said. But they did let slip some details that I think we can use." He related what the Shield had told him, about a rich man who'd lost everything. "On top of that, I figure he'd have to have some connection to the fleet, or ships in general, in order to get it done. If we put those pieces together, we can find this son of a bitch."

Dain grunted thoughtfully. "That could work, provided we can find someone willing to serve it up on the Onnani elite."

"As soon as I got back this morning, I woke Shef and asked him to send for Ash Bookman."

"What makes you think he'll tell you anything?" Rona asked. "He's a part of that world too."

"For now, I'm taking Kar at his word that he wants this situation resolved. After all, it reflects badly on him and his government."

Ide grinned. "Gotta admit, Commander, I'm impressed. Didn't know you had it in you, all this sleuthing."

"It's a bit early to get excited." That was the commander of the White Wolves talking. Liam was bloody *delighted*.

He was in such a good mood that he even tried the shrivelled fish at breakfast that morning. It wasn't half bad. Vastly inferior to bacon, obviously, but edible.

Ash Bookman arrived just as Liam and his officers were repairing to the sunroom. Kar's secretary looked tidy and dignified in a plain doublet and breeches, his smooth young face intelligent and serious. Liam gestured for the secretary to sit. "Thought we'd get started early, if you don't mind."

"Not at all, Your Highness." Drawing an ink bottle and quill from his pocket, Ash placed them on a side table and sat primly, leather notebook at the ready.

"I'm going to start with some questions, and they might sound a little odd."

Ash smiled politely. "I'm sure they won't, Your Highness."

"How many people live in Onnan City, would you say?"

"We estimate approximately fifty-five thousand, Your Highness."

Liam made a face. "Listen, about the *Your Highness* thing. It's not . . . I'd just rather you didn't."

The secretary blinked in mild astonishment. "As you wish . . . er . . . Commander?"

"That's fine. So anyway, the fifty-five thousand . . . I imagine most of them are fisherfolk, bakers, tailors, that sort of thing."

"Yes, Your . . ." He swallowed. "Yes."

"How many men in this city would you consider to be wealthy?"

Ash furrowed his brow. "I suppose that depends. How would you define wealthy?"

A good question. Before he'd taken a second name, Liam would have defined *wealthy* as having a proper bed to sleep in. He glanced at Rona Brown, but she'd probably think of it as having an estate the size of a small country. Somehow, Liam didn't think either of those answers would help.

Dain Cooper came to his rescue. "Able to afford a place like this, say." He made a sweeping gesture, encompassing the gleaming white splendour of Bayview. "Or at least a home in the Ambassador District."

"In that case, very few indeed. There are about fifty homes in this quarter of the city, plus a few estates nearby. Call it seventy or so, to be safe."

That sounded about right, roughly the same ratio as noblemen to commoners back home. "And of those seventy or so," Liam asked, "have any fallen on hard times?"

Ash Bookman's eyes narrowed a fraction. "I'm not sure what you mean, Commander."

Liam smiled and reclined in his chair, all casual charm. "No need to be uncomfortable, Ash. It's a simple question. Have any of the wealthy families in Onnan City lost their fortunes over the past few years?"

The secretary's gaze fell to his notebook, as though he might find the answer there. "I'm not a wealthy man myself," he said. "Such men rarely take me into their confidence."

"You're the secretary of the first speaker of the Republicana," Liam said, still smiling. "You must hear all kinds of things."

"Discretion is a basic requirement of my function. I don't

see what use such gossip would be, and it would be vulgar of me to spread it."

"So you do know, then," Dain Cooper said.

The secretary frowned. "I know many things, which if I thought they were relevant, I would certainly share."

"I was under the impression you were supposed to help me, Ash."

"Please, Your . . . Commander. I'm not being deliberately obstinate. I just don't think it's appropriate for me to traffic in rumours, particularly if I don't see how it could possibly aid your cause."

"You'll just have to take my word for it. Unless you'd rather I asked Kar to send me someone else." Liam raised his eyebrows significantly.

A pained look passed through Ash Bookman's eyes. He twirled the quill in his fingers, black feather spinning. "Very well." He moistened his lips. "Two years ago, a particularly prominent family lost most of their wealth when half of their merchant fleet went down in a storm, along with valuable cargo. A most unfortunate affair. The ships' owner had borrowed heavily to secure that cargo, and it left him in . . . a delicate position." He cleared his throat. "Happily, his friends intervened to purchase his home, leaving him with enough capital to continue his business and his career. Over time, he will buy back his estate, and I'm sure he will recover admirably."

"Name?" Liam asked.

"Perhaps you could ask First Speaker Kar? I would rather not—"

"*Who*, Ash?"

Dark eyes met his, smouldering with resentment. "Welin," the secretary said. "The name is Welin." He snapped the leather-bound book shut. "Will that be all, Commander?"

Liam realised that his mouth had fallen open just a little. "Er, yes, thank you. I'll send for you later if I need anything." Ash Bookman rose and bowed stiffly. Then he turned to Dain and said something terse in Onnani. He left them standing there in stunned silence.

"Wow," said Ide, succinctly.

Liam closed his eyes and rubbed his temples. "Just to make

sure I actually heard that right—did he just say that the man we're looking for is *Defence Consul Welin*?"

"That's what I heard," Ide said. "And something else too. What did he say to you, Dain?"

The Onnani knight frowned at the empty doorway. "He said, *I want no part of this*. I'm not sure what he meant."

Liam had bigger worries. "Welin. Didn't see that coming. In a way, it makes sense."

"But in another way," said Rona, "it doesn't."

Liam looked at her grimly. He had the distinct feeling she was about to rip a huge, gaping hole in his sails.

He was right. "If what Ash told us is true," she said, "Welin was out of immediate financial danger. And he's the heir apparent to First Speaker Kar. Why endanger all that to throw in with the enemy?"

A good point. As a motive for treason, it did seem a little weak. "On top of which," Liam said, "he's the sodding *defence consul*."

"You said he'd need access," Ide pointed out.

"But he has *too much* access," Rona said. "He's the obvious one to blame, politically if nothing else. If there were anything to catch him on, surely his enemies would have found it already."

His enemies . . .

Liam felt something drain from him then, like iron leaking from his spine. "I get it." He nodded, jaw twitching in anger. "I get it now."

Rona sighed. She understood, though her fellow officers hadn't caught on yet.

"Sorry, Commander," said Dain. "Get what?"

Reaching into an inside pocket, Liam drew out a scroll and tossed it on the table. "Chairman Irtok. Worker's Alliance, priest of Olan. *A Shield, fittingly.*"

"And a strong contender for leader of the Alliance," Rona added.

"A rival of Kar's," Liam said, "or at least he was. But Kar has done his two terms as first speaker. So now"—he pointed at the scroll—"he's a rival of Welin's."

"And it was the Shield that gave you the information," Dain said, understanding dawning. "Awfully convenient. With Welin out of the way, they'd be sure of having one of their brothers at the helm of the league."

"And well placed to be first speaker next year," Rona finished.

Liam shook his head. He'd been caught. Thrown a shiny bit of bait, and he'd taken it, hook and all. And now Ash Bookman was on his way back to First Speaker Kar, with news that the nosy Prince of Alden suspected his right-hand man of treason. Liam wouldn't be the least bit surprised if he never saw Ash, or the first speaker, again.

For a handful of hours, there'd been wind in his sails. The idea that maybe, just maybe, he wasn't completely useless after all. So much for that.

I sure hope you're sweeping King Omaïd off his feet, Erik, he thought bitterly. *Because I have a feeling we won't be seeing a fleet anytime soon.*

Liam sat with his chin propped on his knuckles, composing a letter in his head. He'd left off actually writing them days ago. He felt pathetic enough without Alix arriving in Ost to find a library's worth of her husband's whinging. Frankly, the less she knew about his time here, the better. He didn't need her reading a blow-by-blow account of his failures, especially not with Erik's smooth diplomacy to contrast it against, to prove how very *wanting* Liam was in comparison with his regal brother. He couldn't have that, but he did miss confiding in her, terribly. So he sat on his balcony, gazed out at the glittering darkness, and wrote to her in his head.

A knock sounded softly behind him. Rudi sprang to his feet, growling. "Down," Liam said, waving the wolfhound away. Surprisingly, Rudi obeyed.

"Commander." Rona Brown carried a jug and a pair of cups. "I thought you might need a drink."

"Is it the kind that melts your brain and leaves you a drooling idiot?"

She smiled. "I don't think so."

"Pity." He stood aside to let her in.

"Nice," she said, scanning his chambers.

"It's nicer outside." He crooked his neck, showing her to the balcony.

Rona closed her eyes and breathed deeply of the salt air. "You're right, it is nice. I wish I had one of these off my room. The rose window is exquisite." She traced a finger along the fine lead bones of the stained glass.

"Throws some terrifying shadows on the floor, though, let me tell you. Here, let me get that." Liam took the jug. "Wouldn't be very gallant of me to let you pour."

She laughed and settled onto the stone bench overlooking the valley. "Since when do I need gallantry?"

"Every woman needs gallantry now and then." He handed her a cup of wine. "Even if she could kill you with her bare hands."

"I doubt I could kill anyone with my bare hands. Least of all you."

"Yes, I'm quite formidable." It came out more acerbic than he'd intended.

"You are," she said, gazing up at him. The wind carried a slip of hair across her face, catching it on the corner of her mouth. She had her father's eyes, Liam decided, round and dark, with a slumbering fierceness that threatened to flame to life at any moment.

He sank down on the bench beside her. "Sorry. I'm not sulking, really." A grin found its way onto his face. "Well. Maybe a *bit*."

"A little sulking is all right, under the circumstances."

Liam sighed. "I fell for it completely. Everything the Shield fed me. All those carefully dropped hints, the *oh-dear-I've-said-too-much* act. I wanted so badly to believe I was finally on to something."

Rona nodded, sipped her wine. The tendril of hair still hugged the curve of her jaw; Liam resisted the urge to brush it away. "Anyone would have fallen for it, at least at first."

Erik wouldn't have, Liam thought. *Alix wouldn't have.* After all the ruthless politicking on display here, they would have known to question the information they'd been given. To look for the angle. They'd most likely have found it too, before burning their bridges with the first speaker of the Republicana. *Not you, though, you great sap.* "This just isn't me," he muttered into his cup.

"You should be proud of that. It means you're a good man."

"That's a nice varnish to put on it."

"It's not varnish."

Something in her voice made Liam glance over. She actually looked a little hurt, though he couldn't imagine why. "What's wrong?"

"Nothing."

"See, now, not everyone would believe you, but it turns out I'm incredibly gullible."

That earned him a smile. She brushed the stray bit of hair off her face, looking suddenly shy. "It's just . . . I don't like it when you speak that way about yourself. I know this hasn't been easy for you, but you mustn't let it dent your confidence."

"Easy for you to say. You know this world, how to live in it. You saw through the Shield's ruse quickly enough."

"That's different. I was raised at court. You wouldn't pick up a paintbrush for the first time and instantly expect to be a master artist, would you?"

"I'll have you know I am a deft hand at painting. I have a whole collection of stick figures doing battle with vicious beasts that look suspiciously like my dog."

She laughed. "I'd very much like to see those, Commander. But my point is, you have a lot of wonderful qualities, and if being a cold-blooded cynic isn't one of them, maybe you should consider that a blessing."

Her eyes held his, as if waiting for a reply. Liam couldn't think of a damned thing to say except, "Thank you."

He drained his cup and poured another. Rona did the same. "It really is wonderful out here," she said wistfully.

"I haven't enjoyed much about being in Onnan City, but I have enjoyed being near the sea. There's something about the size of it. The . . . indifference, I suppose. It makes me feel better about feeling insignificant, like that's the only reasonable response." He frowned. "If that makes sense."

"It does."

Liam had a feeling he could start bleating like a goat and she'd declare it the very soul of wisdom, but he didn't hold it against her. She was trying to cheer him up, and he appreciated that. "What about you?" he asked. "Is the ocean everything you imagined?"

"I'm not sure. I didn't really think about it much until we were on our way here. I never expected to see it, I suppose." She smiled and shook her head. "I certainly never expected to be here with you. And the others." She took a quick sip of her wine.

"Yes, it did rather sneak up on us, didn't it?"

A companionable silence settled between them. Liam hadn't felt this relaxed in days. *You could have had this all along*, he thought, *if you hadn't shut yourself away from everyone.* It brought to mind something Alix had said about Erik once, about how he always felt the need to shoulder his burdens alone. Maybe Liam and his brother had something in common after all.

Well, he'd had enough of that. He drained his cup again. And again.

Later, when the flickering lights started to go out in the valley below, Liam said, "You lied to me, Rona Brown."

"Never."

"You did. This *is* the stuff that melts your brain and leaves you a drooling idiot."

She leaned in close, pretending to peer at him. "No drool, but I do think there's a hint of insanity there."

"Pay that no mind. It comes and goes."

"Ide was right, you know."

Liam flicked an eyebrow. "About?"

"You do giggle when you've been drinking."

"Nonsense. My laugh is very manly."

Rona thumped a fist against her chest in a sloppy salute. "Aye, Commander."

Commander. He'd almost managed to forget, just for a moment. Sighing, Liam swirled the dregs of the wine in the bottom of his cup.

"Oh, no." Rona gave him a helpless look. "What did I say?"

"Nothing. It's . . ." He shook his head. "I've no idea what happens tomorrow, Rona. I'm completely lost."

She stirred beside him; Liam felt a hand on his arm. He looked over to find her gazing up at him with warm eyes. "You're not lost," she said. "Or at least, you're not alone."

In the garden around them, crickets chirped rhythmically; below that, barely discernible, the distant rush of the sea. Liam was suddenly keenly aware of how light-headed he was. "I'd better turn in," he said, rising.

She looked away, nodded. "Of course. Until tomorrow, then."

"Until tomorrow," Liam said, and he showed her out.

As he lay on his bed, he tried to finish composing his letter to Alix, but he couldn't remember where he'd left off. In fact, he couldn't think of a single thing to say.

TWENTY

"Wake up." A boot nudged Alix's side. "It is time to go."

Without waiting for a response, Sakhr moved on to rouse the others. Alix shuffled to her feet; as always, her gaze sought out Erik first. He was already up, looking out over the valley with an unreadable expression. She could almost hear the gears turning in his head, though she couldn't guess what he was thinking. He'd spoken even less than Sakhr these past two days. He was still, watchful, taking in everything and communicating only in long, reassuring glances. Though his insides must have been swirling with fear, he didn't show it. He wore the royal mask: cool, dignified, utterly inscrutable. Wore it so well, in fact, that if he wasn't careful, he'd give himself away as something other than ordinary. That could be disastrous; if the tribesmen had any notion of who Erik really was, they would more than likely execute him on the spot.

The tribesmen were occupied packing up the camp; judging that they were sufficiently distracted, Alix dared a few words with her king. "Still no sign of Frida?"

Erik's eyes tracked the movements of their captors, ever alert. "The woman, Qhara, is back. I suppose that means she either killed Frida or gave up looking for her."

"Frida's good, but if these tribesmen are half the trackers they're meant to be . . ."

"Still, we shouldn't give up hope."

Alix knew he was right, but that didn't make it easy to follow the advice. "We're still heading southeast."

"I know."

"We've lost days. At this rate . . ."

"I *know*, Alix. We must be patient. Our chance will come."

"Maybe, but if we wait too long, we'll miss it. For all we know, we're only a few hours away from their village. Out here, there are four of us and four of them."

Blue eyes slid to her, and an impatient breath clouded the chill air between them. "Four of them armed with bows and blades, and four of us with our wrists bound, armed with nothing but our wits. Be sensible, Alix. We must wait until the odds shift in our favour."

"And if that doesn't happen?"

"Then we shift them ourselves." So saying, he started across the camp. There was a newcomer, Alix realised, a black-haired woman she hadn't seen before. *Qhara*, Erik had called her. There was something familiar about her, a dark, solemn beauty Alix had seen somewhere before. It took her a moment to place it, but then she glanced over at Sakhr, and she understood. *Siblings.* She'd bet a crown on it.

"Did you find her?" Erik asked. "Our friend?"

The woman didn't answer at first; she regarded Erik impassively, as though weighing whether he merited a response.

"I am worried for her," Erik said. "We already lost one friend to the panther."

"She did not fall to the panther. Sakhr killed it before we caught you."

Alix was relieved to be able to follow the conversation easily. Like most people trying to master a foreign language, she understood far more than she spoke, but she sometimes had trouble with Fahran and Dabir. Fortunately, Qhara spoke clearly, with a milder accent than her kinsmen.

Casually, Erik asked, "How far to the *pasha*?"

The question hadn't got him anywhere with Sakhr, and it didn't get him anywhere now. "You should eat something," the woman said, stooping to pick up a pack.

"I can eat later, when we stop at midday. Or perhaps you will hunt something for supper."

The woman smiled to herself as she stuffed a blanket into her pack. "You think you are clever, Imperial? I will tell you what I wish to tell you, and no more. You cannot trick it out of me."

"My name is not Imperial. It is Erik."

She shrugged indifferently.

"And you are Qhara."

She shouldered the pack and stood. "Erik. What does it mean, this name?"

He hadn't anticipated the question; Alix could tell by the stiffening of his shoulders. The answer could hardly be worse under the circumstances. Telling someone who referred to their own king as *the oppressor* that your name meant *ruler of all* was probably not a good idea.

"It means me," Erik said.

The woman's glanced flicked over him dismissively. She started to walk away.

"Do you know why we are going to Ost?" Erik asked her. He seemed to have decided she was the leader here, or at least the one to whom he should be pleading his case. It was the most talking he'd done in two days.

"I do not care, Imperial Erik."

"You will."

Her expression went cold, and she turned to face him. "And why is that?"

"Because a great danger threatens my land, and yours."

"If you mean the red men, they are no concern of ours."

The red men. She had to be referring to the Trionate, their crimson tabards. They'd come through the mountains before, Alix recalled, on their way to the Blacklands. The tribes had let them pass. Left them to invade from the west, burning and pillaging, sacking Alix's childhood home. She had forgotten that until this moment; it made her blood boil in her veins.

"You are wrong," Erik said. "By the time you realise it, it may be too late."

"It is too late for you to eat," Qhara said. "We will not be stopping."

Damn.

He'd thought he sensed an opening, but apparently he had imagined it. The woman walked away from him as though he were nattering nonsense. Meanwhile, her brother—Erik assumed they were siblings, from the resemblance—was all but smirking at him from across the campsite, as if to say, *Nice try, fool.*

He knew that he had a finite number of chances to get through to his captors. Only so many arrows in his quiver, and he had just wasted one. He would have to choose his openings more judiciously. That would be difficult enough on his own, but he had the others to contend with. He was not worried about Kerta; she was too dutiful to try anything without his leave. Alfred was an unknown quantity. And then there was Alix.

From the look on her face, Erik could tell she was thinking about Blackhold. About the fact that the Harrami tribes—perhaps this very tribe—had allowed the Oridians to pass unmolested through the mountains in order to invade her homeland. Alix was hotheaded at the best of times; with revenge on her mind, Erik worried that she would do something genuinely foolish. He could not afford that. Even if by some miracle they escaped, they would not make it far. Qhara's tribe would hunt them down. And this time, there would be no mercy.

They spent the morning working their way down into the valley. The tribesmen stayed off the main path, leading them through dense pine forest and over steep rocky slopes. The going was slow, at least for the Aldenians. They got caught up in wild rosebushes, slipped and stumbled on loose scree. The Harrami, meanwhile, picked their way over the landscape with the surefootedness of mountain goats, pausing every now and then to cast impatient looks over their shoulders, prompting Fahran, who brought up the rear, to shove the nearest laggard in the back.

Qhara was true to her word: They did not stop until dusk, at a clearing near a small lake. Sakhr went hunting, in spite of the dark. The other tribesmen busied themselves with camp chores, leaving Qhara to stand guard. She lingered near Erik, watching him closely, her expression unreadable as always.

He decided to try again. "Have you ever been abroad?"

Her mouth twisted wryly. "You want to make meaningless talk with me, Imperial Erik?"

"Why not? There is nothing else to do. Unless you are afraid I will trick you after all."

"Why do you care where I have been?"

"I have always wondered what it must be like for you. The tribes, I mean. Not going anywhere, not learning anything of the wider world. It must be very . . ." He paused, searching for the right word. "Limiting."

"You think we are barbarians, yes? That we know nothing of the world?"

"Have you even been to Ost?"

Irritation darkened her eyes. *Careful, Erik.* It was a delicate game he was playing, trying to nettle her enough to talk, but not so much that she would close down. There was a time he would have been confident of managing the balance deftly, but lately, he'd found balance strangely difficult to maintain.

"I have been to Ost," Qhara said. "And I have been to the imperial lands."

"Of course," Alix put in bitterly. "You come to raid."

Qhara fixed her with an icy stare. "I came to look. I raided nothing."

"So you were curious," Erik said, anxious to steer the conversation back on course.

"Even barbarians can be curious, Imperial Erik."

"Just Erik, please. So you have been to Alden, and you have been to Ost. Where else? Oridia, perhaps?"

"I know of Oridia, but I have not been there."

"You know of it." Erik made a point of sounding surprised. That annoyed her. "Do not imagine that just because we choose not to submit ourselves to the yoke of the *mustevi*, we are ignorant. We have maps. We have stories. I know my history."

"Yes, I have noticed," Erik said. "You seem to be rather fixated on history, in fact. Ancient history." That earned him a wry smile, at least. He was making progress, however halting. It was like threading a needle with a trembling hand, only the stakes were life and death. If he could not win this woman's sympathy, they were lost. "I was only surprised that you say you know Oridia, because earlier it seemed you did not. The red men, you called them. You said they were no concern of yours."

"They are not."

Erik shook his head. "I am confused. You say you know the Trionate, and that they are not a threat to you. And yet you say you know your history. One of these things cannot be true."

"Mind your tongue, Imperial!" This from Fahran, who had been eavesdropping by the fire. He was on his feet now, but Qhara waved him off.

She dropped to her haunches in front of Erik. Even in the shadows, he could see the angry glint in her green-gold eyes. "You call me a liar?"

He was on thin ice now, but he forged ahead. "Do you know of Andithyri?"

"Of course. It is the land where the white-hairs fled when we crushed your empire. The leaders of the imperials, the so-called purebloods."

"They are leaders of nothing. Not even their own land. The Trionate of Oridia took it from them. Invaded, two summers ago. There is no Andithyri now."

"Swallowed by an empire? A fitting fate."

"The third country the Trionate has swallowed in ten years," Erik said.

Green-gold eyes narrowed. "And now they will swallow yours, yes? And so you would plead with the *mustevi* for help?" She shrugged. "You would not have got it, Imperial Erik. They are cowards, and they are weak. Had it not been for my people, your empire would still be standing."

"Instead it is rubble!" Fahran crowed. "Shattered into three pieces, broken apart by the might of the *sukhadan*!" He burst into song, waving his arms about as though to rouse an invisible crowd. A battle song, by the sounds of it; Dabir joined in dutifully.

Qhara rose from her crouch. She said something to Fahran about bathing in the lake and headed up the rocky shore, tugging at her clothing as she went. Watching her go, Erik felt a cold weight settle in his stomach. He had failed again. He would not win her over today, and that meant one more day wasted, handed to the Trionate like a gift. How many more could he lose before they were utterly spent? *Perhaps none*, he thought dully. *Perhaps they are spent already . . .*

Fahran and Dabir continued to sing. One of them procured a leather flask, presumably containing some kind of spirit.

"Listen to them," Alix growled under her breath. "You'd think they personally brought down the empire."

"Don't see how the mountain men had much to do with it at all," Alfred added resentfully. "The empire was dying long before these vultures showed up. Slave revolt saw to that. Anyone should be singing, it's the fishmen."

The song subsided, but only long enough for the tribesmen to take a few generous slugs of drink. Then Fahran started up another verse, even more lustily than before. Alix and Alfred exchanged a dark look.

"Why do they hate us so much?" Kerta whispered. "It's not as if we were there."

"I suppose they consider us heirs to the empire," Erik said.

"But we aren't, not really. We inherited the capital, maybe, but the Andithyri were the true imperial race, and they fled Erroman centuries ago. We aren't even their descendants, unless you count a few mixed-bloods like Aldrich the White."

Erik suppressed a bitter smile. His ancestor's dubious claims of Andithyri blood were what brought him the throne; it would be deeply ironic if it were now to bring about the end of his line. Aloud, he said, "I doubt that would persuade our friends. History is not truth, Kerta. It is a story shared."

The singing grew louder. Erik closed his eyes, trying to block it out. There had to be a way to get through to Qhara. If he could just—

A shout sounded. Erik's eyes snapped open. A blur of shadow moved against the fire—Alfred. Somehow, he had managed to get his hands free; he threw himself at Fahran.

"No!" Erik was on his feet now too, but Alfred was past hearing. He crashed into Fahran, sending them both tumbling onto the rocks. Dabir drew his sword, but Alix was there, smashing the heel of her boot into the back of his knee. He buckled, and she struck him in the temple with both hands. She snatched up his sword, but her wrists were still bound, and before she could do anything with it, Dabir had seized her ankles and dragged her down.

Erik had no choice now; he lunged toward Alix, not even sure what he intended to do. It didn't matter; he never got the chance. An arrow slammed into the back of his shoulder. He fell to one knee, pain exploding through the left side of his body. Another arrow bounced off the rocks in front of Kerta, drawing her up short.

Alfred had managed to get on top of Fahran and was raining blows down on the tribesman's face. He didn't even see the arrow that took him; he was dead before he hit the ground.

Alix was oblivious to the danger. She had her arms around Dabir's neck, boots planted in the small of his back, strangling him with the ropes at her wrists.

Erik heard a bow creak behind him. "Stop!" He staggered to his feet, throwing himself between Alix and the weapon trained on her heart. *"Alix, stop!"*

For a moment, he thought she hadn't heard. He thought the bow creaked again. He thought his heart ceased to beat. Then Alix yanked her arms away and shoved Dabir with her boot, leaving him to splutter and cough on his hands and knees.

Footfalls on the rocks. Erik turned to find Qhara, bow in hand, naked from the waist up, striding up the shore. "Do not hurt her," he said. "Please. It was the other one who started it. We had no choice. It was a mistake."

"It was a mistake," Qhara agreed icily. "A very bad one."

TWENTY-ONE

"Our best information puts them in this area," Rig said, tracing a circle, "but that's approximate to say the least."

Vel's eager gaze devoured the map. "Understandable. If your information was better, you would not need me."

"Our scouts have had most luck following this route. There's a game trail through the brush on the far side of the river. Follow it south for about half a day. That should get you far enough clear of the enemy's lookouts that you can swerve back to the highway, about here."

"At which point," Morris put in, "you are a woman alone on the highway, after dark, with the wrong hair colour."

Rig threw a wry look over his shoulder. "Why, Morris, one would almost think you disapproved of this venture."

"I cannot imagine why," Vel said. "It seems like the perfect opportunity to be rid of me."

Morris shifted uncomfortably and looked away. Beside him, Wright forced an awkward laugh. "Joking aside, Daughter, the commander does have a point." Like Morris, he stood back from the map, arms folded in a picture of reluctance— though for very different reasons. "I'm afraid I must renew my protest. This is too dangerous."

"War is dangerous, Commander Wright. Besides, my story is entirely plausible. I would hardly be the first Onnani missionary seeking to soothe spiritual woes in wartime. Or perhaps I am merely heading to Timra to view the relics of the Holy Virtues, as my own brother once did."

"That might help you avoid suspicion with the enemy," Rig said, "but it won't matter a damn to highwaymen or wandering soldiers looking for trouble. On top of which, the gods only know what these Resistance types are like. Don't be under any illusions, Daughter. This *will* be dangerous. If I thought I had a choice, I wouldn't ask it of you."

"You didn't. I asked it of you, remember?"

"*I* remember," Morris said under his breath.

Rig had had enough. "You're dismissed, Commander."

Morris saluted stiffly and withdrew.

"He doesn't trust me," Vel said when he had gone. "How surprising."

"Commander Morris will provide any and all assistance you require. And when you return, he'll be the first in line to congratulate you on a job well done." *Or I'll have his ball sack for a coin purse.*

"Second in line, perhaps," said Wright, laying a hand on

the priestess's shoulder. "This is a very brave thing you're doing, Daughter. May Eldora be your sign."

She inclined her head gravely. "Thank you, Commander. I will see you in a few days."

Wright had not even closed the door before the childlike eagerness returned to Vel's eyes. She leaned back over the map, the corners of her mouth curling just short of a smile. Rig recalled her fervent words the other night, her desire to make a "contribution." Still, he wished she didn't look *quite* so keen. It fed the doubt that gnawed at him.

"You look worried, General."

"I'll say this, I never would have guessed when we met that day on the road that we'd end up here, you and I."

"Here?" She smiled archly. "Alone, in your quarters?" Her enthusiasm was getting to her; the spark in her eyes was almost a flame. "I would not have guessed it either, though if we had known a little about each other, perhaps it would not have been such a leap. We are both of us risk takers." She paused, regarding him curiously. "Tell me something. Why did you conceal your identity that day on the road?"

"I didn't conceal it. I just didn't see the need to mention it. You'd already guessed I was an officer."

"And yet you were no mere officer. I had no idea I was in the presence of such an eminent personage. Commander general of the king's armies, and a banner lord besides!" She fanned her face mockingly. "Why, I practically tremble in awe."

"Obviously," Rig said. "Now if I could just get you to tremble quietly, we'd be getting somewhere."

Her gaze travelled lingeringly down his body. "Oh, but I'm quite sure you *could*, General."

That one got him; he felt himself flush beneath his beard. "Bloody hells, woman, you're relentless."

She laughed, victorious. "At last! I knew it was possible! Even brutes have their limits." She drew in close, face angled playfully to his, gazing up at him through those impossibly long lashes. Rig didn't retreat; he wouldn't give her the satisfaction. "Am I being too forward for you?" she purred, her hand sliding up his back.

He snorted softly. "You just don't quit, do you?"

"I thought you admired my persistence. Besides, things are going my way today. When the wind is in your favour, keep sailing."

"Enough of this, Vel, I'm not—"

She stopped his lips with her own.

Rig froze, momentarily stunned. It had never occurred to him that she would take her little game this far. He'd already given her what she wanted. What was she trying to *prove* anyway? She took his face in her hands, pulling his head down toward her, her tongue teasing his lips. He scowled, sharp words forming in his mind. Would she never stop trying to provoke him? What did she think he was going to do, run away screaming?

He grasped her arms, intending to push her away, but the softness of her skin beneath his callused fingers distracted him. His hands rebelled, refusing to quit the field, revelling in the feel of her. Her scent, spicy and unmistakably feminine, filled his nose. He realised in that moment just how long it had been.

You don't have time for this, he told himself. *If it's been a while, that's because there's a* war *going on. Besides, she's only trying to goad you into . . .*

Oh, sod it.

Rig's arms went around her, his lips parting to let her in. She gave a little sigh as her tongue darted into his mouth. It was about then that his mind stopped working altogether. He was totally unprepared for the *need* that ignited in him, roaring through his veins like a flame put to paraffin. His grip tightened. His kiss grew hungry. She answered with a vehemence that spurred him on still more, prompting a telltale throb below his waist. He had just enough sense left to realise that things were going to get very out of hand very quickly if he didn't do something about it. He broke away; it was like coming up for air after a brush with drowning. She was breathing hard too, but flush with triumph.

"Work to do," he said gruffly, turning away. He leaned over the map and stared until his eyes watered.

"Of course. I should leave you to it." Out of the corner of his eye, he saw her touch her fingers to her lips, a wondering smile on her face. *The beard*, he thought. She'd probably never kissed a man with facial hair before.

When he thought it was safe, he looked up. "Good luck, Vel."

"And to you, General."

She left him leaning over his map, half stunned, still riding the wild current of his blood. He couldn't decide what amazed him more—how brazenly she'd ambushed him, or how thoroughly he'd enjoyed it.

It really had been *far* too long.

The knock startled him out of a fitful sleep. Rig couldn't remember what he'd been dreaming, but the race of his heart and the sweat on his brow suggested it had been battle. Well, either that, or . . . He swept the covers off.

Not battle, then.

He swung his legs over the bed and padded to the door. Opening it a crack, he found Morris, looking grim. "What time is it?" he asked groggily.

"About an hour before dawn, General. I'm sorry to wake you, but we have a fresh report from the scouts, and it's . . ." Morris hesitated, his mouth tightening. "It's disturbing."

The sleep fled Rig in an instant. "Let me get some clothes on."

He found Morris and the watch officer in the common room, speaking in subdued tones with a pair of scouts. The women were fresh from the field, judging from the dust on their leathers, and they looked pale and exhausted. They must have pushed themselves hard to reach the fort at this hour; they hadn't been due back until noon. Even so, they straightened when they saw Rig approaching, heads high and shoulders back.

"What news?" he asked.

"These scouts have just returned from Raynesford, General," Morris said.

"Raynesford." He closed his eyes, pictured the map. He'd pored over it for so long that he had memorised nearly every feature for leagues on either side of the border. "Upriver from Harriston. Near the monument."

Morris nodded. "Seems the enemy crossed the Gunnar there."

Rig felt the blood drain from his face. "I thought that ford was impassable in spring."

"It is. On foot."

"We think they took a small boat, General," one of the scouts put in, her voice trembling a little. At first, Rig took it for nerves, but then he noticed how bloodshot her eyes were. She'd been crying.

"Why would they do that? It would take them a week to get a force of any significance across."

"But only hours to get a few dozen across." Morris's voice had started to shake too—with rage.

"A few dozen? I don't . . ." Rig looked from one face to the next, settling finally on the ashen, downcast features of the woman who'd spoken. "What's your name, scout?"

"Odile, General."

"What did you see, Odile?"

"We saw . . . They . . ." Her eyes started to fill, but she held it together. "They butchered them, General. The enemy. They crossed the river and they . . ."

"The whole village," Morris said. "Men, women, and children."

The air left Rig in a gust. His gaze fell, unseeing, to the floor. "How many?" The question was barely more than a whisper.

Odile shook her head. "We couldn't . . . A hundred, at least. Maybe more. They burned them, and they—"

Her fellow scout choked out a sob, her face collapsing into her hands.

Frost pricked along every vein, every nerve, in Rig's body. It seized the muscles in his jaw, curled his hands into fists. He whirled away from the sight of the weeping scouts, started across the room in great ringing strides. When he spoke again, his voice sounded feral, even to his own ears. "Get my horse."

When he reached the courtyard, he found that Morris had anticipated him, as usual. Alger was saddled and ready, and a dozen cavalrymen were already mounted up. They had obviously heard what happened; a dark silence weighed over the courtyard.

"General."

Rig scarcely registered the sound. *I should order someone to see to those scouts. Brandy, if we've got any left . . .*

"General!"

He spun to find Vel standing beside her horse. Something

in his look must have alarmed her, because she paled and retreated a step. "What . . . What has happened?"

It was Morris who answered, appearing at Rig's elbow. "A massacre upriver."

Her hand flew to her mouth. "Farika's mercy. Where?"

"Raynesford." The word emerged in that same feral growl, ground out between Rig's teeth. He turned away and headed to his horse, mounting up abruptly enough that the destrier shifted uneasily.

"General." The priestess again, her hand on Alger's bridle. "*What*, Vel?"

She swallowed, but held her ground. "I must come with you. Someone must pray for the dead."

"You ride for Andithyri. You should already be gone."

"I will go tomorrow. One more day won't make a difference." In the torchlight, her eyes shone with a fervid light. "Please, General. Someone must pray for them."

Rig couldn't be bothered to argue; he could hardly hear past the blood pounding in his ears. He put his heels to his horse, forcing her to stumble back out of the way. "Do what you will." He rode out the gate and into darkness.

Dawn soaked the sky in blood, seeped between the columns of smoke that rose from the blackened ruins of Raynesford. The crows had already started to arrive, drifting languidly on the warm updrafts from the smouldering husks below. Rig squinted up at them, half tempted to shoot them down one by one. But he knew it would not slake his fury, not by even a small measure. It was not the crows' blood he craved.

The village had been a significant one, by the looks of it. Bigger than anything between here and the citadel, at least. Mud brick and thatch, mostly, but one or two paved streets, a few stone buildings topped with timber. *A hundred, at least*, the scout had said. It would be more, Rig judged. Yet he couldn't see them. Every doorway he stepped through, every window he peered into, empty. The bodies had been burned, obviously— Rig's stomach was sick with the smell of them—but even so, something should remain. Charred flesh. Blackened bones.

Something. Yet he could find no sign. Not even a single dog or panicked chicken.

Here and there, flames still gnawed at scraps of timber, but they had by and large spent their fury. It could not have been much past dark when the enemy fell on Raynesford. Families would have been sitting down for dinner, or gathered in the temple to mark the changing of the guard between Rahl and Olan. They would have had no warning, and no chance.

"There." Morris's voice was barely a murmur, yet it might as well have been a shout in the strained silence. He gestured with his boot at a dark stain in the dirt, sending flies swirling.

"Here too, General," said Commander Gerton, leaning through a burnt-out doorway.

A chill wind sighed through the hollowed shell of the village. It seemed to carry whispers to Rig's ears, echoes of the lives ripped from this place. He squeezed his eyes shut against the stinging smoke and kept moving.

He turned onto a paved road heading into the centre of town. Still no bodies, but signs of the horror perpetrated here began to mount. Blood spattered walls and pooled in the cracks between flagstones. A crossbow bolt protruded from a windowsill. A thick smear of gore left a gruesome trail from a doorway out into the street. *They moved the bodies*, Rig realised dully.

They found them in the village green, the epicentre of a wheeling gyre of crows.

"Gods have mercy."

Rig didn't see who uttered the prayer, but whoever it was, the words caught in his throat. They caught in Rig's throat too, sharp and cold and tasting of bile.

The stack of corpses reached so high that it obscured the awnings of the local bakery. Had he climbed it, Rig could have walked through a second-storey window. *Two hundred*, his mind registered. *Maybe three.* It was hard to tell, for they scarcely looked human anymore, little more than twigs of charred meat and scorched bone tossed like so much kindling in a pile. Arms, legs, skulls with their jaws hanging open in silent agony. How many had still been alive when they'd been consigned to the flames?

"Oh dear gods. Oh *gods* . . ."

Rig turned. What he saw emptied him, scraped out his insides and left him raw and bleeding.

The children had been separated from their parents. They hadn't been burned. Instead, they'd been put to the sword, their bodies left pristine but for the grisly wounds to throat and head and stomach. They might almost have been sleeping, so peaceful were their faces. Boys. Girls. Infants. Laid out in a long row, shoulder to shoulder, to make the counting easier. Whether they'd been forced to watch their parents burn, or the parents to watch their children butchered, was impossible to know.

Above it all, mounted on a spear and snapping majestically in the breeze, was a flag. A banner of black silk.

One of the men doubled over and vomited in the grass. Another took a halting step toward the corpses before freezing midstride, unable to continue. Rig could only stare, transfixed, at the black banner cackling and flapping like a hungry crow above the bodies of dozens of children.

Vel stepped away from the others and made her way across the green, fists clenched at her sides, spine rigidly straight. Tears streamed down her face, but her features were composed, smooth as marble. Smooth as death. She knelt at the foot of the first child, bowed her head, and began to pray.

"Morris." The voice seemed to come from far away, for all that Rig could feel it grating in his throat. "Send a man back to the fort to fetch spades. As many as we've got." Without waiting for a reply, he started across the field. He stared straight ahead as he passed the row of small bodies, unwilling to look. He would face that horror in a moment, but there was something he needed to do first. Grabbing the spear in both hands, he tore it from the ground and snatched the banner down. Then he carried it to a nearby smouldering building, stoked up the ash, and dropped the hateful thing onto the embers.

He stood and watched it burn, letting the smoke swirl in his eyes, letting them stream, as if they could ever be cleansed.

Rig leaned over the map in his chambers, staring at the tiny black dot that marked Raynesford. An insignificant place, seen this way. Inanimate, soulless. A blot of black ink, no more. *That's not right*, he thought. Reaching for the ink bottles lined up on the table, he grabbed the red and dipped a quill. He held it over the map, watching as the crimson liquid ran down the shaft, collecting on the sharpened tip, until a single drop fell onto the parchment. It obliterated the village of Raynesford, leaving only a bloody splash of ink.

"General."

He didn't turn. "Not now."

She ignored him, of course. She did as she damned well pleased, this woman. He heard the door close behind her, heard soft footsteps cross the room. "It's not your fault."

Rig squeezed his eyes shut, ground his teeth together. "Not now, Vel. Don't make me say it again."

"What happened out there . . . it was a tragedy beyond imagining. But it does not lie at your feet." Her voice, always musical, had a soothing cadence to it now, as though she were preaching. It flowed over him like warm water, relaxing the tension in his shoulders. He wanted so badly to sink into it, let it overtake him, but if he did, he would surely drown.

He pushed himself away from the table, away from her. He didn't want to see her. He didn't want to see the woman who'd walked across that field, face shining with tears, to pray over the mangled bodies of children. He didn't want to see the fire in his hearth or the blood on his map. Most of all, he didn't want to see what he saw when he closed his eyes.

"This evil is Sadik's, and no other's," she said.

"The banner," Rig murmured, as much to himself as to her. "It was a message. For me."

"Yes. He's taunting you, trying to—"

"It was a message, and it will not go unanswered."

"That is just what he wants." Rig felt a hand on his arm. "He wants to poison you. To fill you with hate and blind rage, so that you dream of nothing but vengeance—"

Rig whipped around and seized her shoulders. *"It's working."*

She flinched, but she held his gaze. "It can't. You can't let it. What was it you said to me? You don't have the luxury. And it's not who you are."

He squeezed his eyes shut. "You wouldn't say that if you could see inside my head right now, Daughter."

Soft hands touched his face, brushed the hair back from his

temples. "That's not who you are," she repeated in that low, soothing voice. "You are commander general of the armies of Alden."

Warm water, flowing over wounds, easing muscles that ached from the digging of graves.

"I will see you in a few days. Promise me you will not do anything rash while I'm gone. Ardin cannot be your sign in this, General. He *cannot*. You must be guided by wisdom, not passion."

"Eldora doesn't fancy me," he muttered reflexively. Gods, he was so tired . . .

"She does," Vel said softly. "Very much." Something brushed against his forehead. When Rig opened his eyes, she was gone.

Crossing the room, he took up his greatsword and a whetstone. He dragged a chair noisily across the floor, dropped himself onto it, and unsheathed the blade. It was sharp enough to slice through silk, but he didn't care.

Putting steel to stone, he went to work.

TWENTY-TWO

A lix watched, heartsick and powerless, as Qhara tended Erik's wound. The woman worked efficiently, without any obvious care for his pain, tugging at the bandage without even checking to see if it had dried to his skin overnight. Which of course it had, so that when she pulled it free, Erik winced. She grabbed an earthenware cup and poured its contents down his back, washing the wound in something sharp-smelling that made him grit his teeth. Then she smeared on some kind of poultice that seemed to consist largely of moss. Erik endured it all in silence.

"Why do you waste time on him?" Fahran sneered. "He will be dead in two days."

Qhara threw him a dismissive glance. "If he dies, it will be because the *pasha* decreed it, not because of a festering wound."

"What difference does it make?"

"If you have to ask, you are a fool." Ignoring Fahran's glare, Qhara tied off Erik's bandage and put away her things.

They started out along the shore. Sakhr and his sister set a brisk pace as usual, with Fahran and Dabir bringing up the rear. All four tribesmen walked with bows at the ready. No one spoke; the only sound was the rhythmic scraping of boots on rock. To Alix's ears, it was like the tolling of the hour, each one a jarring reminder of the time they had lost, and how little remained.

They followed the path of the lake along the valley floor. The morning shadows retreated gradually up the western slope, sunlight flaring upon snow and harsh ridges of rock. Alix looked for any sign of a village, but all she saw was pristine, undisturbed nature. The lake was a jewel set in golden wildflowers, framed by a luxuriant cloak of pines. A gentle breeze coaxed its waters into shimmering pleats, disturbing the reflection of the row of rugged peaks behind. The serenity of the scene was a surreal counterpoint to the ever-tightening coil of fear that threatened to snap Alix's nerves.

Sometime near midday, they stopped. "I must check your wound," Qhara informed Erik.

"I would rather not stop. Time is of the essence."

She motioned for him to sit, and Erik submitted, squirming as she removed his shirt. "Wash this," Qhara said, tossing the shirt at Fahran.

For a moment, the tribesman just stood there, a look of pure fury sweeping into his eyes. But like Erik, he did what he was told, stomping down to the water's edge. *She's punishing him for something*, Alix thought. He knew it too, and made clear his resentment at this unjust treatment, returning only moments later to hurl the shirt at Erik in a sopping ball. Then he caught Alix watching, witnessing his humiliation. She looked away, but not fast enough; he started toward her. "You," he snarled. "Time to piss."

"I do not need—"

"Now." Grabbing her roughly by the elbow, he dragged her up the shore. "No stopping later, and I will not be washing your breeches." There was nothing Alix could do but comply.

He took her deep into the woods. Alix's breath came quicker. Even supposing Fahran was genuinely concerned for her modesty, which she doubted, the pines were dense enough to offer cover after only a few steps. "I can go here," she said, but Fahran ignored her.

When he deemed they'd gone far enough, he drew a knife and pointed at her breeches.

Alix swallowed. Gesturing away from her, she said, "You wait there?"

Fahran smiled, his green eyes glinting with malice. "You tried to kill Dabir."

"It was . . ." Her Harrami failed her then; she could not think of a single thing to say. Not that it would have mattered.

"He is my cousin," Fahran went on. "This must be punished."

A twig snapped. Alix experienced a brief surge of hope— until she saw Dabir step out of the shadows. He licked his lips, glancing around anxiously. He said something terse to Fahran in their strange dialect, but his cousin only laughed.

"Good things take time," Fahran said, using High Harrami for Alix's benefit. He pointed at her waist again, jerking the knife meaningfully.

Panic started to work its way up Alix's chest, climbing the rungs of her rib cage. Her legs were free; she might be able to knee Fahran in the groin. Maybe she could even get the knife off him. But with Dabir there, armed with bow and sword and knife . . .

Fahran didn't like her hesitation. He struck like a snake, seizing her throat and pinning her to a tree. The back of his knife glided along her temple, pushing away a stray lock of hair. He whispered something in her ear, the same word he'd used that first morning. He laughed and said it again, over his shoulder this time, inviting Dabir to agree. His cousin just smiled nervously.

He pressed the tip of his knife under her jaw; his other hand dropped to the laces at her waist.

"Wait." Dabir took a step forward. He said something that sounded half surprised, half angry.

"What did you think I meant?" Fahran sneered. As before, he used the language Alix knew. He wanted her to understand every word.

Alix glanced helplessly at Dabir, but he just looked away. Fahran started tugging at her laces again. Alix tensed, twisting her body so that her knee was poised to strike. She had no choice. She'd rather die. If Dabir lacked the courage to help her, maybe he would at least stay out of it . . .

A new voice spoke, cool and smooth as stone. Fahran spun to find another of his kinsmen standing in the trees, bow in hand.

Gold eyes met Alix's. "Move away from the tree," Sakhr instructed her.

Alix started to obey, but Fahran shoved her in the chest, held her there. He said something angry in their own tongue.

"You shame us all." Sakhr's tone was perfectly even, yet Alix could sense the cold fury beneath.

Fahran glared at him. "You do not rule me. Neither does your sister, though you both seem to forget it."

"That is so. You are free to do as you will. And so am I." The solemn tribesman drew his bow.

The hand against Alix's chest shook with rage. Fahran hissed something that dripped with venom.

"You humiliate yourself. You need no help from me." Sakhr's gaze shifted to Dabir, who stood by meekly, eyes on the forest floor. "What say you, kinsman?"

Dabir's reply, whatever it was, defeated Fahran; his hand started to drop. Then he slammed Alix into the tree, cracking her head against the trunk. Looking her up and down with contempt, he said, "I would not have touched this filth. I wanted only to put her in her place." He shoved her once more for good measure. Then he walked away, cursing a poisonous streak that required no translation.

Alix shook her head to clear it. When her gaze came back into focus, she found herself alone with Sakhr. His bow was still nocked, though lowered. The solemn tribesman said nothing; he just jerked his head in the direction of the lake.

A tremor started in Alix's hands, spreading through her body to her legs, until she was unsteady on her feet. Her head buzzed, and something that felt like a frozen sob lodged in her chest. She picked her way clumsily through the undergrowth, stumbling and staggering, back to the lake.

Qhara started to pull the shirt down over Erik's head, but he jerked away. "I can do it."

Her mouth twitched in amusement. "Perhaps, but it will hurt very much. The shirt is wet. It will stick to you." She shrugged. "But if you wish to impress me with your toughness, I will not stop you."

"You think highly of yourself. I simply do not wish you to touch me any more than is necessary."

"As you like." She moved away.

Erik started to struggle—painfully, feeling more than a little like a stubborn child—back into his wet shirt, but then Kerta was there, doing her best to help in spite of being bound at the wrists. She took advantage of the situation to whisper in his ear. "I don't like that they took Alix away. That Fahran . . . he had a look in his eye." Erik glanced at the trees where Alix had disappeared. When he met Kerta's gaze, he saw real fear.

"She'll be all right," he said with a conviction he did not feel.

"No talking," Qhara said.

Moments later, Fahran stormed out of the trees, flushed with anger. Dabir followed soon after. Alix was nowhere to be seen. Qhara frowned as she watched her kinsman stalk down to the water's edge. She asked a question of Dabir, but the tribesman just shrugged awkwardly, avoiding her eye.

Erik rose, pulse quickening, but a moment later, Alix appeared, Sakhr in tow. Erik blew out a relieved breath.

It was short-lived. He could see straightaway that something was wrong. She moved haltingly, unsteady on her feet, and her skin, always pale, was bone-white. "Alix?"

"No talking," Qhara said again.

Erik ignored the tribeswoman, making his way over to Alix.

"I'm fine," she said, speaking to her boots.

"What happened?"

"Nothing. I'm fine."

It was obviously a lie. "Alix—"

"Leave it, Erik." She met his gaze, quietly exhorting him to drop it. Erik had a good idea why. *She's afraid of what you'll do. She's afraid you'll get yourself killed.*

Erik turned to look at Fahran and decided that her fear was entirely justified. He stirred.

"Don't." Alix grabbed his arm. "Please. Nothing happened, I swear. Sakhr—"

Qhara pushed her way between them. "No talking." Though it was the third time she had said it, her voice was surprisingly gentle. She took Alix's elbow and steered her away.

After that, their captors took no chances: Fahran, Alix, and Erik were kept as far away from each other as Qhara and Sakhr could manage. Erik could not think straight for the roar of blood in his ears. Never in his life had he craved violence as much as he did now, and the urge to act on it was almost overwhelming. A tiny, malevolent voice in his head seemed to whisper to him, spurring him on. Only Alix's warning, and the fear of what would befall her if he failed to heed it, prevented him. For once, *she* was the one restraining *him*. He had just enough sense left in his seething brain to find irony in that.

They stopped at dusk. Qhara checked his bandage again. She feared infection, though why she should be so concerned when he was very probably marching to his execution eluded him.

"The copper-haired one," Qhara said as she peeled the bloodied bandage away. "She is your woman?"

"My brother's wife."

"You care for her." She glanced up, as if checking his reaction.

"Of course. She is my sister."

A stretch of silence. Qhara dabbed at the wound, adding a new layer of poultice. "She can fight, that one."

Erik didn't know what she was driving at, but it was something. This woman was too calculated for idle chatter. Until he could figure out what she wanted, he thought it safest to hold his tongue.

Later, after they had eaten, Dabir came over to relieve Qhara on guard duty. He settled down near Erik, drawing his curved blade from its sheath and resting it across his knees. He glanced across the fire, as if gauging the distance to the nearest pair of ears. Then, shuffling a little closer, he lowered his voice and said, "I can help you."

Erik's eyes narrowed. "I doubt that."

"I can. Only a little, maybe, but you need as much help as you can get."

Erik considered the tribesman. In the shadows, he was little more than an outline, impossible to read. *There is some trap here*, Erik thought. *Still*, another part of him argued, *it can't*

hurt to play along for a moment, so long as you're careful.
"How can you help me?"

Dabir shot another furtive look over his shoulder, then dropped his voice still further. "The *pasha* will listen to testimony from all of us. Then they will decide your fate. For the right price, I can give you good testimony. Say that you were a noble prisoner, that you did not struggle."

"But that would be a lie, and the others would know it."

"Not a lie, not for you. It was not you who attacked us. You were only afraid for your woman."

"She is *not* my woman," Erik said through gritted teeth—though of course it could not possibly matter.

"I will speak for you, for the right price."

"You have said that twice now. But what do I have to offer you? You have already taken everything I have."

"Not everything. You must have some gold on you, hiding in a pocket somewhere."

Erik almost laughed aloud. "No. I do not carry a purse." Not once in his life, though it would not do to admit it.

"What about the others? One of you must have some."

He shrugged. "You might find some sewn into the lining of one of the saddlebags." Such precautions were common enough among fighting men. Of the half dozen or so surviving saddlebags, it seemed a safe bet that at least one had a few coins stashed away.

Dabir sprang to his feet, grinning. He went straight to the horse, in plain view of everyone, and began rifling through the bags. *After all that trouble to be surreptitious.* Erik had a feeling he had been tricked, though he could not imagine why. If the tribesmen had wanted to know where the gold was kept, they could have just asked. Why should he hide it from them, when they had already confiscated everything he had?

"Here," Dabir called triumphantly, raising a fistful of coins.

"Let me see." Sakhr collected one and brought it close to the fire. He turned it over, examining it in the firelight. "You were right, little sister," he said, adding something else Erik could not follow.

Qhara took the coin and peered at it. She glanced up at Erik, then back at the coin. When she looked up again, her eyes met his.

He understood now.

You fool, Erik.

He had known it was a trap, yet he had walked into it anyway, as reckless as Alix, as mindless as a thrall. *What's happened to you, damn you?* First his barely controlled rage, and now this. He had been so unmoored lately, adrift in a heaving sea of emotions he could not define, let alone weather.

Discipline. Remember who you are. He felt his spine straighten. He lifted his head and gazed defiantly at his captors, to show he was not afraid.

"This changes things," Qhara said.

Fahran had approached the fire now too. He looked from one kinsman to another, frowning, seemingly the only one who did not understand what was happening. "What is it? What has changed?"

Qhara ignored him. "You should have told us the truth, Imperial Erik." She dropped into a low, mocking bow. "Or should I say, Your Majesty."

TWENTY-THREE

Your Majesty.

Okay, that was the easy part. Now what? He glanced down at Rudi for inspiration, but the wolfhound just yawned, showing off a mouthful of wickedly curved teeth.

My enquiries are progressing. That wasn't really true, though, was it?

I regret to inform you of my abject failure. Accurate, but maybe a touch melodramatic.

I have decided that I would rather be bound naked to the prow of a merchant schooner touring every harbour of the known world than continue in this capacity. "Yes," Liam said, tapping his quill against his chin, "I think I'll go with that one."

Rona Brown looked up from the scroll she was reading. "I beg your pardon, Commander?"

"Nothing. Just writing a letter to the king."

Ide peered over his shoulder. *"Your Majesty."*

"It's a work in progress."

Rona sighed and rolled up the scroll. "You're right, Commander, there's nothing here that we didn't already know."

"Thanks for trying, anyway." He'd hoped that Rona might find something in Saxon's notes, some scrap of information he'd overlooked. "I suppose we should head back to the docks. Maybe if we ask around, we'll find someone who saw something out of the ordinary."

"Failing that," Dain Cooper said, "we could talk to Chief Mallik again. You never know—he might have remembered something new since last week."

"Yeah," Liam said, "maybe." And maybe Rudi would sprout butterfly wings and flit gaily around the sunroom.

Shef appeared in the doorway. "I beg your pardon, Your Highness, but First Speaker Kar is here."

Liam's eyebrows flew up. He'd half expected his next communication from the first speaker to be in the form of a letter instructing him to kindly get his royal arse out of the country. "Show him in, please."

"Well," Ide said, "this should be awkward."

Kar entered the sunroom alone. He looked like a man who'd had a falling-out with sleep. His features were as carefully arranged as ever, but it was like a mask with the varnish worn off, all drab colours and frayed edges. "I hope I am not intruding, Your Highness."

"Not at all," Liam said, gesturing for the first speaker to sit. "In fact, I'm glad to see you. I'm not sure if Ash Bookman mentioned it, but—"

"He mentioned it," Kar said. "Right before he resigned."

Liam winced. Apparently, the secretary had been serious when he'd said he wanted no part of this.

"That is why I am here, Your Highness," Kar went on. "I want to make sure there is no misunderstanding."

"There isn't. At least not where I'm concerned." Liam couldn't quite manage to meet the first speaker's gaze. "I was given some information that I thought might help lead us to whoever is responsible for the delays with the fleet, but it seems I was mistaken."

"You weren't mistaken, Your Highness. You were deliberately misled. I have a feeling I know by whom, not that it really matters now. What's important is that you saw through it."

"Straightaway," said Rona Brown. "It was clear to us that it was all a little too convenient." Clear to her, anyway, but Liam saw no need to go into details.

"Defence Consul Welin is no more capable of sabotaging the fleet than I am," Kar said.

Presumably, that was meant to be reassuring. Liam nodded obligingly.

"Moreover, he would have been caught long ago. You can imagine the scrutiny he is under. The opposition has been on the warpath for months. Frankly speaking, Your Highness, it's killing him."

"I can imagine." Actually, he couldn't. In Liam's experience, name-calling was rarely fatal, children's rhymes notwithstanding. *These people have no idea what real war looks like.* If they did, they wouldn't be prancing around like parade ponies while his countrymen died.

"I'm glad we understand each other. In truth, however, I have much more on my mind than Welin. Regrettable though this hateful campaign against him may be, my priority as first speaker is the well-being of the republic. And that means finding out who is sabotaging the fleet."

"So you agree it's sabotage, then?"

"What else could it be?"

Liam knew he should just swallow that and play along, but he couldn't. "If that's what you believe, why didn't you say so from the beginning?"

Kar spread his hands. "Consider my position, Your Highness. Such an act qualifies as high treason, a capital offence. I did not dare make accusations until I was absolutely sure."

Absolutely sure the blame wouldn't fall on your handpicked successor, you mean. Aloud, Liam said, "And you're sure now? What's changed?"

"This." Kar produced a folded piece of parchment and placed it on the table between them.

Opening it, Liam found a series of incomprehensible lines. Did Kar realise he didn't speak Onnani? He felt himself flush.

Dain rescued him before the pause became awkward. "May I, Commander?" He took up the note, translating as he read. "'Gratified that you managed to . . .'" He trailed off, cursing quietly.

"Go on." Kar grimaced as he said it, like a man bracing himself for something painful.

Dain cleared his throat and continued. "'Gratified that you managed to sink it, but do not congratulate yourself too much. That is only the first of many, and they will be on to you now. It will be harder with each one. I am sure you understand why I cannot be involved personally, but I will make sure you are well compensated.'" He paused, jaw twitching in anger. "It's signed . . ."

Liam sprang out of his chair and snatched the note from Dain's hands.

Syril.

The priest of Eldora. The speaker who had humiliated Liam in front of the entire Republicana. "Why am I not surprised?" Liam growled.

"I am." Kar sighed and passed a hand over his eyes. "Very much so. I knew Syril opposed the war, but to go this far . . ."

"Forgive me for asking, First Speaker," said Rona, "but are you certain it's really from him? Couldn't it be a forgery?"

"Quite right that you ask." Kar drew a second note from his robes and handed it to her.

Unfolding it, she held it up alongside Liam's note. The handwriting was identical.

"There is no shortage of examples to compare. Speakers produce dozens of pieces of correspondence a day. It is his hand, I'm afraid. I checked it myself. I could not believe it, you see, even though it was found in his own rubbish bin."

"Found," Ide said. "In a rubbish bin. Pretty lucky, that."

"An individual in my employ came across it."

Ide smirked. "A spy in your employ went rooting through his trash, you mean." Kar didn't deny it; he just shrugged, wearily.

"All right," Liam said, "so what are you going to do about it?"

Kar grimaced again. He really did look awful. "Speaker Syril will be arrested. He will be tried, and if found guilty, he will be hanged. Unless he gives up his co-conspirators, in which case he may simply be confined to prison for the rest of his days."

Liam had seen the inside of a prison once. Given the choice, he'd take the hanging. "When will you take him in?"

"A magistrate is drawing up the papers even now." The first speaker shook his head. "This is a foul business."

"Agreed," Liam said, "and none of it gets the fleet constructed any faster."

Kar collected the note and stood. "There is no apology I can offer that is equal to the task, Your Highness. And now, if you will excuse me, I have an unpleasant duty ahead. I bid you and your officers good day."

After he'd gone, Rona said, "May I see your notes again, Commander? The ones from Lady Alix's spy?" He handed them over, and Rona trailed a finger down the page. "Here. *Speaker Syril, newly minted leader of the People's Congress. A populist of rising fortunes in the Republicana. Priest of Eldora. No known secret society affiliation.*"

"Rising fortunes." Ide grunted sceptically. "You buying this, Commander?"

"Why shouldn't I? Just because it's yet another politician pointing the finger at a rival?"

"So . . . you're not buying it," Dain said.

"I'm not sure. Kar seemed genuinely uncomfortable."

"Could be faking it," Ide said.

"If so," said Rona, "he was very convincing."

Liam was inclined to agree. "On the other hand, if he really believes Syril is behind this, why come to me? He could have informed me after they'd already rounded him up."

"What're you thinking, Commander?" Dain asked.

"I'm thinking whoever found that note was probably hired to dig up something embarrassing on Syril and ended up with way more than he'd bargained for. Kar had no idea he'd find something so damning, and now he's not quite sure what to do with it."

"So what are *we* going to do with it?" Ide asked.

Liam was already heading for the door. "We're going to pay a visit to our favourite priest of Eldora."

They didn't have far to go. Like most of his fellow speakers, Syril lived in the Ambassador District, in a stately home with peaked roofs and large bay windows. Roses climbed the edifice, their petals splashing bloodred on the sparkling white gravel of the courtyard. Populism had its limits, apparently.

"Looks like the speaker is expecting company," Ide said, inclining her chin at the guards clustered around the wrought-iron gate.

"His Highness Prince Liam White to see Speaker Syril," Rona declared in her crisp, highborn accent.

One of the guards stepped forward, a stocky fellow with humourless features. "Speaker Syril is not accepting callers," he said.

A delicate line of disapproval appeared between Rona's brows. "Perhaps you did not hear me. The Prince of Alden—"

"I heard you," the humourless guard interrupted. "No disrespect, but my orders were clear. I must ask you to leave."

"So long as there's no disrespect," Liam said dryly. "Look, I doubt very much Speaker Syril anticipated my coming here, so you might want to check with him before you turn us away."

Another of the guards snorted and muttered something under his breath that set his comrades laughing.

Dain flushed a few shades darker. *"What did you say?"*

The guard looked him up and down, sneered, and replied in Onnani. Whatever he said, it didn't sound very nice, and Dain took it badly. His whole body went rigid.

"Er . . . Dain?" Liam wasn't sure he wanted to know.

His second spoke through gritted teeth. "Commander, this cur has insulted my king, my prince, and my person. I cannot let it go unanswered."

"Got to agree, Commander," Ide said, shifting in her saddle in a manner that not-so-casually positioned her hand above the hilt of her sword.

Liam glared at her incredulously. "You don't even know what he said!"

"Know enough. Dain's not the type to get stoked up over nothing."

Wonderful. As though he hadn't cocked up enough already, it seemed the White Wolves were about to start a brawl with the household guard of a high-ranking speaker of the Republicana. "That doesn't seem like a good idea," Liam said.

"Just him." Dain pointed a gloved finger at the offending guard. "One on one."

Rona tried to reason with him. "Dain, I don't think—"

"If you knew what he said, Rona, you'd have killed him already." He gave her a long, meaningful look that Liam didn't fully understand.

Liam cursed inwardly. The situation was slipping away from him, fast. He couldn't let his second-in-command fight a speaker's guard. But he couldn't forbid Dain either, not in the face of a brazen challenge to his honour. Dain was a knight, a rare distinction for someone of Onnani descent. If Liam allowed such a slight to go unanswered, it could be taken as a sign that he didn't respect Dain as much as an ordinary knight, as if he were somehow less than. That would be a diplomatic disaster too, and not just in Onnan—the ripples would be felt all the way to the front.

When did the world become so complicated? Everywhere he looked, he saw political tripwires, actions tied to consequences tied to other consequences in a tense, vibrating web. Had the war changed everything? Or had it always been this way, and he'd just learned to see it?

Being prince of the realm, Liam decided, was rubbish.

He addressed the leader of the guards. "I really need you to fetch your master now, since things have got just a bit out of hand." If he was going to allow this, he was bloody well going to make Syril understand that he'd had no choice.

Reluctantly, the guard heeded him and headed up the drive.

The Wolves waited. Dain sat stiff-backed in his saddle, his eyes never leaving the guard who'd insulted him. (And Liam. And Erik. And quite possibly the entire Kingdom of Alden.) The guard returned his gaze warily, looking more sulky than belligerent now. He seemed to have realised, too late, what he'd wrought.

Speaker Syril appeared at the door. He paused briefly on

the stairs, taking in the scene before making his way over. "Your Highness." The smooth voice contained no trace of surprise.

"Speaker. I'm sorry to drag you out of your home, but it seems we have a bit of a situation here."

"So I have been informed." Turning to his men, he asked, "Which of you was it?" The offending guard replied in Onnani, but Syril continued in Erromanian. "What did you say?"

The guard looked at his boots and did not reply.

Dain answered for him—in Onnani, presumably to spare the other Wolves having to hear it. Now all the guards were looking at their boots. As for Syril, his expression remained impassive, and for a moment, Liam thought he was going to brush it off. Instead, he turned to the leader of his guards and said, "This man is a disgrace. He will be ejected from the property immediately. Any pay he is owed will be withheld as a fine." He looked back at Dain. "Are you satisfied with this penalty, Commander? Your Highness?"

Liam glanced at his second. Dain's stiff nod was his cue to let out the breath he'd been holding. "I suppose we are."

"Good." Syril paused, as though considering. The clever eyes looked Liam up and down. "I expect you had better come in, Your Highness."

The speaker led them into a well-lit room overlooking the valley. As they entered, a small face peered around a corner of the corridor. A girl of about two watched Liam with round, dark eyes, fingers jammed in her mouth. Liam winked, and she vanished.

Syril sank down on an upholstered chair. He folded his hands in his lap. He stared.

"Thanks for seeing us," Liam said, somewhat stupidly. Syril continued to gaze at him expectantly. "An unfortunate business at the gate."

"Indeed. Please accept my apologies."

"Do you always keep so many guards at your home?"

Syril gave the sort of half smile that wasn't really supposed to pass for the genuine article. "No, Your Highness, I do not. I am expecting a visit from the city guard."

"Oh, really?"

"They will be here any moment, as you well know, so if

you have something to say, I suggest you do not waste any more time." Speaker Syril, it appeared, was rather more direct than his colleagues.

"How do you know they're coming for you?" Liam asked.

A look of distaste flitted over Syril's features. "Whispers and more whispers. It is what the Republicana feeds on, vacuous beast that it is. Whether you want them or not, they fill your ears like a foul odour fills your nose."

"You mean to resist arrest, then?" Rona asked. "Is that why all the guards?"

"And thereby prove my guilt? I think not. The guards are there to protect my family against any . . . excess of zeal."

Liam thought about the little girl peering around the corner, and his guts twisted uncomfortably. "You don't think anyone would . . . ?"

"I don't know, Your Highness, but I don't intend to take any chances. The accusations against me are grave and will provoke outrage all over the country." Though the voice remained smooth, there was more than a hint of worry in his eyes.

"The note was pretty damning," Liam said.

Syril frowned, cocked his head. "Note?"

"The evidence against you."

"That," Syril said, leaning forward intently, "I am very interested to hear."

"They found it in a rubbish bin, if I remember correctly. Something about you being glad they managed to sink it, but it was going to be harder from now on. You promised someone would be well compensated for it."

For a moment, Syril's eyes were blank. Then a spark came into them, and a breath jolted from his lips. He shook his head, murmuring something in Onnani. "By Hew, the man is clever."

"Who, Kar?"

"I have been a thorn in his side, to be sure, but I would not have guessed he would go this far to destroy me."

"If I may interject," Rona said, "I didn't have the impression the first speaker was particularly happy about what he'd found."

"Me neither," Liam said. "If anything, he seemed shocked."

Syril considered that. "I suppose it is possible that he genuinely does not understand the note, what it truly means."

"So it is authentic?" Liam asked. "You wrote it?"

"Presuming it has not been tampered with, yes."

"I'm guessing it's not about the fleet, then." He'd suspected as much, having been treated to two weeks of sailing metaphors.

"No indeed, Your Highness. What was sunk was not a galley, but a motion before the Republicana. The Worker's Alliance seeks to introduce a new law obliging all males over the age of thirteen to submit to military service. Mass mustering, they call it. They insist it is the only way we can be effective in the war." Syril's eyes gleamed fiercely. "Little more than slavery. A betrayal of everything the republic stands for, everything our forefathers suffered and died for. Worker's Alliance indeed."

"Okay," Liam said, "but what about the part where you say *they'll be on to you now*?"

"My opposition to the war has made me . . . unpopular . . . with a number of my learned colleagues. I could not afford to be the banner holder for this latest cause, lest I squander what little political capital I have left. I recruited another face for the campaign, one who is acting quietly, behind the scenes, against the will of his league. In return, I promised compromise on a number of other matters before the Republicana."

"'You will be well compensated,'" Rona quoted.

"Precisely." The thin, humourless smile returned. "So you see, Your Highness, there is nothing nefarious in the note, at least not where the fleet is concerned. First Speaker Kar may simply have interpreted it too literally. That being said, I doubt he put much effort into seeking an alternative explanation, or he would easily have found it."

"That," Liam sighed, "is about what I thought."

Syril's mouth twisted bitterly. "What a proud image of the republic we present. What a recommendation for democracy. How very impressed you must be."

Liam shook his head. "I don't know what to think, except that I've chased another imaginary rabbit down another imaginary hole. I was sent here because my people are in desperate need. They've been dying by the thousands for going on two years now. Without help, we will fall. And I haven't found any help. Not from First Speaker Kar, or Defence Consul Welin, or Chairman Irtok. Not from the Shield or the Sons or the

Worker's Alliance . . ." He paused, looked Syril right in the eye. "And not from you."

The speaker returned his gaze evenly. "That is so. Instead you have been manipulated, just another game piece in a vast political contest that has nothing to do with you. I am disgusted and ashamed, Your Highness."

For all the bloody good that does me. Liam rose.

"Wait." Syril looked up. "There is one thing I can do for you."

"What's that?"

"I can arrange a meeting with the leader of the dockhands union. The dockies, as they are known."

Liam remembered the dockies from his first visit to the shipyard, the hostile looks he'd received. "Why would I want to meet with them?"

Syril hesitated, as though choosing his words carefully. "I'm not sure, Your Highness. But if I were you, I would consider it."

A commotion sounded in the courtyard outside. Liam turned to see a figure flitting past the door, heading for the back of the house.

"It would appear my escort has arrived." Syril stood, smoothed his priestly robes. "Thank you for coming, Your Highness."

Liam regarded him grimly. Whatever else he might be, Syril seemed to be the most genuine person Liam had met in Onnan City. He didn't deserve to be executed over a misunderstanding. Liam could only hope Onnani justice would do itself more credit than Onnani politics. "Good luck to you, Speaker."

"And to you, Your Highness. I daresay we will both need it."

TWENTY-FOUR

"**W**hat put them on to you?" Alix whispered, bending over Erik on the pretence of gathering up her blanket.

The tribesmen stood clustered on the far side of the camp, conversing in low voices. They'd been at it since the night before. Alix had fallen asleep to their murmurs, woken to the same. She should be grateful for it, she knew; it meant they were debating what to do, rather than simply executing Erik on the spot. But the constant buzzing gnawed at her already frayed nerves. She'd tried to put what had happened in the woods yesterday out of her mind, but she was reminded every time her gaze fell on Fahran. It left her raw and exhausted. Still, her king needed her now.

"They could have worked it out in any number of ways," Erik said, eyeing the tribesmen warily. "My name. My demeanour. I was careless, and now we all pay the price."

"You weren't careless. You've been the picture of discipline, as usual."

"What I've been is naïve. Qhara was right—we've always assumed these people were savages, isolated and ignorant. Obviously, we were wrong. If I'd paid closer attention, I would have seen that. Instead, I allowed my assumptions to cloud my judgement."

"You're too hard on yourself."

He laughed, quiet and bitter. "I don't think so, Alix. Not this time. I'm afraid that lately I . . ." He trailed off, shook his head. "It doesn't matter."

Sakhr made his way over. "Time to go," he told them.

"Where?" Erik spoke crisply, with authority, his head held

high. The royal mask was on full display now. He had little choice but to wear it like armour.

"You will be brought to the *pasha*. We are only two hours from the village. To judge you ourselves, when we are so near to their wisdom, would not be right."

Two hours to the village. At last, they would be judged. Perversely, Alix felt almost relieved. One way or another, this would all be over. Another day of counting the lost hours, of clawing at the walls of her mind, would surely drive her mad.

Erik must have been thinking along similar lines, for he merely nodded, getting to his feet and dusting himself off as well as he could with bound wrists. In spite of everything, he looked only slightly rumpled, as though he'd merely fallen asleep in his clothes. He hadn't shaved in well over a week, but the red-gold beard was still tidy enough to look distinguished. It helped that his shirt had been washed, but even so, Alix couldn't help but marvel at his almost preternatural poise. Even Kerta, with her impeccable curls and perfect skin, couldn't compete with that.

They started out, their path still hugging the edge of the lake. Qhara stayed close to Erik, which meant Alix stayed closer, positioning herself between them. Kerta closed with his other flank.

It didn't go unnoticed. "You are his bodyguard," Qhara said, out of thin air.

Alix glanced at Erik, but he just shrugged, as if to say, *the damage is done.* "I did not think it obvious," Alix said.

"Everyone has heard the tale of the red-haired woman who saved the king's life. The woman from the lost hills so near to our lands."

"You knew because of my hair?" Alix asked in dismay.

"There were many clues. It only took me so long to see it because he is not what I expected." Her gaze shifted to Erik. "You are not what I expected."

He acted as though he hadn't heard; he just kept walking, gaze straight ahead.

"I expected the king of the imperials to be soft and lazy," Qhara went on.

"And why would you expect that?" Kerta asked coldly.

"Because that is what men become when they have everything done for them."

Kerta scoffed. "You are quite an authority on kings."

"You had your expectations about us; we had ours about you. We were both wrong, it seems."

"Yet you are still sure we are enemies," Alix said.

Qhara ignored that; she was too busy staring at Erik. "Why come yourself, Imperial Erik? You could have sent someone else."

He answered this time, though he still didn't look at her. "Because I am neither soft nor lazy, and because being king means taking responsibility for the things that truly matter."

The rest of the journey passed in silence. Alix strained her eyes looking at the edge of the lake, but she saw no sign of a village—until, suddenly, she did. It seemed to sprout up out of nowhere, huts of brown and green and gold that blended into their surroundings until you were right on top of them. Bisected by a narrow river fed from a plunging waterfall, the village melted back into the trees, so that it was impossible to tell how large it was, or how many people it held. Terraced fields were just beginning to sprout on the slopes above the treeline, and above that, sheep and goats grazed, the distant tinkle of bells drifting like mist from the falls over the tops of the pines.

Fahran had arrived well ahead of the others, so that a small crowd had already gathered. Alix and Kerta exchanged a nervous glance. As for Erik, he looked much as he had the day he returned to Erroman after months at the front: outwardly composed, taut as the skin of a war drum underneath.

Tribesmen surrounded them in a tight circle, weapons at the ready. "Ready your words," Qhara said. "You will not have much time. The *pasha* come."

So saying, she stepped through the circle of tribesmen and disappeared.

"Sit."

The order came from a striking woman with a deep, authoritative voice. She had just finished addressing the crowd, marking her as someone important. An elder, maybe, though it was hard to tell; the lines around her mouth and eyes suggested she could easily be a grandmother, yet her hair remained raven-black but for a single streak of silver running from her temple. Whoever she was, Alix and the others didn't even consider disobeying her; they lowered themselves dutifully onto the goat-skin chairs that had been arranged for them in the centre of the circle.

Alix did her best to imitate Erik's posture: back straight, head high, expression respectfully composed, as though he were attending a religious service, instead of standing trial for his life. He kept his eyes on the woman, ignoring the crowd gathered around them—the entire village, as far as Alix could tell.

"You do not speak our tongue," the woman said in High Harrami, "so I will translate for you what I have said." Raising her voice as she'd done a moment ago, when she'd addressed the gathering in their own dialect, she said, "We are called here this morning to listen to testimony in the matter of these imperials in our lands. From the people, I have asked for silence. From the *pasha*, I have asked for wisdom. From you, the prisoners, I have asked for respect."

"You shall have it," Erik said, inclining his head at the six men and women seated in a semicircle across from him.

Alix studied the *pasha* closely. They were a fierce-looking lot, dark-haired and sharp-eyed, expressions uniformly severe. Yet they were younger than she would have guessed. Two of them seemed to be over sixty, but most were about the age her parents would have been had they lived, and one looked not much older than Erik. How they had been chosen, she couldn't guess.

The eldest among them was the first to speak. "Where are the warriors who found these trespassers?"

"Here, *pashanai*." Sakhr stepped out of the crowd. "My sister and I led the expedition to monitor the pass." He gestured behind him at the ring of onlookers; Qhara, Fahran, and Dabir all bowed their heads.

"How did you come upon them?" The old man's voice was gusty and crackling, as though his lungs weren't quite right, but the eyes upon Erik were bright and alert.

"Uthal was hunting, *pashanai*, when he was taken by a

panther. We were tracking the animal, and we found these three. There was a fourth who was killed when he attacked Fahran, and one other, a scout, whom we tracked but did not find. I doubt she could survive long on her own."

Another of the *pasha*, the eldest of the women, addressed Sakhr. "The one who was killed—he was trying to escape?"

"Yes, *pashanai*."

"And what did the others do?"

"The red-haired woman attacked Dabir. Qhara subdued the other two before they could do anything."

"I shot the king," Qhara said, to a ripple of laughter.

The old woman eyed Erik with a solemn, golden gaze. "So he tried to escape as well."

Qhara considered that. "I would not say so, *pashanai*. I would say rather that he tried to protect his woman."

Erik sighed and cast his gaze skyward. Alix felt her skin warm. The old woman just grunted, pensively.

"It is true, then?" The old man again, addressing Erik this time. "You are the King of Alden?"

"I am Erik White." A rustle in the crowd, like wind through the trees. Alix tried to read the faces surrounding her, but beyond keen interest, she couldn't gauge the mood.

"You must know that the penalty for trespassing on tribal lands is death. Why have you breached our laws, Erik White?"

"I thank you for asking, *pashanai*, for you are the first." Erik's gaze slid reproachfully to Sakhr and Qhara. "I meant no disrespect. If there had been a way of obtaining permission beforehand, I would certainly have sought it. Just as I would have gladly taken another route, had it been possible. I am sure you are aware that the lands to the south have been overrun by the Trionate of Oridia, with whom we are at war."

"We are aware of this. It is no concern of ours."

Erik nodded slowly. "You are not the first I have heard say this, *pashanai*, but I must respectfully disagree. The Trionate of Oridia is the concern of all free peoples of Gedona."

Alix did not miss the amused expressions exchanged in the crowd. "As far as I am aware, we are the only free people of Gedona," the old man said, "save perhaps for our Onnani brothers. Why should we fear the Trions?"

"Because they are conquerors, and conquerors do not stop. When the rest of Gedona has been swallowed, they will come for you."

The old man smiled, his features vanishing behind a rumple of loose skin. "I shall tell you something about me, Erik White. I am called Ghous, and I have known seventy-two years in this land. In that time, there have been four kings in Ost, and three in Alden. There have been two kings in Andithyri. I would tell you how many times our brothers in Onnan have chosen their king, but"—he made a showy, dismissive gesture—"I do not understand their ways." The crowd laughed with him. "The armies of the *mustevi* have come again and again, and we have repelled them, just as your armies have repelled the tribes who sought to reclaim their ancestral lands in the foothills. None of these things have changed my days. The moon waxes and wanes. The harvest comes and goes. Babies are born and old men die. It is the way of things, and it shall ever be."

Murmurs of agreement among the *pasha*.

"You will be content to have the Trionate rule you?" Erik asked.

Ghous shrugged. "They will not rule us any more than Omaïd does. Why should we care whose pampered buttocks grace the throne of Ost?" More laughter. "But you have not answered my question, Erik White. Why have you come here?"

"We were on our way to Ost," Erik said, "to seek King Omaïd's help in this fight."

The youngest of the *pasha* spoke then, sounding genuinely puzzled. "What help can the *mustevi* be to you? They are not warriors."

"Strength is not measured in the sword alone," Erik said.

"However it is measured, you will not find it in Ost," said the old woman.

"I have little choice but to seek it where I may. I am king, *pashanai*. I am responsible for the lives of my people. I must do whatever it takes to protect them."

"An honourable notion," Ghous said, "if a self-important one. Does it really matter to your people, any more than to mine, who rules in a distant capital? Are their lives not the same whether it is Erik White or another who claims to be king?"

Erik's gaze fell; for a moment, he seemed to withdraw into himself. The *pasha* watched him closely. So, Alix noticed, did Qhara. *She's fascinated by him*, Alix thought.

Erik shook his head, as if to clear it. "There is truth in what you say." He spoke slowly, as though choosing each word judiciously. "Perhaps, if the conquerors at our door were other than they are, I could surrender my crown and spare my people further suffering. But I have seen what the Trions are capable of. I have seen them . . ." He paused, frowning. He seemed to be struggling a little—with the language, Alix supposed. "I have seen them use dark magic to enslave men's minds as well as their bodies. We destroyed the Priest, but I cannot be certain his magic died with him. If I stand aside, who will protect my people from this terrible power?"

Things grew very quiet then. The crowd exchanged unsettled glances, but otherwise kept still. The *pasha* went into a huddle, murmuring in their own tongue.

"So it is true," Ghous said as they drew apart, "what our warriors saw in the pass last winter. The Oridians curse their soldiers."

"Some of them," Erik said. "Mostly, they curse their enemies."

The old woman drew a warding sign in the air. A few of the onlookers did the same.

Sensing an opening, Erik raised his voice a little. "Please, honourable *pasha*. All I ask is free passage through the mountains. I bring no harm upon you. We have lost so much time, yet there is still a chance, and if I succeed, I may even do you a great deal of good."

His words elicited a burst of nervous laughter from the crowd. Ghous fired a disapproving look over his shoulder. "That is"—he cleared his crackling throat—"not an option."

"Why not? What have you to lose?"

"A great deal," came the immediate reply from the youngest *pashanai*. "If we let you pass, you could lead the *mustevi* to our village."

"To release you would be to break faith with the other tribes," said another.

"Imperials do not cross the mountains," said a third. "Ever."

Erik frowned. "With respect, *pashanai*, you just admitted

a moment ago that a host of Oridians passed through here last winter."

The *pasha* traded uncomfortable glances. "That is so," Ghous said. "But we also told you that we have no quarrel with Oridia. They are not allies of Ost. They are not imperials like you."

"Imperial." Erik shook his head, visibly frustrated. "Your warriors called us that too. It is like a curse word in your language. You hate an empire long dead, one that never ruled over you." He gestured at Qhara, still standing behind the *pasha*. "Even your young warriors know the story. They know of the Erromanians, and the white-hairs that ruled them. Why is that, I wonder? Why this obsession with a time long past?"

"It is not an obsession," Ghous said. "It is an education."

Erik's eyes were still on Qhara. "With your permission, *pashanai*, I would like to ask this warrior a question."

Qhara stiffened in surprise. The *pasha* glanced at one another. "It is your choice, granddaughter," said the old woman.

Granddaughter. Alix thought she'd noticed something familiar in the old woman's features, that same solemn beauty that Qhara and her brother wore so well. She had Sakhr's deep-set, golden eyes, Qhara's sculpted cheekbones. Or rather, they had hers.

"He may ask," Qhara said, warily.

"When we spoke, you showed great passion for history. Fahran and Dabir too. You mocked me for being an imperial, and were very proud of the role your people played in the sacking of Erroman. Why?"

"Because it shows we are strong."

That wasn't the answer Erik was hoping for; he shook his head impatiently. "That explains your pride, perhaps, but not your scorn for me. I am sure there are many stories celebrating the strength of the mountain tribes. What makes this one so important, that you still sing about it centuries later?"

"Because . . ." Qhara paused, green-gold eyes narrowing, as though trying to read what Erik wanted from her. "Because we crushed the *mustevi*. The white-hairs who claimed superior blood, who enslaved our brothers on the coast—they fell to our warriors. Their walls crumbled beneath our hooves, and they were no more."

Erik's eyes gleamed. *That* was the answer he'd been looking for. "The Erromanians conquered everyone except Harram. Your country alone, on the entire continent, remained untouched. And yet the mountain tribes rose up anyway. You joined with each other, even joined with your enemies in Ost, to smash the empire."

"What of it?" said Ghous.

Erik's gaze shifted to the old man. "It is only that I wonder, *pashanai*, what makes this situation any different."

The old man's eyes crinkled knowingly, and he chuckled, as if enjoying the antics of a precocious grandchild. "Very well, Erik White, you have said your piece. But we are not here to discuss the Oridians. The *pasha* have been called to decide what to do about *you*. In the matter of trespassers, we have two choices, as agreed by the Council of Twelve. The customary penalty is death. However, it is within our discretion to release you, if we deem you worthy of mercy, in which case you will be escorted back to your own lands."

"I do not know the Council of Twelve," Erik said. "Do they rule here?"

More laughter from the crowd. "They do not," Ghous said. "The Council of Twelve is made up of the elders of each of the tribes. I sit on the Council myself, to represent my people."

"I see," Erik said. "I was under the impression that each tribe ruled itself."

"That is so, Erik White. We make our own decisions, but the will of the Twelve is not to be taken lightly." Beckoning Qhara and the others forward, Ghous said, "We will hear your testimony."

Alix's gaze flicked from one *pashanai* to the next. At this point, it seemed unlikely the *pasha* would call for their execution, but that was little comfort. Sending them back to Alden would be its own sort of death sentence, for without help from their allies, they couldn't hope to repel Sadik's armies. Yet Alix thought she sensed an opening, a tiny wedge of hope pried open by Erik's carefully chosen words.

"Dabir, what do you have to say on the matter of these imperials?"

Dabir's eyes went to Alix, lingering there a moment before

falling to his boots. She couldn't be sure with his dark skin, but she thought he might have flushed. "Thank you for letting me speak, honourable *pasha*. I believe that they behaved as anyone would who was taken captive. They do not deserve to die."

Fahran snorted, shooting his cousin a disgusted look.

"You disagree, Fahran," said Qhara's grandmother. "What say you?"

"I say this one insulted me!" He levelled a finger at Alix. "I say she almost killed Dabir!"

The old woman's mouth quirked. "They vex you in that order, presumably."

Glancing around, Alix saw that the rest of the *pasha*, and indeed the rest of the crowd, were eyeing Fahran disapprovingly. He seemed to realise it too; he shifted on his feet. "They are dangerous, *pashanai*. These are not ordinary imperials. Whatever you decide here, all the tribes will hear of it. All the world will hear of it. And then *they* will judge *us*, decide if we are strong or weak, if we keep faith or are oath-breakers." His words were having an effect; a number of onlookers were nodding, murmuring agreement. That seemed to restore Fahran a little. He straightened, inclining his head formally. "Thank you for letting me speak, honourable *pasha*."

"And you, grandson?" The old woman's golden gaze shifted to Sakhr. "What say you?"

"Thank you for hearing me, honourable *pasha*. I agree with Dabir. The imperials conducted themselves acceptably under the circumstances. But Fahran is not wrong: Whatever we do here today, there will be consequences. I know the *pasha* will consider these carefully."

The old woman raised her eyebrows. "Qhara?"

"Thank you for hearing me, honourable *pasha*." She looked at Erik. Green-gold eyes met blue, a long, drawn-out stare charged with something Alix couldn't read. "I concur with my brother and Dabir. They behaved as I would have. Better, perhaps."

Kerta whispered a prayer of thanks. Alix knew she should join the sentiment, but she couldn't. Exile meant failure. It meant a return to a country at war, and no help at hand.

But Qhara was not quite through. "I also think . . ." She

hesitated another heartbeat. "I think they should be allowed to continue to Ost, honourable *pasha*."

Sakhr's head snapped to look at his sister. The crowd stirred in astonishment. Qhara ignored it all, her gaze still fixed on Erik.

Qhara's grandmother eyed her solemnly. "I thought you might."

"Impossible." The youngest *pashanai* made a sharp cutting motion with his hand. "The Council of Twelve has made its will clear."

"We could convene them," Qhara's grandmother said. "It is our right."

"That would be a mistake," said another of the *pasha*. "Convening the Twelve is not lightly done, and this matter has already been decided. Imperials do not cross the mountains. The tribes are united in this, if nothing else."

Ghous grunted. "Unity does not make truth, Temur."

"I cannot believe we are even discussing this!" The one called Temur gestured angrily at Erik. "What is it to us if he calls himself a king? Why should we make an exception for him?"

"It is not the man I find exceptional," Qhara's grandmother said. "It is the circumstances."

"We have made promises," Temur returned, "and we must keep them. Peace depends on it."

Qhara's grandmother tutted quietly. "We all value peace, Temur, but let us not pretend there is only one path to it."

"We all know what became of the Arsuk when they allowed the Oridians to pass through their lands," Temur said. "Would you have our tribe censured as well? Our elder"—he gestured at Ghous—"removed from the Council, our voice no longer heard?"

Alix's gaze cut back and forth between them. There seemed to be a generational divide here, and surprisingly, it was the younger of the *pasha* who were taking the more conservative part. Unfortunately, the young also outnumbered the old.

"I do not see what we gain by breaking our oath. I see only what we lose." This from the youngest of the *pasha*. Four of them were doing all the talking; the rest had yet to pronounce themselves, watching the exchange as intently as the prisoners.

Ghous sighed and braced his hands against his thighs. "It

appears this will take longer than we thought," he said, rising slowly. "Come, it is no good arguing in front of the entire village. Let us take some drink together and discuss as friends." So saying, he led his fellow *pasha* through the crowd and disappeared.

They were gone a very long time. The onlookers lingered for a while, but eventually dispersed—except Qhara and the others, who seemed to be responsible for keeping watch. Someone brought water and warm bread. The sun slid behind the peaks.

Twilight was falling when the crowd began to gather again, like clouds before a storm. Alix did pray then, if only in her head.

Blessed Farika, goddess of grace, please let them see.

The *pasha* reappeared, looking worn but resolved. One by one, they resumed their seats. "The *pasha* have decided, Erik White." It was Ghous who spoke, his gusty voice raised for the benefit of the onlookers. "Have you anything final to say?"

Erik shook his head.

"Very well," said Ghous. "This is our verdict."

TWENTY-FIVE

"**G**eneral."

Rig turned to find Morris hovering in the doorway, looking uncomfortable. "The priestess has returned."

Thank the gods for small miracles. After five days, Rig had all but resigned himself to the idea that Vel was never coming back. She'd been caught, or betrayed him, or joined the Resistance herself. Any of these had seemed equally possible. Her return was the first good news he'd had since Whitefish Bridge. "You could at least pretend to sound happy about it, Morris."

His second was unrepentant. "I'll be happy if she gives us

anything we can use, General. Anything we can *trust*." He arched an eyebrow significantly, in case Rig had somehow forgotten about his misgivings.

"Fair enough, but I told her you'd at least be grateful. And I told myself that if you weren't . . . well, you don't want to know."

Morris made a wry face. "I'm guessing it involves my notables."

"You're a sharp fellow, Morris. That's why you're my second. Now go fetch her, will you?"

Vel arrived in the company of Battalion Commander Wright. "A great day, General," the Onnani knight said as he strode through the door, eyes lit with something akin to paternal pride.

"Welcome back, Daughter," Rig said. "I was starting to worry."

"How sweet." She had that same look she'd worn the night before she left: almost childishly eager, eyes shining, skin flush with victory.

"Success, I take it?" Rig said.

"I very much hope so. Will you offer us wine?"

One thing you could safely say about Vel: She did not lack for nerve. Shaking his head, Rig fetched the jug from the hearth.

She indulged in a dramatic pause as she sipped her wine. "Hmm," she said approvingly. "You can barely manage to put meat on the table, yet you always have such fine wine."

"Vel."

"I tax your patience, General. Very well." She set down her cup. "I made contact with the Resistance. Or rather, they made contact with me. They took me captive almost the moment I crossed the river. Word had reached them that spies were coming down from the front looking for them. Enemy spies, they presumed, so they set a trap. I fell right into it. Had I not been Onnani, they would have killed me on the spot. Ironic, don't you think?" She smiled sweetly at Morris.

"Ironic, and bloody lucky," Rig said. "Thank the gods."

"Luck is not a Holy Virtue," Vel said airily.

"What did you do?" Wright asked. "How did you convince them not to kill you?"

"I told them the truth. That I had been sent by General Black himself to make contact with them. They could see from the colour of my skin that I was not Oridian. And they had heard that an Onnani battalion had joined the Kingswords at the front. I showed them my priestess's mask, explained how I came to be among you, and asked to be taken to someone who could speak on their behalf. I offered to let them blindfold me, so that I wouldn't know where I was being taken." She turned her smile on Rig. "A trick I learned from you, General."

I'll be damned. Rig could feel a smile beginning to tug at his mouth. "Go on."

"They took me up on my offer. They searched me, blindfolded me, and took me to some run-down farmhouse in the middle of nowhere. That's where I met him." She chose that moment to pick up her cup and take another sip of wine. *She's savouring every bit of this,* Rig thought. Her moment of triumph. Her *contribution.*

Wright could hardly stand it. "Who?"

"He calls himself Wraith."

Rig's eyebrows flew up. "Excuse me?"

"Not his real name, obviously, but all his men call him that. He is a captain of the Resistance. Quite high ranking, from what I could tell. Though"—her voice became reflective—"I am not entirely sure the Resistance acts as one cohesive unit. I suspect there are several branches all over Andithyri, and whether or not they come together under a single leader isn't clear to me."

Morris grunted thoughtfully. "Useful."

Rig could tell from Vel's expression that she was wrestling with a sarcastic reply, but for once, she kept it to herself. "I had to be careful how many questions I asked, lest I rouse suspicion. I was not there to gather intelligence, but to build trust, so I took what information I was offered, and made myself content with that."

"Smart," Rig said. "And so what about this Wraith? What did you get from him?"

"A man of few words. His people asked me many questions before he offered anything in return, and I had to be very careful what I told him. I made it clear that I would not answer questions about the location of the fort, for instance, or numbers and deployments. He understood that. In truth, I think he would have been suspicious if I had spoken of such things. What I did tell him seemed to accord with information they had gathered on their own, which also helped my credibility. After a full day of circling me like a hawk, he finally accepted that I was who I claimed to be, or at least that he could afford to risk it."

"And?"

"And, it appears that he has been as eager to get in touch with you as you with him."

"Then why hasn't he?" Wright asked. "It is not so very difficult for a single person to steal across the border, as you have just proven."

"He was not sure what kind of man the commander general was. Whether he could trust him."

"What did you say?" Rig asked.

"I told him what kind of man you are." She smiled enigmatically.

Morris flashed an impatient glance at the ceiling. "So what's the nub of it, Daughter? Where did you leave it?"

Vel drew a scroll from her robes. "Here is everything they have on the Warlord's movements. It's not much—Sadik is being more careful now. Wraith says it suggests a newfound respect for his enemy."

Rig scanned the scroll. She was right: It wasn't much. The Resistance did seem to have a good eye on Sadik's supply lines, though. That was something. "Says here they're building new siege engines. The old ones didn't fare so well through the winter."

"That's good news," Morris said. "It'll slow them down some."

"More importantly," Vel said, "he gave us a way of contacting him. A falcon, trained to fly to its master with any message you wish to send. I turned it over to your chief messenger."

"You smuggled a falcon back over the border?" Rig couldn't help laughing.

"No, actually. It followed me overhead. A most remarkable bird."

"The white-hairs are known for it," Morris said. "Falconry was the preferred hobby of the Erromanian nobility."

"If we send a message with this bird," Wright said, "how do we receive the reply? Can it find its way back?"

"I'm not sure. But as you said, Commander, it is not difficult for a single man to sneak across the border. Wraith did not trust me quite enough to divulge his location, nor to give me the key to their cypher, at least not yet. But he is willing to coordinate with us."

"He might not have given you his location," Rig said, "but it says a lot that he gave you that bird. If we wanted to, we could follow it right to him. He must have known that. You obviously got through to him."

She flushed with pleasure and let her gaze fall to the map.

"We should send a message straightaway, General," Wright said. "Strike while the steel is hot."

"Agreed. But I don't want to waste a trip, or risk one of their men, for a simple hello. Let's take a couple of hours to think about this. One thing's sure: We need to know how long it will take them to mobilise. I can think of any number of targets I want hit, but I need a better sense of their capabilities first."

"Sensitive information," Morris said. "We'll probably have to give up something in return."

"Let's think about that too. In the meantime, see to it that falcon is secured. I want as few people knowing about it as possible."

"Aye, General." Morris saluted and withdrew.

"Will you pray with me, Daughter?" Wright asked. "Offer thanks to the Virtues for your success?"

Vel gave him a tired smile. "I would like that very much, Commander, but if you don't mind, I would like to rest first. I am exhausted."

"I can imagine. I'll leave you, then. You know where to find me when you're ready."

The tired look vanished from Vel's face the moment Wright closed the door, replaced by barely restrained triumph. She picked up her wine, drained her cup, and helped herself to another. Her skin, already flush, took on a richer colour. It became her; in the low light of Rig's chambers, she was ominously beautiful.

"Careful," he said. "I need you coherent when we meet again later."

"What's this? Could it be that you actually value my advice?"

"You did well," Rig said, hefting his cup in salute. "Bloody well, if you'll pardon my language."

"I will pardon anything from you, General." Dark eyes peered boldly over the rim of her cup.

"I mean it, Vel. Thank you for this. The gods know I needed some good news." He found it difficult to hold on to his smile after that; it slipped away from him like a pleasant dream.

Vel sobered too. "How are the men coping?"

"About how you'd expect. They're hot for Oridian blood. There's grumbling about the fact we haven't retaliated yet. Even among the officers, Morris tells me."

"The slaughter of children will cloud anyone's judgement."

"Tell me about it." Rig passed a hand over his eyes, as if he could wipe away the memory. "It was all I could do not to lead the lot of them across the river the morning you left. It's only the thought of another Raynesford that stopped me. That, and what you said to me." He glanced at her. "Thank you for that too. I'm sure I didn't seem very grateful at the time, but of course you were right. And I needed to hear it."

"You did and you didn't." She set her wine down and drew closer. "What I said was to soothe your mind, but I know you would not have done anything foolish. Ardin's flame burns bright in you, to be sure, but there is more to you than that. Your passions are tempered by something."

"Age," he said sourly.

She laughed. "Actually, I was thinking it was Destan."

He grunted sceptically. "I would have thought honour would side with passion on this one."

"Honour is the first face of Destan, but he is also duty." A hint of the priestess voice now, that musical cadence that thrummed along Rig's spine. "Duty means looking beyond what you want, to what is required of you. It was Destan who whispered in your ear, told you that you had to look beyond your rage and do what was best for your country. Destan, and of course Eldora." She reached for him, fingertips grazing his brow. "She really does fancy you."

Rig sighed. "I'm not sure what you want from me, Vel."

"It does you no credit. I've been rather plain on the subject." She bit her lip, gaze lingering on his mouth.

"Okay, beyond *that*."

Dark eyes met his. "Why does there have to be anything beyond that?"

That, Rig decided, was a very good question. So when she stood on her toes, he met her halfway.

She kissed him lingeringly this time, with none of the wilfulness of the other day. If anything, though, that only made him burn hotter, for he could savour every soft angle of her, every caress of her lips and tongue and the fingertips against the back of his neck. He drew her into him, sighing like a man relieved of an ache. It was like slipping into that warm water he'd been craving, a silken darkness that flowed around him in gently thrilling folds. He kissed her until he didn't know where he was, his blood running gleefully in every direction but up.

At least, until she started tugging on his clothing. That brought him round quickly enough. It seemed he had a decision to make, one his body was voting on rather exuberantly below the drawstring of his breeches. "Vel . . ."

She ignored him, of course, moving decisively enough that he couldn't help going along with it, raising his arms to let her pull his shirt over his head. He was aware, painfully, that the space for decision making was shrinking.

She raked her nails gently down his stomach, making the same approving noise she'd made over the wine. "Just as I imagined it."

He laughed, a little nervously. "Wait—you imagined this? You mean all that flirting wasn't just . . . ?"

"You really are dense, General." Her arms curved around his neck, drawing his head down.

His blood spiked again, sending his hands off on their own reconnaissance mission. His fingers sought the plunging V at the back of her robes, the soft canyon between her shoulder blades. He felt her shiver in his arms. Her robes slid down off her shoulder, offering a new field to explore, satin under his callused hands. An inch more would expose her breast. The tiny bit of Rig's brain that was still working told him that would be the point of no return.

He broke off, leaving just enough space to breathe.

"Do you want me to go?" Her voice was a strained whisper.

"No."

"Are you afraid of what will happen if I stay?"

"I know what will happen."

"Good." She surged into him, a fierce, final push. Her mouth was on his, her hands on his face, every contour of her body pressed into him.

The last remnants of resistance crumbled.

Rig surrendered.

He was turning the corner to head into the courtyard when Morris nearly collided with him. "General. I was just coming to you. There's been an incident."

Rig's blood, still running rampant from the last hour with Vel, slowed to a crawl. "What kind of incident?"

"A fight."

He blew out a breath. "Bloody *hells*, Morris. I was sure you were about to tell me there was another massacre!"

"Sorry, General."

"Men fight," Rig said irritably. "Why do you need me?"

"I can handle it if you like, but I thought you'd want to hear about this. It wasn't just some ordinary fisticuffs, General. The man who got the worse end of it might not make it through the night."

"*What?*" As though they didn't have problems enough, his men were beating each other to the brink of death? "What in the Nine Domains were they fighting about?"

Morris avoided his eye. "From what I gather, General . . ." He cleared his throat. "It may have been about you."

Rig stared.

"That is, about Raynesford."

Swearing under his breath, Rig said, "Show me."

The soldier who'd done the beating was a thick, ruddy fellow with arms like tree trunks. He stood in the courtyard at the centre of a ring of soldiers, scowling at the ground as though it were the source of all his problems. The scowl melted away when Rig appeared before him, replaced by a look that managed to be both sheepish and stubborn. "General," he said, saluting.

Rig gave him a long, hard look, one he hoped even Arran Green would have approved of. "Name?"

"Hagan, General."

"You want to tell me what happened?"

Hagan shrugged like a sulky adolescent. "Soldiers' fight, General. That's all."

"Soldiers' fight. I see. So you figured the enemy didn't out-number us enough, you wanted to lend a hand?"

The man flushed angrily and looked away. Nearby, a clutch of sol-diers muttered angrily, one of them spitting in the dust. Mates of the beaten man, presumably.

"What provoked it?"

Hagan shifted uncomfortably. "Rather not say, General."

"I don't give a flaming fuck what you'd rather. I asked you a question."

Hagan flushed again. "It's only that . . . What Arch said . . . the thing that really got my blood up, I mean . . . It wasn't respectful about you, General. Wouldn't want to repeat it."

"Do I look like the sensitive sort to you?"

The man smiled nervously. "Not really, no, General. More that I'm a bit worried you'll break me in half, General."

"If I'd wanted my sword polished, I'd have said so. Don't make me ask again."

Hagan's eyes travelled the compass of the courtyard. Low-ering his voice, he said, "Called you a coward, General. Said we should be taking it to the Warlord, after what he done. Said you didn't have the spine."

"That's it?"

"More or less."

"And for this, you thought he deserved to die?"

The man shuffled in the dirt. "Didn't mean for it to get that far. Just got my blood up is all."

Rig motioned disgustedly for the man to be taken to the prisoner's pen. He'd decide what to do with him later. Right now, he had bigger problems on his hands. Turning his back on the courtyard, he motioned Morris in close. "You think that sentiment is going around?"

"The men love you, General."

"I don't give a pig's ass about their love, Morris. I need their loyalty, and not just to me. We can't have division in the ranks. It's poison."

"With you there, General."

"Just an isolated incident, do you think?"

"Hard to say. We've talked about the officers, but the rank and file . . . not my cohort anymore, I'm afraid."

Rig nodded absently. He wished Dain Cooper were here.

The Onnani knight, newly promoted, still had a strong network with the common men, and could always be counted on for a weather check. Rig hadn't realised how much he relied on that until this moment. A commander couldn't afford to be oblivious to the mood of his army. Blindness like that could be fatal—for all of them.

"Division in the ranks is bad enough," Morris said, "but I'm worried about discipline too. Herwin, especially. He's a good man, but hot-blooded. All alone up there by the ford, and Raynesford on his patch . . ."

"Yeah."

"If he takes it into his head to avenge Raynesford, he'll have his arse handed to him, and the ford will be Sadik's."

"And we'll be short a thousand men." Rig swore again, ran a hand roughly over his beard. He felt so gods-damned *futile*, sitting here, waiting for Sadik to strike—or for his men to march to suicide. He couldn't even know whether relief was on the way, whether Liam or Erik had secured the aid the Kingswords so badly needed. He might as well have been shackled to a post, forced to watch as the enemy rode past on their way to slaughter and burning.

For a single, glorious hour in his bedchamber, Rig had been free. So much for that.

As if summoned by his thoughts, Vel appeared in the courtyard. She took in the scene, tense knots of soldiers standing around muttering angrily. "What's happened, General?" She lowered her voice. "Do we have a problem?"

"Yeah," Rig said grimly, "we really do."

TWENTY-SIX

Alix gazed out over the valley, her heart in her throat. Below, the world seemed to spill away, flat as far as the eye could see, and no doubt farther. Behind her, the craggy peaks of the Broken Mountains clustered together like the *pasha*, looming over her, pressing at her back, demanding that she move on.

As if on cue, Sakhr said, "Go now." He inclined his head at the valley, like a dog herding a reluctant sheep.

After everything we've been through, Alix thought. She glanced over at Erik. He looked out over the valley too, his expression unreadable. *What must be going through his mind right now . . .*

Qhara came to stand beside him. "There it is, Imperial Erik. Does it not bring you joy to see it?"

"Under other circumstances, perhaps. At the moment, all I feel is determination."

"In that case, I wish you luck. I think you will need it."

She offered her arm, and he clasped it. "I think you are right."

"I see your escort," Sakhr said, shielding his eyes. "Fifty horses." He made a noise of contempt. "As though fifty *mustevi* would be enough if we meant you harm."

He handed over their weapons. Alix let out a long breath as she strapped her bloodblade to her waist, feeling instantly stronger with its reassuring weight at her side. "Thank you," she said. Lowering her voice, she added, "For the other day, too."

Sakhr shrugged. "I did what was necessary to avoid an ugly situation. If I had not intervened, you would have killed him."

That wasn't what she'd expected him to say. "I would certainly have tried," she admitted.

"He would have deserved it, perhaps, but he is still my kinsman."

There was nothing more to say, so she just nodded. "Shall we go, Your Majesty? King Omaïd awaits."

"Tell him we said hello," Qhara said dryly.

"When you return," Sakhr said, "we will ensure your safe passage through our lands, just as the *pasha* have decreed."

"And what of the other tribes?" Erik asked. "I presume there will be consequences for defying the Council of Twelve."

"There will be," Sakhr said, "but they are not your concern. If you take the lower pass as instructed, you will remain on our lands nearly all the way to your border."

"In that case," said Erik, "I look forward to seeing you again."

Sakhr had already turned away. "You will not see us, but we will see you." A moment later, both he and his sister were gone.

"I can't believe we're really here," Kerta said. "I was sure we would never . . ." She trailed off, swallowing.

"We haven't," Erik said. "Not yet. Hurry now, we have lost enough time." *Maybe too much.* He didn't need to finish the thought; it polluted the air like the smell of carrion.

It took almost three hours to reach the valley floor, and by the time they did, Alix's thighs felt like they were made of sponge cake. She despaired of sitting a horse properly, but compared to what they'd just been through, the worry seemed downright decadent.

They emerged from the trees onto the banks of a foaming river swollen with snowmelt. Their escort must have spotted them somewhere on the slope, because a pair of horsemen awaited them on the riverbank, with three more horses in tow. Both riders dismounted as the weary trio approached, their tall frames folding into bows. "Your Majesty," said the taller of the two in Erromanian. "We had begun to fear the worst." Green eyes scanned the three of them, took in their haggard appearances. "Though perhaps that fear was not entirely unfounded."

"No indeed," Erik said. "We had a difficult time through the mountains."

A difficult time. Alix almost laughed aloud.

"We were fifteen when we crossed the border." Erik gestured at the three of them. "You see what remains."

"In that case, Your Majesty, we are even more overjoyed to see you safely delivered, and to welcome you to the Kingdom of Harram, in the name of His High Lordship King Omaïd." The man laid a hand on his breast and dipped his head. "May I offer you some water? Something to eat?"

Erik brushed the offer aside; he had heavier concerns. "Have you any news from Alden?"

"Last we heard, Your Majesty, there was no change. That was two days ago."

Erik sagged in relief. In that instant, he looked ten years older.

"My name is Aarash," the Harrami said. "It will be my honour to lead you to Ost. This way, please."

It was late afternoon by the time they joined the Harrami camp west of the river, and with only a few hours of sunlight left, there was little point in packing up. Though Erik was impatient to reach Ost, even he could not deny that the rest would be blissful. "We should get as much sleep as we can," he told Alix and Kerta. "As difficult as these past weeks have been, what lies ahead may be more trying still. Diplomacy is a delicate business."

"You needn't worry, Your Majesty," Kerta said. "From the masterful way you handled the *pasha*, I can tell you'll be brilliant."

"Let us hope so, because I cannot afford to be otherwise."

"Kerta's right," Alix said, laying a hand on his arm. "There's no one in the world who handles pressure more gracefully than you."

A strange look came over Erik. "I haven't felt very graceful lately. Quite the contrary, in fact. I'm glad things went well with the *pasha*, but I must admit, it was not easy for me. I felt . . ." He shook his head. "Never mind, I'm just tired. I think I'd better turn in." He bid them good night and headed off to his tent, a huge pavilion of silk and stitched leather expansive enough to accommodate a herd of cattle. For Alix and Kerta, a blanket and the night air would have to serve.

"He'll feel better tomorrow," Kerta said as they waited for sleep to claim them. "He'll be wonderful, as always."

"I hope so. If he isn't . . ." Alix didn't finish the thought, but she didn't need to. They both knew what was at stake. The grim truth was that if Erik failed, they might as well have died in those mountains, because without Harram, they were lost.

"**And this wing** of the palace will be yours, Your Majesty," the steward said, gesturing at a long, elaborately carved corridor lined with elaborately carved doors. Alix knew of the Harrami fondness for intricate design, especially where their furniture was concerned—every noble household in Alden had at least one Harrami cabinet, with their extravagant latticework and mother-of-pearl inlay—but she had never before laid eyes upon stonework like this, arch after arch stretching across the ceiling in sumptuous detail, torchlight flickering through tiny holes and casting strange shadows along the walls. This corridor alone must have taken hundreds of hours to create. She wished Liam could have seen it.

"As for your bodyguard," the steward continued, "I imagine you will wish to keep her close. There is a small servants' cell adjoining your sitting chambers. I hope that will serve."

"Admirably, thank you," Erik said. "And for Lady Middlemarch?"

"She will be quartered in the north wing, with the ladies-in-waiting. Unless you would prefer a different arrangement?" The steward, Paiman, raised his eyebrows.

"I'm sure that will be fine," Erik said.

"Shall I lead you through a brief tour of your rooms?"

"That won't be necessary, thank you. Just point me to the bedchamber."

"At the end of the corridor, Your Majesty. The large arched doors. The ablutions chamber is adjoining. Will there be anything else, Your Majesty?"

"No, thank you."

"In that case, I shall leave you. His High Lordship King Omaïd will receive you for dinner. A servant will come to escort you. Rest well, Your Majesty." Bowing, the steward withdrew, leaving Alix and Erik alone with a pair of silent servants who took up posts on either side of the corridor, in case their royal guest should require anything further.

"Will you sleep?" Alix asked.

"Gods, no. I'm heading straight for a bath." He rubbed his bearded jaw, smiling ruefully. "And a shave."

"Me too," Alix said. "The bath part, anyway." She had never looked forward to one more than she did at that moment.

Which made it all the more disappointing when she opened the door to her assigned quarters and found nothing more than a bed, a bucket, and a washbasin.

She stood in the doorway, staring in mild disbelief. *A small cell*, the steward had called it. He hadn't understated the matter. If Alix had been just a few inches taller, her head would have brushed the ceiling. If she lay on the floor spread-eagled, she'd touch all four walls. Her privy at Blackhold was twice this size. And it didn't require her to relieve herself in a *bucket*.

Fury flooded her insides. *Do they know who I am?* But of course they did; Erik had introduced her—as his bodyguard, in accordance with her own wishes. Not Lady Alix Black, for that name was gone, and with it all the things she might have been. She belonged to Erik now, and to Liam. And as far as her hosts were concerned, that meant she was no one of consequence.

The Harrami, Albern Highmount had said, *are very proud.* Evidently, that was putting it mildly. Paiman and the other servants hadn't even made eye contact with her in the courtyard. They'd treated Erik's horse with more deference. Alix knew she shouldn't let it bother her, but it was hard to accept this notion of who she was.

She washed up as best she could with what she had on hand, shivering from scalp to soles as she dragged a cold, wet rag over her body. She spent a good half hour running her fingers painfully through her hair, having lost her comb in the avalanche. She had just finished tying off her customary braid when a knock sounded at her little cell door. Opening it, she found a servant carrying a bundle of letters. "For you," the man said, shoving the bundle at her. "Also, Paiman bade me tell you that the servants eat breakfast in the kitchen one hour before dawn." Without waiting for a reply, he turned his back on her and left.

Alix blinked in astonishment. *Breakfast in the kitchen? With the* servants?

Then she saw the handwriting on the letters, and her outrage was instantly forgotten. *Liam.*

There were half a dozen of them, each one folded into the tiny envelopes carried by messenger hawks. He must have started writing them almost as soon as he'd left her. Grinning like a fool, she started to tear open the first seal. Then she remembered something, and she paused, her smile fading. Liam had given her a letter on the day they'd parted. *Save it for a cold night*, he'd told her. She'd meant to do just that, but then the avalanche . . . Her heart gave a painful twinge. She'd lost her pack in the avalanche, and with it, Liam's letter.

Suddenly, the tiny envelopes in her hand were all the more precious. She tore them open eagerly, scanning each one for the date. The first was over a month old. Her heart gave another pang. *Has it really been so long?* And yet at the same time, it seemed longer.

Dear Allie,

I'm writing you from an inn called the Boar's Tusk. Somewhere in the Greylands, I'm told, which I suppose means we're near the border. Nothing exciting yet, which is probably a good thing. Come to think of it, I hope this ends up being the most boring trip of my life.

Anyway, I met my new second today. Dain Cooper. Decent bloke, from what I can tell, though it's hard to forget that he's displacing Ide. Who says, "Hi," by the way. So does Rona. She's started braiding her hair like yours. Do you suppose she's got a crush on you?

Alix laughed aloud. Liam could be so endearingly clueless sometimes.

As you can tell, I haven't got much to say. We've barely got started, and it's only been a day since I saw you. But I miss you already, Allie. Loads. I wish so much that you could be here with me. Or that I could be there with you. Or better still, that we could be holed up in a cottage in the woods somewhere, just the two of us, raising bear cubs. Doesn't that sound nice? Possibly I should have mentioned that as a lifelong dream of mine before we married, but I was sure you'd understand.

I should probably turn in now. This lamp is running out of oil, and I really don't want to have to call the innkeep. I'm not sure I can stand to see that moustache again. It's genuinely terrifying. It was watching me all through dinner, and when the innkeep nodded off behind the bar, I'm pretty sure I saw it move. I'm afraid it'll come for me in the night. Maybe I'll sleep with a dagger under my pillow.

I'd tell you to take care of Erik, but I know you will. You always do. I hope you're enjoying Ost, lying on one of those big canopy beds with the fancy carved posts.

Be safe, my love.
Liam

Alix could almost hear his voice in her ear. Gods, how she missed it. Smiling, she reached for another.

Her smile didn't make it through the first paragraph.

His abrupt dismissal at the Republicana. The discovery that the fleet was less than half finished. The cynical machinations of politicians whose agendas he just couldn't grasp. No humour, no quintessentially Liam nonsense. Just the unwavering sense that he was failing, again and again.

The letter after that was even worse, and by the time she'd finished all four, it felt as if she'd swallowed a stone.

I don't know what to do, Allie.

He hadn't even signed the last one, as if he couldn't bear to put his name to the defeat he'd narrated in painstaking detail. He'd made no progress, and no friends. Rona and the others couldn't seem to help him. He was alone out there, confused and frustrated, without even a single letter from her to ease his mind. "Oh, Liam," she whispered. "I'm so sorry."

She would send for a quill and parchment straightaway, she decided. If she couldn't be there, she could at least send some comfort from afar. She was in the process of working out how long it would take a hawk to cross the mountains when a gentle tinkling sounded above her head. She looked up to see a small brass bell juddering on the end of a cord that disappeared into the wall. Erik, she supposed, ringing the servants' bell. Folding her letters away, she headed for his chambers.

I wonder how much I should tell him, she thought as she knocked on his door. *Maybe it's better if I—*

The look on Erik's face was enough to drive even Liam from her mind. "Good gods, are you all right?"

"Come in." He stood aside, closing the door behind him. A letter dangled at his side, crumpled into a ball.

"What is it? What's happened?"

He'd just shaved; his smooth jaw showed every taut muscle, every blotch of fury. He held up the letter, his hand showing a slight tremor. "A massacre. On the border."

"Farika's mercy." Alix sank onto a chair. "Where?"

"A village called Raynesford."

"I don't know it."

He hardly seemed to hear. He'd started pacing, boots all but silent on the plush Harrami rug. "I've sent for Kerta. According to this, Raynesford is just upriver from Harriston, which means it's near her family home. She may have lost people."

Alix swallowed a knot in her throat. "Who is it from?"

"Rig." He held it out to her.

Alix scanned the familiar handwriting, her eyes filling. It wasn't just the tidings, though those were awful enough. Her brother's rage, his grief, saturated the page. *I wish I could promise that I will avenge this, Your Majesty, in your name. But the truth is, without reinforcements, there is little I can do. To say that I have failed you would be inadequate.*

Futility. Failure. The same bitter flavours as Liam's letter, the same taste that had sat on Alix's tongue throughout their journey through the Broken Mountains.

Blessed Farika, is there nothing we can do to end this?

A soft knock came at the door. Alix answered it. She could tell from the look on Kerta's face that her friend was already braced for terrible news. Wordlessly, Alix handed her the letter. Kerta wept silently as she read, one hand over her mouth, the other holding the letter as far away from her as she could, as though the distance might shield her from the pain.

"Did you have people there?" Erik asked.

Kerta gave a convulsive shake of her head. "But the Raynesfords . . . They're family friends . . ."

Alix put her arms around Kerta. As she stood there—holding

her sobbing friend, listening to the pacing of her furious king, her eyes still stinging from the grief of her brother—Alix felt something snap, sharp and brittle as an old chicken bone. A single thought, blazing red, formed in her mind.

The Oridians would *pay*.

She would write a letter after all, she decided, but not to Liam. Not yet.

If you require anything of me, do not hesitate to send word.

A rasping voice in a rose garden, like a memory of long ago. She did require something of Saxon after all, something that demanded his particular skills. *Wars are rarely ended by assassination*, he'd told her. That might be true, but surely the death of a Trion would be a staggering blow to the enemy. The more Alix thought about it, the faster her heart pounded, fury and determination and something else she couldn't quite place, something teetering between exhilaration and terror.

Erik would never approve. She knew it, yet in that moment, she'd didn't care. Erik didn't have to know. No one had to know.

Saxon might not succeed—might even refuse altogether—but Alix was determined to try. After all, she wasn't merely some servant. She had resources. She could influence events. After weeks of frustration and impotence, of being a victim, Alix had glimpsed a way out.

The way of blood.

TWENTY-SEVEN

†Liam flopped onto his side and blew out a long, irritated breath. Rudi stirred at his feet, groaning reproachfully. The wolfhound had lately taken to sleeping on Liam's bed, which he wouldn't mind so much if that didn't actually mean *on his feet*, an arrangement that might

have been comfortable if he was sleeping in a lean-to on the highest peaks of the Broken Mountains in the dead of winter but was otherwise disagreeably sweaty.

"This is going to stop when we get back to Erroman," Liam informed the wolfhound groggily. Rudi's ears did not so much as twitch.

Liam sighed. It was no use; he'd been tossing and turning all night, and that wasn't going to change in the last hour or so before dawn. Extracting his feet from under the beast, he tugged on his breeches and headed for the balcony.

He decided to do some sit-ups. It had been ages since he'd had any decent exercise, and he'd be damned if he went home soft around the edges. His wife was quite fond of his edges, so it behove him to keep them intact.

He was nearing a hundred when he thought he heard a noise on the wrong side of the balcony rail. He paused, elbows to knees, listening, but his ears were too full of the sound of his own laboured breathing to discover anything else. He uncoiled, recoiled. Paused. Had he heard it again? Rolling to his feet, he peered over the rail. Darkness sloped away into the distance, pooled in the valley below, the contours of the city barely visible in the weak moonlight. The morning lamps were not yet lit; it must have been earlier than he thought. A sharp breeze swept up from the sea, rustling the potted cedars. *There you go*, Liam thought, turning away.

Pain erupted at the back of his skull. White light flared behind his eyes, and he staggered, slicing his bare feet on broken pottery. Instinctively, he threw himself to the ground, managing to avoid a flash of metal that could only be a dagger. He glimpsed the vague outline of a shape looming over him. It was enough. He blasted his right heel into his attacker's knee, bringing him down. That bought him enough time to roll onto his back, which gave him a disturbingly good view of the sword aimed at his chest. He jerked aside, the tip of the blade ringing off stone and sending sparks flying. Liam swept the ankles and rolled again, this time to his feet.

Frenzied barking from the other side of the door, just out of reach. Liam hoped it would rouse help, because from the looks of things, he'd need it.

There were three of them, just like last time. But this time they were properly armed, and Liam was half naked. The first two had regained their feet, and a third had just hopped over the balcony rail, blade in hand. Two swords and a knife. The closest thing Liam had to a weapon were the bits of flowerpot buried in his skull, and that probably wouldn't be much help.

They spread out. Liam planted his feet and crouched. Everyone waited to see who would go first.

A sword whistled toward him. Liam jerked the upper half of his body back, letting the blade breeze over his chest. He couldn't afford to give ground, not with the balcony rail only a few feet behind him. If he got tied up against that, he was finished. He could jump, but the slope on the south side was a nasty bit of rock, ideal for breaking an ankle. He'd be easy prey after that. As for the front rail, the one he'd gone over with the spy, there was a regrettable number of blades between him and it.

The sword came at him again, and this time it was joined by another, aimed lower. Liam leapt back, losing precious space. The back of his knee hit the stone bench. If he went around it, he'd be pinned in a corner, with nowhere to go but dead. His attackers knew it too; he could see the realisation kindling in their eyes. In a heartbeat, they'd charge, and that would be it.

Liam jumped up onto the bench and sprang at the eastern rail. Pushing off with his right foot, he threw himself into the nearest swordsman, tackling him to the ground before the man could react. He really didn't have a plan for what came next, so it was a good job that things went down like they did.

Glass exploded onto the balcony as Rudi sailed through the rose window. The wolfhound's paws had scarcely touched stone before he was in the air again, launching himself at the man with the knife. The poor fool tried to get his arm up, but that just gave Rudi something to grab on to. Screams of terror turned to screams of pain. Liam didn't pause to marvel. He cracked his attacker's head against stone, twisted the sword from his grasp, and came up swinging before the third man could recover from his shock. Liam had him skewered before the thug even really knew what was happening.

Only one assassin remained now, lying stunned on the balcony floor. Liam wavered for all of two breaths before Rudi made the choice for him, going after the man's throat with terrible enthusiasm. By the time Liam hauled the wolfhound off, the deed was done.

"Bloody hells, dog, did you have to—*ugh*." Liam had seen more than his share of death, but a man with his throat torn out was a new level of gruesome. Moonlight gleamed off the darkness pumping from the wound. Liam eyed the wolfhound warily, half afraid he'd be next, but Rudi just wagged his nub and sat, panting as if he'd had a particularly satisfying walk.

"Commander!" Rona Brown burst through the door, sword in hand, nightgown flapping around her. Dain Cooper was half a step behind, also armed, and quite thoroughly naked. Ide appeared a moment later, blessedly clothed.

"I'm fine," Liam said, patting Rudi down to make sure the knife hadn't touched him. "We're fine."

"What the—oh." Rona grimaced. *"Ugh."*

"Yeah, that's what I said."

"Good boy, Rudi!" Ide dropped to her haunches and ruffled the wolfhound's ears. "Who's a good boy?"

"Can we not encourage him, please?"

"Who were they?" Dain asked, patrolling around the dead men with his sword tip up, as though one of them might recover from having no throat. Rudi had even made sure that the man Liam killed was really, truly dead. Thorough, his dog.

"Not sure." Liam scanned their faces. "This one looks familiar. Might be one of the ones who jumped me the other night. Looks like he meant it this time, though."

"He's got a tattoo," Rona said, gesturing with her sword.

Ide cocked her head. "That a snake, or a rope?"

"It's a maritime knot," Dain said.

She scoffed. "Dumb thing to get inked on your arm, you ask me."

"Nautical tattoos are surprisingly common around these parts," Dain said dryly.

Shef appeared in the doorway, ghoulishly white in the glow of his lantern. "Your Highness! By the gods, is everything all right?"

"Er, more or less, thanks. Nothing we can't handle. Well, except we have a bit of a mess here . . ."

Dawn found Liam's room rather crowded. Servants bustled to and fro, clearing up bodies, blood, glass, and forlorn bits of flowerpot. One particularly intrepid fellow even thought to give Rudi a bath, which proposal the wolfhound declined with a flash of teeth. (Liam promised to do it himself, possibly after donning full plate armour.) The Wolves all stayed put. Dain had put on a pair of Liam's breeches, but Rona was still in her distressingly thin nightgown. Liam had never before made such a conscious effort to maintain eye contact *at all costs*.

"Sure," Ide was saying, "it's got to be the same ones as sent the note, but where does that get us? Got no idea who they are, do we?"

"Or what they really want," Dain said. "Beyond the immediate, I mean. Guess that death threat wasn't just bluster after all. But why are they out for the commander's head?"

"To keep him from stirring things up about the fleet, presumably," said Rona.

"Which means they're most likely connected with our saboteur," Liam reasoned. "Either that, or they really just don't like monarchist bastards."

Rona frowned. "Commander, please. You shouldn't make light. If anything had happened to you . . ."

"Have I ever told you how much you sound like my wife?"

Rona looked down at her feet, her teeth working at the inside of her cheek.

"*Anyway*," Dain said, a little intrusively, "linking these blokes to the saboteurs doesn't help us either, since we're still nowhere on that. Nothing plus nothing equals nothing."

"Yeah, about that." Liam's gaze took a quick inventory of the room. Judging that Bayview's servants were sufficiently occupied, he said, "I had a thought."

The Wolves clustered in tighter.

"Something Syril said the other day has been stuck in my mind. Spent most of the past five hours tossing and turning over it. Remember that motion he mentioned? Mass mobilisation, I think he called it?"

"The one the Alliance tabled," Rona said. "What about it?"

"Syril called it a betrayal. Said it was little better than slavery."

Rona shrugged. "He's a populist."

"Right, and apparently, he doesn't think much of forcing Onnani men to fight someone else's war."

"Won't be someone else's for long," Ide said.

"The point is, Syril thinks it's wrong to oblige his countrymen to fight. He tried to block the declaration of war, and now he's trying to block mass mobilisation."

The Wolves glanced at each other. Ide seemed to be speaking for all of them when she said, "So?"

"So what if it's that simple? What if the saboteur isn't in league with the enemy, or trying to embarrass the government, or anything so complicated as that? What if someone is just prepared to go that little bit further to prevent Onnan's sons from having to march to war?"

"Okay," said Dain, "but that still doesn't tell us *who*."

"I've got an idea about that too. I think Syril was trying to tell me something the other day."

Rona raised her eyebrows. "*Trying* to tell you something?"

"Dain, what do you know about the dockies?"

"Not much. They're a union like any other, I suppose. Though . . ." His forehead cleared, his eyes widening a fraction. "The knot."

"Come again?"

"The tattoo. The maritime knot. I've seen it before!" Dain shook his head in amazement. "I'd forgotten all about it until you mentioned the dockies. Remember when I told you that my father and I used to hang around the docks when I was a boy? We used to watch the dockies working. Twice a day, their foreman would come out to keep an eye on things. He had a sort of uniform, a bright yellow vest with a crest on the back. I'm almost certain it had a knot like that in it."

"You said lots of folk have tattoos like that round here," Ide pointed out.

"Quite a coincidence, though," Rona said.

Liam found himself pacing, just like his brother. "The first I heard of the dockies was when we went to inspect the fleet. They were giving us the sour eye. Then a couple of days later, Chief Mallik mentioned them, how they'd gone on strike and held up the work. I didn't think much of it at the time, but then on the day of his arrest, Syril suggested that I try to meet with them."

"And now this," Rona said. "By Hew, Commander, do you think . . . ?"

"I think . . ." Liam stopped, shook his head. "No, you know what? It's not even about thinking. This *feels* right." He started for the door, striding like a man with a purpose.

"Where are you going?"

"I need to get a message to Syril. He seemed to think he could arrange a meeting, even from prison. I plan to take him up on his offer." Belatedly, Liam realised he was being followed. He paused midstride and looked down. Rudi was at his side, nub wagging, looking up at him expectantly. "Since when?" Liam muttered.

"So, what," said Ide, "you're gonna have a nice sit-down with the blokes who tried to kill you?"

"That's about the size of it, yeah."

"Commander, could I have a moment?" There was a *tone* there, Liam thought, a suspicion that was confirmed when he turned to find Rona Brown glaring at him, hands on hips.

"Okay," he said warily, gesturing for her to join him in the corridor. He closed the door behind him. "What is it?"

She folded her arms tightly over her chest, eyes on her feet. "May I speak freely, Commander?"

"Always."

"I don't think you're taking this situation seriously."

Liam's eyebrows flew up. "You're kidding, right? I'm taking it plenty seriously, Rona, believe me. If I can't fix this—"

She cut him off with a shake of her head. "That's not what I mean. I'm talking about what happened here this morning. I'm talking about everything that's happened up to now. I don't think you realise how much danger you're in, Commander. Those men wanted to *kill* you."

"I got that impression, yeah. The whole coming-at-me-with-swords sort of gave it away."

"You see, that's exactly the sort of—"

"Look, I get it. You think I'm being glib, and maybe I am. That's just how I deal with things. But don't forget, this isn't my first horse race. I've been a soldier since I was thirteen years old. I've faced plenty of men who've wanted to kill me. Except there's usually a lot more of them, and they're better armed and better trained."

"They're also out in the open, right there in front of you brandishing their intentions. They're visible and predictable.

Everything your enemies here are not." She raised her eyes to him, and he saw real fear. "I'm a soldier too, Commander. But I was also raised at court, and I learned very quickly that the enemies you can't see are far, far more dangerous. Whatever's happening here, it involves powerful people with hidden agendas. They're ruthless and ambitious and they won't let you get in the way of their designs. It's a game that's been going on since before you got here, and will keep going long after you leave. Please tell me you understand what I'm talking about."

"I understand."

"If anything were to happen to you . . ."

"I *understand*, Rona." And he did, maybe for the first time. It wasn't exactly news, but Rona was right—he hadn't really thought it through, either. He was so busy worrying about the fleet, he'd forgotten to worry about himself. It was just so easy to pretend that the danger he couldn't see wasn't really there, that it didn't need to be added to his list of things to worry about. Easy, and potentially fatal. She was right about that too. He sighed. "I'll try to be more careful, all right? But you know I can't just walk away. Not until I do my job here."

"I know, and I'm not asking you to. I'm just . . . I just want you to be safe, Commander."

"Me too, oddly enough." He put a hand on her shoulder, gave it a reassuring squeeze. "But in the meantime, I've got to see a man at the docks."

The answer arrived within the hour: Liam and his officers would be awaited at the quay. No escort, no weapons. Should they fail to follow these instructions, they would find themselves alone. There would be no second chances, the message said.

All of which was fine with Liam. His "friends" in the Republicana hadn't done him any good thus far, and while he might have wished for a few moments with Ash Bookman, there was no time to send for the former secretary, and he probably wouldn't have come anyway. As for the bit about the weapons, Liam interpreted that rule as he had done the night he visited the Shield: loosely. He left his knife in his boot, and though he didn't ask, he was pretty sure his officers had done the same.

The appointed place turned out to be a redbrick warehouse with its windows boarded shut. A single, rough-looking man lounged at the door, chewing something that stained his teeth an unsettling red. Wordlessly, he looked Liam and the Wolves up and down, jerked the door open, and cocked his head.

Rough hands seized them the moment they stepped inside. Liam had half expected that, so he endured the patting down in silence, as did Rona and Dain. Ide, meanwhile, cursed with such florid imagination that Liam actually blushed.

"That one swears better than a sailor."

The voice came from the shadows. Liam addressed his reply somewhere over his left shoulder. "Doesn't she? I'm thinking of starting a contest in one of the bigger taverns in Erroman. She'll make us all rich, I think."

An amused snort. "I'll be sure to sign up to the lists if you do. Might need a translator, though."

"Your Erromanian sounds pretty good to me."

"I get by. Not all of us can have posh accents like yours."

The first salvo. Ide met it with an incredulous laugh. "His accent, posh? For a Lower Town smithy, maybe." She glanced at Liam. "No offence, Commander."

"Oh, none taken."

Metal scraped, and the glow of a lantern bathed the hard angles of a rugged, square face. "That's right. How could I forget? You come from humble stock, don't you, Your Highness? Why, you're just like me." His mouth twisted sardonically, in case Liam had missed the sarcasm.

"I wouldn't know," Liam said. "I don't know anything about you. And you don't know anything about me." *For all that you've decided I deserve to die.* He kept a tight rein on that thought. Now wasn't the time; he had bigger issues to deal with first.

The man continued as if he hadn't heard. "That's why they sent you, isn't it? Seeing how you're so close to the *common man* and all?"

"Is that what you are? The common man? I wonder how many dockhands speak a second language."

The square face split into a grin. "Well now, you got me there, Your Highness. My brothers do value a bit of education in their leader, it's true."

"You're Gir, then?"

He sketched a bow. "Chairman of the dockies, at your humble service, Your Highness."

"Can we skip the *Your Highness*, please? I don't like it at the best of times, let alone when it's treated like a dirty word. You've made it clear what you think of me. *Monarchist bastard*, I think it was." A glancing blow, but it was all he dared for now.

Gir stared at him blankly, as if the words meant nothing to him. "Fen," he said, addressing the shadows, "a bit of light, if you please." Another lantern was opened, and another after that, by a pair of unseen hands. The soft light revealed a simple table ringed with chairs; Gir invited them to sit. "So," he said, "Syril said you wanted to talk. I'm listening."

"I'm grateful to the speaker for setting up this meeting, considering how he feels about me."

"You're grateful, I'm surprised." Gir flashed a thin smile. "Considering how he feels about you."

"He must have had his reasons for bringing us together. I expect we should take that as our starting point." Liam paused to let that sink in, studying the square features before him. Sun-baked and salt-scoured, with a thick neck that ran abruptly into wide shoulders, Gir looked like the sort of bloke you wouldn't want to bump into in a dark alley. On the other hand, there was an undeniable shrewdness to his small, beady eyes.

Liam decided to scrap caution. "There's probably a hundred more elegant ways of saying this, but I'm tired and frustrated and running out of time, so here it is: I know that someone is sabotaging the construction of the fleet, and I've a solid notion that someone is you." He left the rest of the accusation unsaid.

Not even a blink. He'd make a good gambler, this one.

Liam forged ahead. "I think you're doing everything you can to delay Onnan entering the war. And I even understand it, in a way. But it has to stop. For the good of my country and your own, it has to stop."

A brief silence ensued, cool and empty as the shadows surrounding them. Gir's expression betrayed nothing save an ironic twitch of the mouth. "That it?"

"That's it."

Gir laced his fingers on the table and leaned forward.

"Supposing the dockies were involved in the delays with the fleet—and I'm not saying we are—well, that would be an act of treason, wouldn't it? Against our government, freely elected by the people. Though not"—his lip curled—"by any dockie, nor any man with pride or sense."

"I suppose it would," Liam said warily.

"So tell me, if the dockies were prepared to defy our own freely elected government, what in the Nine Domains makes you think we'd take orders from the *Prince of Alden*? The days of empire are over, Your Highness, or hadn't you noticed?"

Liam couldn't help it; he laughed ruefully, casting his gaze up to the ceiling in a silent appeal to the gods.

"Something funny, Your Highness?"

"Oh, just appreciating the irony. I've spent the last six months pretending to be a prince. Walking around the palace, dressed in silk and velvet, letting people call me *Your Highness*. I even got a dog so people would think of my grandfather, so they might forget for half a heartbeat that I'm a bastard. Didn't fool anyone. Not for a single moment. At court, I'm a half-breed and always will be." He could feel Rona Brown's eyes on him now, and those of the others too. "And now here I am, in a country still nursing a bitter hatred for the monarchy from the days of the old empire, and suddenly the prince is all anyone sees."

"My sympathies," Gir said. "Would you like a handkerchief?"

"The point is, what I said a moment ago—it wasn't an order. It was a plea. My country is under siege."

"I'm sorry for it. But that doesn't give you the right to enlist slaves to your cause."

Liam's hands twitched into fists under the table. "Not slaves. Allies."

"Slaves," Gir repeated implacably. "This isn't our war. The Oridians have never threatened us. They wouldn't have threatened you if your king hadn't declared war on them. But he did, and now, instead of facing up to what he's brought upon himself, he strong-arms my country into helping him. Once again, Erroman forces Onnan to do its dirty work."

"No one forced the Republicana to do anything," Dain interjected. "They voted freely to join the war."

Gir sneered at him. "Don't be naïve. Erroman's coercion comes in different forms these days—in tariffs and embargoes instead of prisons and torture machines—but it's coercion all the same."

"You must not think highly of your leaders," Rona said. "Could it be that they acted not out of cowardice, but out of wisdom? Or do you honestly believe the Oridians will stop at our border and leave your port untouched?" She tilted her head, as though considering an exasperating child. "The legendary port of Onnan, the finest natural harbour in all of Gedona. Now who's being naïve?"

A brief silence fell. Liam thought Gir might have flushed a little, though with his dark complexion and the orange glow of the lantern, it was hard to be sure. "None of that even matters anymore," Liam said. "The choice was made. Your country is at war with the Trionate. All you're doing is crippling your own forces, putting your own men at risk." He took a chance then, gambling on something he thought he'd seen in the other man's eyes a moment ago. "I think you know that, or you wouldn't be meeting with us now."

Gir's gaze met his, and Liam saw it again—resignation, however bitter. Mingled, he saw now, with fear. "Mass mobilisation, they're calling it," the leader of the dockies said, forcing the words past clenched teeth. "I'm no coward. Me, they can have. My brothers, and even my father if they want his old bones. But my sons . . . my nephews . . ."

Another silence, heavier this time. "How old are they?" Liam asked. "Your sons?"

"Thirteen and fifteen. *Boys.*" He spat the last word like an accusation. "Syril is doing what he can, but now that he's in prison . . ." He trailed off, shaking his head.

"I see." There was a sort of grudging understanding in Rona Brown's voice. "You started off hoping to prevent Onnan from entering the war, but you failed. Now, it's a new fight. You hope to use the fleet as a bargaining chip, is that it?"

"Boys." It wasn't an admission—not quite—but it was close enough.

Too young, Liam thought. *He's right about that.* Even in Alden, with the war in full, poisonous flower, military service was only obliged from the age of sixteen.

Gir's eyes still held his, and there was a message in them now. Somewhere along the way, Liam had become the sort of man who could read these things. "It's extortion," he growled.

"It is," Gir agreed, without a hint of shame.

"Even if I let myself be used like this, I'm not sure it'll work. I'm a foreigner. I don't carry much clout."

"Didn't you just tell me that all anyone here sees is the prince?" Gir smiled, hard and mirthless. "It's time to spend some of that political capital, Your Highness."

Liam hesitated. There was danger here, more than a little. For Alden to interfere so blatantly in the politics of its former slaves . . . He would be spending political capital, all right, a whole lot of it, maybe more than Erik could afford. And he'd be doing it for a man who had tried to have him killed. *But what choice do you have, really? You can't prove anything, and even if you could, he's got a whole union of followers to pick up where he left off.* "If I do this," Liam said slowly, "and I can't promise it will work, but if I try, I need you to do more than just leave the fleet alone. I need you to help Mallik. All of you. I need that fleet finished as soon as possible. Can you do that?"

Nodding gravely, Gir held out his arm.

TWENTY-EIGHT

A soft, almost reluctant knock roused Alix from sleep. She sat up, rubbing the kink in her neck and peeling her dry tongue from the roof of her mouth. *I wonder what time it is?* With no windows in her tiny servants' cell, it was impossible to tell. She hoped she hadn't overslept; the gods knew she'd been exhausted enough when she fell asleep.

She opened the door of her cell to find Paiman, the steward, wringing his hands in a manner highly reminiscent of his counterpart in Erroman. "Your Highness," he said, sweeping into an absurdly low bow, "I am so sorry. So very, very sorry! This is simply mortifying! I most humbly beg your pardon. I cannot apologise enough. Had I but known . . . but they didn't inform me, you see, and I . . ."

He went on like that for some time, the words blurring together in Alix's sleep-sodden brain until she raised a hand in a reflexive gesture that was half warding, half commanding. The steward swallowed audibly and fell silent.

"Sorry, but . . ." Alix rubbed her gummy eyes. *"What?"*

"They told me you were merely the king's bodyguard," he said, almost pleadingly. "How was I to know?"

Ah. They'd apparently realised who Alix was: daughter of a Banner House. Not just any Banner House, either; one in high favour with the king, second only to the Greens in prestige. She couldn't quite prevent the smug twitch at the corner of her mouth.

"Highborn, obviously," Paiman continued, seemingly eager to explain his reasoning, "or a position so close to His Majesty would not be possible, but ultimately a servant."

Alix's eyes narrowed sharply. "Highborn indeed. A *Black*, in point of fact."

The name skipped over him without so much as a ripple. "How could I have guessed that you had recently married His Highness? The chancellor should have told me! It is *his* business to keep abreast of such matters, not mine! Please, Your Highness, I humbly beg your forgiveness." The absurdly low bow again, endangering the tenuous hold of his comb-over.

Alix regarded the top of his head coldly. "Just to be sure I understand, you are apologising to me not because you assigned the daughter of a Banner House to a servants' cell, but because you failed to realise that I was *Liam's wife*?"

The steward's eyebrows rose in assent.

He would never know how close he came to losing teeth in that moment.

"I see," Alix said, the words bristling with frost. "In that case, your apology is accepted."

The bitter sarcasm flew right past his comb-over. "Thank you, Your Highness. Oh, thank you! We are preparing more appropriate quarters for you even now. A hot bath will be drawn, and breakfast laid out . . . Oh no, Your Highness, please, leave all of that! Someone will be along to fetch it for you . . ."

And so on down the hallway, Alix fuming with every step. None of this sudden solicitude was for her. Not for the captain of the royal guardsman, not even for Lady Alix Black. For *Liam*. Apparently, as far as Omaïd's court was concerned, she was no more than an adjunct to her husband.

She'd worked herself into such a froth of temper that when Paiman opened the doors to her new chambers—expansive, opulent, sumptuously beautiful—she had an almost overwhelming urge to break the most expensive thing she could get her hands on. They'd forgive her for it. After all, she was *Liam's wife*.

She managed to hold on to her outrage all through breakfast. Even through the soothing, scented waters of her bath. Then Erik arrived, and he took one look at her petulant scowl and burst out laughing. "Oh, my poor Alix." He didn't even need to be told why she was angry—he knew her too well. "Suffering in silence for a whole night. Why in the Domains didn't you just *tell* them?"

"Tell them what? That I should be in quarters more appropriate for the royal consort?"

The blue eyes grew mock serious. "Oh, dear."

"Oh, yes. They *knew*, Erik. They knew I was highborn, and they didn't care! I'm only here because of Liam!"

He regarded her with a curious smile. "I must say, I'm surprised. I had no idea you were such a proud creature, at least not where rank is concerned."

"I'm not!" To her horror, she felt herself flushing. "Not usually, anyway. But after the way they treated me, like something they gouged out from under your horse's hooves—"

He was laughing again.

"—and now the only reason they repent it is because I'm *Liam's wife*. They couldn't care less who I am, or what I've accomplished. All that matters is who I'm married to, and *will you stop laughing*!"

"You're the one who insisted we use your military rank."

"I know."

"Per your instructions, Lord Sommersdale told them nothing of your station, only that you were captain of the royal guardsmen. If we had at least informed them that you were a Black, you would have been quartered with Kerta."

"I *know*, Erik, but . . ."

He put his arms around her. "It's perfectly right that you're proud of your achievements, Alix, but that doesn't mean you can't also be proud of your bloodline. You very clearly are, or you wouldn't be so offended. Why fight it?"

He was right, of course. If she hadn't been ready to be treated like a commoner, she should have owned up to her name. If she had, the Harrami would never have dared to put her in that tiny cell. On the other hand, they wouldn't have put her in these grand chambers, either. Only Liam's name earned her that privilege. *And there's the nub of it*, Alix realised grudgingly. *Liam outranks you*. Liam, who'd always followed her lead, who was barely visible in her shadow. Now it was she who was barely visible in his.

Erik's arms were still around her. "You're in high good humour," she said, a little sulkily.

"I suppose I am, though the gods know I have little reason to be." He pulled back, still smiling. His hand lingered on her arm, and for a moment—with that crooked grin, those mischievous eyes—he looked very like Liam. "You bring it out in me, it seems." She might have imagined it, but she thought she felt the faintest pressure on her arm.

Just like that, the world swerved under her. It was as though someone had yanked the reins of a fast-moving carriage, veering abruptly, dangerously, in a new direction. Alix swallowed a sudden tightness in her throat. The way he was looking at her . . . It had been a long time since he'd looked at her like that. Though not long enough, it seemed, to completely change what it did to her. Warmth flooded her insides. He saw it; she could tell by his own rising colour. She had no armour against him now. He knew her too well.

They both turned away in the same horrified instant. A brief, tense silence ensued. "I'm for the Grand Library," he said, his voice edged with something Alix couldn't place. He approached the sideboard, fidgeted with the stopper of the crystal decanter in a decidedly un-Erik fashion. For the second time in as many moments, Alix was reminded forcefully of Liam. "I've always wanted to see it, and I don't know when I'll get another chance. If things don't go well tonight, this might be a very short visit indeed."

"You mustn't keep talking like that," she said, trying to find somewhere safe to rest her gaze, somewhere that wasn't Erik and didn't remind her of the man she loved. "I take it you didn't get down to business last night?" She hadn't been able to hear anything from her post on the other side of the door.

"At our first dinner? Gods, no. That would have been uncouth even in Alden. I expect it will come up tonight, though. You will be there, I trust, now that they know who you are?"

"I suppose so. No one has yet informed me of my proper place." A hint of the bitterness crept back in.

"I'll see to it." He paused, then lowering his voice, added, "I need you there, Alix."

That, too, had been a long time absent, and Alix found it affected her nearly as much. She nodded mutely, suddenly overcome.

"Until then."

"Wait . . ." She turned to fetch her armour.

He held up a hand. "The palace guards can accompany me. You should rest." Without waiting for a reply, he fled the room.

"Tired?"

His head snaps up, cheek peeling away from the page of an open book. He rubs eyes bleary with sleep. Embarrassed, he throws a sheepish glance at the door of the library. "I hope you're the only one who saw that."

"Don't worry." She glides under an ornately carved archway, her footfalls curiously silent on the marble tiles. "We're alone." She's standing over him now. Firelight blazes molten copper in her hair, gleams against the smooth white skin of her cheekbones. He fights an almost overwhelming urge to touch her.

She looks away briefly. Bites her lip. A rare nervous gesture, one he secretly loves.

Or perhaps, not so secretly. "About what happened before . . ." she says.

"Don't." He can't deal with this. Not now. Later, perhaps, when the tides of his strangely reckless blood have ebbed, but

*not now. There is something important he must do first—
though for the life of him, he can't remember what it is.*

*A warm touch on his arm. She's tugging at him, bidding
him to rise. Reluctantly, he complies. He tries to avoid her
gaze, but she won't let him—her hands frame his face, forcing
him to look at her. In the torchlight, her eyes are liquid fire.*

*"What are you doing?" He thinks he says it aloud, but he's
not sure.*

*"I can't pretend this isn't here," she says. "Not anymore."
Her lips brush against his, as though sealing a promise. She
lingers there, her breath ghosting along his mouth in a quickening rhythm.*

*Panic and desire collide in a shower of sparks, a hammer
blow against red-hot steel. He tries to pull away, but he can't;
his body refuses to move. He is paralysed, yet every nerve
thrums, vibrating to the whisper of breath on his skin, the soft
glide of fingertips up the back of his neck. He makes a sound
somewhere between anguish and longing.*

"Erik," she whispers.

*It's as if the word is a spell. He moves—painfully,
unwillingly—his arms going around her even as he strains to
prevent it, powerless as a thrall. He tries to speak, but she stops
his mouth with her own, dives in, her tongue soft and perfect.
He's drowning now, no more in control than a man flailing in the
waves, drawing her in in great gasps, like precious air. A wound
opens up somewhere in his chest, bleeding hurt. His throat tight-
ens, his eyes sting, but he's kissing her and it's glorious, it's fire,
it's need. She's backing onto the table, sweeping the books to the
floor, her mouth never leaving his. His lips fall to the sweet white
curve of her throat, back up along her jaw, her cheek, the soft
space behind her ear. Her body arches beneath him in reply.*

He sinks into her, into oblivion, tasting the salt of her tears.

Erik started awake, rustling the page pressed under his
cheek. He shot a furtive look at the doorway, but the palace
guards were nowhere to be seen. He was alone.

We're alone . . .

Dropping his head into his hands, Erik blew out a long,

shaking breath. *What is happening to me? Blessed Rahl, give me strength . . .*

He had dreamed of her before, but never like this, and not since her marriage. *To his brother.*

A wave of guilt crashed over him, cold and poisonous, threatening to drag him off in its dark undertow. It had only been a dream, but the wound inside him was real, and it bled freely. The betrayal—that was real too, as real as it had been on the day his bloodblade cleaved through Tom's neck, ending the life of one brother even as he hoped to begin anew with the other. The other whose wife he had just dreamed of.

Blessed Olan, lend me courage. Blessed Ardin, take your hand from my heart.

He rose unsteadily. The gilded water clock above the hearth showed late afternoon. He needed to wash up. He needed to be ready. The fate of his kingdom could well rest on this night, on a handful of words spoken over braised baby goat and saffron potatoes and fine southern wine. Omaïd was proud, and famously touchy. Erik knew he would have to be perfect tonight. Better than perfect.

He reached inside himself for the discipline he knew he would need, that had always been there to answer his call, even in the worst times. What he found instead . . . a growing cancer, dark and seething, a writhing snarl of flame and whispers . . .

Blessed Farika, have mercy on me.

"Are you sure?" Kerta whispered, as though afraid the walls of King Omaïd's palace were too thin to contain the dangerous words. There was little chance of anyone actually hearing; they were deep in the sitting room of Alix's chambers, surrounded by sound-smothering tapestries and carpets and carved wood panels. Including, outrageously enough, a frieze depicting the sacking of Erroman in grim detail. Under the circumstances, Alix found it wildly inappropriate.

Not that she could afford to dwell on that now. "Yes. I mean, no." She waved a frustrated hand. "Obviously, I can't be sure. I'm not a mind-reader." She couldn't quite meet the other woman's gaze. She would find no censure there, not from Kerta, but even so, her own guilt shamed her. "He didn't say anything improper. It was more . . ." She trailed off, shaking her head.

"The hug?"

"No, not even that." How could she explain it? That it hadn't been anything Erik had said or done, but rather a *feeling*, an unmistakable current running between them. If she admitted that, she'd have to admit that she'd felt it too, in however mingled and complex a form, and that she was *not* ready for. She doubted she ever would be. The only reason she was talking about this at all—even with Kerta, in whom she'd confided so much—was that she worried it hinted at something deeper, something more significant than the lingering pain of a half-healed wound. "Look, whatever it was, it caught him by surprise. And that's what worries me. It's not like him. He's always so poised, so . . ."

"Perfect?" Kerta smiled sadly.

"Exactly!" To the point that it drove Alix a little mad—drove *everyone* a little mad. "It's not like him to let himself get carried away. But these past few weeks, he's . . . different, somehow. Less restrained than usual. More like . . ." *More like me.* It was not a comforting thought.

"He did very well with the *pasha*," Kerta pointed out.

"But you heard him say how difficult it was for him."

"He's only human, Alix. And he's been through a lot, especially these past few weeks."

"I know, and it's not as if I've never seen him falter, but . . ." Sighing, Alix dropped into a chair. "Maybe it's me. Maybe I'm the one who's a bundle of nerves. What's at stake tonight . . ."

"Like the parley with the Raven."

"A lot like that, yes." She smiled ruefully. "Though let's hope with a little less swordplay."

Kerta reached over and patted her knee. "Things will be fine, you'll see. He's under tremendous pressure and he feels vulnerable right now, that's all. When this is over and the Harrami have agreed to help us, he'll be back to himself, ready to lead us around the corner and out of this terrible war."

Alix's gaze drifted over to the frieze on the wall, to the painstakingly carved wooden bodies tangled horribly in a maelstrom of death. Though the scene it depicted had taken place centuries ago, Erroman was still recognisable. The

Elders' Gate, destroyed in the siege last summer, loomed in the background, looking on implacably as Harrami horse archers charged the imperial walls.

She needed Kerta to be right. Needed Erik to be himself. Needed King Omaïd to see reason and agree to join the fight. She needed these things, desperately, but she feared. For reasons she could not have given a name to, let alone spoken aloud, she feared.

TWENTY-NINE

Smuggle the banners across the river under cover of darkness. Maybe a few weapons while we're at it. But can they muster enough help? After what Sadik did to Raynesford . . . If they weren't shitting themselves already, they are now. But without enough bodies, he won't take the bait, and then we're finished . . .

"Sleepless again, my general?"

Rig turned his head on the pillow. Vel lay propped on her elbow, a cascade of black hair spilling over smooth caramel skin. "Sorry," he said, "am I keeping you awake?"

Even in the dark, he could see the sultry little curl of her mouth. "No, but you may, if you wish."

He snorted softly. "You're insatiable, woman."

"I have not heard any complaints from you."

"I'm a very easygoing person."

"Mmm," she agreed dryly. She slid over to curl up on his chest, and Rig tucked her under his arm. It felt good to have her there, he had to admit. In many ways, being with Vel was exactly as he would have imagined it to be—if it had ever occurred to him to imagine it at all. She was lively company, to put it mildly, which was just as well, because Rig found himself embarrassingly voracious. Maybe it was the stress, or maybe it had just been too long; either way, he looked forward to his evenings more than he had in a great many years. Even so, it was all he could do to keep up with Vel. He'd had fierce lovers before—it was something of a requirement for him, really—but Vel was in a category of her own. For her, lovemaking seemed to be a sort of sparring, a contest for dominance in which every inch of flesh was a potential battleground. She would have had him blushing, if his blood hadn't been too busy rushing elsewhere.

Yet as much as he enjoyed the more athletic aspects of their fledgling . . . *situation* . . . he found himself appreciating the quiet moments of intimacy nearly as much. That was something he would *not* have expected, and he still wasn't sure how he felt about it. Having someone to confide in was undeniably comforting, a welcome release at the end of the day. (Especially when it was followed, as it invariably was, by a rather more cathartic form of release.) But he couldn't shake the lingering worry that he didn't really know this woman, not in the ways that mattered.

And then, of course, there was the spy.

"Will you not tell me what troubles you?"

Rig realised he'd been quiet for a long time. "My mind is all over the place, really." He gave her shoulder a reassuring squeeze.

She was too clever to put be off by that. She shifted on his chest, looking up at him with an expression that was half worried, half annoyed.

Before she could call him on his evasiveness, Rig added, "Mostly, I was wondering about the priesthood." A partial truth, at least.

She lifted an eyebrow. "Thinking of becoming an initiate, are you?"

"What's it like? Are even half the rumours true?"

Her expression turned wry. "I suppose I need not ask which rumours concern you."

"I'm not concerned. Just curious."

Tucking herself back under his arm, she shrugged. "We are all drug addicts and sexual libertines, is that it?"

"That's what I hear."

"And now that you have some experience of your own, what do you think?"

He laughed. "I think I know a trap when I see one."

"You would be a poor excuse for a commander general if you did not. And I would not find you nearly so interesting." Her fingertips drifted down his stomach, lightly enough that his muscles twitched. She'd been enormously pleased to discover how ticklish he was. As for Rig, he'd been enormously surprised at the sorts of uses that knowledge could be put to. "The Order of Ardin certainly lives up to its reputation." She traced a finger along his hip bone, over the ugly purple welt he'd earned in the ring yesterday. "The priestesses especially. Given their small numbers, they are rather in demand."

"I can imagine." Every red-blooded Aldenian male could imagine—and had, sometimes more often than was healthy.

"For them, coming together in passion is an act of devotion, celebrating their chosen Virtue."

"They must be the most popular of the orders," Rig said, grinning.

"The most popular in folklore, certainly. But passion is not for everyone."

"Forgive me if I find that less than convincing coming from you." He paused, considering her frankly. "Why did you choose the grey instead of the red, anyway? Ardin seems a perfect fit for you."

She was silent for a moment, and when she spoke again, her voice was unusually diffident. "We do not all choose to follow the Virtue that is closest to our nature. Some of us prefer to immerse ourselves in the tenets of the Virtue we most aspire to."

"And you aspire to wisdom."

Her shoulders bobbed in a small shrug. It was such an incongruously self-conscious gesture that Rig couldn't help marvelling a little. It amazed him how changeable this woman was. Sultry vixen one moment, self-possessed priestess the next. And every now and then, this other, entirely more vulnerable creature, one who seemed always to be waiting for the world to judge her. "That sounds like a more difficult path," he said, "going against your nature like that."

He'd thought that might please her, and it did; he felt her relax in his arms. "Faith should be difficult," she said. "It should challenge us to be better than we are."

"Through enormous amounts of sex."

She laughed. "That's just the Order of Ardin. The rest of us conduct ourselves with more dignity."

"You sure? I've heard a thing or two about the Order of Eldora too. About certain herbs and mushrooms and potions."

"You make it sound so hedonistic. It's not like that at all. If used correctly as part of the holy rites, they allow us to pass through the gates into Eldora's Domain, where we may be given a glimpse of true wisdom."

"The same thing happens to me when I drink too much ale."

Vel *tsk*ed. "Do you genuinely wish to learn, or do you intend to make childish quips the entire time?"

"Can't I do both?" She punished him for that, tracking her nails over the ridges of his stomach. He grabbed her wrist, but not before his body seized under her touch.

"I myself have never managed to cross the threshold," she said. "My mentor says I lack inner discipline."

"Now that I believe." Another tweak of the nails, but this time he was ready, twisting away just enough to avoid the worst of it. "It must bother you that all anyone ever talks about is the mind-altering substances and the sex. People never gossip about . . . I don't know . . . the Order of Garvin, say."

"The Order of Garvin is unspeakably dull. They achieve empathy through prayer circles, in which they pour their hearts out to one another five times a day."

"Five times?"

"A tedious lot. Constantly weeping . . ."

Rig laughed. "I'm getting the sense you all don't always get on."

"We have our rivalries." Soft hair spilled over his chest as she lowered her mouth to his stomach. Rig felt himself stirring. "Still, some orders manage to stay above the fray. The Order of Hew, for example, is well liked by all."

"Really? I've always found them rather off-putting. The piercings, especially. Seems like an awfully *literal* interpretation of Hew's dazzling tongue."

"Oh, but that accounts for much of their popularity." Her mouth was working its way down, slowly, teasingly.

"How's that?" His voice grew husky.

"They make for creative lovers." Her head disappeared beneath the blankets.

"What? I don't . . . *Oh.*"

At which point, naturally, someone knocked on the door.

Rig swore feelingly. Vel merely sighed, sliding out from under the blankets. "The burdens of power," she said languidly.

He rolled off the bed and set about fumbling in the dark for his breeches.

"Shall I conceal myself?"

Rig laughed. "My dear, do you seriously think there's a single person in this fort who doesn't know about us? Aside from the fact that soldiers gossip more than any other creature in creation, you're not exactly the quietest."

"Oh, *really*," she said tartly.

"Maybe they think you're praying. You certainly call on the gods enough." He ducked expertly as a pillow cartwheeled past his head. "I jest!" He held up his hands in laughing surrender. "In earnest, though, the mere fact of you appearing at my door day after day will have led the men to the conclusion that we're . . ."

"Yes?"

He waved vaguely at the bed.

"How very articulate." A self-conscious pause. "You're not worried what your men will think?"

Rig shrugged as he pulled on his breeches. "Fretting about appearances has never been my strength." He could practically hear his mother declaring that to be the understatement of the decade. If only she could see him now . . . she would have been *appalled*.

And speaking of appalled . . . Rig opened the door, knowing full well the expression that would greet him. Commander Morris did not disappoint. He flicked an uneasy glance into the shadowed interior of Rig's room, as if half afraid he might catch a glimpse of the priestess concealed within. "Sorry to disturb you at this hour, General," he said stiffly, "but I have urgent news."

"Let's have it, then."

"The falcon we sent south has returned with a message."

"From the Resistance?"

"That's just it, General. It's not signed. A precaution, most likely, in case the bird was intercepted by a civilian. But we'd best make sure it's the real thing, or we could be blundering into a trap."

"Agreed." It would have been so much better if the Resistance had been willing to trust him with their cypher. He understood why they hadn't, but that still left him with the problem of how to authenticate the message. "Suggestions?"

"The handwriting, maybe. I thought . . ." Morris coughed, shifted on his feet. "Maybe you could ask . . . that is, if you feel comfortable contacting . . . at this hour . . ." Slowly but surely, Commander Morris was turning pink.

"Vel?" Rig ventured blandly.

A pained look crossed Morris's ruddy features. "Yes, General."

"Give me a moment." Rig closed the door.

Vel lit a candle. She lay strewn across the bed, hair dishevelled, bronze curves glowing invitingly in the soft orange light. "I was seriously considering wandering out there stark naked."

"Dear gods, that would have been interesting." At least once a day, Rig still wondered whether this . . . *whatever it was* . . . wasn't just another act of rebellion for her, a way of winding up Morris and anyone else who didn't approve of her. And if it was? How much would it matter to him? Rig honestly didn't know. What he *did* know was that it took every ounce of his discipline not to accost those glowing bronze curves, Morris and his mysterious message be damned.

They found Rig's second in the common room, along with the chief messenger. "Here's the scroll, General," Morris said.

Rig handed it over to Vel. "What do you think? Did you ever see anything written in Wraith's hand?"

"I did, but I can't say I paid much attention. Without a sample to compare it to, we are relying on memory alone." She unfurled the scroll and scanned it. "I think . . ." She bit her lip. "I think this is genuine. Yes." She nodded, as if to reassure herself. "Yes, this is his hand."

"Are you sure?"

Her mouth pressed into a thin line. She wasn't sure.

Rig sighed. "I suppose it was a long shot anyway. All right, let's see what it says." His eyes tracked over the page.

Morris and Emric, the chief messenger, waited patiently for him to finish. Not Vel. She let him get about five lines in before she demanded, "Well?"

He raised his eyes just long enough to communicate disapproval before resuming his reading. "Interesting," he said finally, handing it to Morris.

Vel was fairly dancing with impatience. "Are you deliberately being infuriating? What does it *say*, General?"

"To start with, our friend Wraith claims to have spies deep within the Trionate's borders. In Varadast itself, if he's to be believed."

"It's possible," Emric said, rubbing his beardless chin thoughtfully. "The Andithyrians pride themselves on being learned, so there's probably more than a few of their number with a strong enough command of Oridian to pass for native. They'd just have to pick someone who didn't have white hair."

"Does it say what these spies have learned?" Vel asked.

"Nothing we don't already know," Rig said. "Varad's health is poor, public support for the war is ebbing, that sort of thing. But he thinks one of his people might work his way into a sensitive position soon. He doesn't go into details—too risky without a cypher—but if it's as close to power as he implies, it would be a real boon for us."

"Don't you have spies of your own in Varadast?"

"Of course. My sister's man has an excellent network. But you know what they say—you can never have too many spies."

"Or soldiers," Morris said, finishing the expression. "And what about this other bit, General? About the siege engines?"

"Too risky. Besides, I'm not sure that would work in our favour. Those siege engines might be the only thing holding Sadik on the south side of the river. As it stands now, he's reluctant to start building a third time, but if he loses them, he might as well cross. I'd rather Wraith has a go at the supply lines."

"He's been doing that already," Vel said, her brow furrowing.

"Exactly. And I need him to keep doing it, to establish a pattern. That way—"

"I beg your pardon, General, might I have a word?" Morris drew himself up, as if bracing for rebuke.

Rig had an idea what this was about. So did Vel, judging from the fury flooding her features. Rig crooked his neck, motioning for Morris to follow. "Let me guess," he said when they were at a suitable remove from the others. "You want me to hold my tongue in front of Vel."

Morris avoided his eye, but he still stood stock straight, the very picture of stubborn determination. "I accuse no one, General, but there is too much at stake to take chances, and we can't be certain she is not the spy."

"If she is the spy, I've already said too much."

The older knight met his gaze, steady as steel. "With regret, General, I must agree."

Rig fought down an instinctive wave of anger. Morris was only giving voice to doubts Rig himself still harboured in a dark corner of his mind, a place shielded from the blazing inferno that roared through him every night, incinerating rational thought. Even so, having his second question his judgement at a time like this, when many of his other officers were already grumbling about his failure to answer the massacre at Raynesford . . . it was more than galling. It was dangerous.

"You've made your point," Rig growled. "And it so happens that I agree—the details of the planning will be kept close for now. That means you and me, no one else, at least as far as the Kingswords are concerned. But I'm sure I don't need to remind you that we're already in it up to our necks. It was Vel who brought us Wraith. If she's false, then he is more than likely false too. Any way you look at it, we're rolling the dice."

Morris nodded. "And so we must, because short of a miracle, that's all we can do. I know that, General. And I trust your instincts. That being said"—he shot a look over his shoulder—"you'd hardly be the first."

. . . *to be led astray by his groin.* Morris didn't finish the thought; he didn't have to. "You let me worry about that," Rig said. "Right now, we have a battle to plan. Let's send the others off to bed, shall we?"

The candles had slumped low by the time Rig finished laying it out for Morris, all the details he'd been mulling over for the past few days, combining and recombining them until they came together in his head. It might even have been dawn, though it was impossible to tell in that windowless room. His second had listened attentively, a soldier's blank mask over his features, holding his peace right up to the end. It wasn't until Rig had fallen silent, leaning back in his chair with his eyebrows raised expectantly, that Morris reacted to what he'd just heard.

"That," he said, "is completely insane."

Rig smiled wanly. "I thought you'd like it."

"I know you like to go all in, General, but this . . ." Morris shook his head. "This is beyond audacious. It's irrational. If it doesn't work—and I don't see how it can—we've lost everything. Not just the border. Not just the fort. The *war*, General. We have nothing to fall back on."

"All true."

"Then why—"

"Because we don't have a *choice*!" Rig pounded the table, sending the candles jumping. "We're outnumbered two to one, unless you count their advantage in bloodforged weapons, in which case it's worse. That's if they don't call up more reinforcements, which they could well be in a position to do, because the Trionate of Oridia covers *half the sodding continent*. Sadik can move at any time, choose any field, and be absolutely certain—*certain*, Morris—of smashing us into oblivion. The only reason he hasn't is that we caught him off guard, and our only chance is to do it again."

Morris faced this tirade with the same grim focus he brought to the battlefield. "The reason Sadik hasn't moved on us yet is because we blew the bridge and now he can't get his brand-new siege engines across the water. He's trying to figure out a way to avoid having to start over yet again."

"That's right, and when he decides it's too much trouble, he'll ford the river, and we'll be finished."

"He's got nothing but time, General. What if he's just waiting for you to try something like this? After what happened at Whitefish Bridge, he's got to know you're ready to gamble. If we do this, we could be playing right into his hands."

"We could be," Rig agreed. "And it might not work. But I ask again, Morris, what choice do we have?"

An urgent pounding on the door brought both men to their feet. "Come," Rig called.

Commander Rollin hesitated in the doorway, his face grey beneath his beard. "Word just came in from the ford, General."

Morris swore. "Is Herwin under attack?"

Rollin shook his head, and then Rig knew—knew with a sinking, sickening certainty—what he was going to say.

Morris had tried to warn him. *He's a good man, but hot-blooded. All alone up there by the ford, and Raynesford on his patch . . .*

"He's taken his men, General," Rollin said. "He's crossed the river."

THIRTY

† "It is such a great pleasure to meet you at last," said King Omaïd the Third, hoisting his wine cup. "I told His Majesty last night that I was very much looking forward to it."

Alix smiled awkwardly. She wondered what the king had been told to account for her absence at dinner the night before. Not the truth, she suspected, or he'd have offered some kind of apology. "That is very gracious of you, my lord," she said, following the instructions Ambassador Sommersdale had given her. *My lord, not Your Majesty, and make sure not to show your teeth when you smile. It's considered vulgar.* "I have very much been looking forward to meeting you as well, and seeing the legendary beauty of your palace."

"And? Does it meet your approval?" Omaïd smiled, a faint flicker of the lips, nowhere near reaching his clear green eyes. He was smaller than Alix would have expected—small even for an Aldenian, let alone one of the famously towering Harrami. He looked young too, almost boyish. *He could stand a beard,* Alix thought, though of course that would have been impossible, since no Harrami could grow one. Besides, however fresh-faced he might appear, his eyes gave him away: keen, watchful, reserved.

Those eyes were trained on her now, awaiting a reply. "My approval?" she echoed lightly. "If only I had seen anything comparable, to lend credibility to my opinion. The truth is, we have nothing in Alden to equal the artistry you have here, if my good king will forgive me for saying so."

"I quite agree," Erik said, sipping his wine. "With due respect to our artisans, they are far too attached to the old Erromanian style. They consider Andithyri to be the height of culture, and simply refuse to turn their eyes west."

"Or east, for that matter," said Chancellor Kader, pausing to allow a servant to spoon potatoes onto his plate. "Our Onnani cousins have some truly wonderful woodwork, yet so few of them are employed as craftsmen. It seems their style of carving is not greatly prized in your country."

A swipe, if a mild one, an oblique reference to the lingering prejudices of an empire long dead. Alix had expected a few remarks like this; the Harrami were notoriously self-righteous when it came to Erromanian history. She just smiled blandly. Across from her, Lord Sommersdale did the same, in the time-honoured fashion of diplomats.

Not Erik. "It is strange, isn't it," he said, "how one tends to undervalue the fruits of one's own garden. Take, for example, the complete absence of any art from the mountain tribes in your beautiful palace."

Lord Sommersdale's hand froze momentarily on its way to his wine goblet. Alix grabbed her own cup and took a hasty gulp, forcing herself not to look at Erik.

"And the Grand Library?" Omaïd asked, deftly steering them back on track. "How did you like it?"

"Exquisite," Erik said with a wistful sigh. "Truly, if I had a month, I could spend every hour of it perusing those shelves. Not just the books, but the maps, the tapestries—all of it. Even the architecture is astonishing."

"I am so pleased to hear it," Omaïd said in his soft, inscrutable voice. "We are tremendously proud of it. They say it took the Halla kings four generations to build."

"And more than a little coin, I should think." Erik raised his wine goblet. "To time and gold well spent."

Omaïd lifted his eyebrows in acknowledgement and drank.

Alix gazed down at her plate, a little helplessly. The food

looked and smelled delicious, but she simply couldn't see any way of eating it without surrendering her dignity entirely. It was one thing to pick up a roll of bread, or even a piece of roast chicken, with one's bare hands. But this food was so . . . *saucy*. It was like a sort of stew, but she couldn't see a spoon anywhere, except those the servants used for serving. Alix glanced surreptitiously at Lord Sommersdale, noting the way he tore off bits of unleavened bread to pick up chunks of meat. He had gravy on his fingers. They all did. There was no shame in it, obviously, but she just couldn't shake her mother's voice in her head: *A lady does* not *lick gravy off her fingers, Alix Black!*

"You had a terrible time through the mountains, I hear," said the chancellor. "My condolences on your losses." Omaïd seconded the sentiment with an arch of his eyebrows. Alix still hadn't grown used to this strange affectation. Why couldn't the Harrami simply nod like everyone else?

"It was a trial," Erik admitted. "Quite frankly, I despaired of ever arriving here. It seemed as though all the gods were set against us."

"One can imagine," Kader said. "Such a series of misfortunes. We too feared for your arrival, overdue as you were."

"Some misfortunes are more predictable than others," Omaïd said, sweeping a bite of potatoes into his mouth. "Travelling the pass at the climax of avalanche season was ill-advised. It would have been better to wait until later in the spring."

It would have been better if you hadn't obliged us to come in person. Alix was careful to keep the thought from showing on her face.

"We did not dare," Erik said. "By the time the snows had melted, it might have been too late."

It might already be too late. That thought Alix did not trouble to conceal.

"Even a week would have made a difference," Omaïd said. "You will find the pass a much easier journey on your way home. Besides, one shudders to think what would have become of your kingdom if you had perished in that avalanche."

"They would have persevered. My brother would have ruled in my place."

Alix flinched inwardly. *Oh, Erik, if Liam ever heard you say that . . .* He'd pass out, or throw up, or both.

There was a stretch of silence. Then Omaïd said, "The tribes will be punished, of course. I will see to it."

"I don't think that's necessary," Erik said.

Once again, Alix forced herself not to react. It would have been a presumptuous thing to say to any ruler, let alone a king as famously prickly as this one. Omaïd's boyish face remained expressionless, but Kader shifted in his seat, and Lord Sommersdale stared fixedly at his plate.

"They did let us pass, after all," Erik went on. "It is your prerogative, of course, but—"

"I am so pleased you think so," Omaïd said mildly.

"Forgive me," Erik said, suitably abashed. "It is only that I would grieve to see you put men's lives in danger on my account, when the matter resolved itself on its own."

"The tribes have grown too bold of late." The king spoke softly as ever, but there was a hint of ice there now. "They are no longer content merely to commit treason in the mountain passes. Now, they come down from the hills, into the villages."

"Into the villages, really?" Sommersdale tsked. "That is bold."

"They are mocking us," Kader growled into his wine goblet. "Trying to show how impotent we are, that they may come and go as they please."

"Perhaps they merely want to trade with the villagers," Erik said.

Alix fought an almost overwhelming urge to kick him under the table. Erik had been known to do this before—to play polemicist simply for the intellectual interest of it—but only among his closest confidants. Now was *so surely* not the time. What could he be thinking of?

Omaïd flashed his thin smile, his gaze shifting to Alix. "Is that what they are doing in the Blacklands, Your Highness? Trading with the villagers?"

"No indeed, my lord," she said—a little too quickly, a little too loudly. "They come to raid."

"Though to be fair," Erik said, "they apparently consider the foothills to be part of their ancestral lands."

Alix's mouth fell open. Then—what else could she do?— she laughed. "Now I *know* you're just having fun with us." She reached for her wine goblet, hoping her hand wasn't shaking. "For a moment there, I actually thought you were serious."

Sommersdale gazed expectantly at Erik, a tortured smile plastered to his face. Erik paled, as if he'd only just recognised the dangerous turn the conversation had taken. He grabbed his own wine, lifted it halfway to his lips, visibly casting about for a way to cover his mistake. After a moment's hesitation, he took the escape Alix had given him: He winked, a boyish grin playing about his lips. "You know me better than that."

"But our kind hosts do not, Your Majesty," Alix said, trying for affectionate exasperation, half achieving it. "They may not realise you are only teasing."

"You're right, of course," Erik said. "Please forgive me, my lord."

Omaïd smiled, but the green eyes narrowed slightly.

"It must have been a ghastly experience," Kader said. He was trying to move the conversation along, Alix knew, to get past this frosty silence, but she wished he'd changed the subject altogether.

She jumped in before Erik could reply. "It was. Genuinely harrowing. I thought for certain they were going to kill us. There was one in particular—Fahran, his name was—he was just spoiling for it. And they did kill one of our number, in fact, a member of my royal guardsmen."

"They will be punished, rest assured." Omaïd wiped his fingers on an exquisitely embroidered napkin.

"Savages." Kader shook his head in disgust. "Godless, lawless heathens, fighting among themselves. They build nothing. Create nothing. No order or authority. Content to wallow in their ignorance, to scratch out a living as our ancestors did, in a time before civilisation . . ."

"I found them quite impressive, really," Erik said.

Alix couldn't help looking at him this time, and what she saw confused her almost as much as it frightened her. An angry gleam lit his eyes, and his colour was inexplicably up.

"Did you?" Omaïd tilted his head, as if in mild curiosity. It was the velvet cloth over a curved blade. Alix knew it. Sommersdale knew it. *Anyone* sitting in that room, let alone a diplomat as shrewd as Erik, would have sensed the thin layer of ice cracking under his feet.

And yet he tramped on. "I once thought as you do, Chancellor, but now I see that my attitude was rooted in ignorance."

He said it casually, as though he were chatting to his family back in Erroman, instead of sitting across from the *King of Harram*, praising his bitterest enemies. Worse, Alix could see that his nonchalance was entirely feigned. Beneath that conversational air, Erik was *furious*. For some reason, he'd taken grave offence at the chancellor's words, as though they had been directed at his own subjects, instead of the people who'd taken him captive.

Nor was he alone in concealing a mounting rage. King Omaïd's eyes glittered like emeralds. "We are ignorant about our own people?"

"I can only speak for myself, but I found them to be much more worldly than I had presumed, and much more principled. Neither are they as disorganised as the chancellor suggests. They are quite formal, actually, and highly respectful of their chosen leaders." Erik tore off a piece of flatbread and used it to mop up a bit of gravy. "It is a pity no one has taken the time to study them more closely. Any number of misunderstandings might have been avoided."

"Misunderstandings." King Omaïd arched a raven-black eyebrow. "Do enlighten me, Your Majesty, as to what kinds of misunderstandings might have been avoided. The demarcation of our mutual border, perhaps?"

"Have you considered a form of autonomy? A concession to their local system of governance?"

Alix fought down a growing wave of panic. She cast about for something, *anything*, to say that might avert the disaster hurtling toward them, but she'd already used up the only trick she could think of. Sommersdale was no help; he just stared like a stunned rabbit. It was as if they were trapped in a nightmare, paralysed and unable to speak, watching in horror as Erik slashed his own wrists.

Chancellor Kader barked out a laugh, a clumsy cover for his outrage. "Why, you must be jesting again, Your Majesty! *Their local system of governance?* They have no governance! They are barbarians, pure and simple. Oh, I can see where the simplicity of their traditions might have a certain . . . whimsical appeal. Spending a few days among them might well offer one the illusion that these people are reasonable, can be dealt with as such. But I assure you, Your Majesty, it *is* an illusion.

They are unrepentantly violent, a collection of petty warlords who cannot even pause long enough in their own squabbles to come together for anything."

"They came together once," Erik said, "when they fell upon Erroman. I tried to convince them to do so again, to band together and rise up as their ancestors had done."

And here, at last, was the fatal blow. Alix knew it the moment he'd spoken, even before King Omaïd went rigid in his chair. She closed her eyes.

"You tried to convince them to band together." The King of Harram spoke slowly, deliberately, each word a separate condemnation. *"To rise up."*

"Against the Trionate," Erik amended hastily. "Not against Ost. Of course not against Ost." The anger was gone from his eyes, fled in an instant, replaced by raw dismay. He knew what he'd done. Too late.

Omaïd dropped his napkin onto his plate. "I wish you luck, Your Majesty, in convincing your new friends to come to your aid. Perhaps, when the war is over, you can spend some more time among them, and bestow upon us the fruits of your study." He rose, obliging the rest of them to do the same. Erik couldn't even meet his fellow king's eye; instead his gaze fell, unseeing, to the table, as if he'd woken from a nightmare and couldn't quite believe where he was.

King Omaïd quit the dining hall, sidling gracefully past the startled servants and their beautiful plates of untouched dessert.

"Dear gods, what have I done?" Erik sat on the bed, head in his hands, a note of pure despair in his voice.

Alix didn't know what to say. She couldn't wrap her mind around what had just happened. It was too unreal, too incomprehensible. She had never witnessed a more spectacular diplomatic disaster in her life. That it should be perpetrated by Erik—*Erik*, the most careful, restrained man she had ever known—was unfathomable. "Why were you so angry?" An irrelevant question, surely, yet it was all she could manage.

"I don't know." He shook his head dazedly. "I don't know what came over me. One moment, I was barely listening, trying to think of an elegant way to broach the subject of the war, and the next . . . I can't explain it. When Kader said those things about the tribes . . ."

"Of course he feels that way!" Alix practically shouted the words. She knew she wasn't improving matters, but she couldn't help it. "The crown and the mountain tribes have been bitter enemies for generations! Omaïd, his father, his father's father. For centuries, Erik! Of course he hates them! By all the gods, Rig would have said the same things!"

"And he would have been wrong."

"What does it—?" She broke off, shaking her head. There was no point in arguing about it; the damage was done. She raked her fingers through her delicately pinned hair, paced back and forth on the rug. *Think, Alix. There has to be a way to fix this. Oh gods, please let there be a way to fix this.*

"I've doomed us," Erik said dully.

Alix dropped to her knees before him, heedless of the seam ripping in her dress. "Don't say that. We'll figure this out. You and I can figure this out."

He took her face in his hands, rested his forehead against hers. "My beautiful Alix. So fierce. If only it were that simple."

Impossibly, the world seemed to spin a little further out of control. *My beautiful Alix.* He'd never spoken to her like that, not even before Liam.

"I'm so sorry," he whispered. "I'm so sorry, Alix."

She pulled back to look at him. There were tears in his eyes. *Tears.* Reflexively, she threw her arms around him, and found that he was shaking. *Blessed Farika, what's happening to him?* Her arms tightened around his shoulders, as if she could hold him together, as if she could shield him from whatever demons gnawed at his mind.

Demons. A fleeting thought, figurative. But something was terribly wrong here, something she couldn't define, let alone combat. A blade of fear sliced into her, piercing even through the hurt. She clung to him, stunned and afraid, utterly helpless.

His shoulders convulsed in a silent sob. Alix felt her own tears streaming down her face, dropping onto her broken king, spattering his perfect clothing, falling into his perfect red-gold hair.

* * *

"Where is His Majesty now?" the chancellor enquired coolly.

"Asleep," Alix said. "I asked one of the servants to bring a tonic. It's a testament to his illness that he actually took it. Normally, he refuses any kind of medicine that slows his thinking."

"Perhaps he should have taken it before supper."

Alix sighed. "I know you're angry, Chancellor, and you have every right to be."

"My feelings are irrelevant. It is His Lordship King Omaïd who has been offended, most grievously."

"I know, and His Majesty regrets that from the bottom of his heart. He is unwell, Chancellor. He is not himself."

"And what, pray, is the nature of his illness?"

I wish I knew. "Something that befell him in the mountains. Many of us suffered illness there, of one sort or another. I myself caught a terrible fever, and could barely hold my food down for weeks. It seems that it struck His Majesty a little later, that's all."

"Regrettable." The chancellor crossed his legs, swirled the brandy in his crystal glass. Behind him, a log slumped lower into the fire, sending out a shower of sparks.

Alix drew a deep breath and in her most highborn voice said, "I'm sure you'll agree, Chancellor, that it would be foolish to allow something so trivial to come between longtime friends and allies. Even families quarrel now and then."

"True, though I cannot agree that the matter is trivial. There is no more sensitive issue in this country than that of the mountain tribes." He spoke the last words in little more than a whisper.

"I know that. So does King Erik. As I said, he is not himself."

"King Omaïd is very angry. Nevertheless, given time, I am sure he will forgive the matter."

"That's just it, Chancellor. Time is the one thing we don't have. Oridia will breach our borders any day. We *need* Harram. It would be unspeakable if a few careless words brought on by illness condemned my country to fall."

For the first time, she saw real compassion in the chancellor's eyes. He sighed, swirling the brandy absently. "I sympathise, Your Highness, truly. It would be terrible indeed if tonight's events should lead to so dire a fate. But our good king is not the sort of man to change his mind about such things. I'm afraid . . ." He paused uncomfortably, tossed a mouthful of brandy down his throat. "I'm afraid the assistance of the Harrami legions is quite impossible at this time."

He may as well have thrown the brandy in her face. *Everything we've been through. All that we've lost . . .*

"Perhaps they will not even be necessary," Kader said, as if grasping for some comfort, however inadequate. "Our ambassador in Varadast says that support for the war has reached a nadir. The people are weary. Even Varad's counsellors press him to end it now. They say . . ." The chancellor trailed off; he could see that she wasn't really listening. He sighed again, heavily. "Is there anything else I can do, Your Highness?"

"No," Alix said, the words falling from numb lips. "No, Chancellor, it would seem not. It would seem there is nothing anyone can do."

THIRTY-ONE

† "Thank you for your frank honesty, Your Highness," First Speaker Kar said when Liam had done. Or at least, that was what his lips said. His eyes said, *Where do you get the nerve?* "It is a testament to the strength of our alliance that we can be so candid with each other about matters of domestic policy." Those last two words being the operative ones, obviously. *Mind your own sodding business,* diplomatically speaking.

"I should have mentioned it earlier," Liam said, "but I got

so caught up in this business with the fleet . . ." He spread his hands, smiling. The two men sitting across from him did not smile back.

"Perfectly understandable," said Defence Consul Welin. "After all, that is why you are here." *As opposed to meddling in our lawmaking, you presumptuous princeling.* There was a certain grim enjoyment in learning to speak this language, Liam decided, of stripping these carefully costumed words down to their brittle bones.

"His Majesty was deeply concerned to hear of this measure," Rona Brown said, in a deeply concerned voice, with deep concern etched all over her face. "It weighs heavy on his heart that boys of fourteen and fifteen could be cut down in defence of Alden. He does not want it on his conscience, my lord speakers."

Or at least he wouldn't, if he knew a single bloody thing about it. He didn't, of course; the measure had been tabled after Erik and Alix had already set out for Ost. But the speakers couldn't know that, and Rona had played their trump card flawlessly, laying it on the table with just enough gravitas to remind everyone how much power it represented. Liam couldn't have done it with half so much aplomb. Coming from him, the threat would have sounded childish, like a small boy invoking his big brother to scare away a bully.

Kar shifted uncomfortably in his seat. Traded a glance with Welin. Liam could read the substance of that silent exchange: How much risk was here?

Rona read it too, and she clarified the matter. "Of course, His Majesty understands that the Worker's Alliance does not shoulder the burden of this decision alone. Your learned colleagues in the Republicana have their voices as well, and so they shall be acquainted with His Majesty's views. It is only right that they take their measure of responsibility, don't you agree?"

In case your situation isn't clear to you, let me push you in front of this moving carriage. Once the People's Congress and the other leagues got wind of Erik's opposition to the measure, they would trumpet it far and wide. *Even the King of Alden, whose own borders are under attack, is against it!* Popular support—if there was any to begin with—would be gutted.

The Alliance would be isolated, vilified. All with their precious elections looming on the horizon.

Liam shook his head inwardly. He'd learned the language, but that wasn't nearly enough. It was one thing to know a sword when you saw one; it was another to wield it to perfection. For the tenth time, he thanked the gods for Lady Rona Brown.

First Speaker Kar didn't appreciate her quite so much. "Of course, my lady," he said, voice taut with barely restrained anger. "This is a very serious matter, after all. So serious, indeed, that I doubt the measure will be brought to a vote anytime soon. There is so much to discuss, so many factors to consider. It may be that in the fullness of time, certain amendments are made."

"May Eldora light your way," Rona said gravely.

They were ejected from Kar's offices as summarily as protocol would allow, to find Dain and Ide waiting for them at the bottom of the steps. The moment they were out of sight of the Republicana, Liam turned and planted a kiss on Rona's forehead. "Bloody *brilliant*!"

She blushed fiercely, her self-conscious smile a far cry from the stone-cold look she'd been giving the speakers a few moments before.

"Went all right, then?" Ide asked. Dain, meanwhile, threw an arm around Rona and gave her a squeeze.

"Better than all right," Liam said. "We didn't get a firm yes, but I'd bet gold to granite they're going to water the measure down before it goes to vote, especially on the age issue."

"Will it be enough to satisfy Gir?" Dain asked.

Liam inclined his head in the direction of the docks. "Only one way to find out."

The leader of the dockies was loitering by the doors of the warehouse with a pair of his men when Liam and the others approached. The Wolves must have looked well pleased with themselves, because Gir met them with a grin, his expression echoed unsettlingly by the thug with the stained red teeth. "Well, Your Highness?"

"Don't expect mass mobilisation to go to a vote anytime soon, and when it does, I doubt your sons will be receiving their summons."

"You didn't manage to sink it, then?"

"Not altogether, no. Like I said, I'm a foreigner. Dictating Onnani laws is a little beyond my power."

"So you stalled it?"

"That, and I made it known that the King of Alden would be very displeased if the age of mobilisation was lower in Onnan than in his own country. That's the best I could do, and frankly, it should be more than enough."

Gir grunted. "How do I know you're telling the truth?"

"You obviously have sources," Liam said, "or you wouldn't know about the motion in the first place. Consult them. Or you could just trust that I'm not a *complete* idiot. If I lied to you, you'd find out soon enough. It does me no good to convince you for a day. I need you onside for at least the three months it'll take to finish those ships."

That must have convinced the dockie, because a look of fatherly relief came into his eyes, and he nodded. "Thank you."

"I'm not looking for your thanks," Liam snapped, letting his anger seep through at last. "We had a deal. I expect it to go into effect immediately. If you get your men back on the job today, I'll even throw in a pardon for the whole attempted-murder thing, free of charge."

Gir frowned. "Come again?"

"I suppose I should be flattered you thought it would take three men to put me down, what with me being unarmed and all. Well now, come to think of it, looks like it would have taken more, doesn't it?" Childish, but *oh so satisfying.* "Anyway, what's done is done. I'm a tolerant bloke, and I've got bigger fish to fry"—yes, he'd said *fish*—"but just know that if anything like that happens again, I'm going to be *very* cross."

Gir regarded him searchingly, as though looking for the joke. He turned to the man on his left, the one with the red teeth. "You got any idea what he's—"

"I do," said the third man, and before Liam had even registered what was happening, a knife had buried itself in Gir's ribs. He gasped and staggered into the waiting arms of the red-toothed man.

Instinctively, Liam dropped to retrieve the dagger in his boot—which turned out not to be very clever, because it put his head at the perfect level for the red-toothed man to kick it.

The impact blasted the sense out of him, throwing him to the ground and leaving the top of his brain swirling like water at the bottom of a drain. For a moment, he struggled to process what was going on around him. He heard Rona cry out, heard Dain roar and crash into someone. By the time he was back on his feet, half dazed, dagger in hand, he found himself and the other Wolves surrounded by about a dozen men, all of them armed and ready. Gir lay facedown, motionless in a spreading pool of blood. The red-toothed thug was grappling with Dain, and Ide had an arm around the throat of the third man, the one who'd stabbed Gir. "You're gonna wanna back up, lads," she called to the ring of onlookers, "'less you fancy hearing a neck break."

The dockies hovered warily. Most had their eyes on Dain and Red-Tooth, waiting to see how it came out. One of them, though, a lad of no more than fourteen, took a halting step toward Ide. "Fen?" he said uncertainly.

Fen. Liam remembered the name Gir had called in the warehouse yesterday, the unseen hands that had opened the lanterns.

"My life is not important." Fen spoke in heavily accented Erromanian, words aimed at the Wolves, not the boy. "This is more big than one man. I am happy to die for this. That way, my brothers do not die." He spoke the language poorly, unlike his leader.

Unlike his leader. Liam remembered the note, the awkward phrasing of the death threat. *Gir wouldn't have written that,* he realised grimly. *No wonder he looked so blank. He had no idea what I was talking about.*

As if reading Liam's mind, Fen said, "Gir betrayed us. We do not bargain with you, Prince of Alden. We do not surrender." Ide tightened her grip, but before she could silence him, he shouted something in Onnani.

It was as if some unseen rope had been cut. The dockies surged forward. Ide released her captive, only to sweep a dagger from her boot and open his throat.

"No!" The boy rushed at Ide, knife raised, face twisted in anguish. Before she could react, Liam stepped between them and threw a carefully placed punch, dropping the boy before he could get himself killed.

"Wouldn't've cut the lad," Ide said, annoyed. And that was the last bit of conversation they had time for; she twisted to get under the swing of a full-grown dockie, and it was on.

In these kinds of scrums, incapacitation was more important than killing. It was no good waiting for an opportunity to land a fatal blow when you had two other blokes flanking you. Speed was the thing, and space, and for that, you needed to drop as many as you could as fast as you could. Liam was all elbows and fists and the occasional judiciously placed knee. When he used the blade, it was opportunistic, and he aimed—he wasn't ashamed to admit it—for the soft bits. He blinded one man with a jab, sliced another open from lip to ear with a hook. He reversed the blade for an uppercut, burying his dagger under a man's chin for a quick, tidy kill.

Only when every dockie within his immediate reach was either down or bent at the half did Liam pause—to breathe, and to check up on the Pack. Ide, who was a full head taller than any of her opponents, dropped a man with a hammering blow to the temple before stooping to pick up his sword. The dockies around her took a step back to reassess the matter, which was probably wise. Rona, meanwhile, was pulling a lifeless Red-Tooth off Dain. A half step away, a dockie was on hands and knees, howling, blood dripping from a wound Liam couldn't see.

The boy Liam had knocked out was struggling back to his feet. Liam wasn't the only one who noticed; someone shouted something at him, an urgent order. The lad hesitated a heartbeat, dark eyes fixed on Liam. Then he bolted.

He might have been fleeing, and that would have been fine. But Liam had looked into the boy's eyes, and what he'd seen there hadn't been fear. It had been something else, something fierce. Wherever he was running to, it wasn't safety.

Liam faltered. Shot a glance at the Wolves, still swallowed in the melee. Then Dain cried, "*Stop him, Commander!*" and any lingering doubt vanished. Liam charged after the boy.

Hearing footfalls behind him, the lad found a new speed. He leapt over a stack of crates, graceful as a deer, and swerved around a thick coil of rope. He narrowed his shoulders to crash between a pair of startled sailors, then banked left at a warehouse, breaking Liam's line of sight.

Dread pooled in the pit of Liam's stomach, but it wasn't until he rounded the corner of the warehouse that he realised why: The boy was heading for the shipyard. They were nearly there; already, the lad had begun waving both arms above his head, signalling to someone. The dread in Liam's stomach burst into a flare of panic. He knew what the boy was doing. He knew what was going to happen. He did the only thing he could think of: He stopped, took aim, and whipped the knife.

The boy dropped like a puppet shorn of its strings. Someone screamed. Liam jogged up to the motionless form, the flare of panic already turning to ashes of dread.

He'd been aiming for the shoulder. He'd missed. The dagger had buried itself at the base of the skull; the boy was probably dead before he even hit the pier. Liam stood over the limp form, swaying a little, seized by a sudden wave of nausea. Somewhere nearby, a woman had begun to weep. Sinking to his knees, Liam rolled the boy over, forced himself to look. A smooth, round face. The face of a child. He'd killed a child. He was very nearly sick then, but at that moment a pair of hands grabbed him roughly by the arm, and there were people all over him now, hands wrenching him this way and that, which was fair, which he deserved, and they were shouting and calling him names he couldn't really understand but which were almost certainly justified since he'd just murdered a child.

They yanked him to his feet. That was when he saw the smoke, black, billowing, rising from the shipyard. The stench of burning pitch bit at his nose. In the distance, a bell clanged.

They'd done it. What he'd known in that desperate moment they were going to do, what had made him throw the dagger and kill a child. They'd set it on fire. Three months' worth of half-finished galleys. Alden's great hope.

He'd failed. The boy's death, everything they'd gone through over the past two weeks—all of it in vain. All of it blown away like smoke on the wind.

Closing his eyes, Liam let them take him.

The breeze racing up from the bay was tainted with smoke. Try as he might, Liam could not smell the sea. He couldn't hear the rushing of the tide. Just the occasional snatches of excited babble that still drifted on the wind, carrying word of the dramatic events at the docks.

"Commander."

He didn't turn. He couldn't find the energy.

"Can I bring some ice for your eye?"

"No, thank you." He deserved the wound. He deserved every scratch, every bruise, the crowd had dealt.

A sigh. "Speaker Syril is here."

"Syril," Liam repeated blankly, fingers trailing mechanically through Rudi's fur. When the name registered, he frowned. "Why is he here?"

"I'm . . . not sure, Commander." There was an ache in Rona Brown's voice, a hint of helplessness. Liam registered that absently, as he would the colour of her clothing.

"Does he want to talk to me?"

"I presume so. Shall I send him out?"

"Okay."

Time passed. Liam stroked Rudi's fur and watched the darkening sea. Eventually, a figure appeared at his elbow. "A difficult day."

The sonorous voice roused Liam a little from his daze. He looked up to find Syril gazing out over the valley, hands folded behind his back. The breeze tousled his hair, played with the collar of his priestly robes.

It was only then Liam remembered that Syril had been taken away to prison—what, three days ago? It seemed a lifetime. "They let you out?"

He nodded. "After the city guard took you in, they rounded up as many dockies as they could find. Put them to the question, as the saying goes. Yet another practice the current regime shares with the old empire."

"They confessed?"

"Not without some significant encouragement, I am told." Syril's jaw twitched in anger. "It is a galling thing, Your Highness, to have one's freedom secured at the price of another man's pain. It does not sit well on the conscience. But then"—he gave Liam a halfway pitying look—"I suppose you know a little something about that."

"About what? Having the blood of innocents on your hands?"

"The boy was not innocent, Your Highness. Neither were the men they tortured."

"He was a child."

"And they were men. None of them deserved what they got, but that does not make you responsible. Or me, though that is small comfort for either of us."

"What are people saying?" Liam asked, so softly he almost didn't hear himself. "About the boy?"

Syril was silent for a moment, as though considering his answer. "*They* are saying a great many things. The people of Onnan are divided, Your Highness, more so than ever before. This war has brought discord to our hearts. The dockies are being called heroes by some, traitors by others. So it is with you, and what you did. Some curse you for it. Others say you had no choice."

Liam nodded detachedly. "And you? What are the people saying about that?"

He heard a strange sound; it took him a moment to realise Syril was laughing, though without a trace of actual humour. "Today's events are only a few hours old, the ink on my release scarcely dry, and yet I have already been told by half a dozen of my colleagues what a boon this is to my prospects in next year's elections. Those who sympathise with the dockies consider me their patron; those who do not, a man who was nearly executed as a result of their shameful actions. I alone command the respect of both sides of the political divide, I am told. As though I should celebrate the fact." He shook his head. "Once again, Your Highness, I find myself ashamed in your presence."

Now it was Liam's turn to laugh, just as humourlessly. "I don't see why, Speaker. Seems to me you've come out of all this pretty well. I, on the other hand, have to return to my country in shame. I have to look my brother in the eye and tell him I failed." Actually, that wasn't true; Erik would hear of his failure well before he reached Erroman. Just as well, really—that would give the king time to work out how to hide his disgust. Luckily, Erik was good at that sort of thing.

Syril sighed. "I am sorry, Your Highness. Whatever my views on the war, I have no wish to see your people suffer."

"Thanks, I guess."

There was a long stretch of silence. When Liam looked up,

the speaker was gone. He tugged on Rudi's ears distractedly. The wolfhound hadn't stirred when Syril arrived, or when he'd left. Liam would have been surprised by that, if he'd had the energy.

After a while, Rona came out again. "You should eat something, Commander."

"Pretty unlikely, that."

She stepped in front of him, blocking his view. "You've been here for hours," she said. "You're scaring me."

"Can't a fellow wallow in despair in peace?"

A faint smile flickered across her face. "That's better."

"Seriously, Rona, I'd like to be alone. Sorry."

"Can't do it, Commander. Sorry."

Okay, now he was annoyed. It almost felt good—it was the first thing to puncture through the numbness in hours. "I appreciate the thought, really. And I know what you're going to say, how it wasn't my fault and I had no choice and so on. Can we just skip it, please?"

She dropped to her haunches before him. She had that stony look again, the one she'd used on Kar and Welin. "It wasn't your fault. You had no choice."

"Yeah, okay, that's very witty—"

"You're a soldier, and so was the boy, after a fashion. He chose to fight for what he believed in—or at least, someone chose for him. You did what you had to, what any of us would have done. And as for the fleet—"

"Rona, please—"

"—as for the fleet, there was nothing you could have done to stop it. Gir lost the confidence of his men before you ever got here. That much is obvious, or they wouldn't have been sending death threats behind his back. The dockies had made up their minds to burn those ships, and there were hundreds of them to get it done. Even if you'd stopped the boy, however you'd stopped him, all that would have accomplished would be to rob them of their big symbolic gesture. They'd have done it an hour later, or a day, or a week. You never had a chance, Commander."

The longer she spoke, the coarser the lump in his throat became, until it was all he could do to force words past it. "If I never had a chance, then I didn't need to kill the boy."

"It wasn't your fault," she said again, and for some reason, there were tears in *her* eyes, as though she were the one who'd killed a child, who'd allowed the fledgling Onnani fleet to be burned to ashes.

"How am I going to tell him, Rona? Dear gods, how am I going to tell *her*?"

Rona's head dropped. He couldn't see her face now, just the top of the long braid woven across her scalp. She stayed like that for a long time, head down, face hidden, silent. In the fading light, Liam saw a tear fall onto the balcony.

He tried to think of something to say, something to make either of them feel better, but he came up short. As always.

When she looked up at last, her eyes were clear. She drew a deep, steadying breath. "You can tell them, Liam, because they love you. And that's all that matters." She stood, touched his shoulder. And then she was gone, leaving Liam with his dog and his failure and the smell of smoke on the wind.

THIRTY-TWO

"I recognise that one," Alix said, pointing at the horizon. "The villagers call it the Bull."

Kerta squinted. "Oh, yes, I see it. The peaks on either side look like horns."

"Call that a day's ride, another to the border. Maybe a bit more if we get more rain."

"Two days. We've made good time." Smiling, Kerta twisted in her saddle to look at Erik. "That's encouraging, isn't it, sire?"

He gazed at her mutely, blue eyes dull and distant, just as he had every other time she'd tried to coax him into speaking.

Kerta's smile fell away like a withered bud from a branch. "Well, we should get going."

They continued down into the valley. The slopes were gentler here, and greener, even where a few patches of snow remained. *Almost through*, Alix told herself for the hundredth time. *Almost home.*

There was relief in the thought, but not as much as there should have been. Returning to Alden would seal their failure in Harram. For now, the consequences of that failure seemed remote, abstract. So long as they remained on foreign soil, it would stay that way, as though the rest of the world hung in suspension. The moment they crossed the border, however, the world would waken. The timeglass would turn, and the sand would begin to trickle through, counting down to their doom.

Kerta drew up her horse about halfway down, gazing up at the ugly blotch of clouds gathering in the sky. "Looks like we'll be getting that rain after all."

"Thunderstorm," Alix agreed absently. Unusual for this time of year, but she was past remarking on their ill luck. It had been the way of things since they set foot in this cursed country; there was no reason it should change now. "Looks like there are some shallow caves over there," she said, pointing. "We'd better dig in. These things can come on fast in the mountains."

They weren't caves so much as crevasses in the rock, but they would serve. Alix lowered herself onto her belly, wriggling back until the heels of her boots met resistance. That left a good three feet of overhang in front of her; hopefully it would be enough to keep them dry. "We should be able to sleep here," she said, crawling back out.

"The poor horses, though," Kerta said.

"They're Harrami," Alix said, patting her mount's neck. "They've got thick hides. Now, let's make a fire while we still can."

Erik sat cross-legged on the ledge, inert, while Alix and Kerta gathered wood and moss. He watched the flames as they grew, stared through them as they flickered and danced. He ignored the dried meat Alix held out to him. "At least take the water," she said, unable to keep the edge off her voice. He acquiesced silently.

Kerta shot her a concerned look, one of countless such glances over the past few days. She didn't even bother trying to hide them anymore. But neither could she abide social awkwardness, so as usual, she tried to make conversation. "Do you think our escort will still be there? We're awfully overdue."

"They'll be there. Our letters will have reached Erroman by now, and they'll have sent word on to the guardsmen. By the time we reach the border, everyone will be up to date." *Everyone will know we failed.* Alix didn't need to give voice to the thought; like Erik's silence, it spoke for itself.

"They will be so relieved to see His Majesty safe." Kerta sealed that remark with another futile smile in Erik's direction. His lip twitched into something just short of a sneer, but that was the limit of his reaction. "I suppose there will be another council." Gods bless her, Kerta was going to keep this conversation going if it killed her, like nursing a feeble fire in a rainstorm.

"I hadn't really thought about it," Alix said. Hadn't dared to think about it, was more to the point. "I suppose we're going to hear a lot of *I-told-you-so.*"

"We had certainly better not!" A flash of anger lit Kerta's cheeks. "Not only would that be terribly poor breeding, it would be absolute rubbish! Coming here might have been a risk, but it was our only viable course of action. Everyone knows that."

"They might have known it once," Alix said, "but that doesn't mean they'll remember it. People have a convenient way of forgetting how they felt before everything unravelled. Instead they judge with the benefit of hindsight." She shrugged gloomily. "Human nature, I guess. We all want to believe there must be a way of avoiding calamity, if only we do the right thing. It's so much more reassuring."

"Reassuring and childish. Sometimes there are no good choices."

"Wise words, my friend." Alix smiled weakly. "You do come up with them now and then."

She'd been trying for a bit of levity, but Kerta wasn't having it. "I don't think it takes any great wisdom to see the truth. It's quite simple, really. There was an opportunity to recruit Harram. We tried to seize it. We failed. So what? Are we really worse off than if we'd sat idle? We lost some good people, and that's certainly very sad, but surely it was a sacrifice worth making if there was even a tiny chance of success? This is war, after all. People lay down their lives on such gambits every day."

It was true, every word—Alix knew it. But did Erik? He had, once, before despair had overtaken him. Alix wanted so badly for him to remember it, remember why he'd made the choices he had, but she wasn't even sure he was listening. He was too busy staring into the fire, scrying into a future written in flames.

"Anyway," Kerta said, "I don't believe it's as grim as all that. I'm sure when we hear the news from the front, and from Onnan, things won't seem as bad as they do now."

Erik snorted softly. So he was listening, then.

For once, Alix felt obliged to defend Kerta's relentless optimism. "That's certainly possible," she said gamely. "We've been away for so long—even the news we had in Ost was weeks old. Who knows what might have changed since then?" *The assassination of a Trion, for example?* It was almost certainly too much to hope for—a near-impossible task, even for a spy of Saxon's skill—but at least the wheels had been set in motion. Who could say how many other schemes—Rig's, or Highmount's, or even Liam's—might also be in play?

"Very true," Kerta said. "A week is an age in wartime."

The wind picked up around them, sighing through the pines. A low rumble scudded across the sky. *Won't be long now*, Alix thought.

"I think Chancellor Kader is right," Kerta went on. "The Trionate can't keep this up forever, not if the people are as weary as everyone says. Besides, I have to think that King Omaïd will reconsider his position if the Warlord actually crosses our border. After all, it's only a matter of time before—"

"For the love of all that is holy, *will you please shut up.*"

The words cracked over them like a whip. They were the first Erik had spoken in days, delivered in a voice so rough, so bitter, that Alix barely recognised it. He didn't even turn from the fire; he just glared at it as if it were the most hateful thing he had ever seen.

Kerta blanched. "I . . . I'm sorry, sire, I didn't realise—"

"Didn't realise what?" He turned his glare on her. "That I wouldn't be *delighted* to listen to endless tripe about how everything will be all right?"

"Let's just calm down, shall we?" Alix's cheeks burned, part shock, part mortification for her friend. She could see Kerta was fighting back tears. She'd probably never been spoken to like that in her life. *Erik's probably never spoken to anyone like that in his life . . .*

He didn't seem to hear. "There's a fine line between optimism and foolishness, Kerta, and you crossed it days ago."

Alix sucked in a breath. "That's *enough*, Erik."

His gaze snapped to her, silently furious. When she refused to look away, he shot to his feet and said, "With me." Without waiting for a reply, he skidded down from the ledge and into the trees.

Alix stared after him, too stunned for words. She reached for Kerta's shoulder, squeezed it, and followed Erik down the slope.

He hadn't gone far. He waited with his arms folded, that icy look still in his eyes. "I tolerate your insolence in private, Alix, but I won't have it in front of others. You may be my sister-in-law, but I am still your king."

A year ago—a week ago, even—those words would have pierced her like a lance. Now all they did was provoke her. "You may be my king, but you are behaving like a royal ass." She didn't even give him time to register outrage before ploughing on. "You've been silent as the grave since we left Ost, barely eating, barely sleeping, scaring us both half to death. So no surprise if Kerta feels obliged to sing a merry tune in the hopes it will bring you round. You of all people should know a brave face when you see one. And now you attack her for it? What in the Nine Hells has got into you?"

He started to fire off a heated reply. Stopped. For a moment, it looked as though her words had sunk in. Then the scowl returned. "A bit of an asinine question, isn't it?"

"Not really. You've got every reason to be upset, but that's no excuse for lashing out at someone who's only trying to help you. It's not right, and it's not like you. Not at all . . ." Alix could feel the anger bleeding from her with every word, replaced by the confusion and fear that had stalked her ever since that awful night in Ost, the night her king had broken down in her arms. "Honestly, Erik, I don't know what to make of it anymore. It's as if . . . as if you're someone else lately. I used to know you so well, and now . . ." *And now I barely recognise you.*

He raked his fingers roughly through his hair, grimacing as though he had a terrible headache. "Don't be dramatic. I just can't listen to that treacle. It's killing me. Don't you see? It's a lie, and I can't listen to it."

"Fine, but Kerta's your friend. She's been nothing but supportive, even when—"

"Even when I disappoint? Even when I fail miserably?" The accusing look returned to his eyes, a spark threatening to take light.

"I was *going* to say, even when you're completely unresponsive. Which quite frankly is starting to look good by comparison."

He blinked, and for a moment Alix was sure he was going to erupt again. Instead he blew out something just short of a laugh. "Good gods, woman, you're incorrigible."

And just like that, he was smiling at her, as if nothing whatever were amiss, as if he hadn't just torn into everyone around him like a wounded panther. Alix could not have felt more disoriented if he'd gathered her up and spun her about.

"You needn't look at me like that," he said, frosting over almost immediately. "I'll apologise to Kerta. But please, for all our sakes, take her aside and explain it to her. I simply cannot tolerate two more days of listening to her spin children's tales."

"I'll tell her." What else could she say?

"Good." Erik glanced up. "We'd better get back. It's going to come down any moment."

The first droplets had begun to spatter the rocks when Alix pulled herself up onto the ledge. Kerta had already wedged herself into the crevasse, curled up under her blanket with her face turned away. Alix shuffled in close beside her, but otherwise gave her friend what little privacy their situation afforded.

The rain approached timidly, stealing over them in a muted rush, filling the air with the fragrance of pine. Ribbons of wind darted through the trees; the horses jostled and stamped. Then came the thunder, cracking the sky open, unleashing the full fury of the clouds. Erik stared out through the storm at something only he could see. Beside him, Alix trembled against the cold stone, cheeks wet from the lashing rain, her quiet gasps of grief smothered by the deafening roar.

Aradok fingered the trigger of the crossbow, shifted its unfamiliar contours against his body. He'd fired it a handful of times, and it seemed simple enough. But it was one thing to practice in the quiet confines of his cell, loosing quarrels into a straw pallet, and quite another to do it for real in the vast open space of a holy temple, loosing quarrels into a Trion.

He swallowed hard against the rising bile in his throat. He'd had so little time to prepare this, so little time to consider. What he was about to do . . . It was almost beyond fathoming. Treason, regicide . . . these he could cope with. They were mortal things, inconsequential in the grand designs of the cosmos. True, this act could plunge his country into chaos. The Priest had already been slain, and his underlings were still bickering among themselves for the right to succeed him. Losing a second Trion would be a terrible blow, unprecedented in the history of the Trionate. But Aradok cared little for that. Like many of his countrymen, he had come to disapprove of the Trionate's endless hunger for conquest. If a crisis was what it took to put them back on the path of righteousness, so be it.

But this was more than a crime against his country. This was *blasphemy*. The murder of a Trion, anointed by the gods . . . The mere thought of it made his head throb. It would be a year, a full cycle of the sun, before Varad's soul was reborn, and months after that before the new Priest—assuming he was in place by then—could determine which child born on that day was the reincarnation of the King. Such a journey was for the gods to initiate, not men. Taking it into his own hands would most assuredly not situate Aradok well in the next life.

This is not about you, he reminded himself. *It is about her.*

The gold they'd promised was more than enough. So much, indeed, that he'd almost feared it couldn't be true, that it was some kind of trap. But when they'd told him who ordered the deed, he'd known the offer was real. The royal family of Alden must have mountains of gold at their fingertips, and they were desperate. Desperation was something Aradok knew all about.

A month, the healers had given him. Maybe less, if the growth started to crowd his windpipe. Already, people were turning away from him in the street, disgusted by the sheer size of the cancer that was squeezing the life from him. As for Caria, she did her best to be strong, but he could tell she was terrified. Bad enough to be branded a harlot for the rest of her days, but how would she care for the baby? No one would take pity on the bastard child of a monk, the living embodiment of a shame condemned by gods and men alike.

Footfalls sounded through the passageway, snapping Aradok back to the present. Nausea reared up inside him. *This is it.* The King had come, as he did every day, to bathe in the sacred waters of the fountain. He would be alone. The Crimson Guard would stand watch outside the doors, thinking their Trion quite safe within the fountain chamber. There was only one way in or out, and aside from the fountain itself, the temple contained but one other chamber, a small cell where the caretaker lived. Where Aradok lived.

He swallowed again, painfully. He fingered the trigger of his crossbow. He moved.

As he stepped out of the narrow passageway, his eyes fell upon the King. Varad was undressing—with some difficulty, for his infirmities had become grave. He was half tangled in his robes, face obscured by a billowing sleeve. Aradok raised the crossbow.

The King turned. *He was not alone.*

Aradok registered the fact in the instant before he fired, but it was too late: The quarrel snapped loose. A pair of hands continued to turn Varad about, to help the ailing Trion out of his robes. The servant stepped unwittingly between the quarrel and the King.

There was a scream. It was Aradok's. A Crimson Guardsman charged into the fountain chamber, sword raised.

A servant. There wasn't supposed to be a servant.

The crossbow fell from numb fingers. Aradok sank to his knees. He looked into the eyes of his Trion, saw nothing but empty confusion. A shadow fell over him, crimson reflected in the white marble tile of the floor.

Caria, he thought.

The sword fell.

THIRTY-THREE

†"L osses?" Rig asked.
    "Two thirds, or thereabouts, including Herwin."
Morris's gaze was steady, his voice as impassive as Rig's.
Now was not the time for temper. Save that for the battle-
field. Save that for Sadik.

"Where did his men fall back to?"

Morris dropped a long finger onto the map. "Reckon the
enemy didn't pursue because he was afraid of stretching himself too thin. Better to consolidate his hold on the ford, make
sure we can't take it back."

"Can we?" Vel asked quietly. "Take it back?"

It was Commander Wright who answered. "Not as things
stand, Daughter. Assailing a choke point like that is akin to
laying siege to a castle, which is why General Black was able
to hold the ford for so long against superior numbers."

He wasn't trying to be patronising, but Vel bristled all the
same. "I am aware of the tactical basics, Commander. I simply
wondered whether General Black might have devised one of
those unconventional solutions you claim to admire so much."

Rig touched her arm discreetly, and she subsided. Wright,
meanwhile, stiffened under the rebuke like a soldier being
upbraided by a superior. This in spite of the fact that the man
was more than twice her age. *The power of the clergy*, Rig
thought absently. The Oridians were said to be the same. He
wondered, not for the first time, if he could use that somehow.

But not today. Today, he had other ideas. "We go ahead as
planned," he announced. "Let's get that falcon in the air."

Morris swore under his breath, shook his head. But they'd
been over this too many times, and anyway, he would never

question Rig's orders in front of others. So he just said, "Aye, General."

"Take heart, Morris. The loss of the ford might even play into our hands."

"If you say so, General." He headed for the door.

Silence followed his exit. Commander Wright shifted uncomfortably. Clearing his throat, he said, "I would not presume to disagree with you, General Black. The gods know you have proven yourself time and again, especially in situations in which you are visibly at a disadvantage . . ."

Rig looked up from the map. "But?"

"But you have at least seven hundred fewer men today than you did two days ago. An officer lost. The ford in enemy hands. Whatever you're planning—and I do understand why you haven't divulged all the details—it obviously relies on the Resistance, or you would not have sent that falcon off. But we know so little about them—what they're capable of, whether we can trust them. I must ask, General, is this wise?"

"Probably not, but I hope Eldora watches over us all the same."

"She will," Vel said automatically.

Wright nodded, as if this satisfied him. "Shall we pray, Daughter?"

"Of course," she said. "And you, General? Will you pray with us?"

Rig looked at the map, seeing all the invisible battle lines he'd drawn up in his head. Two nights ago, in the fog of half-sleep, they'd made so much sense. Today, in the dark hours before dawn . . .

"You know something, Daughter? I think I will."

Rig paced the length of the makeshift wall walk, twitching with nerves. He wanted so badly to be out there in the field, under an Andithyrian sky, feeling the Andithyrian breeze on his face. It would have felt like a victory to cross the river with the others, however clandestinely, to set foot behind enemy lines. He would have liked to ride with Morris as they rammed a pike up the enemy's ass. But it was not to be. A commander general couldn't personally lead every mission, especially not one as risky as this. He'd need to be flexible, to think on his feet, and he couldn't do that if he was busy trying to look after his own hide on the battlefield.

He envied Morris. His second would be guiding his destrier down the lines at this very moment, voice pitched to carry, filling Kingsword heads with visions of triumph in the face of steep odds. Honest enough that the men would believe him, but not so honest that they'd lose heart. A hopeless battle is a lost battle, Rig knew.

He followed the walk around the corner of the southwest tower, boards creaking under his boots. Inside, a handful of archers turned away from the arrowslits to smile at him nervously. They had no idea what was coming, but they worried all the same. After all, the fort was near empty, the two thousand men it sheltered having ridden out at dawn, leaving only the Onnani battalion and a few bands of archers. Even more tellingly, their commander general had been around the full perimeter of the fort twice now, scanning the meagre timber fortifications for gaps, weaknesses that could be exploited—as though there were a damned thing he could do about it. Rig knew he was making them anxious, but it couldn't be helped. He'd become adept at hiding his emotions over the years—not as good as Erik, maybe, but better than most—and he'd learned to be especially careful on the cusp of battle. But there were limits to his skill, and he'd reached them. There was simply too much at stake.

So much so that when the cry came, as he'd known it would, Rig experienced a momentary weakness in the knees.

"Enemy spotted at the checkpoint!"

Rig couldn't see the runner, but he could hear her from clear across the compound. So could everyone else: Heads turned, bodies stiffened. From the other side of the fort, Commander Wright sent him a long, hard look. Rig swore under his breath. "Runner! Up here, now!"

She swept off her foaming horse and scrambled up the stairs, thumping out a swift salute.

"You report to me," Rig growled, "not the entire fort."

"Yes, General. It's only . . ." She swallowed, darted a glance over the palisade. "They've never been this close before."

"Yeah, well, tighten your buckles, because they're about to get a whole lot closer."

She paled. "General?"

"They shot down the falcon, I presume?"

"That's right," she said, confusion knitting her features. "But how did you know? I thought I was bringing word. Was someone else quicker?"

"Never mind that. What did the scouts say?"

"Just that the enemy seemed to be waiting for the bird, as if they knew it was coming."

Rig nodded. "Good."

"I . . ." She blinked. "Begging your pardon, General, but how is that good?"

He opened his mouth to explain it to her, to all of them, but he never got the chance. A flaming arrow arced over the palisade. A long-range shot, judging from the angle; it landed harmlessly in the middle of the yard. But it wasn't alone: A whole volley followed, a skyful of shooting stars raining down on them in a fiery deluge.

Shouts went up all over the fort. The men in the courtyard scattered. The rest, including Rig, hunkered down and nocked their arrows.

"They're here," the runner gasped, eyes round with fear. "How did they find us?"

Rig didn't have time for chatter. He craned his neck, peering between the sharpened tips of the palisade. He couldn't see much through the trees, but if they were in bow range, they were in ballistae range. Over his shoulder, he cried, "*Catapult, long, go!*"

A rattle of wood and a *whoosh*. A slab of stone sailed over the walls. There was a long breath of silence, followed by the crash of branches in the distance. No screams. Cursing, Rig started to look between the stakes again, but the enemy's answer was already upon them: Another flaming volley slammed into the fort. Arrows studded the palisade, the towers, the roof of the barracks. The catapults took a heavy barrage, but the Kingswords were ready, dousing them with pails of water and snapping off the shafts to keep the mechanism free. Infantrymen jumped down from the wall walk to smother the bourgeoning flames on the roof, and archers poured buckets from the towers. At the well, half a dozen Onnani soldiers took turns at the crank, keeping the water flowing.

"*Catapult, medium range!*" Rig uttered a silent prayer as darkness passed over him, sudden and swift, like the shadow of a hawk. Then he heard the screaming, and he knew the gods had answered. "*There it is! Let them all go!*"

Now that they could be sure of not wasting precious ammunition, the Kingswords held nothing back; three arms snapped to in rapid succession, flinging boulders the size of sheep. More screaming floated up from the trees. From the ramparts too, as Kingswords slumped over the parapet or tumbled from the wall walk, feathered with arrows. Manageable losses for now, but they wouldn't be able to hold out for long. A wooden fort was no great citadel, and it was especially vulnerable to flame. Already, a tendril of smoke threaded its way through the southwest tower.

Rig decided it was time to answer fire with fire. "*Short range! Light them up!*"

He wondered if the advancing Oridians could smell the pitch. He hoped so. He hoped they smelled it, saw it smeared on the bark of the trees, so that when the flaming missiles started raining down, they'd know exactly what came next.

It was almost beautiful, the way the woods took flame in a perfect arc. They might have been able to set the fire without the aid of pitch, but it was springtime, and conditions were wet; Rig hadn't been willing to chance it. He'd had fifty men working to the predawn hours to get it done. They'd painted the briar patch as well, the thicket of sharpened logs lying in wait at the bottom of the trench ringing the fort. Rig would light them up too, if it came to that.

For now, they'd rely on arrows and catapults, pelting the enemy ranks while Sadik's army tried to find a way past the flaming perimeter. It wouldn't save the besieged defenders, not in itself, but it would buy them time. And time was what Rig needed, time for Morris to move his men into position.

Drawing a long, steadying breath, Rig nocked an arrow to his bloodbow, took aim between the stakes, and fired.

Morris lifted the visor of his helmet and spat in the mud. An old habit, going back to his earliest days of King's Service. *More than twenty years ago now*, he realised with a flicker of surprise. Twenty years of spitting in the dirt and bracing for a fight. He couldn't even remember how it started, but it didn't matter; he wouldn't dream of going into battle without it. It was as much a part of his ritual as the war paint on his horse, and a soldier knew better than to muck about with ritual.

He twisted in his saddle to look behind him, satisfying himself one last time that the men were ready. Four thousand of them. No great host, but if the gods were kind, it might just be enough. Not that Morris expected kindness. Riggard Black had pressed his luck too far and too often; no man could get away with that for long. Especially not with a plan like this. Too clever by half, with too many pieces in play. For it to work, they needed the spy to behave just so, and the Resistance too. Needed Sadik to take the bait. The fort was a tempting target, to be sure; Morris had no doubt the Warlord would jump at the chance to take it, and the gods knew he had more than enough men to get it done. He could attack the fort, fend off the Resistance at the grain silos, and still have a sizeable force sitting idle on the Andithyrian side of the river. That was just what the Kingswords were counting on. But all it would take was one enemy scout to blow Morris's position, and that would be the end of them. Their surprise attack would be thwarted, the fort would fall, flags down and good night.

No sense crying about it now. Either it would work, or it wouldn't. And if it didn't, he wouldn't live long enough to mind.

"Commander." Rollin pointed a gauntleted finger at the sky. "Smoke. It's time."

Morris slammed his visor back down. "Let's do the king proud, then. This might be our last chance."

He urged his horse to a trot. Behind him, the infantry marched double time, jogging through the trees as quietly as four thousand armour-clad men can manage. They had a lot of distance to cover, and they had better do it fast. The fort couldn't hold out long against an all-out assault. If Morris didn't engage the enemy's rear soon, the commander general's forces would be overwhelmed.

He tried not to think about it. That wasn't his job. He had his orders, and he'd follow them.

They'd gone less than half a mile when it all went wrong.

"*Shit!* Did you see that?" Rollin drew his blade.

"What?"

"Enemy scout! Bloody vermin is on horseback too!"

A blur of movement up ahead, the rustle of undergrowth. Morris spat out an oath. "Archers!"

Arrows whistled through the air. They'd got their shafts off quickly, he was proud of them, but it wasn't good enough. The scout had vanished into the trees.

"Rollin!"

The younger man didn't need to be told; his horse was already springing forward. "Jarold! Searle! With me!"

The three knights thundered off in pursuit. But the enemy scout had a healthy head start, and a forest full of trees to lose himself in. On top of which, there was no telling if he was alone, or how far he had to go before he could signal the enemy . . .

Can't say I didn't warn you, General, Morris thought, even as he spurred his own horse to a gallop. *Can't say I didn't know how this would end.*

Flags down and good night.

THIRTY-FOUR

† "We can't get it out, General!" The frantic cry came from the base of the northwest tower. They'd managed to douse the fire to the south, but the men operating the bucket line couldn't keep pace, not even after Rig had written off the stables. A minor loss, that; with the cavalry out in the field and the stables a safe distance from anything else, they could afford to let it go. Not so the tower, or the other parts of the palisade that were burning out of control. With the outer defences breached, the fort would be easy prey, even with a ring of fire keeping the enemy at bay.

"Find a way!" Rig cried, knowing he was potentially condemning dozens of his men to death. They had to hold on a little longer. *Just a little longer* . . .

For the hundredth time, he thanked the gods they'd managed to destroy Whitefish Bridge. If the enemy had been able to get siege engines across the river, the fort would have fallen in a heartbeat. As it was, the Kingswords were being ground down by attrition. The Oridians had long since stopped trying to advance. Even the flaming arrows had ceased to fall. Spent the last of their pitch, most likely. Not that it mattered; the damage was done. Worse, the wind had changed direction, pushing the creeping wall of fire to the northeast. The flames were in danger of jumping the wide clearing that protected the fort. All Sadik had to do now was wait.

Rig started to raise his bloodbow, to force his arching arm to draw and his bleeding fingers to grasp the bowstring, but there was no point. It had been ages since he'd seen a target. The Oridians were sheltering in the trees now, protected by branches and shields and gods knew what else. Hazarding a blind shot would be senseless, a waste of a good arrow. Like his enemy, Rig could do nothing but wait.

He glanced at the sky, at the pitilessly slow track of the sun. *Come on, Morris.* The worst part was, he couldn't be sure how much time had passed, couldn't even be sure there were enough men on that field in Andithyri to make a difference. So many unknowns . . .

Morris had warned him. They'd all warned him. Rig had listened, at least on the surface, but he'd already made up his mind. Sometimes, it seemed as though he'd made up his mind in the cradle. *As bold as a Black.* He'd worn that old saying like ancestral armour, but he'd always known that someday it would be the end of him. "What do you think, Morris?" he murmured, his voice lost amid the cries and the *whoosh* of the catapult and the distant roar of the flames. "Is today the day?"

A long, tortured groan sounded from behind him. Rig whirled in time to see the northwest tower buckling. The outer wall tore away in a shower of flaming debris, taking a handful of screaming soldiers with it. Men and timber tumbled down the slope toward the briar patch. The inner wall remained intact, Rig saw; only a few tongues of flame still licked at what was left of the tower. They could be doused easily now. *A stroke of luck*, he thought. *The collapse spares the rest of the tower.* Such a callous attitude would have horrified him a year ago, but the commander general of the king's armies could not afford to be sentimental.

"General!" The voice came from below, a runner scrambling up the ladder to the wall walk. "Word from Andithyri!"

This is it. The news he'd been waiting for. A bitter, metallic taste on Rig's tongue told him just how much he feared it. He'd posted two scouts up a tree with a pair of longlenses and orders to watch the enemy's movements on the Andithyrian side of the river. *If they so much as glance east, I want to hear it straightaway.* It would be the only sign, the only way of knowing whether Morris had managed to move his men into position without being seen. If he hadn't . . . If the Oridians spotted him and repositioned in time . . .

"The enemy's rear lines have peeled off," the runner said breathlessly. "Almost half of them have turned round!"

Rig's limbs felt weak. "Where are they headed?"

"We saw Kingsword banners over the rise, on the Andithyrian side. I don't know how you smuggled those men across the river, General, but the Oridians have spotted them. They're moving to intercept. With the time it took me to get here . . . I guess they'll have engaged by now."

Rig nodded. His head swam with disbelief, but he made himself move, putting one foot in front of the other until he'd reached the southwest tower. The archers stood aside to let him peer out the arrowslit, but it was a waste of time—he couldn't see anything through the smoke. The wind had continued to push the fire north, edging it slowly toward the fort. *If it keeps up like this, they'll be able to manoeuvre around it to get at the walls.*

"What happens now, General?" The question, softly spoken, came from one of the archers. A slip of a girl, no more than eighteen, with wide hazel eyes that reminded him of Alix's.

I don't know.

The answer, however truthful, was not one he was prepared to give. He was still casting about for something to say when he heard the horn.

Rig closed his eyes and muttered something between a

prayer and a curse. "Better late than never, Morris." He looked through the arrowslit again, though of course it was too soon to see anything. His head spun, still dizzy with disbelief. It had actually *worked*. "Ready your bows," he told the archers. "They're coming."

"The enemy?" The hazel eyes widened in surprise. "But the fire . . . won't they run straight into it?"

"With eight thousand Kingswords driving at their rear?" Rig smiled darkly. "Let's hope so. If not, I owe Commander Morris what's left of my estate." A grim joke, that, since neither of them would be alive to settle the bet.

They're too many, General, Morris had said. *So you dress the Resistance up in armour, have them fly Kingsword banners. What then? Even supposing Sadik takes the bait, the most it'll draw off is a few battalions. That leaves fifteen thousand at his fingertips, and they still hold the ford.*

Unless, of course, more than half of them could be lured across the river. With the Kingsword fort in his sights at last, Sadik would not be able to resist. He'd come at them hard, leaving only a few thousand men behind to protect his position in Andithyri. But when Kingsword banners were spotted on the Andithyrian side of the river, he'd be obliged to split his host, leaving his rear dangerously vulnerable. Sadik wouldn't think twice about it, confident that Rig couldn't possibly cover more than two fronts at a time. He would never expect the attack from behind, pinning his men between the Kingswords and the fort. Between eight thousand men and a wall of fire.

"General!" Commander Wright's voice sounded urgently from the wall walk above.

Movement in the trees, shadows drifting, ghostlike, behind the curtain of smoke. A horse screamed. Rig tore out of the tower and up onto the wall walk. Oridian cavalry swarmed on the far side of the flames, searching for a way around. It was their first good look at the enemy since lighting up the perimeter, and Rig didn't hesitate. He nocked an arrow and fired, sending an enemy cavalryman tumbling from his horse.

A second shaft followed Rig's, burying itself in one of the ghostly riders. The hazel-eyed archer appeared at his side, already drawing for another shot. On his other side too, a pair of archers sighted through the smoke, and beyond, he saw

Commander Wright draw his own bow. All around him, Kingswords and Onnani came out from under cover to punish the enemy for straying so near to the fort. In the distance, he could hear the clash of metal as the southern battalion drove into the enemy's rear. From the north, he knew, a second battalion was sweeping down in a pinching manoeuvre, led by Morris himself. Beset on two sides, pinned between the river, the flames, and the fort, the Oridians had nowhere to go.

So many unknowns, so many things to go wrong. But they hadn't. For once in this gods-damned war, they'd gone exactly right.

Rig drew a deep, satisfied breath. Smoke had never smelled so sweet to him. Flames had never been so beautiful. The pain in his arms and fingers was forgotten, replaced by the subtle thrum of the bloodbond as he drew on his enemy.

For Raynesford, Sadik, you son of a bitch.

When Rig judged that the fort was out of danger, he left Wright in command and called for his horse. By then, only a handful of enemy stragglers could be glimpsed from the palisades, and they paid the price. Most of the rest had fallen or fled. Bodies littered the forest floor, charred or bloodied or both. A few had actually made it past the wall of flames, only to blunder into the briar patch. Through the veil of smoke, their twisted limbs were scarcely distinguishable from the sharpened logs that had ended them.

Rig wended his way cautiously through the woods, the naked edge of his bloodblade glinting in the occasional shaft of sunlight slanting down through the trees. His knights flanked him, eyes raking the shadows for any sign of threat. In the madness of combat, even a friend could be an enemy. Yet they saw no one, friend nor enemy—at least not living. Here and there, a rustle of branches or a ring of metal would turn their heads, but these individual struggles, these small dramas, could not distract Rig now. Instead, he sought out the distant staccato rhythm of hundreds of blades glancing off each other. It drifted up from the south, borne by the wind and the smoke. The battle for the ford continued, though it could not be long now. With the Kingswords sweeping in from the west, cutting off the enemy's escape, Rig had the advantage. He might not win the ford, but he wouldn't lose it, either.

He found the trail that followed the riverbank, urging Alger to a lope. Here they did find the living, fleeing Oridians trying to make their way across the river, or back upstream to rejoin their comrades. Rig cut down any of them foolish enough to get in his way.

The ford was just ahead now, and Rig could tell from the sounds that they'd won it: the low-throated horns urging the Kingswords on, the shrill trumpets sounding the enemy's retreat. *Bloody well done, Morris.* Rig swerved north to come in at the rear of the Kingsword lines, his gaze already seeking out the White standard.

When he saw it, his guts turned to lead.

The banner stood well behind the rear lines, under heavy guard. Morris never led from behind. Rig spurred his horse.

"Took you long enough," Morris rasped as Rig pushed his way through the ring of knights. He lay on his back, pale as bone, hands folded over his belly. Rig didn't look at the wound. He didn't have to.

"Funny, I was going to say the same thing." Rig's voice sounded odd to his own ears, thin somehow. *Nobody would obey that voice,* he thought, irrelevantly. Strange the things that came to one's mind in moments like these.

He knelt beside his second. Morris curled over himself a little, scowling down at his wound as though it were terribly inconvenient. "Spear," he said, lying back with a grimace. "Barbed, of course, the bloody savages. Suppose I should be grateful it wasn't poisoned too."

Rig cleared his throat. Started to say something. Stopped.

"Well, now," Morris said, "this day will certainly go down in history. The day Riggard Black was lost for words."

Rig laughed, a strained, strangled thing. "Yeah, well, I'm bloody exhausted. Somebody had to keep the enemy busy while you were faffing about."

"Sorry about that, General. Guess my speech was too long—" A hiss of pain cut him short; Morris squeezed his eyes shut.

Rig glanced over his shoulder. The rear lines had moved even farther away. On the far side of the river, they were still sounding the retreat.

"Looks like I owe you some gold," Morris said between gritted teeth.

"Damn right, so don't even think about dying before you pay up." Rig was still trying not to look at the wound. Instead, his gaze strayed to the armour they'd cast aside, but that was no better, for it told the story well enough. The spear had taken him between breastplate and faulds, punching through the bottom of the cuirass. It had been torn out again, from the looks of things. Morris's guts would be in shreds; it was a miracle he'd lived this long.

The thought must have played clearly across Rig's face, because Morris said, "Not long now, I reckon, so I need you to listen."

Rig dragged his eyes from the ruined armour, forced himself to look at the ruined man.

"You got him today, General—"

"*We* got him."

Morris scowled impatiently. "Will you shut it and let me finish? He's going to come at you hard, you know that. But what you did here today—*don't*, damn it, just listen—what you did here today will make this army stronger than it's ever been. You're invincible in their minds now, General. Use that. You can—" He seized up again, choking off whatever else he might have said.

Rig grabbed his hand, his own jaw clenched so tight it hurt. "Enough. Just rest."

Morris relaxed a little. He swallowed, throat working again and again, eyes tracking across the sky as though searching for something. He tried once more to speak, but all he managed was a cough.

Morris died with his hand in the shaking grip of his commander, who couldn't find a damned thing to say.

He was a good man," Commander Wright said, as one did. Rig murmured agreement, as was expected of him. His mind was already elsewhere, trying to work through what came next, and after that, calculating how long it would take the Warlord to regroup. He wished Morris were here.

He downed a cup of wine in a single draught, a private toast to one of the best men he'd ever known.

"He was with you a long time," Wright said. Beside him, Vel winced; she knew Rig well enough by now to guess how little he wanted to talk about this.

She did her best to change the subject. "How long will it take to repair the fort?"

"Weeks." Rig poured himself another cup. "The good news is that Sadik will need time to regroup. He lost a lot of men today."

"Any word from Wraith?" When Rig glanced over, Wright shrugged. "I heard about the diversion the Resistance was planning. Half the fort seems to have known about it. Deliberately, I suspect."

Rig didn't bother to deny it. "I've heard from him, yes. They lost a few in the attack on the grain silos, but the decoy got away unscathed. Melted into the fields the moment Sadik's men moved on them." The thought of the enemy marching on a bunch of farmers in mismatched armour, only to have them scatter like dandelion fluff at the first sign of advance, was enough to bring half a smile to Rig's face.

To Wright's face, though, it brought only confusion. "But I thought the attack on the grain silos *was* the decoy?"

"That's what he wanted us to think," Vel said, looking as if she were torn between pride and pique. Rig hadn't told her the truth, either. He was going to pay for that later, he knew.

"It was *a* decoy," Rig said, "just not the only one. We also had a host of Resistance fighters flying Kingsword banners in Andithyrian territory. Convincing enough from a distance. Sadik figured I'd smuggled a battalion across the water somewhere downstream. And being Sadik, he sent at least twice as many men as he needed to smash it."

"You leaked the information about the grain silos," Vel said. "That made the false Kingswords the more convincing, because Sadik would take it for the main event, the thing you were trying to distract him from. You leaked the location of the fort too, didn't you? You intended for that bird to be shot down. All those preparations—you told us it was just in case, but that wasn't true, was it? You expected him to come. You wanted him to."

"Decoys and lures and diversions." Wright shook his head. "A rather elaborate plan, General."

It wasn't a compliment, Rig knew. Wright might lack experience, but it didn't take a veteran to know that the more complicated the plan, the greater the odds of it going wrong. "There were a lot of pieces in play," he admitted, "but I couldn't see any options. As you've no doubt realised by now, I have a spy in my ranks. I decided to use that to my advantage."

"It certainly does seem that there is a spy," Wright said. "The question is, what are we going to do about it?" Rig noted the *we*.

"There are two thousand men in this fort, and another seven thousand in the immediate area. Ferreting out a single man—that's assuming there's only one—is going to be all but impossible."

"Is it?" Wright rubbed his beardless jaw thoughtfully. "The spy must have a way of communicating with Sadik. There are not many options. Perhaps if we fabricated another bit of tempting information—about the Resistance, say—and then watched the river and the skies . . ."

Rig shook his head. "After what happened today, the spy will know we're on to him. If he has any sense at all, he'll keep a low profile for a while. For now, there's nothing to do but live with it."

"Hardly comforting," Wright said.

"That's putting it mildly." It was, in fact, like a physical weight pressing down on Rig's shoulders, just one more stone added to the load.

Sighing, Wright said, "Still, at least we know the Resistance is a force to be reckoned with. I would not have guessed they had the numbers to mount two separate diversions. It is encouraging."

Rig could have taken the wind out of his sails—told him that fewer than half the men flying Kingsword banners had been fully fledged members of the Resistance—but it seemed wiser to keep that information to himself for now. Instead, he just shrugged and said, "Looks like the white-hairs still have some balls left." That much, at least, was Destan's own truth.

After Wright had gone, Vel poured herself a generous helping of wine. It was the first time they'd been alone together since the battle, and Rig was fully expecting an earful.

He got one.

"You lied to me. You lied to my *face*. Will you lie again now and tell me you don't think I'm the spy?"

"I don't think you're the spy."

She scoffed, threw her wine back. "You think I might be, or you would have told me the truth."

"No, I wouldn't have." He took her shoulders, turned her around. Not the most dangerous manoeuvre of the day, but not the safest, either. Fortunately, she was content to glare up at him. It was, he had to admit, a very good glare. He nearly said so, but she wasn't in the mood for levity, and for once, neither was he. Besides, there was never going to be a good time to say this, so he might as well get it over with. "Whatever this is between us, Vel, it doesn't change the fact that I am commander general of the Kingswords. I have responsibilities, and that includes keeping secrets. That might change after the war. It might not. If you can't accept that, I understand." He left the rest unsaid.

Vel turned away from him, cradling her cup in both hands. "Do you have any idea what it's like to cower behind the walls and wait for the world to end?"

He did, actually—he'd done more or less exactly that during the Siege of Erroman. But that wasn't what she wanted to hear, so he held his tongue.

"To be so powerless, while you're out there . . ."

"You aren't powerless. You did your part. You gave us Wraith. Without you, none of this would have been possible."

She laughed bitterly. "You are a fool, Riggard Black, do you know that?"

"It's occurred to me."

"You think this is about my pride?" She turned back to him, dark eyes haunted. "Yes, I wanted to make a contribution. To do my part for the struggle. Do you think any of that mattered to me today? You think that sitting in this room, on your bed, while you were out there on the walls, I could think of anything but . . ." She stopped, hugging herself as though to stave off a bitter wind.

Rig paused. She was telling him a great deal, maybe more than she meant to. Her words sat between them like an offering. But Rig wasn't ready to take them up. Not yet. He wasn't ready for where that might lead them. It would have been complicated enough before the war, when his only responsibility was to his banner. Now . . .

She saw it in his eyes; she turned away again.

A wave of exhaustion swept over him. Exhaustion, and something else—something like loss. He would have to cope with that loss one day, maybe soon. But the ache that it brought was more than he could take just then. Though he knew it was selfish, he couldn't stop himself: He slid his arms around her, pulling her close and tucking his chin into the curve of her neck. He drew in the scent of her, listened to the slow, heavy draw of her breath. It was shelter, however temporary. It was peace.

After a moment, she relaxed; her hands slid up his arms, clasping him tight.

"Thank you," he whispered. He wondered if she understood what he meant.

A long pause. Quietly, she asked, "What happens now?"

Rig's gaze drifted over to the fire, to the twisting, inscrutable shadows it threw on the wall. "I don't know," he said, and he buried his face in her hair.

THIRTY-FIVE

A lix drew up the reins so hard that her horse skittered backward, nickering in protest. She didn't even wait for the animal to settle before swinging down from the saddle and throwing herself into the waiting arms of her husband.

"Allie. Thank Farika you're safe." He'd heard about what happened with the tribesmen; she could tell by the hitch of his breath, the way he clutched her to him in a grip that was painful even through her armour.

In Liam's arms at last, it was all Alix could do not to burst into tears. But once again, they were surrounded by people, and Alix couldn't afford to let herself go. She forced it down—the grief, the fear, the rushing tide of relief—though she felt as if it might split her apart.

Liam looked her up and down as though inspecting her for damage. "You're all right?"

"I'm fine, but . . ." She glanced over her shoulder, to where Erik waited at a polite remove. *Not now, you fool*, she scolded herself. *Certainly not now.*

"Your Majesty," Liam said. "You'll forgive the breach of protocol, I hope."

"Just this once." Erik started forward, but a snarl froze him in his tracks. He looked down, mildly astonished, to find Rudi standing between him and his brother, teeth bared. "What's this? I thought we were friends."

Embarrassed, Liam grabbed the wolfhound's collar. "Sorry, I don't know what's got into him. I guess a few weeks is all it takes for him to forget you. He's thick as an oak, this dog." He glanced at Alix. "Er, would you mind?"

She hesitated, expecting Rudi to snap at her as well, but the wolfhound let her take his collar without protest, and even sat obediently beside her.

"He remembers you perfectly well, it seems," Erik said dryly.

"It's good to see you," Liam said, embracing his brother. "When I heard what happened—"

"It's over now. We're home."

"Just in time, too," Liam said, grinning. "I've been in charge two whole weeks, and I've already started to go mad. You're lucky you didn't come back to find the whole place burned to the ground and me wandering around half naked and muttering about banquet menus."

Erik laughed, but it sounded strained to Alix's ears. "What's this? You were in charge?"

"My doing, Your Majesty." Albern Highmount descended the steps of the keep to bow, gingerly, before his king. "I thought it best to have the Whites restored to the crown as soon as possible."

"Did you? Transition upon transition. Yes, I can see where that aids the cause of stable government." Shaking his head,

Erik moved past his astonished first counsel and mounted the steps of the keep.

Liam's eyebrows flew up as he watched his brother disappear through the palace doors. "Wow. Someone's a bit touchy today."

Alix pursed her lips, but it still wasn't the time. What she had to say on the subject of Erik's mood could only be said in private. Besides, Liam had just spotted Kerta and was already shouldering his way through the courtyard to greet her.

Highmount, meanwhile, was still staring after Erik. He'd schooled his features back to their customary impassivity, but Alix knew he would still be wrestling his surprise. Not so long ago, she would have taken petty delight in seeing him publicly upbraided like that, but not now. Not like this. *Should I tell him?* She resolved to ask Liam about that too.

Sensing her eyes upon him, Highmount turned. "I am pleased to see you looking so well, Your Highness. We all had quite a fright when we heard what happened in the Broken Mountains."

"Thank you, Chancellor."

"And what of our news—did that reach you on the road?"

Alix cocked her head. "I don't think so. What news is that?"

"Varad has been assassinated."

The air left Alix in a gust. She stood there, mouth hanging open, for what seemed like forever before she finally closed it with a snap. *Saxon did it. He actually did it!*

"Told her about Varad, did you?" Liam appeared at her side, sounding oddly grave.

"*When?*" she breathed.

"About a week ago," Highmount said. "In the Temple of the Fountain. One of the monks, if you can believe it." Like Liam, he spoke in subdued tones, and when he glanced back at the palace doors, his expression was unmistakably worried. "His Majesty will not be pleased."

Alix all but laughed in her disbelief. "Why in the Nine Domains not? We've killed another Trion! It's a huge blow to our enemies!"

"*We*, Your Highness?" Highmount arched a bushy grey eyebrow.

"I mean . . . I presume one of our allies . . ." Alix swallowed, glanced away. "At any rate, we are the ones who benefit."

"I hardly see how. Varad was the weakest of the Trions, and the least committed to expansion. That was *before* his health began to fail. His death gains us nothing. On the contrary, it has become a rallying point for the Trionate. By all accounts, the Oridian public and even some of their top advisors were urging an end to the war. Now, they cry for our blood, since of course everyone assumes Alden was behind the deed."

"Bad luck, huh?" Liam said. "Someone murders the old man, and everyone blames us."

"As though we would stoop so low." Highmount shook his head in disgust. "Assassination of a *king*! Simply not done!"

"But surely," Alix said weakly, "in times of war . . ."

"I could perhaps be convinced of that, Your Highness, but it is not merely the morality of the thing to consider. Removing a head of state is deeply unwise, for it is all but impossible to guess what will follow, whether the enemy will be weakened or strengthened by it. In this case, we need not wonder. The Oridians are unified as never before. To them, Varad is a living god, a divine soul housed in mortal flesh. Killing him was not merely murder, but blasphemy. In the eyes of the Oridians, we have proven that we are the heathens Madan always claimed we were, in desperate need of civilising. If the Priest's death weakened their resolve, the King's has restored it entirely." Still shaking his head, Highmount headed for the stairs.

"Allie, are you all right?" Liam touched her arm. "You look ill, love."

"I . . ." *Dear gods, what have I done* . . . She put a hand to her stomach, tried to control her breathing. "I'm fine. I just . . . it's a shock, that's all."

"You're telling me. For a moment there, it looked like we might live to see an end to this thing, and now . . . On top of which, I got to be the lucky sod in charge when the news hit."

"Oh gods." Alix doubled over. She was going to throw up, she was sure of it.

"Hey, now. Come inside, love. We can talk in there." Liam took her by the shoulders, casting a nervous glance about the courtyard.

He's afraid you're making a scene. Liam, impervious to

nearly all forms of embarrassment. Her husband, who wouldn't know a political implication if it slapped him in the face. *Blessed Farika, the world is inside out.*

Numbly, Alix let herself be ushered inside.

People passed by in a blur, saluting and bowing and smiling. Liam led her on, his voice sounding oddly distant as he offered vague pleasantries and excuses to the various well-wishers. Alix followed in a daze. It wasn't until Liam threw the latch on their chamber door that she came round, blinking as though she'd just woken from a bad dream. "Liam—"

He stopped her mouth with his own, a kiss almost desperate in its urgency. Alix wilted in his arms. *I'm home.* For a moment, every other thought fled from her, and she let herself be swaddled in the cocoon of Liam's love, soft and warm and safe. Then he pulled away, and the worry in his eyes brought the world crashing back down.

"You heard what happened in Harram?" Alix asked, swallowing.

He nodded. "What about you? Did you hear . . . ?" His gaze dropped to his boots.

She reached up, brushed her fingers through his unruly hair. "It wasn't your fault."

"On some level, I know that." He sighed. "You'd think that would help, wouldn't you?"

"Give it time. It's too raw right now."

"See, that's why I need you around." He drew her in again. "You always know what to say to me."

"I wanted to write you a letter . . ." An ache was working its way up Alix's chest, choking off her words. "You were so good about writing to me, and . . ." She trailed off, gazing up at him miserably.

"What?"

Her eyes filled with tears. "That first one you gave me, on the road . . . I never . . . I lost it . . ." She broke down at last, a sob tearing from her like a weed dragged out by its roots, leaving a gaping hole behind.

Liam's arms tightened around her. "Hey, what's this, love? It's all right. It's only a letter . . ."

And of course it was just a letter, but it was *his* letter, his love poured out on the page so that she could hold it close wherever she went. Imagining it buried in the snow out there, lost and forlorn . . . It seemed such a tragedy to her in that moment, such a crushing loss, that she couldn't bear it. It was the feather that brought the whole stack of firewood crashing down. She wept bitterly, Liam holding her close, rocking her and whispering to her and doubtless thinking she'd gone completely mad.

Later, when she'd settled, curled up beside him on an oversized upholstered chair, cup of tea in hand and wolfhound at her feet, Liam went looking for the source of her madness.

"What happened out there, Allie?"

"So much," she whispered, her gaze on the rippling surface of her tea.

He waited for her to elaborate. When she didn't, he said, "What about King Omaïd? Couldn't Erik get through to him?"

The choice of words almost made Alix laugh—which would no doubt have dissolved instantly into tears. She blew on her tea, composing herself. She'd been thinking about this moment for days, deliberating over how to put into words the fears she almost didn't dare acknowledge to herself. "Erik made a mistake," she said. "Several, actually, each worse than the one before. By the end, Omaïd was barely speaking to him. I wasn't even sure he would be there to bid us farewell when we left."

"Gods. What did he *say*?"

"Among other things, that he thought the mountain tribes should join together and rise up."

Liam's mouth fell open.

"He meant against the Trionate, of course, but it didn't matter. The idea of the mountain tribes banding together for any cause is anathema to Ost. The fact that Erik openly admitted encouraging them to do it was more than Omaïd could take."

"Well, of *course* it was! Even I could have guessed that, and I'm the man who managed to alienate half the population of Onnan! What was Erik thinking?"

Alix took a sip of her tea. Once she said these words, there was no unsaying them. But she had to tell someone, and she trusted Liam more than anyone in the world. Even so, when she finally did speak, her voice was thin and trembling. "Something is wrong with him, Liam. Very wrong. I think . . ." She swallowed. "I think Erik might be going mad."

Liam drew back. For a long moment he just stared at her, his gaze fearful and searching. "Allie . . ."

"I know that's a lot to process—"

"It's *treason*, is what it is." His voice, already a whisper, dropped even lower. "Why would you say something like that?"

"Because it's what I believe." Her eyes started to fill again, but she kept herself together. "You saw him in the courtyard. He's like that all the time now. Not just moody, but erratic. Fearful. It started in Harram, but it's been getting steadily worse. Almost as if the closer we got to home, the more he came undone. By the time the escort met up with us, he was snapping at everyone. You should see the way the men were looking at him by the end. Like they didn't even recognise him. And why should they? I don't."

Liam took her by the shoulders. "Alix, Erik is the sanest man I've ever known." He said it firmly, gazing deep into her eyes as though *she* were the one who'd gone mad.

"I know, and I can imagine what this must sound like to you. But I'm telling you, I know him better than anyone in the world, and something is wrong with him."

"Okay. Maybe he's ill, or maybe . . ." Liam stood, shoved a hand through his hair. "Remember how the Raven was. His moods. And their father . . . our father . . . he was addle-brained in the end. Maybe it's a family trait."

"Maybe it is, but that doesn't change the fact that he isn't himself."

Liam paced the length of the hearth and back. Rudi yawned at his feet, as though he'd seen this kind of thing before. "So what do we do?"

"I don't know. Watch him, I suppose. Try to help him."

"Help him how?"

"I don't *know*, Liam. We just . . . try to be there for him. Let him know he's not alone, whatever he's facing."

Liam stopped pacing. Blew out a breath. Rudi got up and went to him, nub wagging, bumping up against his master's leg. Liam patted him absently.

"That's new," Alix said with a weak smile.

But Liam wasn't ready to change the subject. "If he's as bad as you say, he isn't going to take the news about Varad very well."

The sick feeling reared up inside Alix again. For a moment,

she'd managed to forget about the assassination of the Trion. The assassination she'd ordered. *Oh Alix, what have you done?* She looked up at Liam, the concern weighing his brow. She couldn't bring herself to add to that burden. Not yet. She'd have to tell him eventually, but there was nothing to be gained by doing it now. For today at least, she was on her own. "I'm going to have a bath," she said. "And after that, if it's all right with you, I think I'll take Rudi for a walk."

He was barely listening. "I suppose I'd better find Highmount, see if there's something I'm supposed to sign or anything now that Erik's back . . ."

Alix brought her tea to her lips, but it had gone quite cold.

Saxon was waiting for her in the rose garden, as she'd known he would be. He had good instincts; it was one of the things that made him an excellent spy.

Rudi growled at the unfamiliar figure on the bench, but Alix put a hand on his head, and he subsided. "The famous Rudolf," Saxon said in his grating voice, the hood rippling as he tilted his head to consider the wolfhound. "He is excessively large."

"And a bit edgy, unfortunately, so I wouldn't make any sudden movements."

"Always so much excitement with you, Lady Black. If only all my clients were this interesting."

"I don't think civilisation could cope with having too many clients like me," she said dully, dropping down beside him.

Saxon said nothing to that. He stared straight ahead, features obscured within the depths of his ever-present hood.

"How did you do it?"

"Now, now, Lady Black, you know better than that. Suffice it to say that everyone has a weakness, and a good spy network makes it their business to learn the weakness of those in key positions. In case the need should ever arise."

"I suppose it doesn't matter. The job was done, however much I might rue it now." Her voice didn't sound particularly rueful. It didn't sound like anything at all. It was utterly barren. *This is the worst thing you've ever done.* How would she explain herself to Erik? To anyone?

He turned to look at her, but once again held his tongue. *I must look as bad as I sound*, Alix thought, *if he's declining the opportunity to say* I told you so.

She decided to say it for him. "You warned me." She shook her head, dragged the toe of her boot through the gravel. "You tried to tell me that it was no way to stop a war."

"You give me too much credit. I said that wars rarely end in such a way—not that they could not, or should not. I couldn't have guessed what effect Varad's death might have on the war."

"But I could have. I knew the King was the weakest of the Trions. I knew it was the Priest who set the Trionate on the path to conquest, and the Warlord who revelled in it. Highmount is right; we had little to gain from Varad's death. And of course his murder would only rally his people." She would have seen that, if only she'd paused a moment to think. But instead she'd done what she always did, rushing in, letting herself be guided by raw emotion instead of good sense. She'd been so angry, so tired of feeling powerless . . .

One of these days, your recklessness is going to cost you dearly. Cost all of us, perhaps. Erik's words, a lifetime ago. He'd known she would do something like this someday. The memory only deepened her shame.

"I cannot say what you should or should not have known," Saxon said. "I am no diplomat, only a humble spy."

"A very effective one, it seems."

He grunted. "I wondered. I suppose the rumours would not yet have reached you on the road."

"What rumours?"

"I may not be as effective as you suppose. My network in Varadast has reason to believe that the attempt we set in motion was a failure."

She frowned. "I don't understand."

"Neither do I. No one can confirm whether the rumour is true, but they say the monk was killed by a member of the Crimson Guard before he could finish the job."

"That makes no sense. Varad is dead. If the monk didn't do it . . ."

"I'm still trying to find out what happened. Varad was old and unwell. Perhaps he died of a heart attack, or some other nervous affliction. Perhaps someone saw an opportunity in merely letting the public believe he was murdered." He shrugged. "I truly do not know. Not yet. But I vow that I will do everything in my power to find out."

Alix nodded, but in truth she didn't much care. Whether the assassin she'd paid for had succeeded or not, Varad was dead, and Erik blamed for the deed, so it amounted to the same thing in the end. *The worst thing you've ever done.* She would have to tell Erik. How he would react in his current state was anyone's guess.

It was as though Saxon read her thoughts. "There is something else you should know. Another rumour."

"Go on."

"Your arrival is barely two hours old, and already word is spreading that His Majesty is . . . unwell. That his ordeal in the Broken Mountains has left a terrible mark on his nerves."

Alix's spine went rigid. At her feet, Rudi stirred, as though sensing her distress. "The king is unwell, it's true," she said, choosing her words carefully. "A fever, such as afflicted many of us. I had it myself, and it's no small thing. It . . . inflames the emotions. Makes one nervous. But it will pass."

The spy considered that. "What you have just told me—is this something you wish to get about?"

Alix feigned an indifferent shrug. "As you like. It's not very important."

He glanced over, but he'd looked away again before she could meet his eye. There was no way of telling whether he believed her. "Is there anything else, my lady?"

"I would say we've done quite enough," she said bitterly, "wouldn't you?"

Saxon rose. He started to walk away, but then he paused, looking back at her. "I told you once that it is a delicate business, being a spy. But it would seem it is not half so delicate as being Lady Alix Black. Do not punish yourself unduly."

Alix watched him go, wishing to all the gods she could take that advice.

"It was a bold stroke," said Highmount, "and highly successful. Lord Black estimates that the Oridians lost several thousand men. Still a long way from achieving parity, but a tremendous victory nonetheless. It will be some time before the enemy is able to regroup. Needless to say, it could not come at a better time, considering developments in Harram and Onnan."

"The Harrami were always a long shot," Erik said, "but the loss of the fleet is crushing."

Liam's gaze dropped to the floor. "At least we stopped the saboteurs." Scant comfort, but it was all he could offer. "The construction should move quickly now."

"Six months is not my definition of quick," Erik said. "Still, it's something. In the meantime, we will have to find a way to swell our ranks."

Highmount lifted an eyebrow. "What did you have in mind, Your Majesty?"

"I'm not sure. I need time to think. At a minimum, we need to reduce the age of recruitment. Fourteen, perhaps."

Liam swallowed down a bitter laugh. The irony was just too much.

As for Highmount, his left eyebrow climbed even higher. "Perhaps a consultation with Lord Black would be in order before reaching any decision, sire."

Perhaps you would like to reconsider that truly awful idea, sire. Liam's newly acquired language skills really were coming in handy.

Erik shrugged. "You're right, of course. Rig may have another brilliant solution tucked away somewhere. He never does cease to amaze." He smiled at Liam. "We must think of a suitable way of rewarding your brother-in-law."

Liam tried to return the smile, though he suspected it looked a bit mangled. He was doing his best to observe his brother closely without being obvious about it, but he wasn't at all sure he was pulling it off. He thought Erik might have given him a funny look earlier, but maybe he was just being paranoid. Treasonous thoughts did that to a fellow.

"Riggard Black is a banner lord and commander general of the armies of Alden," Highmount said dryly. "One struggles to imagine what additional honours we might bestow."

"Gold is always popular. Rig lost rather a lot of it when Blackhold fell, as I recall."

"Indeed, but regrettably, the royal treasury is not what it once was."

"That's putting it mildly," Liam said. "We took a look in there a few days ago, and let's just say you have a spacious new room in the palace. You could barrack the better part of a battalion in there."

Erik gave him a cold look. "That amuses you, does it?"

Liam shifted uncomfortably. "Well, no, obviously. Just trying to lighten the mood."

"At a spectacularly inappropriate moment. How very unlike you."

Sweet Farika. Liam had been on the receiving end of a few of those looks from Arran Green, but he'd never had it from Erik. Never seen *anyone* have it from Erik. Alix was right, something was definitely not right here. Even Highmount let his eyebrows twitch just enough to betray unease. "Sorry," Liam said. "I tend to babble when I'm nervous."

The ice-blue eyes narrowed. "Why should you be nervous?"

Because you're starting to remind me of the Raven, and just the sight of him made me whimper like a kicked puppy. "Just haven't seen you in a while, that's all."

Highmount cleared his throat. "Perhaps we could move on to the matter of Varad's death."

"What is there to discuss?" Erik said. "It's not as though we can do anything about it."

"We should issue a proclamation. Deny any and all involvement."

"I don't see why. It won't do any good. Besides, we may stand to gain from this rumour."

Highmount's lips parted, but no sound came.

"Sorry, but"—Liam glanced at the struggling Highmount—"how exactly do we stand to gain?"

"We look strong," Erik said. "First we took out Madan. Then Varad, then we smashed Sadik at the Gunnar, one event hard upon the other. Two Trions dead, the last humiliated. It will give our enemies pause."

"The Warlord is not a man to pause, Your Majesty," Highmount said, all but spluttering in his incredulity. "As the sole remaining Trion, he is greatly strengthened by Varad's death. A new King cannot be named until a full year has passed, and the priests show no sign of overcoming their deadlock and appointing a successor to Madan. For the foreseeable future,

Sadik rules alone, and without Varad's restraining influence, he will be more bloodthirsty than ever."

"I have to say, Erik, I agree." Liam regretted the words as soon as they were out of his mouth. Erik gave him another of those *looks*, only this time, there was an added bit of menace to it, a sort of *open-your-mouth-again-and-I'll-see-your-head-on-a-pike* quality.

"Thank you for your opinion, Liam," Erik said. "Now may I ask you to leave us? The chancellor and I have much to discuss."

"No problem," Liam said, already halfway out of his seat. "Enjoy."

He headed straight for the royal apartments, his step as brisk as he could make it without drawing attention to himself. He had to find Allie. They needed to talk.

They needed to *do something*.

"I suppose I don't need to tell you," Erik said when his brother had gone, "that I am not pleased with your decision to put Liam in charge in my absence."

Highmount brushed at some imaginary dust on his breeches. "You have made your sentiments clear, Your Majesty. I regret the error. Obviously, I had not anticipated your concerns."

"Quite frankly, Chancellor, that baffles me. After the wreck Liam made of the Onnani situation, I cannot understand how you thought it a good idea to make him regent of my country."

"The Council all agreed. His Highness is very well liked, and after all, he is a White."

"Half."

Highmount paused a beat. "With respect, Your Majesty, not anymore. You made certain of that last year."

Erik squeezed his eyes shut and massaged his temples. His headache was growing worse. "Though it pains me to admit, Highmount, I'm afraid you were right. I should not have acknowledged Liam in the middle of a war. It was sheerest folly. My position is too weak to have this kind of destabilising factor come into play."

The old man grunted. "Be that as it may, it is done now. There is no going back."

"I don't see why not."

"I . . . pardon?" Highmount sat forward a little in his seat, as though he was not quite sure he had heard correctly. It was possible he hadn't; he really was very old. Past his prime, certainly, but perhaps worse than that. *I'll need to replace him soon*, Erik thought. But was there anyone else he could trust? Tom had poisoned so many against him . . .

Aloud, he said, "I'm sure we can find a discreet way of keeping my half brother out of trouble."

"I am not sure I follow."

"He has only been in the palace a short time. No one would notice if he were to spend a little time . . . away."

"Away, sire?"

"I don't like it any better than you do, but the situation is getting out of hand. Anyway, it doesn't have to be anything drastic. He can be made comfortable, wherever we put him."

"Put him?"

"Good gods, man, is there an echo in here?"

"I am simply astonished, sire. Where do you propose to *put him*? And what in the Domains would you do about his wife?"

"I can handle Alix."

The chancellor gave a manic sort of laugh. "I am not certain what brought this on, but now is definitely not the time to quarrel with your brother. If nothing else, think of how it will look."

"I know how it will look," Erik snapped. He also knew how Liam had looked, the surreptitious little glances he'd been throwing Erik's way for the past hour. Erik had seen those looks from a brother before, though he hadn't recognised them at the time. He had trusted Tom blindly, and very nearly paid for it with his crown. He would not make that mistake again.

Highmount pressed his palms together, pleadingly. "Your Majesty. Erik. You cannot move against your brother without moving against his wife, who happens to be your bodyguard—"

"Bodyguards can be replaced, if necessary."

Highmount winced. "—and you cannot move against Lady Alix without moving against her brother, who is *commander general of your armies*!"

He doesn't understand, Erik thought. *He doesn't see the danger.* Or did he? Perhaps Highmount had already been corrupted.

Liam had had the chancellor to himself for two whole weeks. Who knew what he might have offered in exchange for loyalty?

Erik forced a smile. "I can see this discussion has upset you, Chancellor. Let us shelve it for now; we can pick it up again another time. It's late; you should try to get some sleep."

Highmount's piercing eyes remained fixed on Erik, as though trying to read his mind. At length, however, he rose. "I shall indeed try to rest, Your Majesty, and I suggest you do the same."

"I will," Erik said. And he would, eventually. For now, though, he had no time for rest. The situation was spiralling out of control; he needed to regain his grip, and quickly.

He needed to make plans.

THIRTY-SIX

"Maybe you're right," Alix said. "Maybe Erik is suffering from the same affliction as Tom." She lay curled against Liam, tucked into his body as though he could shield her from her fear. For some reason, Rudi lay draped across her feet, which was something they were going to have to discuss at some point.

"I'm not sure about that anymore," Liam said. "When I squired for Arran Green, I spent a lot of time around the Raven, and this feels different to me. Prince Tomald was moody, to be sure, and he had a vile temper. But what I saw in there today . . . I don't even know how to describe it. Not only was Erik talking nonsense, he kept giving me these looks, like he didn't trust me."

"Are you sure you're not the one being paranoid? I put a lot of ideas in your head . . ."

Liam fell silent for a while, lost in his own thoughts. Alix had started to doze off, lulled by the steady rise and fall of his breath, when he said, "I had a thought."

"Okay."

"You're not going to like it."

"Under the circumstances, I think that goes without saying."

"What if it's the bloodbond?"

The words splashed over her like cold water. Alix sat bolt upright. For a moment, she could only stare at him, aghast.

Liam propped himself up on his elbows. "What if Highmount is wrong, and the Priest did pass on his tricks after all?"

"But this isn't anything like the Priest's magic. Erik isn't acting like a thrall. Not even close."

"Okay, but what if this is just a different way of doing it?"

"You're not making any sense. Where would they get the blood?"

"Yeah, I thought about that." He sat up, his expression frighteningly earnest. "Remember Boswyck? Erik lost his bloodblade. What if the Oridians found it? What if they could use the blood in his sword somehow? That might explain why the effect is different."

"Impossible," she said reflexively. But the truth was, she had no way of knowing. She had no idea whether the bloodbond or some other, hitherto unknown magic might be to blame. A part of her even wanted to believe that it was, for it meant Erik wasn't responsible for what had happened in Harram. Any of it.

"It sounds far-fetched," Liam said, "and maybe it is. All I know is, I've never seen Erik behave the way he did today, and it scares nine kinds of hell out of me."

"Me too."

They slid back down beneath the covers, lapsing into uncomfortable silence. Alix stitched her limbs through his, pressed herself against his warmth. But her mind continued to churn, and she stirred restlessly. She couldn't seem to burrow in close enough, couldn't keep her hands from wandering over his body, as if to anchor herself. He answered, wrapping himself around her and stringing soft kisses across her brow.

It had been a long time since they made love, and even longer since they made love the way they did that night: slow, subdued, an act of comfort more than passion. They'd clung to each other like this on the eve of the Siege of Erroman. And not since that night had Alix fallen asleep in her husband's arms with tears wet on her cheeks.

"**Good morning, Your** Highnesses." Nevyn rose from his breakfast table, smiling warmly. "I am so pleased to see both of you back at the palace."

"Even this early in the morning?" Alix tried her best to return the smile. "We're sorry to come upon you unannounced like this."

"Terribly bad breeding," Liam added. "Me, especially."

"Please, finish your breakfast," Alix said. "We'll wait for you at the forge."

"That won't be necessary, Your Highness. May I offer you some tea?"

"No, thank you. And we won't keep you long. We just had a few questions, if you don't mind. About the bloodbond."

Nevyn's eyes took on the guarded look they always wore when people posed questions about the bloodbond. Not for the first time, Alix wondered if there was some clandestine bloodbinder code out there in the world, an agreement never to share the most vital secrets of their art. Nevyn was a kind soul, and he always answered her questions, but evasively enough that she never came away feeling she'd learned much of anything. "May I offer you a seat?" the bloodbinder asked politely.

"Thank you."

"So, the reason we're here," Liam said, "is that I heard some rumours on the road to Onnan that worried me, and Alix and I thought you were the best person to ask about them."

"I see." Nevyn's brown eyes tracked warily from Liam to Alix and back. *He's worried about discussing this without Erik present.*

Liam saw it too. "That way, we'll have more complete information to present to His Majesty." He said it smoothly, sealed it with his most charming smile. He'd learned a thing or two in Onnan, it seemed. "What I heard—and of course it's just a rumour, so it may be nothing—is that the Priest may not have been alone in knowing how to bind men to his will."

Nevyn sighed. "That is certainly possible. Once a thing has been discovered, it cannot be undiscovered. Madan may have taught others, or they may simply have worked it out for themselves."

Alix wanted so badly to ask if Nevyn had worked it out for himself, but now was not the time. Instead, she said, "There's more. Tell him, love."

Liam continued with the story they'd worked out. "This is just tavern gossip, mind, but the rumour is that the Oridians combed the field after the massacre at Boswyck, collecting bloodweapons."

"Could there be a danger there?" Alix forced herself not to lean forward in her chair, to let her eyes widen in anticipation of the answer. "Could a bloodweapon be reverse engineered somehow, used to control its owner?"

Nevyn laughed gently, the way a parent might laugh at a particularly fanciful suggestion from a child. "Certainly not, Your Highness. For the bloodbond to work, the blood must be unadulterated at the moment of its joining with the materials that will make the weapon. Once the bond has been forged, it cannot be unmade, and therefore the blood cannot be reused in any way. There is no danger from lost bloodweapons."

"You're absolutely certain?"

"Absolutely. Moreover, to forge a bond powerful enough to control a man, Madan would have required a great deal of blood. More than would ever be used to forge a bloodweapon. Even if it were possible to reuse the blood—and I assure you it is not—one would never find enough in a single weapon, even in a greatsword."

Alix and Liam exchanged a look. It was good news, of course—it meant Liam's theory couldn't possibly be correct—but it also meant they were no closer to finding out what was wrong with Erik.

"What if you could find some other source of old blood?" Liam asked. An absurd, desperate question, and of course it took Nevyn aback.

"Old blood, Your Highness? I don't follow . . ."

"Never mind. I'm being paranoid. I just want to understand the possibilities, you know? The risks."

"I empathise, Your Highness. The perversion Madan created is a terrifying thing. The gods know it has robbed me of many a night's sleep. But we can take some comfort in the fact that in order to be made a thrall, a person must fall into enemy hands. The only way to forge a bloodbond is to have access to a significant quantity of a man's blood." He shrugged. "Or his twin's, obviously."

"Okay," Liam said. "Thanks."

Nevyn considered him with a bemused little smile. "I was under the impression I just gave you some good news, Your Highness, and yet you look like a man bound for the gallows."

"Sorry." Liam smiled weakly. "It's just . . . this talk of thralls makes me a little ill."

"Perfectly understandable."

Alix rose. "Thank you for your time, Nevyn."

"Well," Liam said as they made their way down the corridor, "that got us nowhere."

"You know what we have to do now."

"Are you going to say *talk to Highmount*? Please don't say *talk to Highmount* . . ."

"We have to tell him. He's chancellor of the realm, he needs to know."

Liam sighed. "It just feels like a betrayal. This is *Erik* we're talking about. He's my brother, Allie."

"I know, but there's a bigger duty at stake here. We're at war. We can't afford to keep this to ourselves." The words seemed to come from someone else, someone whose heart wasn't breaking with every step she took.

"You're right, of course, but . . ."

But this could be the end of everything.

They crossed the courtyard under a coldly blazing sky, heading for the chambers of Albern Highmount.

"I see," said the chancellor. He had listened carefully, without interruption, his expression revealing nothing of his thoughts. Alix had done her best to match that expression, though her heart was pounding in her ears, and her head felt sickeningly light. Liam, for his part, stared at the floor, fidgeting every now and then but otherwise holding his peace.

"We would not have come to you if we weren't terribly afraid for Erik," Alix said for the second time. "But whatever this is, whatever he's dealing with, he needs our help. And . . ." She drew a deep breath. *No going back now. It's already too late.* ". . . and Alden cannot afford for her king to be suffering such an affliction right now."

Treason. This is treason. Her head felt as if it might float away.

Highmount's gaze pierced her like a spear. He still wore that damnably blank expression, hands forming a steeple on his desk. At length, he said, "You have done the right thing, Your Highness." He rose and went to a trestle table to fetch a pitcher of water. "Please," he said, offering her a cup. Alix took it with a shaking hand. "The truth is, I had already come to much the same conclusion. I have known Erik White since he was a boy, and though he can be accused of any number of failings, paranoia is most certainly not one of them. If anything, he has been dangerously cavalier, at some detriment to my intestinal health."

"I never said he was paranoid—"

"I did. His behaviour last night was uncharacteristic in the extreme. Frankly, it was alarming. I do not wish to go into details, but it is clear to me that his judgement is impaired. I have just spent a sleepless night trying to decide what to do about it. If you had not approached me, Your Highness, I might very well have approached you. You spend more time with him than anyone. If you tell me that his mind is unwell, I believe you, in spite of your obvious incentives for lying."

"My . . ." Alix spluttered, heat flashing to her cheeks. *"What did you say?"*

Highmount raised a hand in a mollifying gesture. "Stow your umbrage, Your Highness. I simply mean that Prince Liam would obviously stand to gain a great deal from his brother's downfall."

"Oh, is that all you meant?" Liam snapped. "Do you honestly think I'm the sort of man who would betray his own brother?"

Highmount met their joined wrath with a bland expression.

"If I did, both of you would be in the Red Tower by now. Please, Your Highnesses, compose yourselves. We are in a delicate enough place without fits of temper. Now, have you any theories?"

"None," Alix said, a sullen note still clinging to her voice. The *nerve* of this man . . . "We thought perhaps the blood-bond, but Nevyn dismissed that notion."

Highmount's eyes widened in horror. "You have spoken to others about this?"

"Of course not. *Stow your umbrage*, Chancellor. We merely asked certain pointed questions about the bloodbond, to see if we might learn something that could explain Erik's behaviour."

"And?"

"And nothing, as I said. In order to forge a bloodbond, you need the man himself to be in your custody, and obviously that hasn't happened. I haven't left Erik's side since we quit Erroman."

"To be precise," Liam said, "what he told us was that you'd need a *significant quantity* of a man's blood, or his twin's. But like Alix said, she's been with him the whole time, and he doesn't have a twin, so . . ."

"Actually, he does," Alix said. "Or rather, he did." Liam's gaze snapped to her. Highmount, meanwhile, had gone quite pale. *He's surprised you know.* She couldn't help taking a certain petty satisfaction in that. "A sister," she said. "Still-born. Erik told me about her last year, while he was recuperating at Greenhold."

"Wow." Liam sat back in his chair. "That's unexpected. Doesn't help us any, though. It only works with identical twins, and she was a girl."

"In fact," Highmount said, passing a hand over his eyes, "he was not."

Silence.

For a long moment, Alix could only stare at Albern High-mount, ears ringing, the stunned aftermath of a lightning strike. She forced herself to speak. "What do you mean, *he*?"

Highmount shook his head. "I warned him," he muttered, as if to himself. "I told Osrik that these things never really go away, that it would haunt his family forever if he did not muster the strength to do what was necessary. But he was so sentimental, Osrik. Just like his son . . ."

"Highmount, what are you talking about?" Alix was halfway out of her chair, fists balled, voice quavering. When he didn't react immediately, she seized the front of his doublet in a perfect imitation of her brother. *"Speak, damn you!"*

"Keep your voice down, Your Highness." He extricated himself from her grasp. "What I am about to tell you is the most closely guarded secret in the realm. Even King Erik himself knows nothing of it." He went back to the trestle table, but this time, it was wine he poured, three generous cups. Though it was early in the morning, Alix did not even consider refusing. She would need it, she knew.

"Rodrik White was born only a few moments after his brother. Straightaway, the midwife saw something was wrong. His right arm was withered, just over half the length of the left. Choked by the cord, the midwife said, but who knows? Blessedly, the woman had the presence of mind to fetch His Majesty straightaway, and of course King Osrik summoned me.

"Identical twins. *Firstborn* identical twins, and boys in the bargain. A more wretched eventuality for a king cannot be imagined. Even Osrik, who delighted in mocking me for my supposedly exaggerated caution, saw the danger immediately. Even so, he would not countenance the obvious solution. Queen Hestia would never forgive him, he said. So he contrived to have the boy sent away, somewhere remote enough that he would never be discovered. As though such a thing could ever be guaranteed." The chancellor shook his head scornfully, took a long pull of his wine. "He granted me one concession, at least: that the child be exiled from Alden altogether. It was not foolproof—nothing short of destroying the boy could accomplish that—but at least, if the child were raised in a foreign land, the chances of him one day being recognised would be greatly lessened.

"To add to his protection, we enlisted the aid of the King of Andithyri. He would ensure that the boy was sent somewhere suitably removed from civilisation. Guards, posing as ordinary farmers, would take up residence in the nearest hamlet, with orders to silence anyone who learned the truth of the boy's identity. Needless to say, this was a great deal to ask of an ally, especially one with whom we were so recently reconciled. King Berendt was far too cunning to let such an opportunity pass him by, so naturally, he asked for something in return. Something hugely significant. Again, I counselled against it, and again, I was overruled."

"The Treaty of Imran," Alix whispered, her hand going to her mouth. "Oh my gods . . ."

Her memory travelled back in time, to the words of a departed friend around a crackling campfire. *Scholars everywhere are still puzzled about what old King Osrik was thinking,* Gwylim had said. *It doesn't make sense to risk Alden's security for Andithyri, especially when the Trionate was already showing signs of expansionism. Andithyri could never protect us if the situation were reversed, so what did we get out of the deal?*

"A foolish commitment," Highmount said. "I told him the cost was too high, but he would not listen. That damned treaty sealed our fates nearly thirty years ago." He gazed up at the ceiling, shaking his head. "Ironic, is it not? The price of protecting Rodrik White's identity was the very treaty that committed us to this war, and it is because of that war and the invasion of Andithyri that his identity has somehow been discovered. The guards, I expect. Taken captive in the course of battle, tortured, or perhaps merely looking to secure their release." He sighed. "We will never know, I suppose."

"And Erik knows nothing of this?" Liam's voice was rough, his skin flushed.

"He was told that he had a twin sister who died at birth. He was also told that this was a great secret, one he must never reveal. Apparently, however, he did not take that injunction to heart." Highmount shot a wry look at Alix.

"And the queen?" Liam asked.

"She knew the truth. She had already seen the baby, held him and named him. She begged His Majesty not to send him away. She never got over the grief, poor woman. It is what took her in the end, I believe."

Alix was scarcely listening anymore. "That's got to be it," she said numbly. "The Oridians have Rodrik, and they're using him to warp Erik's mind." Saying it out loud sounded absurd, but there was no other explanation.

A wave of guilt crashed over her. Liam must have seen it, because he said, "It's not your fault, Allie. You couldn't have known."

"Couldn't I?" Memories flashed through her mind, a dozen instances of Erik behaving strangely. His raw fury in the moments before they were captured. His disgust with himself for letting slip his identity, and later, his admission of how he'd struggled with the *pasha*. The way he'd looked at her, his touch on her arm . . . All of it *before* the disaster with Omaïd. How many other moments, hints she hadn't picked up on or been privy to? "I should have seen. I should have helped him."

"Even had you known," Highmount said, "there was nothing you could have done for him."

But that wasn't quite true. She could have been more compassionate. She could have been there for Erik, instead of berating him, and later, avoiding him. He'd deserved the benefit of the doubt, earned it a thousand times over, and she hadn't given it.

It's done now, she told herself, drawing a deep breath. There was no point looking back. "So what do we do?"

"We have to find them," Liam said, as though it were the simplest thing in the world. "Rodrik. The bloodbinder. Rescue one, kill the other."

"How?"

"We know where Rodrik lived, don't we? We can start there. I'll take the Pack and—"

Highmount was already shaking his head. "You cannot leave the capital, Your Highness. Not now."

"Why in the hells not?"

Highmount turned to Alix. She knew what he was going to say, and it made her ill.

"Tell me the truth, Your Highness. If you say he can do this, I will believe you."

She looked helplessly at her husband.

For a moment, Liam just stared back at her. Then, slowly, understanding dawned. "No." He sprang out of his chair as if it had scalded him. "No way."

"Liam . . ."

"*No way*, Allie. How could you even . . . either of you? Have you both lost your minds?"

She rose, spreading her hands as if to calm a wild animal. "It would only be temporary. You've already done it once. This would be no different."

"No different?" His eyes were white-rimmed, like a terrified horse. "It was *two weeks*, and Erik wasn't even here. What you're talking about . . . it's *treason*. Even worse treason than before, I mean. This is *really* treason. *Huge treason*."

"It would be preferable if you would stop saying that word at *quite* such a volume, Your Highness," Highmount said between gritted teeth, "unless you would like to see us all beheaded."

"See?" Liam stabbed a finger at the chancellor. "Exactly! Beheaded, Alix! That doesn't sound like a good outcome to me!"

She dropped into her chair, cradling her head in her hands. "Sit down, please. We need to think."

"Yeah, you do need to think, both of you. A lot more."

Alix ignored that. "What would we tell people?" she asked Highmount.

"The truth. That His Majesty is ill and needs time to recover. After his ordeal in the Broken Mountains, no one will question it."

Liam glared at both of them. "And while I'm poncing about pretending to be king, who's going after Rodrik? Or do you plan to tell someone else about this lovely little development?"

"I will," Alix said. "I'll ride down to the front first. Rig needs to know what's happening."

"Agreed," said Highmount. "We cannot have any confusion about who is giving the orders."

"So, what," Liam said, "your plan is to go alone? Into enemy territory? Do you honestly think I'm going to allow that?"

She scowled. "There, you see? You're getting the hang of this king business already."

"Allie—"

"Don't *Allie* me. Unless you're planning on poisoning me again, you can't stop me."

Liam folded at the waist, arms clasped over his head as though bracing for impact. "This is a nightmare."

"Yes," Alix said, "it is. But we're living it, so unless you have a better idea, this is the way it has to be."

The silence that followed felt thick, polluted. Alix dragged it in and out of her lungs, willing her head to quit swimming. Highmount stared at his desk. Liam remained curled over himself, features obscured within the shield of his arms. He was still in that position when he broke the silence. "What about Erik?"

A pained expression crossed Highmount's face. "The royal apartments can be sealed off from the rest of the palace. A quarantine, if you will." He glanced at Alix, and she was struck by how impossibly ancient he looked in that moment. "Your guardsmen. Are there any you can trust with this?"

"I lost some of my best men in the mountains. But yes, there are a few."

"If we do this," Liam said, "I want the Wolves with you. Give me that, at least, Allie."

She nodded wearily.

"Very well," Highmount said, straightening. "We know what we must do."

Epilogue

Torchlight licked at the rough stone surface of the walls, filtered through deer antlers to throw strange veins of shadow along the dining table. The figure lying atop it was pale as death, wrists and ankles horribly bruised from the bonds, but his chest rose and fell steadily. He looked peaceful lying there, drugged out of his wits. Watching him brought peace to Sadik's breast too. It was so easy to imagine that he was Erik White, captured and broken, utterly at the mercy of the Trionate. Sadik took comfort in that, even if he wished it were another, darker-haired man in his place. Having Erik White in the palm of his hand was a delightful feeling, but having Riggard Black—that would have been glorious.

Then again, he could not deny there was a certain pleasure in having such an enemy out there in the field. It made the anticipation that much sweeter. He had cursed his luck at having Arran Green taken from him, but perhaps his anger had been premature. Green's successor was proving himself a most diverting opponent. Perhaps his skull would be worthy of Sadik's mantel after all.

Things really were going wonderfully, he decided. The battle at the fort had been an unfortunate turn of events, but the fates had more than compensated him with the botched attempt on Varad's life. The existence of the plot was a stroke of luck, the imbecility of the would-be assassin an even greater boon. But that it should be Kurya, the cleverest, most ambitious of Sadik's Crimson Guardsmen who should stumble upon the event—what more proof could be needed that the gods favoured his designs? Kurya had seized upon the opportunity, for he had served in the Crimson Guard long enough to see what a millstone Varad had become. Moreover, Sadik had instructed him to be on the lookout for just such an opening, though admittedly he had assumed it would be more in the nature of a pillow to the old man's face.

And now Sadik was free. The last remaining Trion, and if he had his way, the last of the Trions altogether. It was time for a new order—past time, really—and now, thanks to the goodwill of the gods, he was nearly there. What was a petty skirmish at an insignificant fort compared to that?

"My lord." The soft voice at the door drew Sadik from his musings. "I did not expect to find you here."

Sadik's gaze drifted over the figure on the table. "I like to watch him, Dargin. It pleases me."

Light footsteps crossed the solar. "It is nearly time for his tonic." Dargin reached over the table and tucked his fingers under the red-gold beard, feeling for a pulse. He nodded to himself, satisfied.

"And Erik White? What can you tell me about how he fares?"

The bloodbinder smiled, revealing his unsettlingly white teeth. "It is much easier, my lord, now that he is back in

Erroman. At such a great distance as he was, the best I could do was inflame his emotions. Rather like a bellows to the coals, if you will forgive an analogy. I could not create a spark, but I could stoke it into an inferno."

"I have little patience for analogies," Sadik growled. In truth, he had little patience for the bloodbinder—for his soft, doughy features, his obsequiousness—but there was no denying the man's usefulness.

The bloodbinder bowed his head. "Apologies, my lord. It was not my intention to be obtuse. What I meant, my lord, is that physical distance matters to the bloodbond. It is one of several factors influencing the strength of the enchantment, along with the freshness of the blood, its quantity, and the skill of the bloodbinder. The greater the physical distance from the subject, the more muted the effects of the bloodbond. Erik White's voyage to Harram temporarily weakened my hand."

"How so?"

"My control over him was limited. I could not compel his actions, nor even plant thoughts in his mind. But I was able to magnify his emotions, make them infinitely stronger."

"And what did you accomplish with that?"

Dargin shrugged. "No way of knowing, my lord. At that distance, the bloodbond does not offer a clear view into the mind. I could sense his feelings—fear, or anger, or desire—but I knew nothing of his actual circumstances, whether fuelling those feelings would hurt him or aid him."

Sadik scowled. "What good is that?"

"In general, my lord, I have found that rampant emotions are rarely helpful. Thus inflamed, his self-control would have been severely compromised, and so his judgement. Even when I was not acting upon him directly—when I was asleep, for example—his emotions would still have borne the mark of my interference. He would still have been raw, so that the effect was in some way cumulative over time." Dargin gestured at the figure on the table, at the bleeding wrists. "Not unlike these rope burns, if you see what I mean. When first the ropes are applied, they are merely a mild discomfort. But each tiny movement wears a little more at the flesh. Over time, it develops into a gaping wound."

"And what were your designs with this . . . interference?"

"Why, to ruin him, of course. We can safely assume he made any number of poor decisions as a result, hopefully some of them important. Perhaps he took unnecessary risks, or shied from taking necessary ones. Perhaps he alienated an ally, or undermined confidence in his leadership. Perhaps he undermined confidence in himself. I certainly sensed that he grew fearful, conscious that something was very wrong with him, but unable to account for it. Not only was he afraid, I sensed such despair as to convince me that my efforts were not in vain. Something changed while he was in Harram, something devastating to him."

Sadik grunted. Fear and despair were always useful. Yet there was too much vagueness here, too much uncertainty. Wars were not won with *perhaps*. "I had hoped for more," he said.

"I am sorry, my lord." Dargin gestured at the table again. "If we had found this one sooner, before the enemy king left his capital . . . But things are different now, as I said. Now that he is back in Erroman, with less distance between us, I can be more . . . directive. Already, I have begun planting ideas. Notions he would never have considered before, yet now holds with such conviction that he does not even question where they come from. At this point, he no longer realises anything is wrong with him."

"And?"

The white teeth flashed again. "He sees enemies everywhere, and with a little luck, he will begin moving against them."

"Moving against his friends, you mean."

"With a little luck, my lord."

Sadik walked over to the hearth and fetched down his flagon of ale. "Tell me, Dargin, what if I were able to get you even closer to Erik White? Into Erroman itself, even?"

"We would have to bring this one," he said. "I need the blood to be fresh."

"That should not be a problem."

"Well, then, I would have him in body as well as mind. He would be altogether mine. That is"—Dargin bowed—"altogether yours, my lord."

"In that case, begin preparations for moving. Not too quickly, mind you. The gods have blessed us with this moment, Dargin. It would be a sin not to savour it."

The bloodbinder bowed again. Moving to his table of implements, he fetched a knife and a shallow silver bowl. "Will you stay, my lord?"

A foolish question. How could anyone walk away now, with that blade against that flesh, silver on white, poised with promise? How could he not draw closer, breath suspended, pupils dilated, bewitched by that slow, flashing caress that coaxed the reluctant blood forth? *Beautiful*, Sadik thought, watching the rich crimson glide into the bowl, run along the edges of the runes.

So beautiful, he almost wanted to weep.

GLOSSARY

THE KINGDOM OF ALDEN
CAPITAL: Erroman

Feudal monarchy, ruled by the Whites since the disintegration of the Erromanian Empire more than four centuries ago. Aldrich the White, claiming descent from the royal bloodline of Erroman, fought a brutal campaign to unite what was left of the empire, founding the Kingdom of Alden and naming it after himself. He awarded his closest ally, Konrad, a banner of green silk. This historic event marked the foundation of the Banner Houses; forever more, Konrad's descendants would be known as the Greens. Since then, only four more banners have been awarded—Black, Grey, Brown, and Gold.

King Erik White
Prince Liam White (commander of the White Wolves)
Prince Tomald White (deceased)

Riggard Black (banner holder, commander general of the
    king's armies)
Alix Black (bodyguard to the king)

Raibert Green (banner holder)
Arran Green (deceased)

Alithia Grey (banner holder)
Sirin Grey
Roswald Grey (deceased)

Rona Brown (banner holder, White Wolf)
Aina Brown
Adelbard Brown (deceased)

Norvin Gold (banner holder)

THE TRIONATE OF ORIDIA
CAPITAL: Varadast

Theocracy ruled by a triumvirate, fiercely committed to expansion in the name of religious conversion. The King is said to be a living god (Varad), whose soul is reborn through millennia. When his mortal body dies, Varad's soul passes exactly one year in the heavens before being reincarnated as a newborn baby. It is the Priest, appointed by his peers, who identifies the reincarnated Varad, assembling all male children born on the designated day and subjecting them to various tests until he is certain he has recognised the anointed one. The Warlord earns his place through victory in battle and single combat.

The King, Varad
The Priest, Madan (deceased)
The Warlord, Sadik

THE REPUBLIC OF ONNAN
CAPITAL: Onnan City

Democratic republic. Political parties, known as *leagues*, are elected by district, each district being represented by a speaker. The league with the most seats is said to be *in power*, its leader becoming First Speaker. Most speakers are also priests, reflecting the deep religious convictions of Onnani society. However, it is said that the real power lies with the secret societies, most of which were founded as underground revolutionary movements during the time of the empire, when the Onnani were enslaved by the Erromanians. The slave revolt—known in Onnan as the Great Revolution—marked the beginning of the end of the empire.

First Speaker Kar (Worker's Alliance)
Chairman Irtok (Worker's Alliance)
Defence Consul Welin (Worker's Alliance)
Speaker Syril (People's Congress)

THE KINGDOM OF HARRAM
CAPITAL: Ost

Feudal monarchy, ruled by His High Lordship King Omaïd. Protected on all sides by mountains, sea, and arctic, Harram holds itself aloof of affairs on the wider continent of Gedona. While politics are generally stable, Ost has never been able to extend effective control over the mountain tribes, whom it views as savages. Because of its imposing geographical barriers, Harram was the only kingdom never to succumb to Erromanian rule, though it did play an important role in the empire's demise. The mountain tribes are generally credited with dealing the death blow to the empire, uniting for the first (and last) time in history to sack Erroman more than four hundred years ago.

THE KINGDOM OF ANDITHYRI
CAPITAL: Timra

Feudal monarchy, ruled by King Berendt until his execution by the Warlord, now under the stewardship of Governor Arkenn of the Trionate. Andithyrians claim direct descent from the Erromanian nobility. During Erromanian times, the so-called purebloods were easily distinguished by their white hair; when the empire collapsed, this trait became deadly, marking them out for reprisals as chaos gripped the former empire. The imperial race fled in droves, founding their own small country on the southern border of modern-day Alden. To this day, most Andithyri have white hair, though this is slowly changing over time due to intermarriage. Andithyri is the most recent country to fall to the Trionate of Oridia, but rumours have begun to stir of an underground resistance movement.

THE NINE VIRTUES

RAHL (STRENGTH) SYMBOL: the sun. Also associated with power, leadership.

OLAN (COURAGE) SYMBOL: the moon. Also associated with determination.

ELDORA (WISDOM) SYMBOL: the all-seeing eye. Also associated with temperance, experience.

DESTAN (HONOUR) SYMBOL: the ram. Also associated with duty, integrity.

FARIKA (GRACE) SYMBOL: folded hands. Also associated with mercy.

ARDIN (PASSION) SYMBOL: the flame. Also associated with impetuousness, boldness.

HEW (WIT) SYMBOL: the crow. Also associated with guile, cleverness.

GARVIN (EMPATHY) SYMBOL: tears. Also associated with solidarity, generosity.

GILENE (FAITH) SYMBOL: the star. Also associated with devotion, truth.

LOOK FOR THE NEXT GREAT BLOODBOUND NOVEL

THE BLOODSWORN

AVAILABLE IN PAPERBACK AND EBOOK
FROM ACE IN OCTOBER 2016!

Erin Lindsey is on a quest to write the perfect summer-vacation novel, with just the right blend of action, heartbreak, and triumph. The Bloodbound series is her first effort. She lives in Brooklyn, New York, with her husband and a pair of half-domesticated cats. Visit her online at erin-lindsey.com and twitter.com/ETettensor.

THE ULTIMATE IN FANTASY FICTION!

From magical tales of distant worlds to stories of those with abilities beyond the ordinary, Ace and Roc have everything you need to stretch your imagination to its limits.

Marion Zimmer Bradley/Diana L. Paxson

Guy Gavriel Kay

Dennis L. McKiernan

Patricia A. McKillip

Robin McKinley

Sharon Shinn

Steven R. Boyett

Barb and J. C. Hendee

penguin.com/scififantasy